GREAT LIVES

Human Culture

Human
Culture

GREAT LIVES

David Weitzman

Charles Scribner's Sons · New York

Maxwell Macmillan Canada · Toronto
Maxwell Macmillan International
New York · Oxford · Singapore · Sydney

For all my students over the years
who have been my teachers

Charles Scribner's Sons Books for Young Readers
Macmillan Publishing Company · 866 Third Avenue, New York, NY 10022

Maxwell Macmillan Canada, Inc.
1200 Eglinton Avenue East, Suite 200, Don Mills, Ontario M3C 3N1

Macmillan Publishing Company is part of the Maxwell Communication Group of Companies.

First edition   10 9 8 7 6 5 4 3 2 1
Printed in the United States of America
Cover illustration © 1994 by Stephen Marchesi. All rights reserved.

Library of Congress Cataloging-in-Publication Data
Weitzman, David L.
    Human culture / David Weitzman.—1st ed.
        p.   cm.—(Great lives)   Includes bibliographical references (p.   ) and index.
    Summary: Presents biographical profiles of twenty-seven anthropologists and archaeologists, including Jane Goodall, Zora Neale Hurston, and Richard Leakey.
    ISBN 0-684-19438-4
1. Anthropologists—Biography—Juvenile literature.
2. Archaeologists—Biography—Juvenile literature.
[1. Anthropologists. 2. Archaeologists.]   I. Title.   II. Series.
GN20.W45   1994   301'.092'2—dc20   93-16791

Contents

Foreword

Some of the people in this book are anthropologists and some are archaeologists. They probably would not have cared much what they were called; they just wanted answers to questions that wouldn't leave them alone. They were all interested in human culture—the way people live: their customs, beliefs, language, art, families; what kinds of dwellings they build to live in; how they fit into their environment; their social relationships; how they make their living; their daily lives.

It's sometimes hard to distinguish between anthropologists and archaeologists. They often seek answers to the same or similar questions; it's just that they go about their work differently.

Anthropologists ask questions about the lifeways of living people and cultures. Their questions may be historical—where did this custom come from? why do they make puppets just that way?—but they ask them of living people who even today carry in their faces and in their memories and behavior almost the entire history of their culture. Some anthropologists specialize. Ethnologists, like Robert Harry Lowie, study and compare human behaviors. Folklorists, like Zora Neale Hurston and Mary Kawena Pukui, are especially interested in the stories people tell about themselves—their songs, jokes, tall tales, chants, and myths. Ethologists, like Jane Goodall, study animals to find clues to human behavior. All of them work in similar ways. They observe, ask questions, even take part in daily life and rituals while all the time, with pencil and paper, film and videotape, and tape recorders, they record what they see.

Archaeologists are curious about lifeways, too, but the people who interest them lived hundreds, perhaps thousands of years ago. To answer their questions, archaeologists must dig to find the remains of cultures—clay tablets, palaces, tombs, crumbled house walls, weapons, jewelry, tools—buried by drifting sand and by new cities built atop old ones. There's even a special kind of archaeologist, called a paleontologist, like Louis S. B., Mary, and Richard Leakey, who digs down to find traces of human life and lifeways from millions of years ago, back close to the time of our human origins. Sometimes archaeologists act like anthropologists, observing people alive today for clues to the lives of their ancestors many generations back. Sometimes archaeologists become philologists—speakers and readers of ancient languages—and philologists, like Jean-François Champollion and Michael Ventris, must sometimes be archaeologists. In this way they can give voice to long-dead languages and even make ancient flutes and harps play once again.

Anthropologists and archaeologists, as you'll soon discover, can be found all over the world; there might even be one in your own backyard right now. Many anthropologists, like Margaret Mead, have gone to faraway places, to Bali and Samoa in the South Pacific, while others, like Hortense Powdermaker, have studied the culture of Hollywood, rural Mississippi, or the Lower East Side of New York City. Some archaeologists dig in places like Iraq, Egypt, Greece, Mexico, or China. Some can be found deep under the torn-up pavement of San Francisco or out in the middle of an Illinois farm. They will go wherever they must in order to answer their questions.

And who are these people? Who becomes an anthropologist or archaeologist? Have you ever wondered about people who accomplish things, whose life stories are included in books like this? Have you wondered what they were like as kids, if they had problems with their parents, or if they got into trouble or didn't do so well in school? I did. I remember as a kid looking at the gray hair and wrinkled faces in my history books. They were so ancient—about the age I am now—so stern and serious. I wondered if they were so different from me when they were young, if they thought about the same things, had the same childhood cares and joys I had.

The lives of the people in this book were all very different and most, like you and me, were just regular kids when they were in school. Sitting next to any one of them in class, you might not notice anything special about him or her. Lord Carnarvon (George Herbert), who, along with Howard Carter, made the archaeological discovery of the century, was considered "idle" and slow by his teachers. Howard Carter never went to college. Neither did folklorist Mary Kawena Pukui or paleontologist Mary Leakey, who was finally thrown out of school when she set off two explosions in chemistry class and staged a fit, rolling and kicking on the floor, spitting up soap suds. Alfred Kroeber painted several statues in Central Park red, white, and blue one night; and Austen Henry Layard threw a glass inkwell at his teacher. The schoolmaster beat him with a ruler and locked him in the cellar. Mortimer Wheeler found school intolerably boring. Jean-François Champollion did so badly in class that his brother took him out and tutored the boy himself. Arthur Evans kept a pet snake in his coat and, while he was reciting in front of class, his back to the schoolmaster, the snake popped out of his collar, disappeared, and then came out his sleeve.

Just as these famous kids were not always well behaved, neither were they all from happy, storybook families. Layard lived in terrible poverty while apprenticed to his uncle. Heinrich Schliemann once pretended to be sick and checked himself in to the hospital so that he could get warm and have something to eat. Ruth Benedict's father died when she was a child and she remained always alienated and distant from her forever-grieving mother. Hortense Powdermaker and Elsie Clews Parsons never felt part of their families and rebelled, unable to accept their parents' values. Alice Cunningham Fletcher finally escaped her abusive stepfather when a friend's parents hired her as a nanny and took her in. Ironically, it may have been these troubled childhoods, with the need to adapt and to separate themselves from the hurt, that made these kids such perceptive social scientists.

You will get to know these accomplished, talented people when they were children. You'll find out about that moment in life when they decided to become what they became (for several, it was a surprise). The twenty-seven lives in this book are all quite different, some not what you would expect. But all of these children who grew up to become social scientists shared one important trait—an unquenchable curiosity about, and desire to explore and discover, the world.

Ruth Benedict

1887–1948   American anthropologist; student of Native American culture

All over the world today countless anthropology students are reading Ruth Benedict's *Patterns of Culture*. That's true even though the book was published some sixty years ago. For two generations now, the book has served as an introduction to the study of culture. Chances are that if you decide to study anthropology you will read it, too, probably in your very first course. The book has been translated into twelve languages. Since it was first published in 1934, nearly two million copies have been sold in English alone. But even before the book made her famous, Ruth Benedict had made her mark. She was one of the first women to be recognized the world over for her work as a social scientist.

Benedict's   friend   anthropologist Margaret Mead has called her one of the first humanists in anthropology. Benedict was interested in anthropology because it helped her to answer a serious question about life. Her question was not easy, then or now. Scientists generally agree that despite some physical differences—skin color, size, and shape—all human beings are the same. And yet, the cultures that shape them and which they, in turn, shape are so different. What, Benedict asked, accounts for the many different kinds of cultures we see around the world? "The trouble with life isn't that there is no answer," she wrote in her journal, "it's that there are so many answers."

Ruth Fulton Benedict's interest in the questions posed by life began when she was a child. "The story of my life," she wrote later (published in *An Anthropologist at Work: Writings of Ruth Benedict* by Margaret Mead), "begins when I was twenty-one months old, at the time my father died." Her father, Frederick S. Fulton, was a surgeon who died very young of a strange, unknown disease. It wasn't that she remembered him exactly, in every detail. "My memories have to do, instead, with a worn face illuminated with the translucence of illness, and very beautiful." As young as she was when he died, Benedict remembered him her whole life. "I have very little idea what he was really like, but the part he played in my childhood, and still plays," she wrote when she was in her forties, "was none the less great for that."

In a way, Benedict also lost her mother. For her whole life after her husband died, Bertrice Shattuck Fulton grieved. The deeper she withdrew into her grief, the more Benedict withdrew from her mother. The family—which included a younger sister, Margery—lived on the family farm in northern New York State, not far from Benedict's grandparents' farm. Her mother, who had graduated from Vassar College, supported the family by working as a teacher, a principal, and a librarian. The Fultons moved to Missouri, and then to Minnesota and back to New York State, but every summer they returned to the farm. This farm was home to

Benedict, the home she would remember her whole life.

Having lost her father and turned away from her mother, Benedict lived in daydreams and fantasy. "Happiness," she wrote, "was in a world I lived in all by myself, and for precious moments. These moments were my pearls of great price."

She fought constantly with her mother, who punished her and then wept over her. Benedict often had violent tantrums. She remembers sadly once smashing a friend's doll to pieces without any reason—and then becoming confused. She just couldn't understand where the anger and violence within her came from. The little girl's mother demanded that Benedict explain her actions. "I couldn't; I couldn't even guess myself why I had done it. I was horrified and humiliated; I had done something without the slightest will of my own, something that made no sense. For years I used to dream about it."

To add to her confusion, Benedict was deafened by the measles. She couldn't hear as well as other children, but it wasn't until she was five that her hearing loss was discovered. Before it was discovered, her mother often punished her for not answering when she was spoken to.

In later years Benedict recalled that her life was not all sorrow and anger.

There were also good feelings that she associated with "holding a sleeping kitten on my lap on the woodhouse steps looking out over the east hills, and with shelling peas for the family—there were thirteen or fourteen to feed and it was a long job—at peace on the front porch while everybody else was busy in the kitchen." She recalls, too, finding peace in her Bible. "I loved the story of Christ, and I knew it better than the ministers before I was ten. . . . Christ was a real person to me, and my favorite company. I learned most of what I knew about life from the Bible."

Like many children, Benedict found peace also in a make-believe world. "In this happy world I lived in by myself I had several different games. The one I remember best was the beautiful country on the other side of the west hill where a family lived who had a little girl about my age. This imaginary playmate and her family lived a warm, friendly life without recriminations and brawls. So far as I can remember I and the little girl mostly explored hand in hand the unparalleled beauty of the country over the hill." It was while she was living in this secret inner world that Benedict later began to write. She kept a journal and, in high school, wrote poetry. Some of her poetry was published under one of her pen names, Anne Singleton.

Benedict and her sister, like their mother, attended Vassar College, graduating together in the class of 1909. Benedict majored in English literature. College, as she put it, "kept me lit up mentally like a Christmas tree for four years." Vassar was a place to learn, but college for young women in those days had an even more important meaning. When Benedict's mother attended Vassar, it was rare for a young woman to go to college. Now, only twenty years later, the number of young women attending colleges and universities had more than tripled.

At college, young women learned to be independent and experience for the first time some of the freedom men enjoyed. Theirs was the first generation of women to ride bicycles around the campus and beyond. For Benedict, being able to ride a bicycle was more than just being able to have fun. It meant freedom from tight clothing and skirts that almost touched the ground. It meant freedom to explore the city and countryside alone and with friends. For the first time women were free to take up sports. Vassar women played tennis, field hockey, and basketball, ran and jumped in track-and-field events. They swam in the summer and went ice-skating and sledding in the winter. Benedict and thousands of other women in college saw themselves as new women of a new century.

For Benedict it also meant the freedom to find her identity, to become an individual. At Vassar were women she could look to as role models. Her teachers were considered "strong minded," even "dangerous," women. They were interested in ideas; but they were not content with only teaching. They were activists who sought social change.

Every day now, Benedict was in the presence of successful, talented women scholars. She especially liked one of her English teachers, Florence V. Keys. Keys had studied at universities all over Europe. She spoke out for women's suffrage, a woman's right to vote. Many years would go by before Benedict would realize how important Keys had been to her. Keys encouraged her students to think about what they were learning, to apply "the social test of the value of all knowledge." Later, Benedict would apply that test to everything she did in her life. She would also remember Lucy Salmon, a great history teacher, who reminded her students over and over, "You have a mind, use it." Philosophy and psychology teacher Margaret Washburn encouraged Benedict to do original work, to look at questions and problems no one else had asked about.

Benedict met and heard many famous people who came to Vassar to teach or to speak. One of these was the naturalist John Burroughs. Benedict had joined an outdoors group called the Wake Robin Club. Once or twice a year they would visit Burroughs at his home in the woods. He'd take them for walks through the woods and teach them how to see things: birds and insects, flowers in bloom, and the tracks of animals. John Burroughs was an elderly man with a flowing white beard, who reminded Benedict of the grandfather she loved so. He taught her to be observant, a skill she would use and excel in later in her own work. But most important to Benedict, his ideas were like those of Ralph Waldo Emerson and Henry David Thoreau, two writers she admired very much.

Benedict felt depressed and worried much of the time. Burroughs, too, often felt depression, what he called his "blue devils." It made Benedict feel better about herself to know that someone she admired had the same feelings. His cure? Work, original work that you love. "When you feel blue and empty and disconsolate, and life seems hardly worth living, go to work. . . . The blue devils can be hoed under in less than half an hour." Benedict would use his cure often all her life.

It was at Vassar, too, that Benedict and her sister took on their social values. Later, Benedict would work for charities and the poor. She had always been sensitive and caring about others, but Vassar increased her social consciousness. There she was taught that education was a privilege and that with the privilege came a responsibility to work to improve society. Many Vassar students helped the poor by doing settlement and mission work. Benedict was too shy to actually go out and work herself, but she vowed that she would improve lives with her writing. She would, she hoped, make people aware of the working and lower classes and of the responsibility to help them.

College was also a place for Benedict to make friends. Her deafness and her anger had isolated her as a child. Now she had friends and also became closer to her sister. They found themselves "going through," as Margery Fulton later wrote, "all the experiences of life together, and discussing the significance of each endlessly." Benedict and her sister attended suffrage meetings. Benedict worked on the college yearbook and had her writings published in the *Vassar Miscellany*. She also chaired the Bible Study Committee. Among the many friends she made in these activities was Agnes Benedict, later to become a social worker and a writer. Agnes Benedict introduced Ruth Fulton to her brother, Stanley Benedict. Ruth would later marry Stanley and take his name.

After graduation, Benedict traveled in Europe briefly. It was a marvelous trip, but her return was a letdown. At her graduation a speaker had told the class, "the graduate of this college dare not let her life be a failure; she is under bonds to do things in the world." The freedom Benedict had enjoyed at Vassar and then traveling in Europe was, she discovered sadly, not possible in the real world.

Vassar created a dilemma for its graduates. For four years women were encouraged to learn, to be free and independent thinkers. They lived in an exciting climate of ideas and possibilities. They were educated to take on important responsibilities, to be leaders, to make changes, to make life and society better. But graduation from their protected college haven was a terrible shock for Benedict and her classmates. The world—a man's world—would neither accept their help nor give them opportunities to use their learning. There were limits to the possible. Educated women, Benedict realized, would have to make their own way. "So much of the trouble is because I am a woman," she wrote in her journal. "To me it seems a very terrible thing to be a woman."

Benedict helped where she could. She got a job doing social work for the Charity Organization Society in Buffalo,

New York. As a caseworker she visited families in the slums, often immigrant families, and then tried to get help for them from public agencies. It was painful work. Women watched their children and husbands die of tuberculosis. Families lived on bread and water and a few potatoes. Mothers were starving because they gave what little food they had to their children. Benedict felt how terrible and humiliating it was to be poor—but worst of all was the hopelessness of it all. There were so many poor and hungry, more than she could possibly help. She had to deal every day with life-and-death problems, and always it seemed that what she had to offer was just too little, too late.

Benedict left social work to teach in a girls' school. She had always believed that teaching was one way to bring about social change. She taught for three years, but still she had not found the life she wanted. Despite the promises of her Vassar years, she felt unable to control the direction of her own life. She had decided to quit her job at the Orton School for Girls, and so she went to tell Miss Orton of her decision.

Anna B. Orton, the school's founder, was also a Vassar graduate. Benedict expected Miss Orton to tell her what other older women had told her, that this was life and that she must learn to do the best she could with it. But

that's not what happened. Miss Orton sympathized with her young teacher and told her not to accept a life that was painful to her. She encouraged Benedict to change her life so that it suited her better. "She gave me a self-respect I had not had for months—years," Benedict wrote in her journal that night, "and I think it was because she never once implied that it is our business to live placidly through *anything. . . .* She hadn't treated me as if I were a child. . . . She talked with me as with an equal who had a right to his own distastes and tried to help me plan my year more pleasantly. God bless her!"

Benedict returned to teach the next year. And then she fell in love with Stanley Benedict, the brother of her friend from Vassar. It seemed to her that the security of a marriage and a family was all that she had ever wanted. She would have a husband to care for her. She would be free from the struggle to be somebody. She could forget the pain of not having found out who she was. And no longer would she be tormented by dreams of doing something original. She would be a wife and a mother and that would always be enough. But for Ruth Benedict, it was not enough. She returned to social work and began to write.

Like most American husbands of the

time, Stanley Benedict could not accept the idea of his wife having a life of her own. As a renowned professor of biochemistry, he lived almost entirely in the life of his work. Wouldn't it strengthen their friendship and love, his wife argued, if she had her own interests as well? Then they could come together as equals, and a marriage of equals is always stronger. Stanley could not agree. He forbade Ruth to work outside their home. Benedict felt suffocated and became more and more depressed. Her husband had his place in life. "I must have my world too, my outlet, my chance to put forth my effort," she confided in her journal.

Benedict found her world. At thirty-two, she began attending lectures at the New School for Social Research in New York City. She decided to take courses in anthropology taught by Elsie Clews Parsons and Alexander Goldenweiser. Goldenweiser was impressed with the originality of Benedict's work and her intense interest. He suggested that she work on a doctorate in anthropology and sent her to a friend, anthropologist Franz Boas at Columbia University. Anthropology was a new field then, and it seemed to Benedict that it was what she was looking for. She saw that there was a place for women in anthropology. She could use her talents and her experience in sociol-

ogy. It would help her to understand some of her own personal questions about life, and through anthropology, she hoped, she could learn ways of bettering society.

Professor Boas advised Benedict on her studies and also served as a role model for her. He posed problems and raised questions in a way that stimulated students' minds. He made his department a community of scholars who shared their work and ideas with one another, almost like a close family. From the beginning, it was clear that here was where Benedict belonged. Her first paper was published in the *American Anthropologist*, the most important anthropology magazine in America. The article, about the culture of the Plains Indians, was widely praised. Benedict completed all her course work for her Ph.D. in three semesters. A year later, in 1923, when her dissertation was published, she became Dr. Ruth Fulton Benedict. She was one of only forty women in the United States to earn a Ph.D. in the social sciences that year. Franz Boas called her dissertation "an excellent piece of work." Other scholars began referring to her material in their writings. The renowned linguist Edward Sapir wrote Benedict, "I read your paper yesterday in one breath" and congratulated her on "a very fine piece of

Ruth Benedict in her office at Columbia University. *Vassar College Library. Photograph by Helen Codere.*

research" and a "notable addition" to anthropology.

All of Benedict's work for her papers had been done in the library. Now Dr. Benedict would do her first work in the field. She spent a summer on the Morongo Indian Reservation near Banning, California. Her work was guided by another important anthropologist of the day, Alfred Kroeber of the University of California at Berkeley. She went to the reservation to try to gather up what was left of a disappearing way of life. She talked with informants, elderly Serrano Indian men and women who still remembered the past. She gathered information on how the Serrano lived before the coming of white civilization. The elders told her about the foods they used to eat and showed her how they prepared them. They told her about the ancient ceremonies, about kinship and the tribal laws.

Now that Benedict had completed

her first fieldwork, she was ready to go out and do work on her own. She spent summers with the Zuñi and Cochiti and worked among the Pima Indians. She supervised the work of student anthropologists among the Blackfoot in Montana and Alberta, Canada; the Apache; and the Blood. Some of her informants spoke English. Others told their stories to Benedict through interpreters. As much as she wanted to learn the languages of the people with whom she talked, her deafness made it impossible. She struggled to hear the elders' quiet voices and then to record with pencil and paper her informants' every word—verbatim. One of her informants remembers of Benedict: "She always put her right hand on her ear while she talked with somebody and often asked them to speak louder."

Benedict enjoyed this active, adventurous outdoor work. It was a rare opportunity for a woman of her day, and one of the reasons she found anthropology so exciting. She often wrote to her friend Margaret Mead about her life in the field. Each letter, like this one describing her journey to Cochiti Pueblo, shows her love of the land and of the lifeways she was recording.

The cart came, and we lunged across the river and up to this quite charming pueblo. I'm glad I spent so much time with my mountains in Peña Blanca, for here, being so near them, we can't see them at all. My house is next door to a half-underground kiva with its ladder thrust up to the sky. An adobe stairway ascends from one side. It's quite effective. The houses many of them have twisted acacias to sit under in front, and porches covered with boughs whose leaves have turned just the color of the adobe.

The Indian people Benedict talked with year after year changed her life. Their lives became part of hers. Even with the long hours of writing, she found time for her first love, writing poetry. Now her poems included images of the tribal life she recorded in her notes, like this one she called "Myth":

A god with tall crow feathers in his hair,
Long-limbed and bronzed, from going
   down of sun,
Dances all night upon his dancing floor,
Tight at his breast, our sorrows, one by
   one.
.   .   .   .
And all alone he dances, hour on hour,
Till all our dreams have blooming, and
   our sleep
Is odorous of gardens—passing sweet
Beyond all, wearily, we till and reap.

It was after her many experiences with Indian peoples that Benedict decided to write a book. In this book, she would look at three cultures—the Zuñi she knew so well, the Kwakiutl of the

Ruth Benedict on a 1939 field trip, with two members of the Blackfoot tribe. *Vassar College Library.*

Northwest Coast whom Boas had studied, and the Dobu people of the South Pacific. This was the book that became *Patterns of Culture*. To most people then, especially nonanthropologists, cultures seemed to be just strange kinds of random behavior. It was hard to see any patterns or wholeness about them. Part of the problem was that so few cultures had been studied in detail. But now anthropologists were watching people carefully, scientifically, living among them for long periods of time.

Benedict came to several important conclusions in *Patterns of Culture*. Each was quite new for its day. First of all, she concluded, cultures are not just collections of strange, chaotic behaviors. Instead, she observed, cultures have direction and purpose. It is these that shape the culture. What's more, the culture shapes the individual, shaping each person's behavior and thoughts. Also, she said, cultures are not forever the same. Individuals can change patterns of the culture. Suddenly, with Benedict's insights, cultures not only in other parts of the world but also in the United States had new meaning.

Before Benedict's ideas were read, there had been a different view of human behavior. Scientists believed that biology determined behavior. They believed that every trait they saw in humans could be explained by chemistry, the genes and hormones in the body. And, since the chemistry of the body could not be changed, then behavior could not be changed either. Being poor or rich, being a master or a slave, being educated or uneducated, all were thought to be determined by biology. It was this kind of thinking that led to some people being called inferior. But worse, it led people to believe that if they were "inferior" there was no way to improve their lives—that's just the way they were. Benedict's work changed this view. It was culture, she had proven—not biology—that shaped human life. Yes, she agreed, some behavior was transmitted biologically. But the culture into which we are born and grow up, more than anything else, shapes our behavior.

Benedict had hoped that through anthropology she might better our lives. From her work on cultural patterns came new ideas about education and change. Unlike biology, culture offered the possibility of social change. No longer do people *have* to be poor. No longer do people *have* to live in poverty. No longer can we accept the idea that some people are inferior and others superior. Culture is human-made, and so culture can be changed.

With the publication of *Patterns of Culture*, Americans began to see new hope for humankind. At first Benedict's findings were known only to a small group of social scientists. But then, in 1946, *Patterns* was published as a twenty-five-cent paperback book. Millions of people all over the world read this first anthropological best-seller. It changed our views of other cultures and, surprisingly, of our own. "I have the faith of a scientist that behavior, no matter how unfamiliar to us," Benedict wrote, "is understandable. . . . And I have the faith of a humanist in the advantages of mutual understanding among men."

Franz Boas

1858–1942   Anthropologist and linguist

When Franz Boas died, one of his distinguished students, Alfred Kroeber, said, "the world has lost its greatest anthropologist, and America one of its most colorful intellectual figures." So important was Boas that it is impossible to imagine anthropology without him. He was one of the first to set up and teach university courses in anthropology. He trained the very first Ph.D. in anthropology in the United States. And many of the anthropologists whose stories are told in this book found their life's work when they met up with Boas. He trained almost all of them. Ruth Benedict decided to become an anthropologist when she took her first course with Boas. So did Margaret Mead, Zora Neale Hurston, Alfred Kroeber, and Robert Harry Lowie. But Boas was always more to his students than just a teacher. He remained a close friend and adviser long after they took their last class with him. And they referred to him fondly, even addressed him in their letters as "Papa Franz."

Very little is known about Boas's youth. He talked only occasionally about his growing up. He never wrote an autobiography or, apparently, reflected much on his childhood. His students recall that his only interest was the present and the future. Unlike the others whose stories are told in this book, Boas as a boy cannot be envisioned. His look is so serious and stern that we can't even imagine calling him "Franz" rather than "Professor Boas."

A few things we do know. Franz Boas was born in the town of Minden, West-

A photograph of Franz Boas during his early professional life.

phalia, in Germany on July 9, 1858, one of six children. His father, Meier Boas, was a prosperous businessman. His mother, Sophie Meyer, was interested in new ways of educating children and set up the first kindergarten in their town that was operated according to the philosophy of the pioneer educator Friedrich Froebel. Young Boas attended school in Minden up through the *gymnasium* ("high school"). His first interest was botany, and he spent much

of his time collecting and classifying plants. He loved to play the piano, which he continued to do into his old age. He once told his student Ruth Benedict that he'd rather have written a good poem than all the books he'd ever written—to say nothing of a good movement in a symphony.

Boas didn't start out as an anthropologist. He probably hadn't even heard of the subject when he was a student in college. He studied physics and mathematics, and after four years at Heidelberg, Bonn, and Kiel universities—in Germany it was customary to attend more than one university then—Boas received his doctorate in physical science. He learned to apply the scientific method in his studies. He would make observations, analyze the problem, try to prove that what he had discovered was correct, repeating his experiments as many times as was necessary to come up with an answer. While a student he became more and more interested in natural sciences, especially cultural geography. Still, those first years as a physicist would shape his mind and whatever he chose to study.

It was by way of cultural geography that Boas eventually found his way to anthropology. When he was twenty-five, he made a trip to Baffin Island, in northeast Canada on the Arctic Circle. It's not certain why he chose to go to this part of the world. It may be that he had read articles in the Minden newspaper about a German explorer who was traveling through the Arctic. And there were probably articles about the German meteorological station in the Arctic. In any case, Boas had very little money, so he paid for his trip by writing articles about his travels for a German newspaper.

Boas went to the Arctic with an idea, a theory, in mind. It was generally believed in his day that the human mind was shaped by the natural environment. Since the environment of the Inuit is so extreme, it must have seemed to Boas to be a good place to test out his idea. He expected to find that the cold and snow, the long, dark winters and brief summers, were what mostly shaped the Inuit personality. But that's not quite what he found. Environment did shape the Inuit culture, but there were other things going on as well. The human mind often creates a kind of reality that has nothing to do with the outside world. It was a discovery that changed Boas's ideas about the mind. Eventually, through Boas's work, it changed much of the way we all think about the human mind.

The young scientist proved to be a fine traveler and explorer. Boas traveled widely through the uncharted ter-

ritory by dogsled with Inuit guides, finding his way by the stars. From his astronomical observations Boas was able to draw a more accurate map of the Baffin Island coast than explorers had up to that time. He discovered two freshwater lakes and made other discoveries about ice and the movement of currents around the island. Boas loved the Arctic world of ice and snow. He was especially interested in the Inuit and was intrigued at the happiness and fullness of Inuit life in a place that seemed an impossible environment for humans. Throughout his life, even when he was old, whenever Boas heard about an expedition to the Arctic, he felt a nostalgia for his youthful wanderings and dreamed of going back.

His reports on the Inuit were Boas's first anthropological writings. He had discovered his interest in ethnology, the comparative study of people and their lifeways. He also did his first work in linguistics in Baffinland. He learned to speak Inuit and then began writing down phonetically what he heard, becoming the first person to record the language. So it was that when he returned to Germany, Boas did not seek a teaching position in geography or physics. Instead, he applied for a position at the Ethnological Museum in Berlin. There he met a group of Bella Coola Indians from the Northwest

Boas on his way to Baffin Island, Canada, in 1883. *American Philosophical Society.*

Coast of Canada and was intrigued by their culture. From his studies of the Bella Coolas came publications about their culture and language. Boas was now becoming a linguist as well as an anthropologist. Moreover he was feeling the tug to travel and explore again. This time he would sail for the coast of British Columbia and the land of the Bella Coolas.

On his way to the Pacific coast, Boas made some important acquaintances in the United States. There was Frederic Ward Putnam, one of America's first anthropologists and teachers of anthropology. Boas was also asked to be the assistant editor of the journal *Science*, in which he published some fifty articles over the next two years. Perhaps most important, now he had work and a living. He decided to move to the United States, to marry, and to work full time on his research and explorations. Later in his life, Boas talked to some friends about why he had decided to leave his native country. His parents, especially his mother, were ardent believers in democracy and individual freedom, and they raised their children in this family tradition. As a scholar, as an individual, and certainly as a Jew, Boas looked to America for the freedom he could not find in his own country. He had made his decision.

Over the next few years Boas re-turned again and again to British Columbia and his study of the Indians there. He also received his first academic appointment, at Clark University in Worcester, Massachusetts. Clark was a new school then, patterned after the German university model, and so Boas felt at home. It was here that he trained America's first doctor of anthropology, Alexander Francis Chamberlain, who later succeeded Boas at Clark. This was also a time of tremendous writing activity for Boas. He wrote dozens of papers on folklore, traditions, and linguistics. He was the first to describe the languages of the Chinook, Salishan, and Chemakuan peoples and translate their folktales. He observed and wrote about children growing up in North American tribes.

Boas left Clark to become assistant to his friend Putnam, who was preparing for the World's Columbian Exposition in Chicago. Among the new buildings built for the exposition would be one to house a great anthropology collection, the Field Museum. When Putnam left to go on to the Peabody Museum of American Archaeology and Ethnology at Harvard and the American Museum of Natural History in New York, Boas remained as curator of anthropology of the Field Museum, which grew into one of the greatest museums in the world. Later, Boas would follow

Putnam to the American Museum of Natural History and be given his first solid academic post, lecturer in physical anthropology at Columbia University. By now Boas's interests ranged from the Inuit to the Plains and California Indians to field studies in China. He opened new exhibit halls reflecting his personal view of how exhibits should be arranged.

"Boas was first of all a scientist," is the way his student Margaret Mead remembered him. He demanded of his students the highest standards—his standards. "The stern training his students received from him," Mead remembered well, "was designed to set them on their own feet." He insisted that his students gather enough data, get as many facts as they could first, before making any generalizations. "You don't just *have* theories," he told his students. "Your materials furnish your theories." Rather than baby them, Boas assigned his students to tasks, real work in anthropology, and let them work out a method. He was always available to his students when they needed him, but sometimes they had to work things out on their own.

Ruth Benedict wrote to him once, "All summer I've worked on the mythology and I don't suppose a day has ever passed that I haven't wished fervently I could ask you some question,

or wondered what you thought. . . ." Boas assumed, too, that his students would learn the languages they needed to do their work, as Ruth Benedict discovered. "I've been acquiring enough Spanish to read the untranslated tales," she wrote him. "You knew I'd have to do it, but I smiled at your tact in letting me find it out for myself. . . ."

Boas himself had learned many languages. "The number of wholly different languages investigated by Boas, in nearly all cases from a completely fresh start with personal recording," commented Alfred Kroeber, "is almost unbelievable." In some of his letters to Ruth Benedict, however, Boas makes it clear that learning to speak languages was not easy for him. Still, along with everything else he did, he learned over twenty Native American languages. In his book *Handbook of American Indian Languages* he analyzes nineteen languages, almost entirely his own work.

For Boas, language was the anthropologist's basic tool. Among the courses he taught were several in American Indian languages. One of these was the first course Alfred Kroeber took from Boas. Later, Theodora Kroeber wrote about her husband's memories of that first class. "Boas was a curator of anthropology at the American Museum of Natural History; he had his students come each Tuesday evening to his home on

82nd Street, close to the museum, where, at the dining table lighted by a fringe-shaded lamp, he held his class." That was the class, Alfred Kroeber remembered, which sparked his interest in anthropology and linguistics. "We spent about two months each on Chinook, Eskimo, Klamath, and Salish, analyzing texts and finding the grammar (with help and some straight-out presentation by Boas)." Later that year Boas invited an Inuit woman to his class, giving Kroeber and the other two students their first experience working with a living informant.

Boas taught his students that one of their most important skills was learning how to ask questions. He often cautioned them that asking the wrong question could result in the wrong answer. Ruth Benedict cautioned her students in the same way, for she had learned her lessons well from Papa Franz. She used to quote to her students from *Hamlet*:

We know the answers, all the answers
It is the questions that we do not know.

To Boas, a wrong question is one based on the modern point of view, modern perspective. To ask the right question the researcher must learn all about the people being studied—customs, language, how they think—and then must frame the question as they would. Since language is so much a part of how people think, it is a must that anthropologists learn the language of their subjects. Only then, Boas felt, are the right questions likely to be asked.

As Boas's students got better at asking questions, they also came up with better answers. He and his students who became the next generation of anthropologists changed greatly our view of native peoples. Before trained anthropologists began going out into the field, our impressions of native peoples in Asia, Africa, and other faraway places was that they were "strange," and their lifeways unexplainable. That's because our first impressions of these cultures came from missionaries and travelers who did not know how to ask the right questions. Their study of the people was not scientific. They knew no systematic way of observing others. But most important, they simply weren't interested in understanding others. Their purpose was to change the people, to make them Christian, to "civilize" them. These people had no intention of learning from the native peoples. Even if they had, most would have asked the wrong questions. Before Boas, anthropologists often used travelers' and missionaries' impressions to form their own ideas about native people.

Boas criticized these anthropologists who "thought that scraps of data from here, there and everywhere were enough for ethnology." Perhaps his greatest contributions to human understanding were the methods he devised to study people and their ways. His first stay among the Inuit made him realize he did not have a scientific way to study them. He had instruments and mathematics to study ice and snow, air and water, wind and currents. But human thoughts and beliefs, folktales and songs cannot be explained by mathematics. He had, he realized, no scientific measures of humanity. Finding these was a lot of what the rest of Boas's life was all about. He came to realize that if our purpose is to understand the thoughts of a people, then our conclusions must be based on *their* thoughts, not ours. Today that seems obvious. But in Boas's day it was an extraordinary idea.

For Boas, the most important quality of an anthropologist was this ability to think the thoughts of others. It didn't matter who you were, this was what you needed. And so at a time when women were just beginning to enter graduate studies, Boas encouraged them to become anthropologists. It was more than just fairness. Boas considered that women might actually be better at anthropology than men, es-

pecially in the field, where they often observed and talked with women and children. In a letter from Boas to Ruth Benedict we get a glimpse of him working with one of his colleagues in the field in British Columbia. "We are getting on quite nicely now," he wrote. "Julia is making friends with the women and has been learning matting and basket making. Now she is learning cats cradles [making figures with a loop of string on the fingers of both hands] of which there are hundreds here. She is picking up village gossip etc. The language comes pretty hard to her. I talk with difficulty and understand after I write it. I follow conversation only partly. It goes too rapidly, but I am getting into it again—There are now feasts without end."

Ruth Benedict, among others, respected Boas greatly for accepting women as colleagues equal with men. The statistics are startling. During the years that Boas was at Columbia University, twenty men and nineteen women received Ph.D.s in anthropology there. In that time Harvard graduated fifty-three male anthropology Ph.D.s and no women. The University of Chicago graduated twenty-eight men and two women. Unlike many men of his day, Boas could as easily accept a challenge from a woman as from a man. When Gladys Reichard discovered that her reading of the Coeur d'Alene language did not agree with Boas's, she confronted him. "I said to him, 'I'm afraid your *i-a* theory of Salish languages is wrong. What can we do about it?' Like a flash he came back, 'Change the theory!'" For Boas, integrity, skill, and intelligence were important in a student, not gender.

One of the ways you might appreciate Boas's work is to notice certain things the next time you visit a museum. He brought about important changes in the ways museums display the things they collect. To do this, he also changed the way museum curators thought about their collections. That change probably makes it easier for you to understand what you're seeing at the museum. Before Boas's ideas took hold, museum displays were often haphazard, just stuff gathered for display. Some museums presented "comparative" displays. Weapons, or clothing, or tools, or house models from all over the world were put together in a single hall. The visitor to the museum was expected to compare them and see how they evolved from more simple to more modern. It would be like showing stone hammers evolving eventually into a giant pile driver.

Boas disagreed with this idea. First of all, anthropologists were beginning to understand that not everything has

A Bella Coola Indian sun mask from British Columbia, collected by Franz Boas and George Hunt in 1897. *Department of Library Services, American Museum of Natural History (Neg. No. 101258). Photograph by J. Kirschner.*

to evolve. A hammer is the simplest, easiest way to drive a nail. It's simple because it works, not because it's primitive or old-fashioned. Another example would be a comparative display of Plains Indians' tepees and a model of a modern brick house. The tepee, anthropologists now understand, is not a primitive dwelling just waiting to evolve into a brick house. The tepee is an ingenious house—simple, easy to carry around, just the right shelter for a nomadic people. The last thing nomadic people need is a brick house!

But Boas had another problem with museum exhibits of the day. To him the most important reason to have a public exhibit—maybe the only reason—was to show how people all over the world live. Museum directors argued that the purpose of a large museum was research, not instruction. Boas agreed that research is an important part of what a museum does. But he argued that there are at least two more things museums provide —"healthy entertainment and instruction." Boas wanted museums to "popularize their exhibits," but he did not mean that exhibits should be slipshod and inaccurate. On the contrary, everything should be done well and always with thoroughness. Materials should be organized and displayed so that they could be enjoyed and understood by a visitor who happens not to have a Ph. D. in anthropology—that's most of us.

To make his point, Boas himself installed the Northwest Coast hall at the American Museum of Natural History. Here he brought together materials from a group of tribes having similar cultures. He focused the visitor's attention on specially chosen pieces that expressed what he wanted the visitor to know. The visitor might learn how different tribes use decorative motifs on the things they make. Or Boas might demonstrate cultural borrowing, show-

ing that peoples who live close together are more similar in their lifeways than peoples who live at a distance. Over the years, Boas's ideas have been refined and extended to other kinds of exhibits, but his basic ideas are still used in almost every museum in the world.

Although Boas is best known for his work among peoples of the Pacific Northwest, his interests extended south as well. He helped found the International School of American Archaeology and Ethnology in Mexico. He lectured at the school and did field studies in archaeology and linguistics in Mexico and Puerto Rico. Working in the Valley of Mexico, Boas was the first to discover the sequence of the ancient cultures that had lived there. From this work came a dozen reports and papers, several of which he wrote in Spanish. A colleague of those days gives us an idea of how hard Boas worked his whole life: "Almost every moment of an eighteen-hour day, seven days a week, was filled with activity. In addition to our all-day archaeological collecting trips, his supervision of excavations, his lectures at the University, and his linguistic researches on Aztec, he personally numbered, and I think washed, almost every one of the thousands of potsherds and fragments collected on our excursions."

If we could ask Papa Franz what was the most difficult of his studies, he would probably say the "problem of race." During Boas's lifetime, millions of people around the world suffered and millions more were put to death because of their race. We're all well aware of how the issue of race affects American life. A whole people were enslaved because of their race. Their acceptance in America today, even by the law, is still not certain. In the past race determined whether people were free or slave in much of the world, and it still does. In Boas's native Germany, Jews were classified as a "subhuman" race, and this classification became an excuse for murdering millions of them. But to him and most anthropologists today, *race* has no meaning. It is not a scientific way of classifying people.

Boas didn't like the term. He preferred the phrase *physical type*. He recognized that there are different physical types and that the anthropologist needs words to describe them. But *race*, as the word was being used, was, to Boas, not a useful term. He fought with all his energies against the idea that one group of people could be superior or inferior to another. There was no scientific proof and there still isn't. Over seventy years ago Boas tried to make us understand, and insisted that "Negroes have a right to be treated as individuals, not as members of a class." His book *The Mind of Primitive Man* was among

the books burned in Germany by the Nazis.

The problem, as Boas saw it, was perspective. Black people in the United States were being judged by our knowledge of them here, in America. They were made slaves here, and we continued to see them as slaves. But black history in Africa is another history. Anthropologists, archaeologists, and historians had already, in Boas's day, discovered the greatness of Africa. They knew about the beautiful ironwork of Benin, the history of the great kingdoms, the native systems of law, the art, the music, and the lifeways. Some of the renowned artists of the twentieth century, like Picasso, looked to African art for their inspiration. And yet even this knowledge had not changed our view of African Americans. Was the problem education? Boas didn't think so. He was not hopeful that Americans could solve what they saw as their race problem. "It would seem that man being what he is," he wrote in 1921, "the Negro problem will not disappear in America until the Negro blood has been so much diluted that it will no longer be recognized. . . ." New generations of anthropologists have continued his work, teaching us that we are all the same—human beings. Whether or not Boas's pessimistic prediction comes true is up to us.

James Henry Breasted

1865–1935   American Egyptologist

May 1878. It is a warm spring morning in Downers Grove, Illinois, out a way from Chicago. In one room of the little red-brick schoolhouse a class of boys and girls, their heads bent in concentration over the copybooks on their desks, write slowly, carefully. The room is quiet except for the scratching of the steel-nib pens on paper. Now and then the children pause to look up at the blackboard, dip their pens into the little glass inkwells set into each desk top, and begin writing again. On the blackboard, in the teacher's neat hand, is chalked "Monthly Examination in Geography and Arithmetic."

Among the children is Jimmy, a slim boy with thick brown hair that hangs down over his forehead. He's thirteen. He looks up at the board, and as he reads question 2, he silently shapes the words with his mouth: "Name the bodies of water you would sail on, in going from Cairo, Illinois, to Cairo, Egypt." Jimmy dips his pen into the inkwell and begins writing, his hand forming the slants and loops of his very best longhand: "Mississippi R., Gulf of Mexico, Florida Strait, Atlantic Ocean, Strait of Gibraltar, Mediterranean Sea, and Nile R."

The boy's eyes return to the blackboard for question 3, "Tell something about the Bedouin." With another dip of the pen Jimmy sets down his answer: "The Bedouin are inhabitants of the deserts of Arabia who look with contempt on the inhabitants of the towns. They are wandering pastoral tribes, hospitable, but revengeful, and addicted to plunder."

Jimmy's work that morning was not

exceptional. His grade was 88, and his rank in class was fourth. It would be difficult to guess what might come of Jimmy Breasted.

James Henry Breasted grew up to become the greatest American Egyptologist of his time. He was invited by Howard Carter and Lord Carnarvon to be there with them the moment they opened the tomb they had discovered. Earlier they had asked him to help with the difficult task of deciphering the seal impressions they found chiseled into the great block of stone protecting the entrance. Breasted studied the characters carefully, the syllables moving silently across his lips. And then he read aloud for the first time in centuries the pharaoh's name: Tutankhamen. He read the heiroglyphs as effortlessly as he might read his own name in English. Breasted had taught himself to read the ancient Egyptian signs when he was a young man.

This remarkable man saw nothing remarkable about himself at all. Unlike many archaeologists, Breasted refused to write his own story. His son Charles often urged him to write an autobiography; Breasted said he was just too busy to take the time. Besides, he argued, who would be interested? He never understood why he deserved the many honors he received. It was, he said in all seriousness, like a case of mistaken identity. He would listen to the pre-

senter of an award and "wonder who the other fellow can be for whom it was all without doubt intended." He told his son about the day he was awarded an honorary doctorate from Oxford University. He was fifty-seven years old. There he was in a scholar's scarlet robe. The Public Orator was telling the assembled guests of Breasted's accomplishments. "I listened to a lot of impossible nonsense in polished Latin, all of which was of course intended for somebody else. I saw a dusty, bare-footed youngster standing at the door of a cluttered smithy in a little village in northern Illinois, watching the big blacksmith shoeing his father's only horse. And here was a learned Oxonian in a similar scarlet robe, saying all these ridiculous things to this lad!"

Finally Breasted agreed to help with a biography. "But you would have to do it, my son," he insisted. Charles Breasted did write a biography of his father. Had he not done that, we might never have known James Henry Breasted's personal story.

Breasted was born in Rockford, Illinois, on August 27, 1865. His father, Charles Breasted, was a partner in a successful hardware and general merchandise business in Chicago. His mother was Harriet Newell Garrison. Among his earliest memories were playing on the covered wagons Grandfather

Garrison had brought back from Colorado, where he had gone in search of gold and silver. And he remembered the books his father read to him at night—The Leatherstocking Tales by James Fenimore Cooper, Daniel Defoe's *Robinson Crusoe*, the *Pickwick Papers* by Charles Dickens, and stories of the sea.

He also remembered days in early October of his sixth year, when gloom and despair gripped the family. Chicago, a great city of wooden buildings, burned to the ground. In the ashes lay his father's business. Charles Breasted was ruined.

Charles Breasted had just enough money to move the family from Rockford to Downers Grove and build a modest house. They had a small farm and here Breasted enjoyed a happy midwestern boyhood. He milked the cow and looked after the family's horse. He hoed weeds in the family garden and helped raise asparagus, which was sold at a street market in Chicago. He collected birds' eggs and butterflies and learned woodworking from his father. He loved to make and fly kites, and he was learning to play the flute.

Breasted took after his father in his love of books. He read Shakespeare and Plutarch's *Lives*. But there was one book he loved more than any other: Austen Henry Layard's *Ninevah and Babylon*. Layard's beautifully illustrated book described his discovery of the great cities of the Bible. It was published just a few years before Breasted was born, and it fired the imagination of many a young reader. Layard's enchanting descriptions of his digging appeared with page after page of drawings of great kings and splendid palaces, ranks of warriors with drawn bows, ships with oarsmen all in a row, and armies on the march. There were wonderful images of everyday life, of houses, the clothing the ancient people wore, their farm animals. And most exciting of all to Breasted were the pages of cuneiform, the ancient wedge-shaped writing on clay tablets.

"My early 'education,' was wholly haphazard and without a pattern," Breasted remembered years later. He attended the little red-brick schoolhouse until he was fifteen, when his parents sent him to what was then called Northwestern College. What interested him most were chemistry and botany. Breasted apprenticed in a local drugstore while he attended college and began his study of Latin. He enjoyed the practical chemistry and went on to become a registered pharmacist. For a time he worked in drugstores, but then his life was to take another turn.

Breasted had an aunt Theodocia (actually, she and her husband were friends of Breasted's father), who was a religious woman and devoted to Breasted. She often encouraged him to enter the ministry—"the service of God," as she put it. One day in church Breasted thought of his talks with Aunt Theodocia and suddenly had a thought, a feeling, as he explained in a letter to his sister, May, that "The Lord hath need of me." His mind was made up. "I would rather be a useful man than a rich man," he wrote. "The world appears very beautiful now that I have a mission in it, and life has new meaning. I begin studying in Chicago, at the Congregational Institute, next Tuesday." So Breasted began his study of the language and literature of ancient Israel.

Breasted had decided that he would master Hebrew—not just learn it, but master it. That was Breasted's way. He wrote Hebrew words and phrases on one side of hundreds of small cards— flash cards we'd call them today. On the other side he wrote the English translation. He was never without a packet of cards. On streetcars, on trains, at mealtimes, whenever he had a few minutes, he would go through his cards, training his eyes and his mind to recognize the Hebrew. If he made a mistake or hesitated too long, out would come that card for special drill later on. It became his personal method for learning languages. Later, in the same way,

he taught himself to read Egyptian heiroglyphs, Greek, and Latin, several languages of the ancient Near East— Aramaic, Syriac, Babylonian and Assyrian cuneiform, Arabic—as well as French and German. He was able to repeat whole books from the Old Testament and even began to *think*, he said, in Hebrew.

It was the study of Hebrew that was setting the course of Breasted's life. In his second year at the seminary a contest was announced. A prize of one hundred dollars would be given to the student who got the highest marks in a written and a public oral examination in Hebrew. Breasted and two others entered. On the day of the examination, Breasted, nervous and unsure of himself, completed the written examination quickly. Afraid he had made mistakes, he went back over his translations, checking and rechecking his answers. That evening the oral examination took place in the chapel. Breasted arrived to find the pews filled. He was the last one to be examined. Among the examiners was his professor, Dr. Samuel Ives Curtiss. Breasted remembered the questions and his answers happening so fast that he could scarcely believe the examination was already over. "That will be all, Mr. Breasted," the examiner announced.

The judges returned in a few minutes. Dr. Curtiss spoke to the people who filled the chapel, anxiously awaiting the announcement of the winner. "Because both his written examination this afternoon and his oral examination this evening have been without a single error, the judges have unanimously awarded the prize to Mr. Breasted." As Breasted stepped forward to accept the envelope, Dr. Curtiss congratulated him and then whispered, "I would like to see you in my office tomorrow morning."

Breasted lay awake all that night, wondering why Dr. Curtiss wanted to see him. The next morning he went to Dr. Curtiss's office. The elder scholar asked Breasted to be seated and then came straight to the point. "I have guessed, my young friend, that you are wavering away from the ministry." Dr. Curtiss looked kindly upon the young man before him. Breasted was one of the most talented students he had ever had. "You are torn at the moment because the pulpit appeals emotionally to your imaginative and somewhat dramatic temperament. But intellectually it confounds you with doubts which will only grow. You could be a successful preacher, but it would never satisfy you. You have the passion for truth which belongs to the scholar.

"You made a fine showing last night." Breasted blushed, overcome by a warm rush of embarrassment at such praise. "You have it in you to make of yourself one of the outstanding Hebrew scholars of America. Hebrew would be only the beginning of a career in oriental languages, culminating, perhaps, in Egyptology—a vacant field. We have great need of Orientalists. The path is thorny, the positions are few, and the financial rewards are meager. But there is always a place for a first-rank scholar—and at best, scholarship is its own reward."

Dr. Curtiss had seen through to the conflict in Breasted's heart. But even beyond that, he would help the young scholar take his next step. He had written to Professor William Rainey Harper at Yale University about Breasted and suggested that the two should meet. "I hope you will decide to make oriental languages your life work and will continue your studies under Professor Harper. Possibly he might even secure a fellowship for you. But whatever you do, I could not wish you greater success if you were my own son."

Breasted was deeply troubled by the decision he had to make. Dr. Curtiss was right, of course; it was what Breasted wanted. But there was the problem of money. He could not ask his parents to help him go to Yale. His father was ill and the family quite poor. Breasted felt he should be helping out in some way. Besides, his aunt Theodocia and his mother had their hearts set on him becoming a minister. How could he disappoint them? His family were down-to-earth, practical people. Being a minister was something they could understand. But being an "Orientalist"? What was that? And is it, they would ask timidly, possible to earn a living doing that? Still, Breasted knew there was only one answer now, and somehow he'd have to tell them. He knew, too, they would respect his decision even though they might not understand it.

One day, Breasted found the opportunity to tell his mother. He was at home, translating a passage from the ancient Hebrew text of the Old Testament. He had checked his translation against the King James Version, the Bible used by almost all the churches. Its history goes back to 1604, during the reign of King James I of England. There were, at that time, many versions of the Bible in use. The king decided to bring together a group of scholars to do a new translation that would be used in all churches. The new Bible, the King James Version as it was known, was published in 1611. In Breasted's day it was still the standard for scholars.

While Breasted worked, his mother sat quietly sewing at the window. Suddenly, he found a way to say what he had wanted to say for months now. "Mother, I'm going to tell you some-

thing which will trouble you, and you must try to understand: I've decided that I cannot be a minister." Much later in his life Breasted remembered how her hands dropped into her lap and her bit of mending slipped to the floor. She looked up at him, stunned, unbelieving, her eyes imploring him, But why?

"Let me read you this, Mother." Breasted read aloud the translation he had just made from the Hebrew. "What I've just read is correct. Now listen to this." James read the same passage from the King James Version of the Scriptures. "Do you see that it's full of mistakes which convey a meaning quite different from the original? I've found scores and scores of such mistakes. I could never be satisfied to preach on the basis of texts I know to be full of mistranslations. It's my nature to seek the sources of everything I study. The Hebrew writers fascinate me. I shall never be satisfied until I know their entire history and what forces created them."

So it was that in September 1890 Breasted found himself getting off the train at the New Haven station. He blinked in disbelief that he was actually there, picked up his heavy bags, and began walking toward the Yale campus. Harriet Breasted had juggled the family budget and borrowed a little from here and a little from there to come up with enough money to get Breasted started. "I understand the part that matters, Jimmy," she had told him. "We must fix things for you to study at New Haven." And even Aunt Theodocia, disappointed as she was, managed to come up with a little money for him. Now, at twenty-five, the pharmacist who almost became a minister began his new life as a scholar.

Life at Yale was more than Breasted could have dreamed of. He made friends with students who shared his passion for scholarship. Professor Harper treated the young scholar like a son, guiding him through his studies. Harper had been asked to be the first president of the new University of Chicago, and one day he asked Breasted what he planned to do after he was finished at Yale. He told Harper he hoped to go to Germany, whose universities were known the world over as teaching and research centers for ancient languages. "There isn't a single professorship in Egyptian in any university in the United States, and there never has been," Breasted reminded Harper. "Samuel Ives Curtiss once called my attention to this and asked me why I didn't go into Egyptian. What do *you* think of this suggestion?"

Harper turned and gazed intently at Breasted, excitement gleaming in his eyes. "Breasted, if you will go to Ger-

many and get the best possible scientific equipment, no matter if it takes you five years, I will give you the professorship of Egyptian in the new University of Chicago!" Once again Breasted's happiness and dreams were clouded by worries about money. His father was ill again, but soon recovered and seemed to Breasted to be his old self. Charles and Harriet and Aunt Theodocia wanted Breasted to fulfill his dream. And they saw to it. In July 1891 Breasted joined Professor Harper and his family and a small group of students on the steamship *Normannia* and sailed with them for Germany.

At Berlin University Breasted was introduced to the greatest Egyptologist in Germany, perhaps in the whole world, Adolf Erman. Breasted found the man kind and good-humored. Erman would see to it that his students got the most rigorous possible language training. "And so the hieroglyphic war is on," Breasted wrote home to his family. "Besides the work in Egyptian I have Coptic, Hebrew and Arabic. One is obliged to offer for his degree, *three* languages and philosophy. I will present Egyptian, Hebrew and Arabic."

It would take three years. In the meantime Breasted mastered the German language, which, to the amazement of his professors, he now spoke like a native. Erman befriended

Breasted and invited him to vacation with him and a few other students in the mountains. It was an honor for a German student and one rarely extended to a foreigner. Breasted was astonished and embarrassed by the great respect and regard Erman had for him. Still he must have found time for other activities besides studying. He attended concerts of the Berlin Philharmonic Orchestra and the Royal Opera. And he became engaged to be married to Frances Hart, a music student from San Francisco.

The date was set for Breasted's doctoral examination: July 19, 1894. In the meantime Professor Erman offered him a special opportunity. A team of scholars from the Royal Prussian Academy were going to Egypt. Their task would be to compile the first ever dictionary of ancient Egyptian. Erman invited Breasted to join the team. For any scholar, but especially for a foreigner, this was an exceptional honor. During the evening of July 19, Charles and Harriet and Aunt Theodocia received a two-word cable from Germany—"PASSED WELL." Only one other American before Breasted had ever graduated *cum laude* ("with distinction") from Berlin. Jimmy was now James Henry Breasted, Doctor of Philosophy in Egyptology.

Breasted and Frances Hart were married on their way to Egypt. And although he had never been there before, Breasted felt at home. After so many years of being submerged in Egyptian history, everything was familiar to him. He discovered that still, after thousands of years, life went on much as it had in the days of the pharaohs. But there was no way that he could have anticipated his emotions. Every day brought the excitement of finding himself surrounded by the story of Egypt's ancient past written on the hieroglyphs he now read expertly.

Breasted had many duties. Before leaving Berlin, he had received a letter from William Rainey Harper telling him of his appointment as instructor in Egyptology at the University of Chicago. The first chair in Egyptology at an American university had been created. What's more, Breasted was given the responsibility of collecting objects for an Egyptian museum to be created at the university. But his principal task was to translate many of the important inscriptions that covered temples and monuments all over Egypt.

Breasted and Frances were breathless with their first view of Luxor. Everywhere were stories from the past. "For three days, from dawn to dark," he wrote in *Pioneer to the Past*, "I never lost a moment copying inscriptions—and on one night at Karnak I copied by moonlight. The silver light streamed down through the broken roof of the vast collonnaded hall, splashing with bright patches the dusky outlines of the enormous columns. . . . Imagine a forest of 134 columns, the middle two rows sixty-nine feet high and twelve feet thick, with capitals eleven feet high; and carved upon them in deep relief the tall figures of gods and kings, with legends in hieroglyphic, and myriads of royal cartouches [oval rings within which were written the names of Egyptian kings]. I shall remember that evening until my dying day."

Soon Breasted was introduced to a new experience. He met the archaeologist W. M. Flinders Petrie, who had been digging in Egypt since 1881. For several days Petrie showed Breasted around his excavations, explaining every detail of his work. Petrie was impressed with the young Egyptologist and sensed in him a kindred spirit. He proposed that they work together on an excavation. Breasted made no commitment, for he was beginning to see more clearly what his life's work would be. It would *not* be excavating, he realized, but the reconstruction of the ancient past from writing. No one had done that, and he wasn't yet sure how he would go about it. "I have tried to find some phrase which would sum up what I want to do, or *can do*," he wrote to his father. "It is this: I want to read

to my fellow men the *oldest* chapter in the story of human progress."

Breasted returned to an idea he had had back in his student days in Berlin. He would collect *all* the historical sources of ancient Egypt wherever they were in the world. Then he would translate them all into English. That's exactly what he did. Beginning in 1899 and for the next ten years, he sought out every Egyptian text he could find—even if it was a lone hieroglyph—in museums and private collections anywhere in Europe and the United States. His wife and their young son, Charles, were his constant companions on his travels around the world. When he finished in Europe and the United States, he traveled the Mediterranean and then copied and photographed every inscription along the Nile Valley. He made thousands of photographs on glass plate negatives. (He could not afford the new "film.") Eventually Breasted's translations—not counting the pen-and-ink copies of the originals—filled ten thousand pages.

What was it all for? Breasted's dream from his student days was becoming real. "Behind all this preliminary work looms my history of Egypt," he wrote to his mother. "But before I write a history based on the original monuments, I intend to find out, to the last jot and tittle, *what the monuments say.*

The great hall of Karnak, Egypt, looking toward the Nile River. *Griffith Institute, Ashmolean Museum, Oxford.*

James Breasted in a photograph taken around 1935. *Hulton-Deutsch Collection Limited, London.*

This is what the other fellows have not yet done."

While still traveling, Breasted received a letter from Charles Scribner, a New York publisher. "Mr. Scribner expresses the desire that they may be 'privileged' to examine my *History*," he wrote to his mother. "I can only hope he does not expect a definitive history of Egypt to prove as fascinating as the latest summer novel!" Mr. Scribner decided to publish *A History of Egypt*. Eventually the book was published in German, Russian, French, Arabic, and Braille editions. Later, Breasted's five-volume study *Ancient Records of Egypt* was published by the University of Chicago.

All told, Breasted wrote over twenty books. His *Ancient Times: A History of the Early World*—a high school history textbook—was translated into Swedish, Arabic, Malay, Chinese, and Japanese. Through this book Breasted shared his learning with untold thousands of schoolchildren. He would write hundreds of articles. He would receive more than a score of honors. The little museum at the University of Chicago that he helped build eventually became the Oriental Institute. It is one of the great museums of the world.

One of Breasted's favorite remarks in his later years was "if I were only twenty years younger." He always felt that even with all he had done, it was not enough, that there was still so much more that needed to be done. "We are like some frontiersman in the night," he wrote just before he died, "holding up a torch over a dark stream and imagining that the circle of its hurrying current revealed by the torchlight is all there is to the stream."

Howard Carter (1873–1939)
George Herbert, Fifth Earl of Carnarvon (1866–1923)

English archaeologists who discovered the tomb of Tutankhamen

Sometimes buried history has to be discovered two or three times before archaeologists actually realize they've found what they've been looking for all along. It may be discovered the first time, only to be ignored as insignificant. And sometimes important clues get hidden away in museums, where they sit unknown to other archaeologists. When other archaeologists do come along, covering the same ground, entirely unaware that something's been found there before, their work would of course be much easier if they knew about the first discovery. They don't, and so they continue in doubt. But maybe these archaeologists are more careful or more observant, and so when they find something, they recognize its importance. That's the story of the quest for Tutankhamen's tomb.

Historians had long been intrigued by Tutankhamen. Many important events happened during the young pharaoh's short reign and short life. He was born about 1343 B.C., but nothing is known of his parents. Apparently, he was married to the pharaoh Akhenaton's daughter, Ankh-es-en-pa-aton, when he was very young. Upon the death of Akhenaton, Tutankhamen became pharaoh of one of the greatest kingdoms of all time. He was nine years old. He inherited not only the great pharaoh's crown and his immense power, but many of the problems Akhenaton had left behind.

Akhenaton had brought many fundamental changes to Egypt. Before him, Egyptians had worshiped many gods and goddesses, including Amon, who was the chief, or state, god. We know the gods from the stone statues, tomb paintings, and writings the Egyptians left behind. Some of the gods were depicted in human form, like Amon; Ptah, god of artisans; and Meskhenet, goddess of childbirth. Others had the body of a human and the head of an animal. Among them were Horus, the hawk-headed sky god; Ra, the great sun god with the head of a falcon; Heket, the frog goddess; and Thoth, the divine scribe, with the head of an ibis.

But Akhenaton changed this. He proclaimed Aton, the god in the sun, to be the only god. He believed that the most appropriate symbol of Egypt was the sun, upon which the whole of life depended. Then he moved the capital from Thebes to Amarna and encouraged a new style of art. But so strong was the opposition against the changes brought by Akhenaton that the young pharaoh Tutankhamen was forced to undo them. He returned the capital to Thebes and Amon to the high position he had held before. Tutankhamen's story was carved into a stone monument at one of the temples of Karnak. "I found the temples fallen in ruin," he says, "with their holy places overthrown, and their courts overgrown with weeds. I reconstructed their sanctuaries. . . . I cast statues of the gods in gold and electrum, decorated with lapis lazuli and all fine stones."

Tutankhamen died, at about the age of nineteen, around 1325 B.C., and for thousands of years the details of his life were obscured by time. To find out more about this boy who ruled Egypt, archaeologists would have to find his tomb. And there, in the artifacts and in the writings and paintings on the walls, they hoped, could be read the story of his life and times.

If Tutankhamen's tomb could be found, it would be in the Valley of the Kings. Here, in a deep gorge cutting through the rocky desert near Luxor, archaeologists would eventually find more than sixty tombs. Earlier pharaohs had built immense pyramids of stone for their tombs. Later, about two hundred years before Tutankhamen's reign, the pharaohs began to be buried in caves hewn from the rock cliffs of the gorge. Pyramids had proven too easy for grave robbers, and the architects of the tombs sought "a solitary place where no one could watch and no one could listen." Some of the tombs were unbelievable. The largest was 470 feet long and plunged 180 feet below the desert floor. But the cave tombs did little to deter grave robbers. Every tomb found over the years had been robbed, and there was little hope that Tutankhamen's tomb would be found undisturbed. But cave burials did make the archaeologists' work considerably more difficult.

Pyramids, of course, jut out of the ground, so they're easier to find. But you can be standing on top of a cave tomb and never know it. That's what happened to the leader of one expedition, who discovered some small jars buried in the sand. Inside were a few items—linen bags filled with chemicals, a few pieces of cloth, some utensils, and dried but still beautiful floral collars—"trifles" is the way he described them. He put them aside. And then they sat in the Metropolitan Museum of Art in New York for several decades, ignored. Later, Herbert Winlock, curator of the Egyptian department at the museum, realized the importance of the find. What the expedition leader and the museum staff had failed to notice was that on one of the jars was the impression of Tutankhamen's seal. The "trifles," it turned out, had been used thousands of years earlier in the young pharaoh's embalming ceremony. What's more, they marked almost the exact location of his tomb.

The next chapter in the search for Tutankhamen's tomb begins with the meeting of two remarkable men, Howard Carter and Lord Carnarvon. George Edward Stanhope Molyneux Herbert, fifth earl of Carnarvon, was, even as a child, interested in antiquities. His sister, Winifred, recalled the interests of the young earl, "Porchy," to his family and close friends. "Curiosity shops had been his happy hunting grounds. As a little lad, besides the stereotyped properties of the average schoolboy, the inevitable stamp album, and a snake— the latter housed for a whole term at Eton in his desk—when he had a few shillings to spare, blue and white cups, or specimens of cottage china, would be added to his store of treasures. He was still at Cambridge [University] when he began collecting French prints and drawings. . . ."

Young Carnarvon was a terrible disappointment to his teachers. "Before he left home for school," his sister recalled, "tutors and governesses had pronounced Porchy to be idle; and probably, as in the case of most active young creatures, it was no easy task to hold his sustained attention. Yet, judged by the less exacting standards of the present day, a child of ten would now scarcely be considered backward who was bilingual—French being the language used with mother and teachers—was possessed of a fair knowledge of German, the Latin Grammar, and the elements of Greek, and sang charmingly to the old tin kettle of a schoolroom piano." Winifred reflects on the reasons for Porchy's lack of enthusiasm for schooling. Perhaps it was the perfection and scholarship demanded by the boy's father. Or, perhaps, it was just bad teaching. "Labels are fatal things. . . . It is one of life's little ironies on which schoolmasters should ponder, that a man destined to reveal a whole chapter of the Ancient World to the twentieth century, frankly detested the classics as taught at Eton."

Carnarvon was recognized as an expert yachtsman and, at the age of twenty-three, sailed around the world. He had a passion for cars, fast cars, and was the third person in all of England to receive an automobile license. In fact it was his automobile, or rather his fast driving, that caused him to go to Egypt. Badly hurt in an automobile accident, Carnarvon could no longer endure the English winters. He began traveling to Egypt in the winter of 1903 for the warm climate and there discovered his interest in archaeology. While visiting archaeological sites in the Valley of the Kings, he decided that this was what he had been looking for, a way to combine his love for art and collecting and travel, and his passion

for adventure. And it was here that he would meet his future colleague and lifelong friend Howard Carter.

Howard Carter was born in Norfolk, May 9, 1873. His father, Samuel John Carter, earned a living painting pictures of animals. The family could not afford to educate Carter at school, so he was tutored at home. Samuel taught his son to sketch and paint, and Carter became an expert draftsman. As a youngster he earned pocket money from his paintings of the pet dogs, cats, canaries, and parrots of his father's clients. It was this training in art that started him on the path toward archaeology.

When Carter was seventeen something wonderful happened. Professor Percy E. Newberry, who was then on the staff of the Cairo Museum and taught Egyptian history at the University of Egypt, happened to be visiting one of the people for whom Carter had painted animal pictures. Newberry recalled the day some years later in his memoirs: "I was then in need of assistance in inking-in the mass of pencil tracings that had been made the previous winter at Beni Hasan, and Lady Amherst of Hackney, with whom I was staying at Didlington Hall, Norfolk, suggested that Howard Carter, who was at that time living in the neighboring village of Swaffham, would be most useful for this purpose."

Newberry was so impressed with the young man's portfolio of drawings and his interest in archaeology that he hired him on the spot and set him to work at the British Museum. The staff at the museum were also impressed with Carter's work, and in three months he was on his way to Egypt. It was there that he met and was invited to join the staff of Sir William Matthew Flinders Petrie. It was Petrie who, perhaps more than any other, established archaeology as a science. As a youngster he was fascinated by mathematics and chemistry, and he was the first to apply his scientific training to solving archaeological riddles. And now he had on his staff a young man with the same curiosity and enthusiasm.

In Petrie, Carter had found the best possible teacher. While he made his careful drawings, Carter also had the opportunity to work alongside the renowned Egyptologist. For four months he received training in the art of excavating. And rather than just learning conventional techniques, Carter was introduced from the very first day to an entirely new approach to archaeology, the scientific archaeology of the future. To student archaeologists of today, Petrie's suggestions would seem basic, but in those days they were nothing less than revolutionary. Petrie later wrote down his basic principles in his book

Ten Years Digging in Egypt, 1881–1891. "The main requirement," he instructed his eager young student, "is plenty of imagination. . . . Every ounce of earth [must be] examined. . . . Pottery is the very key to digging. . . . Never dig anywhere without some definite aim. . . . The most trivial things may be of value, giving a clue to something else. . . . Keep a record of where everything is found. . . . Soak all finds to prevent the corrosive effects of salt. . . . Wrap finds in wax to preserve from air. . . . One-fifth of the time of excavation is spent in packing a collection. . . . Finding things is but sorry work if you cannot preserve them and transport them safely."

Petrie saw that young Carter had talent. Carter was appointed as draftsman to the staff of the Archaeological Survey and worked on two important excavations. A year later he joined the staff of another great archaeologist, Édouard Naville, with whom he worked for six years. He drew hundreds of exquisite line drawings of sculptured scenes and inscriptions uncovered in the temple of Queen Hatshepsut. Later Carter's drawings were published in six beautiful volumes by the Egypt Exploration Society.

It was now clear that Carter was not only a skilled draftsman, but a talented archaeologist as well. He led excavations in the Valley of the Kings and discovered the tombs of two important Egyptian rulers, Hatshepsut and Thutmose IV. So it was that Carter came to the attention of the director-general of the Service of Antiquities of Egypt, Sir Gaston Maspero. The professor was so impressed with Carter that he appointed him, at the age of twenty-five, inspector-in-chief of monuments in Upper Egypt and Nubia. The young draftsman-turned-Egyptologist became curator of what must have been the largest open-air museum in the world. It included the cities of Thebes, Karnak, and Luxor, the Valley of the Kings, and many more of the most important archaeological sites in Egypt.

Carter was in charge of restoring temple ruins and was the first ever to put electric lighting deep into the rock tombs, which made it possible for people to come from all over the world to view the wonders of ancient Egypt. Perhaps most important, he influenced the methods of other archaeological teams coming to excavate. Most were using the shotgun method, digging haphazardly here and there and everywhere, hoping to find something, anything. He encouraged them to adopt instead the techniques he had learned from Petrie—what Carter called a "systematic exploration in the Valley."

It was about this time that Carnarvon

appeared in Egypt and applied to Maspero for a permit to dig. "It had always been my wish and intention even as far back as 1889 to start excavating," his sister quoted him in her biography of Carnarvon, "but for one reason or another I had never been able to begin. . . . I may say that at this period I knew nothing whatever about excavating. . . . There, for six weeks, enveloped in clouds of dust, I stuck to it day in and day out. Beyond finding a large mummified cat in its case, which now graces the Cairo Museum, nothing whatsoever rewarded my strenuous and very dusty endeavours. This utter failure, however, instead of disheartening me had the effect of making me keener than ever."

Maspero kept an eye on the new arrival and was impressed with the seriousness of his quest, to say nothing of his lack of experience. He recommended to Carnarvon that he take on an experienced excavator. Maspero introduced him to Carter with the recommendation that the young Carter be superintendent of the excavations.

Their partnership turned out to be a happy one. Carter had all the skills and experience Carnarvon lacked. He had learned well the lessons of Petrie and Newberry, two of the best archaeologists of the day. In addition to archaeology and Egyptology, Petrie had

Lord Carnarvon with Lady Evelyn Herbert and Howard Carter. *Copyright © Times Newspapers Ltd.*

taught Carter the logistics and economics of running an archaeological dig. Carter had taught himself to speak Arabic and to read the ancient hieroglyphs. His superb drawings were the very best of the draftsman's art (and are collected today). And he had conducted extensive excavations on his own. Most important, the two men shared a reverence for things from the past.

Carter explained that reverence in his book *The Tomb of Tutankhamen,* which he dedicated to Carnarvon.

It was slow work, painfully slow, and nerve-racking at that, for one felt all the time a heavy weight of responsibility. Every excavator must, if he has any archaeological conscience at all. The things he finds are not his own property, to treat as he pleases, or neglect as he chooses. They are a direct legacy from the past to the present age, he but the privileged intermediary through whose hands they come. . . . Destruction of evidence is so painfully easy, and yet so hopelessly irreparable. Tired or pressed for time, you shirk a tedious piece of cleaning, or do it in a half-hearted sort of way, and you will perhaps have thrown away the one chance that will ever occur of gaining some important piece of knowledge.

In every way these two men, who had known one another for only a short time, had actually spent their lives preparing for this endeavor and were ready to go to work.

That work took many years and included many disappointments. They had actually reached the point, after several seasons of failure, when Carnarvon was ready to give up. Perhaps, he thought, they should listen to the voices that had been saying all along that there was nothing more to be found, that the age of discovery in the Valley of the Kings was past. Carter argued for more time and finally convinced his friend to stay with it one more season. Carter returned to the valley and on November 1, 1922, began what was to be the last season of digging. On the fourth morning of the dig it happened—"the dramatic suddenness of the initial discovery left me in a dazed condition," Carter later recalled.

Carter arrived at the site that morning to a strange scene. "The unusual silence, due to the stoppage of the work, made me realize that something out of the ordinary had happened, and I was greeted by the announcement that a step cut in the rock had been discovered. . . ." Carter and his men dug feverishly the next day, clearing away the sand and broken rock that filled the stairway. November fifth: "It was clear by now beyond any question," Carter later wrote, "that we actually had before us the entrance to a tomb." The many previous disappointments kept Carter from being too hopeful. "I watched the descending steps of the staircase, as one by one they came to light. . . . Work progressed more rapidly now; step succeeded step, and at the level of the twelfth, towards sunset, there was disclosed the upper part of a doorway, blocked, plastered, and sealed."

"A sealed doorway—it was actually true, then!" For the answer to what lay behind the doorway, Carter would wait several days until Carnarvon arrived from England. Carter had wired his friend the news so that they could make the discovery together. Work resumed just before Carnarvon's arrival so that they could get down into the staircase without delay. "By the afternoon of the 24th the whole staircase was clear, sixteen steps in all, and we were able to make a proper examination of the sealed doorway. On the lower

Entrance to the tomb of King Tutankhamen. *Griffith Institute, Ashmolean Museum, Oxford.*

part of the seal impressions were much clearer, and we were able without any difficulty to make out on several of them the name of Tut-ankh-Amen."

Carter bored a peephole into the door and found behind it a passageway filled with stones and rubble. After photographing the door and its seal impressions, the workers broke through and began clearing away the rubble. "The day following (November 26) was the day of days, the most wonderful that I have ever lived through, and certainly one whose like I can never hope to see again. Throughout the morning the work of clearing continued. . . ." Carter, Carnarvon, his daughter, Lady Evelyn Herbert, and Egyptologist A. R. Callender stood by in suspense. "Then in the middle of the afternoon, thirty feet down from the outer door, we came upon a second sealed doorway, almost an exact replica of the first. The seal impressions in this case were less

Howard Carter cleaning off the inner coffin of Tutankhamen, having raised the lid of the outer coffin. *Brown Brothers.*

distinct, but still recognizable as those of Tut-ankh-Amen and of the royal necropolis." Fortunately, Carter has left for us these vivid accounts of the final days and moments of discovery.

Slowly, desperately slowly it seemed to us as we watched, the remains of the passage debris were removed, until at last we had the whole door clear before us. . . . With trembling hands I made a tiny breach in the upper left-hand cor-

ner. Darkness and blank space, as far as an iron testing-rod could reach, showed that whatever lay beyond was empty, and not filled like the passage we had just cleared. Candle tests were applied as a precaution against possible foul gasses, and then, widening the hole a little, I inserted the candle and peered in, Lord Carnarvon, Lady Evelyn and Callender standing anxiously beside me to hear the verdict. At first I could see nothing, the hot air escaping from the chamber causing the candle flame to flicker, but presently, as my eyes grew accustomed to the light, details of the room within emerged slowly from the mist, strange animals, statues, and gold—everywhere the glint of gold. For the moment—an eternity it must have seemed to the others standing by— I was struck dumb with amazement, and when Lord Carnarvon, unable to stand the suspense any longer, inquired anxiously, "Can you see anything?" it was all I could do to get out the words, "Yes, wonderful things." Then, widening the hole a little further, so that we could both see, we inserted an electric torch.

Surely never before in the whole history of excavation had such an amazing sight been seen as the light of our torch revealed to us.

Once in the antechamber, Carter and Carnarvon found a jumble of royal treasures, hundreds of beautiful objects— a golden throne with a picture of the pharaoh and his queen made of colored glass, cups and vases of gleaming white alabaster, a little ebony-wood chair in- laid with gold that recalled the pharaoh's childhood, beds whose legs and frames were legs and bodies of fantastic animals, life-size statues of Tutankhamen. But as splendid as all this was, the objects seen through the hole in the door turned out to be just the beginning. There was another sealed door beyond the roomful of treasures, leading to a golden shrine, and another door to the treasure chamber, and yet another to an annex as full of wondrous things as the antechamber. And there was a wall that, when carefully dismantled, revealed the greatest treasure of all. "With intense excitement I drew back the bolts of the last and unsealed doors; they slowly swung open, and there, filling the entire area within . . . stood an immense yellow quartzite sarcophagus, intact . . . just as the pious hands had left it." They had found Tutankhamen.

Jean-François Champollion

1790–1832   French philologist and Egyptologist who deciphered the Egyptian hieroglyphs

The story of how the Egyptian hieroglyphs were deciphered is not the story of one man. True, it was the great mind and energies of Jean-François Champollion that brought to life voices that had been mute for centuries. But archaeological and scientific discovery can be likened to a staircase. Someone mounts the first step toward understanding, someone else the second, and so on until enough is known and someone further along finally puts it all together. Seldom do great discoveries come from a sudden flash of inspiration. Decipherment of the Egyptian hieroglyphs, like the cuneiform of ancient Sumer (see the chapter on Georg Friedrich Grotefend) and other ancient languages, was the work of many.

This story begins in 1798, when Napoleon sailed with a French fleet of 328 vessels carrying 38,000 men, all bound for Egypt. Napoleon's objectives were not archaeological—he was bent on conquering Egypt, as his hero Alexander the Great had done two thousand years earlier. Still, he had personally attended a meeting of scientists and invited them to accompany him to Egypt. Among the thousands of soldiers were a number of chemists, historians, poets, painters, astronomers, mineralogists, and mathematicians. With them came a huge library of books on Egypt and crates of scientific instruments.

This was Napoleon's style. And no matter how one feels about him as a leader or a general—the Egyptian campaign ended in disaster—he did this

47

kind of thing well. Among Napoleon's "learned civilians" was an artist, Dominique Vivant Denon, who was the emperor's personal choice. Denon drew all that he saw. He rendered it beautifully and, most important, accurately, in precise detail. He was especially fascinated by the writing with pictures, the hieroglyphs, that covered every surface of the temples and monuments he saw. These he copied as faithfully as everything else. He could not read the hieroglyphs or make out from them a single sound of ancient language. No one could. But he saw that there were different styles of writing and began choosing with purpose the subjects he would draw.

Little was known of Egypt in the Europe of this time. Few travelers had made it as far along the Nile as Denon and none of them, apparently, had his eye for historic detail. Very few Egyptian relics had yet made their way to museums. In this day of air travel, photography, and high-speed printing presses, it's hard for us to imagine a time when there were places totally unknown to the rest of the world. When Denon's drawings were published back in France, they epitomized Egypt to countless curious minds who had never seen these wondrous things before. So accurate and evocative were his drawings that they were used for years for the study of Egyptian writing, art, and architecture.

Something else of great importance to our story happened during that ill-fated military venture. Some French troops, digging in the vicinity of Rosetta in the Nile Delta, unearthed a large, flat slab of black basalt. The stone, which is now in the British Museum, is about four feet high and three feet wide. Fortunately, one of the soldiers recognized it as possibly something of importance. He was right. The stone, though broken all around in jagged edges, was complete enough to show inscriptions in three different scripts. Two of the scripts—the hieroglyphs and another of squiggly lines—were undecipherable, but the third was Greek! And the Greek was easily translated by one of Napoleon's generals. It had been written in 196 B.C., a decree by the priests of Memphis praising the king, Ptolemy V. Keep that name in mind—it will be important later.

Before we go on, you need a lesson in ancient Egyptian. The Egyptian language is so old and goes back so far that no one really knows how it began. Scholars today see that Egyptian was similar, especially in the way it was spoken, to ancient African languages. And they see similarities with Semitic languages, like Arabic and Hebrew. It's probable that written Egyptian began

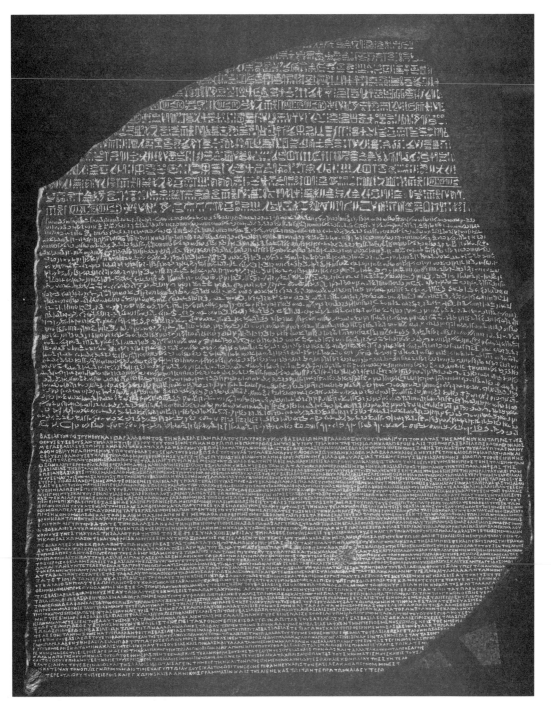

The Rosetta Stone. *British Museum.*

as a pictographic or picture language. On the earliest pottery found at archaeological sites are drawn little images of people, animals, boats, plants, birds, and other objects that are not just pictures, but writing.

Pictographs are fine when you are communicating about things. But what happens when you want to write about feelings, or thoughts, or concepts like truth and honesty, or dreams and fantasies? Pictures don't work for these, so you come up with symbols that represent these abstract ideas. And then there are symbols that neither are pictographs nor stand for abstract ideas, but tell us how to pronounce a word. The pictographs and symbols that come to mind when we hear or read about Egypt are called hieroglyphs, "sacred carvings." That's because this writing was engraved on temple walls.

Now you can see the problem with deciphering hieroglyphic writing. Does a picture of a falcon, for instance, stand for *bird*, or does it mean *flight*, or does it stand for the sound *B* (as in *bird*) or *F* (as in *falcon*)—or might it do all three things? Is it possible that the picture of a bird no longer has anything to do with birdness but now has a totally unrelated meaning? Is each picture a word or is each picture like a letter? Is a group of pictures a word or a long thought? Do you read left to right?

Right to left? Top to bottom? And how do you figure out how the language sounded and which symbols go with which sounds? Not easy.

The little pictures in the inscription at the top of the Rosetta Stone were recognizable as hieroglyphs. And the language of the inscription at the bottom was clearly Greek. But what about the squiggly writing in the middle? This kind of writing is called demotic, or popular writing. Hieroglyphs might have been fine for writing on temples and monuments, but what happened when someone wanted to write a letter, or a receipt, or a long story, or a poem, or a military order? Writing in hieroglyphs was too slow, and, besides, it was so hard to learn that few people learned it. What evolved, then, was ordinary writing for everyday life, demotic writing. It's sort of like the cursive writing you learned after you could print. And by the way, the hieroglyphs, reshaped by the Phoenicians, given vowels by the Greeks, and then reshaped some more by the Romans, are the basis of our own alphabet.

What's very important to our story is that when the Rosetta Stone was discovered, scholars were beginning to read demotic writing. They were even more intrigued by the possibility that all three inscriptions—hieroglyph, demotic, and Greek—were the same document written in three languages. All of this was a prelude to the eventual decipherment of the hieroglyphs. It's just that no one knew it yet.

By the time Champollion was eleven years old, most of the pieces needed to complete the puzzle of the hieroglyphs were coming together. That was the year the eminent mathematician Jean-Baptiste Fourier visited Champollion's classroom and was so impressed with the boy that he invited him to his home. Fourier showed Champollion some of the things he had brought back from Egypt, including a drawing of the Rosetta Stone. Champollion would never forget that moment he first saw fragments of papyrus with the mysterious black script and stone tablets with hieroglyphic inscriptions. "Can anyone read them?" he asked Fourier. The mathematician shook his head. "I am going to do it," Champollion announced with the confidence of a grown-up. "In a few years I will be able to. When I am big."

Fourier knew enough about the boy not to doubt him. At eleven, Champollion was already practically a grown-up. He was well on his way to mastering Latin and Greek and had begun the study of Hebrew. When he was twelve he was studying the Old Testament in the centuries-old original. And he was not learning these languages at school.

In fact he was doing so poorly in school that his brother, twelve years older and himself a talented linguist, took Champollion out of school and took personal charge of his education. The next year the boy wrote his first book, *History of Famous Dogs*, and put together his own history of the world, his "Chronology from Adam to Champollion the Younger." When he was thirteen, Champollion took up the study of Arabic, Syrian, and Chaldean. He also began studying Coptic, a later development in the Egyptian language, written in Greek characters and using some Greek words. Within a year he was writing his personal journals in Coptic and spoke it so well that he once remarked, "I speak Coptic to myself." Eventually he spoke Arabic so well that Arabs he met took him for one of their own. Soon he would be studying Zend, Pahlavi, and Parsi—dialects from ancient Persia—and Sanskrit, the ancient language of India. Once, when he was away from home, he wrote his brother asking him to send a Chinese grammar book "for amusement."

Even at this early age, Champollion was not only learning all he could, he was doing original research. When he was seventeen he drew up a chart showing the succession of pharaohs. There was no such chart in existence at the time. Champollion compiled it on his own, using information he gleaned from the Bible and fragments of text in Latin, Arabic, Hebrew, and Coptic. It was this year that he applied for admission to the lycée, an academically rigorous secondary school, in Paris. And instead of writing the usual schoolboy's essay on his application, he submitted the outline for an entire book, which he titled *Egypt Under the Pharaohs*. He was then invited to read the introduction to his book to the assembled faculty of the lycée. He was subsequently admitted to the lycée—but not as a student. The faculty was so impressed with his knowledge, his theses, and the logic of his arguments that they elected him to the faculty! "In making you a member of the faculty," the president announced, embracing Champollion, "we of the lycée are taking into account your accomplishments to date. Yet beyond that we are counting on what you will do in the future. We are convinced that you will justify our hopes. . . ." In a matter of minutes, Champollion had graduated from student to teacher.

In the meantime, important new information had come to light. The French scholar Antoine Silvestre de Sacy had begun making comparisons between the Greek and demotic texts on the Rosetta Stone. De Sacy could reach only a partial solution, but the next year, other scholars took major steps toward deciphering the demotic. Swedish diplomat and philologist J. D. Åkerblat, comparing the Greek and demotic writings, identified all the proper names and the words *temple* and *Greeks*. Then an English physicist and physician, Thomas Young, realized that the clusters of characters enclosed in lozenge-shaped rings were the names of royalty. The rings are called cartouches, and understanding their use made it easy to find names in the inscriptions. The scholarship was remarkable; slowly, piece by piece, the puzzle was coming closer to being finished. Still, none of these men was able to make the breakthrough. Although it was becoming clear that the demotic script was "alphabet writing," no one was able to accept the idea that so was the hieroglyphic. They were all working under a false premise.

The prevailing wisdom of the time was that the hieroglyphs were picture writing. Several ancient writers had said so. Herodotus, the great Greek historian, had said it, and he had actually been to Egypt. And Horapollon, who lived in the fourth century B.C., had described Egyptian as picture writing. Since he lived so much closer to the time when hieroglyphs were used (though he couldn't read them either), it just seemed that he ought to know. So everyone assumed that the answer to deciphering the hieroglyphs was in understanding the symbolism of the little pictures.

There's a problem about ideas that become so set in our minds. They interfere with our reasoning, especially if they are wrong. For a long time people's ideas about hieroglyphs kept them from seeing any alternatives—but not for Champollion. When he was just twenty-five, Champollion began to have concerns about Horapollon's conclusions. "This work [by Horapollon] is called *Hieroglyphica*," he wrote in a letter, "but it does not contain an interpretation of what we know as hieroglyphs, but rather of the sacred sculptural symbols—that is, the emblems of the Egyptians—which are quite different from the real hieroglyphs. . . . The sacred sculptures distinctly show the emblematic scenes mentioned in Horapollon, such as the snake biting the swan, the eagle in characteristic posture, the heavenly rain, the headless man, the dove with the laurel leaf, etc., but there is nothing emblematic in the real hieroglyphs." In other words, Horapollon was confusing the sacred symbols of Egypt with the symbols of the hieroglyphs.

Champollion had some advantages over the others attempting to decipher the hieroglyphs. He was able to put out of his mind the centuries-old belief

Jean-François Champollion.

that the hieroglyphs were picture writing. As soon as he did this, his mind was open to possibilities that others were closed to. Then there was his amazing grasp of languages, especially Coptic, which proved crucial to his work on the hieroglyphs. By the time he was eighteen years old, Champollion had mastered twelve ancient languages. Perhaps most important was his knowledge of philology and the structure of languages. The other scholars were try-

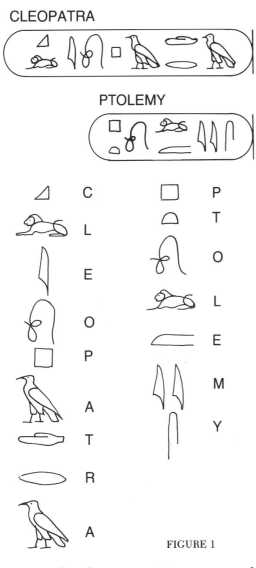

FIGURE 1

phonetic. If this were true, he reasoned, then the individual signs stood for letters and sounds. To test his hypothesis, he would try to spell with hieroglyphs the royal names in the cartouches. He had the name Ptolemy from the Rosetta Stone. Now there was a new find, a small obelisk on which were inscribed the names of Ptolemy VII and his wife, Cleopatra, in both Greek and hieroglyphs. Champollion placed the two cartouches one above the other (see Figure 1).

He noticed something immediately. The two names have two signs in common: the square and the lion. Champollion guessed, from the position of the letters in the names, that these signs might stand for the letters *P* and *L*. So he tried them, and the letters fit in the right places. The square (at the upper left of the Ptolemy cartouche) is the sign for *P* and the lion is the sign for *L*. Once he had done this, Champollion could guess what the other hieroglyphs were. For instance, the letter *A* is used twice in *Cleopatra*. Since the falcon appears twice in Cleopatra's cartouche, it must be the sign for *A*. The segment of the circle and the hand seemed not to work. Then Champollion guessed that they must be homophones, two signs having the same sound: *T*.

Champollion also found that the

ing to decode ancient Egyptian word for word. But Champollion was grasping the underlying system of the language.

Champollion became convinced, beyond a doubt, that the hieroglyphs were

Greek spelling (Ptolemy) was different from the Egyptian spelling, but the two were close enough for Champollion to see that they denoted the same person.

As Champollion went further and further into deciphering the hieroglyphs, he began to realize how complicated they were. Some of the signs were indeed pictographs. Others were phonograms, signs that stand for sounds. The hieroglyphic writing, then, had both sense signs and sound signs. Ancient Egyptian writing, like Arabic and Hebrew, did not have symbols for the vowels. But vowels aren't really necessary. Wth lttl prctc y cn lrn t rd by pttng th vwls n yrslf. The writing, Champollion discovered, was done in three directions—left to right, right to left, and top to bottom.

Champollion's achievement showed that there is nothing mysterious about hieroglyphs. The language—though not easily pronounceable—has a grammar that can be learned. And it has the special qualities of being both pleasing to the eye and intriguing to the mind. Many people have learned to read hieroglyphs and many students at universities today are learning to read Egyptian and other ancient languages. They owe this special opportunity to read the literature of ancient Egypt to Jean-François Champollion.

Champollion died in 1832. Fortunately, he had completed his book *Egyptian Grammar*, which made it possible for Egyptologists all over the world not only to read the hieroglyphs but also to write in Old Egyptian. Happily, he had an opportunity to visit Egypt before his death. Friends who were there said he dressed in native clothing and that he was so excited walking among the temples and great statues. People came from all over to see the man who could read the hieroglyphs. Surely it must have given Champollion great joy to look upon the walls and give voice once again to the writing of ancient Egypt.

Arthur Evans

1851–1941   English archaeologist who found Knossos

If you look at a map of Europe and find Greece, and then look to the south, in the Mediterranean Sea, you'll find the island of Crete. Here, a long time ago, from about 2600 to 1100 B.C., lived the ancient ancestors of the Cretans of today. They called themselves Minoans, a name taken from their legendary king Minos, and the centers of their civilization were the great palaces at Knossos, Mallia, Phaistos, and Zakros.

The Cretans were farmers and fishermen. They raised barley and wheat, olives, grapes, sheep, goats, and pigs. Some Cretans lived in villages and towns and were artisans known all over the world for their beautiful carved alabaster figures, goldwork, bronze tools and swords, and decorated eggshell-thin pottery. They painted colorful wall frescoes of their sports, religious life, animals and plants, and the sea around them. They had a written language. They knew metallurgy, knew how to alloy copper with tin to make bronze. And they built fine ships that carried Cretan manufactures to ports all around the Mediterranean.

The ships returned with wondrous things from all over the world: copper from Cyprus; lapis lazuli, an exquisite deep-blue stone from Afghanistan; ivory from Africa; gold and gemstones from Egypt. Crete was wealthy and powerful. But then, suddenly, sometime around 1100 B.C., the civilization just disappeared. All that remained were piles of stone and rubble and a few legends handed down from Greek storytellers. And so it was for thousands of years, until the early twentieth century, when the English archaeologist Arthur Evans went looking for Minos's legendary kingdom.

Evans seems to have spent his entire life preparing for his work. As a child, he was already becoming a skilled historian. He spent his days studying the fascinating objects his father collected. He was even then serious about everything he did. "Arthur," his father wrote in his diary, "has announced his intention of becoming a poet and an astronomer." In another entry he noted that "Arthur is taking very diligently to drawing coins and writing letters."

Evans's home was like a museum. His father had many interests, and so the house was filled with wonderful old things to enchant a curious boy. John Evans was a numismatist, a coin collector, and his broad interests included archaeology, geology, and anthropology. He had a huge collection of coins, and as a young man was already an expert on gold coinage in Britain before the days of the Roman invasion. So, in Evans's house were fossils, ancient flint axes, stone tools and bronze weapons, Roman glass and jewelry, old weapons and pottery, dazzling rocks and minerals.

But John Evans was not just content to read and collect. He was a member of the Geographical Society, and he wrote articles on coins regularly for historical journals. He was also an explorer, and one of the few in his day knowledgeable about paleontology, the study of fossil animals and plants from early geological periods, millions of years ago.

Once he traveled to Amiens, France, to a place where he had heard stone tools could be found. As usual, he took his son Arthur with him. "We proceeded to the pit," he wrote in his diary, "where sure enough, the edge of an axe was visible in an entirely undisturbed bed of gravel and eleven feet from the surface." The ax was an important find in itself. But John Evans knew that even more significant was the depth at which it was found. It meant that the humans who had made the ax lived much longer ago than anyone had guessed.

Of all the things Evans enjoyed, he was happiest when he and his father explored history together. They would go out looking for fossils, and when he was nine Evans went along with his father on a dig. They worked side by side with pick and shovel, carefully digging, freeing pottery shards from the side of a cliff. Later, John Evans would show his son how to clean, classify, and match the pieces of a broken pot and then, like working on an immensely complex puzzle, try to put them back together again. When Evans was twelve, the two of them went off on another archaeological expedition. Again, when he was fourteen, they spent ten days together digging in northern France. The next year, Flint Evans, as John was known to his friends, brought his son with him to a meeting of the Society of Antiquaries, an association of scholars and amateur historians. There Evans sat in the audience and listened proudly as his father stood up at the podium and read a paper on the artifacts he had found while digging in Ireland.

As a teenager Evans was already on his way to becoming a historian. When he was a student at Harrow, he became secretary of the Scientific Society, the oldest student natural-science club in England. He organized an exhibit of artifacts, minerals, coins, and fossils from his father's collections, some of which he had helped find. He published a catalog of the artifacts with his own pen-and-ink drawings of his favorite pieces. And, like his father, he stood before the group and read papers he had written on his own research. One he titled "The Antiquity of Man."

But there was another side to Evans, and one his father definitely disapproved of: his playful, mischievous side. His friends at Harrow were unable to control their laughter—and his teachers

their irritation—at Evans's antics at school. He had a pet snake that he had trained to crawl up the sleeve of his jacket. Then, sometime in the middle of math class, the snake would pop its head out through Evans's collar. Evans also published on his own a little magazine he called the *Pen-Viper* (a play on the little cloths students kept at hand to wipe their pens). It was full of advice to younger boys in the school; for instance, "be as noisy as you can. That pays more than anything, and if you carry it out well, you are sure to be popular."

All of these things were part of Evans's childhood. He read the books in his father's library and studied and drew the artifacts he and his father had collected together. He learned where each came from, the probable date they had been made, how the tools were used. Evans found all this a lot of fun, probably not realizing yet that he was also learning skills that many scholars didn't have and that, someday, would lead him to make important discoveries on his own.

After graduating from Harrow, Evans went on to Oxford University, but he would probably agree that the years at Oxford were not the most important in his life. Instead he would remember always the year 1883, when he met the renowned archaeologist Heinrich

Schliemann. Scholars of Schliemann's generation considered the works of the Greek poet Homer, the *Iliad* and the *Odyssey*, to be myth, beautiful stories to be sure, but not to be believed. Schliemann, however, believed in his heart that at least part of Homer's epic poems was true, that there really was a city called Troy. And, what's more, he vowed to find it.

Evans visited Heinrich and Sophia Schliemann at the site of their discovery. The Schliemanns told him the story given in detail elsewhere in this book. Evans was a little amused with the quaint Germans. But now he had seen firsthand the wondrous things the Schliemanns had unearthed, magnificent objects of gold. In his mind, he was already beginning to put together plans to devote his life to archaeology and uncovering long-lost cities and cultures.

Evans didn't go to Crete to find Knossos. Except in legend, nothing of King Minos's palace was known. He went the first time, in 1893, in search of inscriptions, ancient writings cut into stone or written on clay tablets, that might help him decipher the language of ancient Crete. Did the Cretans speak and write Greek? Or did they have a language of their own? Was it possible their language came from somewhere else? To try to answer these questions

Evans returned in 1900 to find more examples of writing. The Minoans wrote in hieroglyphs, little pictures, but beyond that nothing was known of the language. Evans was unable to find any clues to the pronunciation and meaning of the mysterious script. It would be another fifty years, several years after Evans had died, before the code would be broken by a young amateur, Michael Ventris. What Evans did find when he started digging was beyond his wildest dreams.

Evans, like Schliemann, had few historical facts to go on. There were the legends that were considered no more than that—just stories, fanciful stuff. Yet Schliemann had shown that legends were not to be discounted, that they were at least partly true and, if read carefully, might provide maps to discovery.

Evans, like every English schoolboy of his day, knew the story of King Minos and the Minotaur, the monster, half bull and half man, who lived in a labyrinth, a bewildering maze, in the great palace. The old story tells of Minos, king of Knossos, and how his son, Androgeus, a great athlete, went to Greece to take part in the Athenian games. Androgeus was so strong and skilled that he won every event. This angered Aegeus, king of Athens, and he murdered the young athlete.

Enraged, King Minos sent his great fleet of warships to Athens, invaded and captured the city, and exacted a terrible punishment on the Athenians. Every nine years, the Athenians were to choose seven of their finest young men and seven of their finest young women and send them to Knossos, where they would be sacrificed to the Minotaur.

King Aegeus had a son, Theseus, who had shown himself a great hero in battle. Theseus included himself among the young men and women on their journey to Crete, determined to kill the monster and put an end to the sacrifices. Their boat was outfitted with black sails. But if the returning boat displayed white sails, it would be a signal to King Aegeus that his son had killed the Minotaur and survived.

When the Athenians landed in Crete, Ariadne, daughter of Minos, saw the handsome warrior, Theseus, and fell in love with him. She offered to help him in his mission. She gave him a sword. She also gave him a ball of wool yarn and held tightly to the loose end. Theseus wound his way through the labyrinth, playing out the yarn behind him until, at last, deep inside the palace he confronted the dreadful monster. There was a terrible struggle, but Theseus killed the Minotaur, and then he followed the yarn back through the maze to where he had begun and where Ariadne awaited him.

Rejoining the other young Athenians, the lovers sailed back to Athens. But in all the excitement, Theseus forgot to change the sails. Awaiting his son's return on the shore, King Aegeus saw the black-sailed ship appear on the horizon and, believing his son dead, threw himself into the sea and drowned.

How much truth is there in the myth? Evans wondered if he could find the palace, the black-sailed ship, the labyrinth and, perhaps, even evidence of the Minotaur.

Wandering over the island, Evans noticed here and there piles of stones and rubble. The stones were quite large and obviously not the remains of the simple dwellings ordinary Cretans lived in. He became fascinated and, putting aside for the time being his quest for the meaning of the writing, began to wonder about the meaning of these great ruins. When he began digging, he found more clay tablets with inscriptions—and something even more exciting.

Evans began work in March 1900. He chose to dig at a mound that he recognized as the sort of place where, over thousands of years, successive settlements might have been built on the same site. After one settlement had been destroyed or abandoned and fallen into ruin, another would have been built on top of it, using the rubble of the old buildings for foundations for the new ones. When Evans dug down into the mound with pickax and shovel, he began digging down through the years, revealing levels—much like the layers revealed in cutting through a cake—but the layers revealed by Evans's digging were layers of settlements. The most recent settlements were on the top and the oldest toward the bottom. These layers are called strata, and for an observant archaeologist, they are a way of telling historical time.

From the beginning, the mound revealed to Evans secrets of Crete's ancient past. Masonry walls showing the shapes of rooms were found just below ground level. On the second day of digging, workers uncovered the remains of a building. As the excavations continued, it became clear to Evans that this was not just a house, but an immense palace. Among the fragments of stone were some from a painted fresco. On the third day the workers uncovered huge pottery jars, the kind in which the ancient Cretans would have stored wine and olive oil. More frescoes appeared: paintings of a large fish and a branch with leaves.

Every day brought new discoveries. Hundreds, at first, and eventually over a thousand, clay tablets with the mysterious writing were found. Evans described one of them in his notebook as "a kind of baked clay bar rather like a stone chisel in shape, though broken at one end, with a script on it and what appears to be numerals." And then he realized he had seen similar tablets before: "I at once recalled a clay tablet of unknown age that I had copied at Candia, also found at Knossos. Also broken." Evans still could not read the script, but on some of the tablets he found pictographs, characters that are actually pictures of the things they represent—chariots, wheels, daggers, pots and vases, and horses' heads.

Day after day, new discoveries were unearthed. One day a worker called out excitedly for Evans and the others to come see what he had found. He had dug into what seemed to be a narrow corridor, and on the floor lay two pieces of fresco, the colors so bright they could have been done the day before. A few days later the workers dug into another chamber. In the rubble were more pieces of paintings. More digging uncovered a chair finely carved from stone, and later two stone benches. Who had sat in this magnificent chair? Evans wondered. Could this be the throne of King Minos himself? Then he realized that the many rooms of the palace were forming a maze. And everywhere there were images of the bull. We can imagine Evans recalling over and over the story of Theseus and the Minotaur, and smiling to himself with great satisfaction.

Other rooms were excavated, and

Excavation of the Throne Room in the palace at Knossos. *Ashmolean Museum, Oxford.*

more pieces of plaster showing traces of paint were found. When the pieces were put together, like the pottery puzzles Evans had learned from his father how to solve, they brought back to life wonderful scenes from the ancient past: griffins with the heads of eagles on the bodies of lions; scenes with hills and a river, and flowers; peacock feathers; and a great horned bull. In still other rooms workers found pottery decorated with starfish, sea urchins, and an octopus. They found walls across which swam blue dolphins and other marine life. One fresco depicted a dancer wearing a richly embroidered jacket and ruffled skirt, her hair in long braids. In another, boys and girls wander through meadows, gathering flowers. Colorful spiral patterns covered the ceilings, and painted stucco reliefs of papyrus plants framed each doorway.

The frescoes and painted reliefs, the carved stone furniture, and the pottery showed the Minoans to be fine artists and craftsmen. But Evans was also dis-

Sir Arthur Evans at an exhibition of his findings at the Royal Academy, London, 1936. *Hulton-Deutsch Collection Limited, London.*

covering that they were innovative engineers and architects as well. Unlike most of the people of Evans's day, the Minoans had indoor bathtubs and toilets, flushed with water carried in small clay pipes. Everywhere were signs of the most advanced engineering. A system of terra-cotta pipes carried waste water from the rooms of the palace to huge stone sewers large enough for a person to walk through. And that's why they were so large—to make it easy to clean them out.

Evans was particularly impressed with the clay pipes he found. Ingenious in design, they were far in advance of anything known from this early period. The pipes were tapered, narrower at one end, wider at the other. The smaller end was inserted into the larger end, tapped tightly into place, and then the joint was sealed with cement. But there was even a further refinement. Cast a small distance from the smaller end was a raised shoulder that stopped the pipe from being pushed too far into the larger end. And on the larger end was another shoulder to strengthen the pipe and prevent it from splitting when the small end was forced into it.

Evans and his crew even discovered something about a Cretan meal long ago. The fields around Knossos have been fertile for thousands of years. Olive oil, herbs, honey, raisins, and wine were plentiful. But what other kinds of foods might ancient Cretans have eaten? Workers found a clay grater like the kind used to grate cheese (Cretans still eat many kinds of cheese today). Fish bones were found in another vessel. And in one of the jars excavated were still some dry beans. The Cretan workers recognized immediately what they were: Egyptian beans, which were still being imported into Crete from Alexandria.

There was one thing Evans did not find, and for a long time it puzzled him. Usually, great palaces were surrounded by fortifications, but he could find no ruins that would suggest high walls surrounding and protecting Knossos. Fur-

ther digging revealed the remains of ships. These were the ships that carried goods back and forth between Crete and other ports on the Mediterranean. But they could also be used as fighting ships. King Minos needed no walls to protect his kingdom. His navy was powerful enough to repel attacking ships and armies before they ever reached the shores of the island. Was it possible, Evans must have wondered to himself, that these were also the remains of the mighty navy Minos sent to defeat Troy?

By now Evans knew what he had discovered—though not exactly. He estimated that he would need about a year to finish his work at Knossos, but he was wrong. Eventually he unearthed the palace and an entire village surrounding it, all linked by a system of paved roads. The palace alone covered over five acres. And Evans would devote not a year, but a quarter of a century—much of the rest of his life—to finishing his work at Knossos. He had found the palace of Minos.

Alice Cunningham Fletcher

1838–1923   Pioneer American anthropologist and archaeologist

Alice Cunningham Fletcher was America's first woman anthropologist and archaeologist. She was not content with reading about Native Americans in books and learned journals. She insisted on studying their ways firsthand. At a time when women's lives and spirits were restrained by suffocating social attitudes, corsets, bustles, and hoop skirts, Alice lived among the Indians as one of them. What's more, she was probably the first not only to do fieldwork, but to record her work through the photography of her friend E. Jane Gay.

Fletcher was born on March 15, 1838, in Havana, Cuba, where her father had gone to rest and try to regain his health. She was named Alice for her grandmother and Cunningham after her mother's closest childhood friend. Thomas Gilman and Lucia Adeline Fletcher actually lived in New York City. There, Thomas was building a promising law practice when he was stricken by tuberculosis. He became very ill and died of the disease when Fletcher was only twenty-one months old. Fletcher couldn't really remember her father; she had feelings about him, though. He seemed caring in spite of his terrible illness. And her mother had told her what a talented flute player he was so many times that Fletcher could almost remember hearing him play. Did she actually recall her father's love of reading, or was it her mother who told her how much her father had loved to read Charles Dickens? Lucia, now a widow, settled in Brooklyn

Heights, where Fletcher spent her childhood and attended a new boarding school called the Brooklyn Female Academy (later, Packer Collegiate Institute).

Fletcher's education was unusual for a girl in those days. The academy had been founded by families concerned that their daughters get an education as good as young men could get. The school's director had exciting new ideas about educating children. Rather than the customary memory drill, students were expected to write original compositions and speak well in oral examinations. The intent of the school was to give girls an English and classical education. Fletcher studied history and geography, Latin, arithmetic, natural history, and philosophy. Every student was instructed in vocal music. The scientific training the young women received was considered even better than that offered at most men's schools. There was a chemistry and science lab. For the study of astronomy the school had built a telescope of the finest quality. "Little Alice," as she was known, was the youngest pupil in the school. Her early years at Packer shaped her life. She had a lifelong interest in natural science, and she could sing or speak before large audiences with ease and confidence.

Fletcher was close to her mother and grandmother. Lucia was a bright, well-educated woman and expected her daughter to be the same. Whenever Fletcher looked back on those years, she was aware of these expectations and, at times, how she failed to live up to them. Once she joked that her mother "who never misspelled a word looked upon my failings in that respect with a sort of wonder. I think she sometimes suspected that her daughter was a changeling." Fletcher always remembered the joy of listening to her mother and grandmother talk about their lives. One of her fondest memories was "of an afternoon when my grandmother sat beside the pretty Chippendale worktable arranging the lace on one of her caps, for in those days, old ladies wore caps, she and my mother were in a reminiscent mood and were recalling the mirthful evenings when my father read aloud from [Charles Dickens's] Pickwick and they laughed until they cried."

Memories like these suggest a happy, loving family. But they seem to be the only happy times Fletcher can remember. She cherished these moments of happiness, it appears, because they were so few. The only other memory that she ever recorded is that as a child she was forbidden to read fiction. Then one day, when she had been very ill and was resting, the ban was lifted and she was allowed to read stories. She read *The Pickwick Papers* and all the other Dickens works she could. Later she would recall that it was Dickens who determined her life's course, which was always to help others oppressed and less fortunate than she. But why was it that a woman who wrote so well and so perceptively about others wrote so little of her youth? We know a lot about later times in her life. Was there some meaning to the silence?

Fletcher's friends thought they knew. A few years after the death of her husband, Lucia Fletcher remarried. Little is known of the new husband, Fletcher's stepfather. His name was Oliver C. Gardiner, and he is most often described as straitlaced, strict, and unfeeling. It was most certainly Gardiner who forbade Fletcher to read fiction and her beloved Dickens. Fletcher's mother would have never done such a thing, but Lucia was too helpless and weak to protect her daughter. Fletcher talked about her life one day to a friend, Caroline H. Dall, older than she and a writer. Dall wrote in her diary that night about their talk: "I heard for the first time the terrible story of her life. . . . Pursued by a stepfather's fiendish malice, she had a tough fight for life." In those days such things were never talked about, so that even Fletcher's closest friends couldn't have known. But people who knew her later recognized her behavior as the lasting scars of a horribly abused child.

Fletcher's childhood left her with many scars. She grew up feeling somehow different from others, set apart, even bad. She felt as if everyone else were better than she. But out of her pain came an inner strength and a wish to survive and succeed. Her childhood experiences had taught her that the world was a hostile place, threatening and dangerous, and that she had better look after herself because no one else would. Some people saw her determination and strength as stubbornness. They said Fletcher didn't know how to compromise. Others, especially women who recognized themselves in Fletcher, understood why she had to be that way. But Fletcher did not become bitter. The pain only strengthened her desire to do good and help others.

Fletcher was able to escape from her family when she was eighteen. Her closest friend at school, Elizabeth, must have told her parents of Fletcher's plight, and they came up with a way to save her. Claudius and Eliza Ann Conant hired Fletcher to be the governess for their two younger daughters. So she moved in with the Conants and their ten children. Mr. Conant paid her a good salary, but most important, they accepted her into the family as one of them. They became her lifelong friends and more her parents than her own. Fletcher enjoyed the comfort and security of her "family" into her early thirties, when she decided to go off on her own.

Fletcher traveled in Europe for a while and then returned to New York to teach in private schools. Still uppermost in her mind was a desire to be helpful, to devote her life to bettering the lives of others. This was not easy for a woman in nineteenth-century America. Few schools and fewer professions were open to women in those days. Even the school Fletcher had attended, Packer, did not envision its graduates becoming leaders. They would become women of intellect, character, and taste, to be sure, but homemakers, mothers, and a few of them teachers. So Fletcher had become a teacher and, yet, somehow it wasn't enough for her. Limited as a woman's role in the United States might be, she needed to do more, much more than was expected of her, to feel she had really accomplished something.

For a woman at that time, accomplishing something meant volunteer work for an organization with a cause she believed in. So it was that Fletcher was attracted to Sorosis, a club founded to encourage women to be "helpful to each other and useful to society." Among its members were women writers, journalists, scientists, and physicians. Fletcher was elected recording secretary. She organized a three-day meeting of over four hundred prominent women from all over the United States, which resulted in the formation of the Association for the Advancement of Women (AAW). It was an important beginning. For the first time women were coming out of isolation. They were meeting and talking with one another, sharing ideas about what it was possible for women to accomplish.

The women Fletcher met at her meetings made her realize the possibilities of her own life. From Julia Ward Howe she learned the power of public lecturing to bring issues like women's rights and suffrage to the public. Her friendship with one of the physicians, Dr. Mary Putnam Jacobi, suggested the possibility of a career in science.

One of the subjects Fletcher enjoyed lecturing about before women's groups was American history. And she discovered that what interested her audiences most was prehistoric America. This was a time when the new theories of Charles Darwin and Charles Lyell on evolution were arousing public discussion. Most people also were first hearing of the chipped-stone tools discovered in Europe. One of Fletcher's talks was a series of eleven "Lectures on Ancient America," illustrated with watercolor drawings. She talked about the earliest traces of humans in North America, the ceremonies of the mound builders of the Ohio Valley, the people of the pueblos, and the coastal tribes. She compared their material cultures to those of Greece, Egypt, Assyria, and India. She concluded the series with a talk on the value of studying anthropology. Anthropology as a discipline didn't really exist yet, but Fletcher was becoming an anthropologist.

Fletcher's information on early humans came from reading books and scholarly papers. She wrote letters to museums asking them to send her information on the latest discoveries in archaeology. One of those letters was answered by Frederic W. Putnam, director of the Peabody Museum of American Archaeology and Ethnology.

Putnam might be called the father of American anthropology; he is the one credited with giving the new science its name. At the Peabody he created a new kind of museum, one devoted solely to the study of humanity. He set up graduate programs in anthropology at Harvard and Columbia Universities and helped establish several great museums, including the American Museum of Natural History in New York and the Field Museum in Chicago. He encouraged women to become some of the very first anthropologists. It was he who hired the great scholar Franz Boas at Columbia. And he was probably the first to encourage Native Americans to become anthropologists. Now, impressed with her scholarship and energy, Putnam invited Fletcher to work with him at the Peabody.

That was the way you became an anthropologist or archaeologist in those days when there were not yet graduate programs in those fields. You could become an anthropologist or archaeologist by working as an apprentice to a scholar or museum director. That's what Putnam was inviting Fletcher to do. At first she turned him down, feeling that she was neither serious enough nor worthy of the great man's attentions. "I hardly feel myself entitled to accept so valuable a gift," she wrote him. But Putnam was insistent, and Fletcher could no longer resist the wonderful possibilities. She could become a scholar or, perhaps, a scientist like her friend Maria Mitchell, who was setting an example for women everywhere. Fletcher began visiting the museum regularly. She was assigned to work with Lucian Carr, one of Putnam's assistants, who taught her the basics of archaeology. Now Fletcher's lectures were based not just on her reading but on her own archaeological excavations of shell heaps in Maine and Massachusetts.

Fletcher's work at the Peabody Museum took her into an exciting world of new ideas. And while this was satisfying, she still needed to be helping, bettering the lives of those who could not help themselves. A new direction in her life would come from a chance meeting with some remarkable people, two Omaha Indians—Susette (Bright Eyes) LaFlesche and her brother, Francis—journalist Thomas H. Tibbles, and the chief of the Ponca Indians, Standing Bear. The group was on a speaking tour across the country to tell people how the government planned to remove the Poncas from their tribal lands and to ask them to protest the removal. Tibbles had brought the planned removal—from the Dakota Territory to Indian Territory (present-day Oklahoma)—to public attention with his articles. Fletcher met up with them in Boston, whose citizens took the plight of the Poncas to their hearts.

Plans were made for Fletcher to travel west with Bright Eyes and Tibbles (who were now husband and wife). She hoped that once she had learned her way around she would head out on her own. Fletcher sought the advice of Frederic Putnam, but there was really no way for her to prepare for her adventure. She would simply have to make her own way. She did know what she wanted to do. "I know that what I am toward is difficult, fraught with hardship to mind and body," she wrote to Lucian Carr, "but there is something

to be learned . . . that will be of value not only ethnologically but help toward the historical solution of 'the woman question' in our midst. . . . Even if you tell me that I 'aim my arrows at the sun' I must earnestly reply I must still aim." She met her friends in Omaha, Nebraska, and together they traveled and camped among the Sioux.

Fletcher did not begin this new career until she was forty-three. And yet, with this journey in 1881 she was headed in a direction no woman had ever taken before. Several men had traveled and even lived among the Indians for as long as two years. There were women who had lived among the Indians as teachers and as the wives of missionaries or traders. But Fletcher was the first woman to live with the people, to study and learn their ways, to record scientifically what she observed, and then to publish her findings. Putnam and Lucian Carr had taught her a scientific approach to archaeology that included detailed record keeping. She would use these same methods now for the study of ethnology. She listened and watched and wrote down what she heard and saw. She taught herself to be an anthropologist and as she went along discovered what later came to be called doing fieldwork.

The Indians were amazed at Fletcher's spunk. Though she had only known

Alice Fletcher *(center)* camping during one of her journeys to visit Indian groups. *Idaho State Historical Society. Photograph by E. Jane Gay.*

the comforts of city life, she adapted easily to the harsh life of the Great Plains. Joseph LaFlesche, Bright Eyes's father, described Fletcher as "a remarkable woman; in thought and expression she is more like a man than a woman." From Wajapa, their Omaha guide, Fletcher received an Indian name, *Ma-she-ha-the*, meaning "the motion of an eagle as he sweeps high in the air." This was a great honor, even more so because the eagle was the name of his family. Tibbles wrote about their travels "through a steady series of rainstorms, broken whiffle trees [the bar to which

the traces of a harness are fastened for pulling a wagon], muddy roads, balky spells of a pony, thunderstorms during our night camping, and winds which burned our ethnologist's face to a blister. But that city-bred lady stood everything without one complaint."

She did not complain outwardly, but to her journal Fletcher confided that it was not easy for her. "I was very weary in mind and body," she wrote. "How hopeless seemed the effort of living as far as my life is concerned—but one can't die, and work may be done." And another time: "Today it seems as though my heart would ache itself out of my body. Why can't I die?" Fletcher was lonely, often thinking of "the desolation of life when the heart has no echo . . . the vanity and solitariness of life." Fletcher was certainly experiencing what today we would call culture shock. Her experience, living so long among another people, would become familiar to others who followed in her path, but Fletcher was feeling it for the first time. "The strain of being day and night with a different race, always alert, ever trying to keep the peace and not offend is very wearing, particularly added to the very hard and trying mode of life."

While Fletcher was becoming an anthropologist, she was feeling more and more the unfairness and brutality of the white man toward the Indians. She realized that Indian life was being destroyed by the relocation and imprisonment of the people on reservations. At one place she visited, the Rosebud Agency, almost seven thousand Sioux had been forcefully encamped, unable to live free. They lived on rations. Each month they were given meager amounts of beef, flour, coffee, sugar, milk, and bacon—nothing they were used to eating. She walked among them over a "horrid, desolate path," disgusted by their treatment. "Nothing can describe the lack of cleanliness and order of Rosebud Agency," she wrote

in her journal. And then a question arose in her mind that would not leave her alone. "How can Indians do better, hemmed in as they are at the agency deprived of their native life . . . and not fully introduced to our ways. They are stranded between two modes of life."

It was at Rosebud that Fletcher heard the first call for help. She and her friends received a message from the great chief Sitting Bull. He was a prisoner at Fort Randall, six days travel to the east. After being lied to by the United States government and having their treaties ignored, the Sioux, led by this brave man, had attacked and defeated General George Armstrong Custer at the Battle of the Little Bighorn. Sitting Bull had fled to Canada, but was forced to return and surrender.

Now Fletcher was seated in Sitting Bull's tent. She was immediately impressed by the fifty-year-old chief, the leader of the Hunkpapa Sioux. Speaking through her interpreter, Buffalo Chip, Sitting Bull told Fletcher about his decision to give up the old ways, ways now destroyed, and encourage his people to plow and cultivate the ground like the white man. Then he looked at his wife, sitting by the fire, and at Fletcher, and sat quietly a few moments. "You are a woman," he said suddenly, speaking slowly, thoughtfully to Fletcher.

"You have come to me as a friend. Pity my women. We men owe what we have to them. They have worked for us . . . but in the new life their work is taken away. For my men I see a future; for my women I see nothing. Pity them; help them, if you can." With that, Sitting Bull took a ring from his finger and gave it to Fletcher, to remind her of the favor he had asked.

That night Fletcher wrote in her journal, "God help me to help them." It was yet another beginning for her. From talking with the Indians she knew their greatest fear was that they would be driven from their homes and lose the land so sacred to them. All they wanted, they pleaded with Fletcher, was to be given individual legal title to their lands, no more nor less than the white man had. Fletcher understood how painful all this must be to them, this division and ownership of the land. She herself had struggled to understand just what the relationship was between Indians and the places in which they lived. It was not easy for white people whose lives were divided up into pieces, lots, and blocks, homesteads, towns, cities, townships, counties, states, and territories. "I have taken much pains to get at the Indian ideas of property, of the use and occupation of land," she once wrote to Putnam. "Owning it, they never dreamed of. . . . They would as soon [have] thought of owning air or rain."

Fletcher helped the leaders of the Omaha write a petition to the United States Senate asking that they receive full title to their land. She wrote to as many people as she could, asking for their support, including Henry L. Dawes, the senior senator from Massachusetts. Then she went to Washington to personally lobby among members of Congress for Indian rights. She spoke in meetinghouses, churches, and homes—wherever she could get an invitation—but mostly to wives and daughters. In one of her audiences was Harriet Hawley, wife of a Connecticut senator, Anna Dawes, daughter of the Massachusetts senator, and Mrs. Teller, wife of the secretary of the interior. All were impressed by Fletcher's plea and the authority with which she spoke. After all, she had been there, lived among the Indians, and spoken with them. Soon Fletcher was speaking before the congressional committee on Indian affairs.

Women's organizations led the struggle for Indian rights in the 1880s. One group, the Women's National Indian Treaty-Keeping and Protective Association, collected over one hundred fifty thousand signatures in just three years on petitions to be sent to government officials. They urged the keeping of trea-

Alice Fletcher *(seated at table)* consulting with Indian families about land allotments. *Idaho State Historical Society. Photograph by E. Jane Gay.*

ties. And they asked that one hundred sixty acres of land be given to each Indian on the reservations, that schools be set up for Indians, and that they be given the protection of the law. It was a woman, Helen Hunt Jackson, who exposed the government's treachery in dealing with the Indians. Her book *A Century of Dishonor* was the first many Americans had read about the violation of the Indians' human and civil rights. Fletcher was not alone. All America was becoming aware of what had happened, and the government seemed ready to

do something about it. Fletcher had begun fulfilling her promise to Sitting Bull.

When legislation passed the Senate, Fletcher's work was not over. She was asked by the United States Indian Commissioner to go back to the reservation and divide up the land among the Omahas. She received an official appointment from President Chester A. Arthur. So she returned, now to work months in the field, surveying and assigning the land allotments. But she knew that land ownership alone was no solution to the Indians' problems. She suggested ways they might use their lands, such as keeping some land in common for grazing. She helped young Indians get into the Carlisle Indian School in Pennsylvania and the Hampton Institute in Virginia. She made speeches urging the government to set up Indian schools, to make loans available so that they could build homes on the reservations.

Through all of this—Fletcher also made all the land allotments for the Winnebagos and the Nez Percés—she continued her fieldwork in anthropology. She was now accompanied on many of her travels by E. Jane Gay, a friend going back to her days in school. Gay had taught herself photography and fully recorded not only Fletcher's work allotting land to the Indians, but her anthropological studies as well.

Another constant companion was Francis LaFlesche, who helped her put together the largest collection of Indian music ever recorded. The Omahas sang many of their songs for them. At first Fletcher and LaFlesche transcribed each song, writing it down exactly as it was sung, and then translated it. Eventually they began using the new graphophone—an early phonograph that cut wax records—to record the sounds. Fletcher published many articles on her work and several pioneering studies of Indian life, including *The Omaha Tribe, Indian Story and Song from North America,* and *The Hako: A Pawnee Ceremony.*

Fletcher always respected the Indians she met, and they, in turn, had the utmost respect for her. While collecting relics among the Omaha, Fletcher was entrusted with their most sacred secrets and ritual objects. The chiefs gave her their sacred pole and other articles from the sacred tent of war to be put into safekeeping at the Peabody. The Omaha performed secret ceremonies for her, never seen by anyone else outside their nation. They sensed that she had become one of them in spirit. "Living with my Indian friends," she wrote, "I found I was a stranger in my native land. As time went on, the outward aspect of nature remained the same, but a change was wrought in me. I learned to hear the echoes of a time when every living thing, even the sky, had a voice. That voice devoutly heard by the ancient people of America I desired to make audible to others."

Fletcher died in 1923 at the age of eighty-three. She was a pioneering American archaeologist and anthropologist. She had tried to help the Indians preserve their lands and lifeways. More than anyone else, perhaps, she helped Americans understand, appreciate, and

Alice Fletcher with Chief Joseph of the Nez Percé and James Stuart. *Idaho State Historical Society. Photograph by E. Jane Gay.*

respect Indian life. Perhaps she is best described by a newspaperman who followed her as she lobbied in Washington on behalf of the Indians. She was a "quiet force," he wrote, "a plain, gentle, modest little woman. . . . She didn't fight—any more than a snowflake and a sunbeam fight. Like them, she Just Kept On." But Fletcher summed up her life more modestly. "There is no story to my life," she wrote. "It has always been just one step at a time— one thing which I have tried to do as well as I could and which has led on to something else. It has all been in the day's work."

Jane Goodall

1934–   Ethologist and authority on chimpanzee behavior

"Since dawn I had climbed up and down the steep mountain slopes and pushed my way through the dense valley forests. Again and again, I had stopped to listen, or to gaze through binoculars at the surrounding countryside. Yet I had neither heard nor seen a single chimpanzee, and now it was already five o'clock. In two hours darkness would fall over the rugged terrain of the Gombe Stream Chimpanzee Reserve." To Jane Goodall (as quoted here, from her book *In the Shadow of Man*) it seemed that this day, too, would end in failure. Every day for over half a year, she had tried to get close enough to observe the chimpanzees, and every day it was the same. She would get to about a third of a mile from the chimps—still too far away to observe them—and then they would flee, just vanish into the forest.

Today, it seemed, would be no different. As Goodall crept up closer, to where she had heard the chimps, she noticed the tree branches were empty. All was quiet. The chimps must have fled, she thought. Once again she felt frustrated and depressed—until she looked just below the trees. "Then all at once my heart missed several beats."

Less than twenty yards away from me two male chimpanzees were sitting on the ground staring at me intently. Scarcely breathing, I waited for the sudden panic-stricken flight that normally followed a surprise encounter between myself and the chimpanzees at close quarters. But nothing of the sort happened. The two large chimps simply continued to gaze at me. Very slowly I sat down, and after a few more moments, the two calmly began to groom one another.

As I watched, still scarcely believing it was true, I saw two more chimpanzee heads peering at me over the grass from the other side of the forest glade: a female and a youngster. . . . Without any doubt whatsoever, this was the proudest moment I had known.

Goodall was now on the way to realizing her dream. She would be the first person ever to live among the chimpanzees and observe and record their behavior over many years.

Goodall was born in London, England, on March 4, 1934. Her father, Mortimer Herbert Morris-Goodall, was a business executive. Her mother, Margaret MyFanwe Joseph, later wrote a novel, *Beyond the Rain Forest*, under the name Vanne Morris Goodall. Goodall's interest in animals goes back to her childhood, back to an age most of us can't even remember. "When I was just over one year old my mother gave me a toy chimpanzee, a large hairy model celebrating the birth of the first chimpanzee infant ever born in the London zoo. Most of my mother's friends were horrified and predicted that the ghastly creature would give a small child nightmares; but Jubilee (as the celebrated infant itself was named) was my most loved possession and ac-

companied me on all my childhood travels. I still have the worn old toy."

Jubilee was the beginning of her fascination with animals. Goodall grew up in London and in Bournemouth, England, where she attended school. Even as a child she spent most of her free time watching and making notes on the behavior of animals and birds in her neighborhood. She read everything she could about animals and spent her pocket money on used zoology books. "One of my earliest recollections," she wrote in her autobiography, *In the Shadow of Man*, "is of the day I hid in a small stuffy henhouse in order to see how a hen laid an egg. I emerged after about five hours. The whole household had apparently been searching for me for hours, and my mother had even rung the police to report me missing.

"It was about four years later, when I was eight, that I first decided I would go to Africa and live with wild animals when I grew up."

Goodall attended school until she was eighteen. She left to take a job so that she could save money to go to Africa. She worked as a secretary at Oxford University and as an editor for a documentary film studio in London. And then she got her chance. A school friend invited Goodall to stay at her parents' farm in Kenya. She quit her London job—it was impossible, she realized, to save money in London—and went to work as a waitress in Bournemouth. At the end of the summer season Goodall had saved enough money to head for Kenya.

All this time Goodall had not given up her dream to live with and observe animals in the wild. In Africa someone told her, "If you are interested in animals, then you should meet Dr. Leakey." So it was that one day in 1957 a young, slim, blond woman showed up at the National Museum of Natural History in Nairobi, Kenya. She had come, she said, to ask Dr. Louis S. B. Leakey, the famed archaeologist and the museum's curator, for a job. Leakey was used to young people just showing up at the museum and asking to work with him. He found work for them whenever he could. "Somehow," Goodall recalled, "he must have sensed that my interest in animals was not just a passing phase, but was rooted deep, for on the spot he gave me a job as an assistant secretary."

Goodall became more than a secretary. The naturalists and archaeologists working at the museum taught her about their work. She was soon invited by Leakey and his wife, Mary, on one of their expeditions to Olduvai Gorge. The Leakeys were searching for fossils of our earliest ancestors, going back hundreds of thousands of years. And

Goodall was there. "The digging itself was fascinating. For hours, as I picked away at the ancient clay or rock of the Olduvai fault to extract the remains of creatures that had lived millions of years ago, the task would be purely routine, but from time to time, and without warning, I would be filled with awe by the sight or the feel of some bone I held in my hand. This—this very bone—had once been part of a living, breathing animal. . . ."

As Leakey got to know Goodall and watched her work, he began to see her as the one to do a study he had been thinking of. She was a careful excavator and very observant. But, most of all, he saw her love of animals and their attraction to her. She seemed to be able to relate to animals in a way he hadn't seen before. And she was always having remarkable encounters in the wild. She would come upon gazelles and giraffes and dik-diks, miniature antelopes not much bigger than hares, and once they saw a black rhinoceros. And then there was an evening walk Goodall would never forget. "Once we came face to face with a young male lion: he was no more than forty feet away when we heard his soft growl and peered around to see him on the other side of a small bush. We were down in the bottom of the gorge where the vegetation is comparatively thick in parts; slowly we backed away while he watched, his tail twitching. Then, out of curiosity I suppose, he followed us as we walked deliberately across the gorge toward the open, treeless plains on the other side. As we began to climb upward he vanished into the vegetation and we did not see him again."

Leakey realized that Goodall was more interested in living things than in fossils, though she found the digging exciting. He was impressed by her fascination with animal behavior. And for months he had watched how easily she adapted to the difficult conditions at Olduvai. He began telling her from time to time about his idea for a study of chimpanzee behavior. Leakey's discoveries were now pushing back human history hundreds of thousands, even millions, of years. He was finding fossils of early creatures who might have been apes or, perhaps, very early humans. How human was their behavior? he wondered. Did they live in families? Did they hunt together? Did they make tools? Did they talk to one another?

The answer to Leakey's questions might be answered by the chimpanzees. Of the countless animals on this earth, none resembles the human being as much as the chimpanzee does. "The chimpanzee is our closest living relative," Goodall observed. The circuitry of the chimpanzee brain is similar in

many ways to circuitry of the human brain. Although not as human-looking as the gorilla, chimpanzees are closer to humans in intelligence. They learn in much the same way we do. The chemistry of their bodies—their immune system; their blood; even the structure of their DNA, the molecules of heredity—are similar to ours. So is it possible, Leakey wondered, that their behavior might hold some clues to the evolution of early humans? What if we could observe them, not in a zoo, but in their natural home? What if we could watch long enough to see a baby chimpanzee grow from a juvenile to an adolescent to an adult? Would we see patterns of growth similar to ours? Is it possible that watching chimpanzee behavior would shed light on the behavior of our Stone Age ancestors? Could we look at chimpanzee behavior and imagine life a million or more years ago?

Chimpanzees are difficult to observe. They are frightened away long before the observer is close enough to watch them for any length of time. What's more, they live in the upper and lower stories of dense forests. Much of their life goes on out of sight. Only one person had ever tried to observe chimpanzees closely. Back in the 1930s Henry Nissen had spent two-and-a-half months observing chimps in French Guinea. But that was too short a time,

Leakey felt. It would take at least two years. Nor would it be of any use to observe chimpanzees at the zoo: Confining animals in a zoo changes their behavior to something quite different from the way they act in the wild. It seemed like an impossible or, at least, discouragingly difficult task.

But Leakey knew of a good place for a study of chimpanzee behavior. At the Gombe Stream Reserve on the shore of Lake Tanganyika, some two hundred chimpanzees lived, not deep in the forest, but along its fringes, more in the open. Their habitat, Leakey realized, was very similar to that of the hominids whose remains he was unearthing at Olduvai Gorge. Today the Gorge is hot and dry, with only scrubby vegetation. Hundreds of thousands of years ago, however, when the first humans lived here, it was green with grasslands and forests. What intrigued Leakey even more was that some of his fossils of early apes and prehistoric people were found right on the very shores where the chimpanzees now lived. That made it even more likely that their behaviors would be similar. To answer all his questions would take a very special approach and a special person. Leakey believed that Goodall was that special person.

Goodall agreed. So Leakey sent her back to London to study with Dr. John Napier at his primate unit at the Royal Free Hospital. Dr. Napier was an authority on primates, the order of mammals that includes humans. It was to Napier that Leakey sent many of his fossils of early primates for identification. Goodall would study primate anatomy and behavior and also observe at the London zoo before beginning her own work. She studied hard and within a year was becoming an expert herself. In the meantime, Leakey was looking for sponsors who would pay for Goodall's study. He had to convince people who were used to sponsoring scholars to sponsor Goodall, who had only a high school education. He came up with a sponsor who gave Goodall three thousand dollars. That was enough to pay for a tent, a boat, some supplies, and her airfare, with just enough left over for six months in the field.

Goodall had her wish. In June 1960 she returned to Africa to set up her camp at the Gombe Stream Reserve. Leakey insisted that someone go with her, and so she was joined in her work by her mother, Vanne Goodall. Vanne took care of the camp for Goodall. She ran a one-woman medical clinic for local fishers and their families. And she gave Goodall lots of support and encouragement, especially after long days in the field when the chimps would not let her anywhere near them.

African children visit Jane Goodall at her camp. *Baron Hugo van Lawick. Copyright © National Geographic Society.*

At first, the closest she could get was about five hundred yards. That was still too far away for detailed observations, even with binoculars. Each evening, when Goodall returned to camp and her mother, she said, "the same old feeling of depression clawed at me." Together, Goodall and her mother suffered another, more deadly danger of the forest. They both caught malaria and lay in their cots, delirious, for over a week with 105-degree temperatures. Both were too sick to get to a doctor, who was hours away. Goodall and her mother pulled through, though, and af-

terward were told by the doctor that they were lucky to be alive.

Goodall was persistent, and each week that went by brought her closer and closer to the chimps. Eventually her patience was rewarded with glimpses of chimpanzee life, more intimate glimpses than anyone had ever had before.

I saw one female, newly arrived in a group, hurry up to a big male and hold her hand out toward him. Almost regally he reached out, clasped her hand in his, drew it toward him, and kissed it with his lips. I saw two adult males embrace each other in greeting. I saw youngsters having wild games through the treetops, chasing around after each other or jumping again and again, one after the other, from a branch to a springy bough below. I watched small infants dangling happily by themselves for minutes on end, patting at their toes with one hand, rotating gently from side to side. Once two tiny infants pulled on opposite ends of a twig in a gentle tug-of-war.

As the days passed, the chimps became less and less afraid of Goodall. In fact she had such frequent contacts with them now that she was beginning to recognize different individuals. She decided that she would give them names so that she could get to know them and record their behavior more easily. Some of the chimps reminded her of people she knew. One of the first chimps she got to know she named Old Mr. McGregor. Mr. McGregor was between thirty and forty years old, getting old for a chimpanzee. He was very belligerent and threatening toward Goodall whenever they crossed paths. "He reminded me," she wrote, "of Beatrix Potter's old gardener in *The Tale of Peter Rabbit.*"

One by one Goodall named over fifty members of the extended family of chimps and noted their relationships to one another. Soon she was seeing their individual faces and habits as clearly as if they were people. There were Flo and her two-year-old daughter, Fifi, and her son Figan. Flo was often seen with another mother, Olly (named for Goodall's aunt Olwen), and her brother William. Then there was Baby Flint, and David Graybeard and Goliath. One chimp, whom Goodall described as being robust, high-ranking, and usually good-natured, she named Leakey. David Graybeard took a liking to Goodall, which helped her. Whenever he accompanied her, David's countenance calmed the others, and Goodall could get closer to them. By the end of her first year she was able to get within thirty feet of an individual or a group. Within two years, the chimps would come to visit her camp for bananas. They had become members of what she called her "banana club."

Beyond her wildest dreams, Goodall became not only an observer, but was accepted by the chimps as one of them. It seems that, once she had gained their trust, they accepted her into their family. Goodall tells how one of the young females, Melissa, actually brought her new baby for Goodall to see. "Melissa came right up to us, quite unafraid for her infant." Melissa cuddled her baby and then removed her encircling arm so that Goodall could see it. "The baby's head fell back on her knees, and Me-

Jane Goodall with one of her chimp friends. Ms. Goodall explained that sometimes "we hid bananas under our shirts." *UPI/Bettmann.*

lissa, looking down, stared long at the tiny face. Never had we imagined such a funny twisted-up little face. It was comical in its ugliness, with large ears, small rather pursed lips, and skin incredibly wrinkled and bluish black rather than pink. His eyes were screwed tight shut against the fading light of the sun and he looked like some wizened gnome or hobgoblin. We christened him Goblin on the spot. Melissa gazed down at her son for fully two minutes before she placed one hand behind his back and set off to make her nest for the night."

What came of Goodall's work was a record of chimpanzee behavior more detailed than was ever before possible. Chimps had always been thought to be vegetarians and fruit eaters who occasionally ate insects and small rodents. Goodall discovered David Graybeard one day sharing with his family a young bush pig he had killed. Over the years of her observations, Goodall saw chimps hunt, kill, and eat small antelopes called bushbucks, monkeys, and baboons. She watched chimps throw stones with surprising aim. She also discovered that they walk upright more than was thought. Like humans, chimps have a complicated social system, more complex than anyone had thought possible.

Goodall's studies were beginning to attract a lot of attention. The National Geographic Society especially became interested after she had reported on chimpanzee behavior no one had ever observed before. They began funding Goodall's work and they also sent a Dutch photographer, Baron Hugo van Lawick, to record her chimpanzees on film. Hugo made several beautiful films and took thousands of stills over the years he spent at Gombe. One film entitled *Miss Goodall and the Wild Chimpanzees* was shown on television and made people all over the world aware of her important work. Goodall and Hugo were married and continued their work together. Their son, Hugo Eric Louis—better known as Grub—grew up with his mother and father among the chimpanzees. As a child he spent his days with his mother and father playing on the sandy beaches and swimming. "Grub is happy at Gombe," Goodall wrote in *In the Shadow of Man*. "He repeatedly tells everybody that it is his 'favorite place in all the world.'"

Goodall's discoveries have taught us about the "humanness" of animals we consider less important in the world than us. She has given us names and faces for animals that, before her work, we would have thought of as just "animals." Her observations of chimpanzee mothers and their children especially remind us of our own lives. Like us, chimps are comforted by the reassuring touch of a parent or friend. There were

4b. Full closed grin   5. Horizontal pout

4a. Full open grin

Chimpanzees' facial expressions. *Illustrations from* In the Shadow of Man *by Jane Goodall.* *(Boston: Houghton Mifflin, 1971.) Copyright © 1971 by Hugo and Jane van Lawick-Goodall.* *Reprinted by permission of Houghton Mifflin Company. All rights reserved.*

many such episodes, but one Goodall records in her wonderful book *In the Shadow of Man* is quite familiar. "Once when Figan was about eight years old he was threatened by Mike. He screamed loudly and hurried past six or seven other chimps nearby until he reached Flo [his mother]; then he held his hand toward her and she held it with hers. Calmed, Figan stopped screaming almost at once."

The ethologist's interest in animal behavior is more than just scholarly curiosity. Much can be learned about ourselves from observing other animals, especially those most closely related to us. For Goodall there is much to be learned from chimpanzees—clues to human aggression and violence, mothering and child rearing, even growing up. "In humans, adolescence is a diffi-

cult time; it also is," Goodall discovered, "for chimpanzees. If we can learn more about the effect of physiological body changes in chimpanzees at puberty and how this affects their behavior, we may be better able to understand and help our own teenagers."

Goodall's most important discovery surprised and delighted Louis Leakey. Before her study, it had been assumed that humans alone of all the animals were toolmakers. In fact, the presence of tools near a fossil primate was the definitive evidence of humanness. But all that changed the day Goodall came upon David Graybeard in the tall grass. "He was squatting beside the red earth mound of a termite nest, and as I watched I saw him carefully push a long grass stem down into a hole in the mound. After a moment he withdrew it and picked something from the end with his mouth. I was too far away to make out what he was eating, but it was obvious that he was actually using a grass stem as a tool. . . . Goliath once removed at least fifteen yards from the heap to select a firm-looking piece of vine, and both males often picked three or four stems while they were collecting tools, and put the spares beside them on the ground until they wanted them." The chimps were making and using tools to collect insects.

Goodall knew that chimpanzees had been observed using objects as tools. She'd watched chimps using rocks as hammers to break open nuts. She had seen a chimp use a little twig as a toothpick and another a stout stick to pry open a box of bananas. But David Graybeard and Goliath were taking yet another step. To her surprise, she saw that "on several occasions they picked small leafy twigs and prepared them for use by stripping off the leaves. This was the first recorded example of a wild animal not merely *using* an object as a tool, but actually modifying an object and thus showing the crude beginnings of tool *making*." On other occasions Goodall watched chimps crumple up and chew leaves and use them as sponges to sop up water in rock crevices and other places too narrow or deep to get their tongues into. The chimps

had learned that crumpling up the leaf made it more absorbent.

Goodall's discoveries forced anthropologists and archaeologists to redefine humanness more precisely. "Or else, as Louis Leakey put it, we should by definition have to accept the chimpanzee as Man."

The work at Gombe has continued, with many assistants, up to the present day. Goodall left only when she was called upon to lecture and teach. One of the times she left her "banana club," it was for a very special honor. She had gained entrance to Cambridge University and over the years worked on her own toward a doctorate. Her friend Leakey felt it important that she have a degree so that she would be taken more seriously by scholars and scientists. And it was he who saw to it that she was admitted to Cambridge. Finally, in 1965, she submitted her thesis, based upon her work, "Behavior of the Free-Ranging Chimpanzee." Goodall was only the eighth person in the long history of the university to be allowed to work on her Ph.D. without first having gotten a B.A. And how would Flo and Goliath, David Graybeard, Melissa, and McGregor feel about her now that she was Dr. Goodall? She felt that the chimpanzees seem to regard her as an inferior primate—on a level with the baboon—but a superior source of bananas.

Georg Friedrich Grotefend

1775–1853 German schoolteacher who was the first to decipher Sumerian cuneiform writing

The first translation of the oldest written language in the world began, as the story goes, with a wager. It seems that Georg Friedrich Grotefend, a teacher at the Göttingen city school, bet his friend Fiorillo that he could find the key to the translation of Sumerian writing. The agreement was that Fiorillo, who was secretary at the Royal Library at Göttingen, find for Grotefend all the information that had been written on the subject. His friend took him up on his bet, and the young schoolteacher— he was then but twenty-seven—set to work.

Examples of Sumerian script, called cuneiform—from the Latin *cuneus*, which means "wedge"—had been discovered over the years. The name comes from the wedge-shaped charac-

ters that were pressed into soft clay tablets by a short length of reed with a triangular end. Each tablet was like a piece of paper. One tablet might contain a whole document; other documents might cover several tablets. If the scribe needed to keep one copy, then two identical tablets would have to be made. After the scribe was finished writing on a tablet, he would put it out in the sun to bake dry. This presented problems for archaeologists. Since the tablets were only dried in the sun, rather than baked hard in a hot oven, they absorbed water from the ground and returned to soft clay. Some tablets had been baked hard. But archaeologists themselves had to bake the majority of the tablets dug from the ground (see the chapter on Charles Leonard Woolley) before they could safely clean and handle them.

Inscribing characters in soft clay tablets was slow and cumbersome compared to writing with a pen or pencil on paper. But clay tablets had one important advantage: They carried their message through the ages to us, over five thousand years, and remained legible. It's unlikely that pen or pencil on paper or even parchment could do that.

One of the first to publish cuneiform texts was the German geographer Carsten Niebuhr. His book *Description of Travels in Arabia and Neighboring Lands* included a drawing of reliefs he found at the ancient palace at Persepolis in Mesopotamia—six lines containing a total of forty-two characters. Although a geographer who was seeing the writing of Sumer for the first time, Niebuhr made some remarkable observations about the language, which later helped others to make sense of it. First of all, he deduced that the characters were letters, each representing a sound. He realized this when he found that there were only a few characters, repeated over and over again. Just as we use only twenty-six letters to create hundreds of thousands of words, Niebuhr figured that the Sumerians wrote with forty-two characters. And he was very close; scholars who translate Sumerian writings today recognize an alphabet

of thirty-nine signs. But although Niebuhr recognized the writing as being cuneiform, he was not able to translate even one word. Still, without Niebuhr's work, the work of translation probably would not have been possible.

Deciphering the characters would come later. And it would come in small steps. First, a German scholar, Olav Gerhard Tychsen, discovered a small but very important mark, an oblique wedge, which he guessed was a word divider. It was, and once he recognized this mark, the script no longer looked like row upon row of endless signs. Now he could see individual words marked off by the divider, though he still had no idea of the meaning. He also discovered that the inscriptions and tablets from Persepolis were from the Achaemenid dynasty, a fact, as you'll soon see, that helped Grotefend with his work.

The first important steps in the decipherment of cuneiform came from an unlikely young man. Grotefend was born on June 9, 1775, at Münden, Germany. He was a teacher and a scholar, having studied language and literature at Göttingen University. He taught at the municipal school in Göttingen and later became vice-principal of the Frankfurt am Main grammar school. His last position was that of director of the Lyceum, the secondary school at Hannover. He knew Greek, but scarcely anything of ancient languages or modern Near Eastern languages. Nor was he a linguist. Grotefend had not even had an opportunity to study cuneiform texts before he made his wager. Nor would he have the opportunity to see the large number of tablets already collected. All he would have to work on would be some poor copies of the inscriptions at Persepolis.

But Grotefend did know ancient history, and it was this knowledge that enabled him to make some brilliant assumptions that got him started on the right track. First of all, he decided, as had Niebuhr, that the language was alphabetical, that each group of signs stood for a sound. He agreed with Niebuhr's conclusion that the three different inscriptions appearing side by side in three columns were three different systems of writing. He also made the assumption, like Niebuhr, that although the writing might be different, the subject of all three inscriptions was the same. Finally, he knew from the work of another scholar that the middle column of the three might be the simplest to translate and, perhaps, important since it had been placed in the middle.

If Grotefend had no formal training in ancient languages, he had instead a wonderful resourcefulness. One of the first problems that he confronted was which way the writing ran. When you pick up something written in any language in our alphabet, you instantly and without even thinking turn the writing so that the letters stand up the right way. But what if you don't recognize the characters, have never seen them before? How do you hold the tablet? Which is the top of the tablet and which is the bottom? Which is the left and which the right side? And in which direction do you read it—left to right, right to left, back and forth, top to bottom, bottom to top, beginning at the upper left or the upper right?

One of the first things Grotefend noticed about the characters was that the points of the wedges were positioned three ways: to the right, diagonally downward to the right, or downward. In this he found the clue to how the writing should be read and which way the tablets should be held. "They must be held in such fashion that the tips of the vertical wedges point downwards, those of the oblique wedges to the right, and the openings of the angles also to the right. If this is done, it will be found that no cuneiform writing is written vertical, but always in a horizontal direction. . . ." From this he concluded also that the writing was read from left to right.

What Grotefend had actually done

Lithograph of Georg Grotefend by von C. Kiesel, from a painting by Winkelmann. *Historisches Museum, Hannover, Germany.*

was recreate the rules of writing used by the scribes of long ago. For efficiency and speed in writing, the wedges were made in only three directions: perpendicular, horizontal, and oblique. One more stroke, which looked something like an arrowhead, was made with the tip of the stylus. Only these four strokes could be used. No others were allowed.

Now that Grotefend had decided that the text was read left to right (though, remember, he was still guessing), the hard work began. How do you begin reading characters that have no relationship to any language you know? If Grotefend had been a linguist, educated in the languages of the ancient Near East, he might have approached cuneiform as a language puzzle. He'd have tried to figure out the arrangement of words in the sentence, the placement of subjects and verbs. For example, scholars now know that the language of the Sumerians was related to Sanskrit, the language of ancient India. If you knew Sanskrit, then you might try to plug in words in the same order they appear in Sanskrit to see if the pattern worked. Here's a simple example of confronting a new language that uses words and patterns similar to your own:

Meine Mutter und Vater sind in dem Haus.

You probably recognize some cognates here, words that look and sound like English words, especially if you read the sentence out loud.

						in		*house.*
	mother		*father*			*in*		*house.*
My	*mother*	*and*	*father*			*in*		*house.*

And, at some point, you see the pieces of the puzzle that fit.

My mother and father are in the house.

Two things about the new language helped you translate. The sounds of some of the words are familiar and even look like English words. And the syntax—the order of the parts of speech—in this German sentence follow the same pattern as English (as a matter of fact, English and German are linguistically related).

But Grotefend didn't recognize any of the words in the cuneiform texts; the alphabets of German and Sumerian are entirely different. And he knew nothing of the syntax; he knew nothing of the language at all. So he decided to use a mathematical approach. He would decipher the cuneiform writing as a cryptographer deciphers a code to be broken. Rather than work with sounds and meaning (as we did in the German example), he would have to work with the symbols.

There were some things he did know, not from his study of language, but from his knowledge of ancient history. The

Greek historian Herodotus had reported ancient king lists, so that Grotefend already knew the names and genealogies of the kings of ancient Persia. Also, another scholar, Antoine Silvestre de Sacy, studying later texts near Persepolis, had discovered a curious pattern in the inscriptions. The genealogies always included phrases that were repeated over and over again, chronicling the succession of rulers. Even though these were later inscriptions, Grotefend guessed that their pattern might go back to much older times.

The pattern was:

X, great king, king of kings
X, great king, king of kings; son of
Y, great king, king of kings; son of Z

In mathematical symbols Grotefend would write it like this:

X<Y<Z

and so on. (He also knew that Persian kings were not modest men!)

You've probably noticed, as Grotefend did, that the word *king* is repeated three times in each line and, if the cuneiform text follows the same pattern, then it should be easy to find the character for *king*.

You've probably also noticed that the name of a king begins each line, and that X is the name of the son, Y the name of the father, and Z the name of the grandfather. Therefore, Grotefend reasoned, because he knew the Greek names of the kings from Herodotus histories, if one of these names could be read, the other two would be known as well. But he was also hoping to find a very special line. Notice that Z does not have anything following his name. He perhaps was not a monarch, and therefore was not entitled to the honorific "great king, king of kings."

That made it easier. Because now Grotefend was looking for a king whose father was a king, but not his grandfather. What's more, because he guessed, like Niebuhr, that each character stood for a sound, then he needed also to find kings whose names had the same number of characters as X, Y, and Z. "Fully convinced that I would have to look for two kings from the Achaemenidian dynasty," Grotefend later explained, "I began to check through the royal successions to find out which names most nearly fitted the inscriptional characters. They could not be Cyrus and Cambyses, because the two names in the inscription did not have the same initial letter, nor could they be Cyrus and Artaxerxes because the first of these names, compared to the characters, was too short, the second too long."

Now Grotefend was using a process of elimination. It's like when you're faced with four answers to a question and you don't know the right one. You go through all four, eliminating the answers you know can't possibly be right and, therefore, settle on the remaining answer as the correct one. That works on tests and it is also a common technique in deciphering. "There were no names left to choose from but Darius and Xerxes, and they fitted so easily that I had no doubt about making the right choice. This correspondence was clinched by the fact that in the son's inscription the father's name had the sign of royalty beside it, whereas this character was lacking in the father's inscription. This observation was confirmed by all the Persepolitan inscriptions."

So, first Grotefend tried out one of the most celebrated son-father-grandfather successions of ancient Persian history, Cyrus < Cambyses < Cyrus, and that didn't fit. The three names in the cuneiform script do not begin with the same character. So, then he tried Darius < Artaxerxes < Xerxes, and that didn't fit either; the names, as he said, not being the correct length. His inspired guess was that the son-father-grandfather succession that would work was Xerxes < Darius < Hystaspes, and it did. There were the correct number of characters in each name. And the last name in the series, Hystaspes, fit. Xerxes' grandfather had

begun the royal line of succession, but was not himself a king. Grotefend had it: "Xerxes, great king, king of kings, son of Darius, great king, king of kings, son of Hystaspes." What's more, Grotefend could now give sounds to some of the signs:

Persian:	(cuneiform signs)
Grotefend:	D. A. R. H. E. U. S
Correct reading:	D. A. Ra. Ya. Va. U. Sh

Grotefend, however, was not finished with his work. He had sounds for a few of the characters. Now he was going to try to give phonetic values to the remaining unknown letters in the Sumerian alphabet. He had already proved that the Greek spellings of the names of Persian kings worked in his decoding. He could now plug the known letters and sounds into other names and, from the Greek, assign sounds to the characters he did not yet know. Grotefend explained how he did just that: "Since a correct decipherment of names had already given me over twelve letters, including all the letters of the royal title except one, the next move was to put names known only in Greek into their Persian form, in order to get a correct value for each character in the royal title and so divine the language in which the inscriptions were written. I now learned from the [sacred Persian writings] that the name Hystaspes was pronounced Goschasp,

Gustasp, Kistasp, or Wistasp in Persian. This gave me the first seven letters of the name Hystaspes in the Darius inscription, and the last three I already knew from a comparison of all the royal titles."

And so it was that Grotefend became the first man in thousands of years to read from cuneiform script the name of a king of ancient Persia, whom the Greeks called Darius.

Zora Neale Hurston

1891–1960   African-American anthropologist and folklorist

"Like the dead-seeming, cold rocks, I have memories within that came out of the material that went to make me. Time and place have had their say.

"So you will have to know something about the time and place where I came from, in order that you may interpret the incidents and directions of my life."

That's how Zora Neale Hurston begins her autobiography, *Dust Tracks on a Road*. It is the story of an amazing journey, which begins with Zora leaving home at the death of her mother and traveling as a maid with a Gilbert and Sullivan musical troupe. As the story unfolds, she becomes a short-story writer and novelist, a student at Barnard College, and a graduate student at Columbia under the eminent Franz Boas. Then, as an anthropologist, she collects African-American folklore and stories about voodoo in Jamaica, Haiti, and Bermuda. She works on plays with Langston Hughes, teaches drama at a college, and becomes a staff writer at Paramount Studios in Hollywood. In all she publishes seven novels and scores of short stories and journal articles. She is perhaps best remembered and loved for collecting and preserving the traditions, the lore and oral history, the soul of her people.

Hurston was born in Eatonville, Florida, on January 7, 1891. "I was born in a Negro town," as Hurston tells it. "I do not mean by that the black backside of an average town. Eatonville, Florida, is, and was at the time of my birth, a pure Negro town—charter, mayor, council, town marshal and all.

It was not the first Negro community in America, but it was the first to be incorporated, the first attempt at organized self-government on the part of Negroes in America." Her father, John Hurston, was a wayfaring carpenter and Baptist preacher from "'over the creek,' which was just like saying on the wrong side of the railroad tracks. John Hurston had learned to read and write somehow between cotton-choppings and cotton pickings," Hurston tells of her father. "I know I did love him in a way, and that I admired many things about him. He had a poetry about him that I loved."

Lucy Ann Potts was fourteen years old when she married John Hurston. Lucy's parents didn't approve of her choice of a husband. They never accepted him, or ever mentioned his name for that matter—"regular hand-to-mouth folks" were his family. John and Lucy bought land in Eatonville, built a house, and planted their crops. Hurston grew up in a "house full of young'uns." Besides her, there were Robert, Sarah Emmaline, John Cornelius, Richard William, Clifford Joel, Benjamin, and Everett. Reverend John was a strong presence and was elected to three terms as mayor of Eatonville.

Living in an all-black town, Hurston grew up in security and comfort. "There were plenty of orange, grapefruit, tangerine, guavas, and other fruits in our yard. We had a five-acre garden with things to eat growing in it, and so we were never hungry. We had chicken on the table often; home-cured meat and all the eggs we wanted." The family lived in an eight-room house on a large piece of land covered with trees, gardenia bushes with hundreds of blossoms, and flowers. Lucy had been a country schoolteacher before she was married, and she saw to it that her children had schooling. "After supper," Hurston recalled, "we gathered in Mama's room, and everybody had to get their lessons for the next day. Mama carried us all past long division in arithmetic and parsing sentences in grammar, by diagrams on the blackboard. That was as far as she had gone. Then the younger ones were turned over to my oldest brother, Bob, and Mama sat and saw to it that we paid attention. You had to keep on going over things until you did know. How I hated the multiplication tables—especially the sevens!"

John Hurston didn't share his wife's interest in bettering the children's lives. He felt that too much ambition and independence and spirit was dangerous. Hurston remembers her father warning her angrily that white people would hang her or that "somebody was going to blow me down for my sassy tongue." Being "sassy," to Hurston's elders, included asking questions. She was full of curiosity and was always being ignored or punished by adults who were upset with her questions. "If telling their questioning young to run off and play does not suffice for an answer, a good slapping of the child's bottom is held to be proof positive for anything from spelling Constantinople to why the sea is salt." Still, Lucy prevailed and encouraged all her children to "jump at de sun," to be strong and do their very best. "We might not land on the sun," said Hurston, "but at least we would get off the ground."

From as early as she could remember, Hurston always had her eyes set in the distance. She saw things there that other children never noticed. She played in the bright light and shadows of moonlit nights, delighting in the way the moon "followed" just her. When asked by her father what she wanted for Christmas, she answered, "I want a fine black riding horse with white leather saddle and bridles."

Hurston had dreams of exploring beyond her small world. "I used to climb to the top of one of the huge chinaberry trees which guarded our front gate, and look out over the world. The most interesting thing that I saw was the horizon. Every way I turned, it was there, and the same distance away. Our house, then, was in the center of the world.

It grew upon me that I ought to walk out to the horizon and see what the end of the world was like." Hurston almost had her closest friend, Carrie Roberts, talked into going with her to the horizon. But Carrie was too scared, and Hurston became scared, too. "It looked so far that maybe we wouldn't get back by sundown, and then we would both get a whipping."

Hurston didn't reach the horizon that time. It would have to wait for another day. "When we got big enough to wear long dresses, we could go and stay as long as we wanted to. Nobody couldn't whip us then. . . . I couldn't give up. It meant too much to me. I decided to put it off until I had something to ride on, then I could go by myself."

Hurston was beginning to realize very young that Eatonville was a small place in a lot of ways. "The village seemed dull to me most of the time," she wrote later. "If the village was singing a chorus, I must have missed the tune." She kept reaching out toward the horizon, which still seemed so far away. All the time, her father called her "brazen" and threatened her with what would happen to a black girl who didn't know her place, "always trying to wear de big hat," as he put it. But people seemed fond of her; or, at least, this bold little girl intrigued them. And she became bolder. "I used to take a seat on top of the gate-post and watch the world go by. One way to Orlando ran past my house, so the carriages and cars would pass before me." The white travelers would wave to Hurston and call out greetings to her. But sometimes she called out to them, asking, "Don't you want me to go a piece of the way with you?"

"They always did. I know now that I must have caused a great deal of amusement among them, but my self-assurance must have carried the point, for I was always invited to come along. I'd ride up the road for perhaps a half-mile, then walk back. I did not do this with the permission of my parents, nor with their foreknowledge. When they found out about it later, I usually got a whipping." Once again Hurston was trying to break away from what she called "the fixity of things."

Hurston went to the local school after being taught at home by her mother. She did well, but couldn't honestly say she liked it. "I liked geography and reading, and I liked to play at recess time. Whoever it was invented writing and arithmetic got no thanks from me." She also hated the long, stinging palmetto switch the teacher used as a "squelcher." But she did love to read and she was the best reader in the class. One day, two young women from Minnesota visited her class, and the teacher asked Hurston to read from her lesson the Greco-Roman story of Pluto and Persephone. She must have read beautifully, for the visitors asked the teacher if they could meet and talk with the young reader. For Hurston they had words of praise and encouragement, an Episcopal hymnbook, a book of fairy tales, and a copy of *The Swiss Family Robinson.*

She loved her new books. But then there was another big surprise. One day there came in the mail from the two ladies back in Minnesota a big box of clothes and books. She opened the box and took out the clothes quickly and without much interest. Then she saw the books: *Gulliver's Travels, Grimm's Fairy Tales, Greek and Roman Myths,* Kipling's *Jungle Books,* some Hans Christian Andersen, Robert Louis Stevenson, and *Norse Tales.* These were her favorites. "Why did the Norse tales strike so deeply into my soul? I do not know, but they did. I seemed to remember seeing Thor swing his mighty short-handled hammer as he sped across the sky in rumbling thunder, lightning flashing from the tread of his steeds and the wheels of his chariot." Hurston would fly like that some day.

But then something terrible happened, and Hurston's sweet life at home would end forever. "I knew that Mama was sick. She kept getting thinner and thinner and her chest cold never got any better. Finally she took to bed." Hurston's mother was soon dead. Within a very short time her father remarried, and Hurston and the rest of her brothers and sisters were sent off to live with aunts and uncles and other family members. The grieving little girl, barely over the shock of her mother's death, found herself on a train to Jacksonville, where she would live with her older brother Bob. Hurston found the big city to be a very different place. "Jacksonville made me know that I was a little colored girl." She enjoyed school and did well. "But I was deprived of the loving pine, the lakes, the wild violets in the woods and the animals I used to know. No more holding down first base on the team with my brothers and their friends. Just a jagged hole where my home used to be."

For the first time Hurston knew poverty. "There is something about poverty," she wrote later, "that smells like death. Dead dreams dropping off the heart like leaves in a dry season and rotting around the feet. . . . People can be slave-ships in shoes." Hurston was forced to leave school and find a job. She was fourteen years old, and she knew that from now on she would have to pay her own way. She worked as a maid, and as a receptionist in a doctor's office, and as a live-in maid with her brother's family. Hurston hated the work. Then she found a job that was fun and where the people cared about her. She was hired as a wardrobe girl for a singer in a Gilbert and Sullivan light opera company touring the South. She traveled with the group, seeing new places, having new experiences, and reading during every spare moment. She felt like a member of the family. One of the tenors, a Harvard graduate, loaned her books from his traveling library. She listened not only to light opera but also to grand opera since many of the performers had classical training. But more than anything else, she wanted to go back to school. Her singer friend arranged for her to attend a good high school, so she left the company in Baltimore.

Hurston was sad to leave her friends. "Before this job I had been lonely; I had been bare and bony of comfort and love. Working with these people I had been sitting by a warm fire for a year and a half and gotten used to the feel of peace. Now I was to take up my pilgrim's stick and go outside again." Supporting herself as a waitress, Hurston went to night school at the Morgan Academy. She was given a place to stay and a job in the home of a local minister and his wife, the Baldwins, while she attended school. She liked her new home. "They had a great library," she recalled, "and I waded in. I acted as if the books would run away. I remember committing to memory, overnight—lest I never get a chance to read it again—Gray's 'Elegy in a Country Churchyard.' Next I learned the 'Ballad of Reading Gaol' and started on the 'Rubaiyat.'" She graduated two years later and, taking up her "pilgrim's stick" once again, headed for Washington, D.C., where she enrolled at Howard University.

Howard was more than just a school for Hurston—it became her new way of life. She visited the home of the black poet Georgia Douglas Johnson for evening literary discussions. During the day she attended classes in philosophy, paying her way as a manicurist. It was at Howard that Hurston got the very first inkling of what she might like to do with her life. There was one professor, in particular, who inspired her. "Listening to him, I decided that I must be an English teacher and lean over my desk and discourse on the eighteenth-century poets, and explain the roots of the modern novel."

Hurston was accepted into the campus literary club and then published her first short story, "John Redding Goes to Sea," in *Stylus*, the club's magazine. With this first published writing, Hurston's life changed overnight. Black

magazines wrote and asked her to send them her stories. She published two short stories and a play in *Opportunity Magazine*, a journal whose pages would introduce readers to new black writers. Still, despite the success, she was poor once again. But rather than give up, Hurston headed for that distant horizon. This time she went to New York, arriving with "$1.50, no job, no friends and a lot of hope."

Hurston arrived in New York at the time of what was called the Harlem Renaissance—a gathering of black writers, musicians, singers, poets, and artists from all over the country. She was invited to an *Opportunity* awards dinner and found that she had won second prize for one of her stories. At the dinner she met novelist Fannie Hurst, who hired Hurston as her live-in secretary. She also met another writer, Annie Nathan Meyer, who also happened to be one of the founders of Barnard College. Meyer got Hurston a scholarship so that she could go to Barnard, and two years later, at the age of thirty-seven, she graduated with a B.A. degree.

College broadened Hurston's choices. She had majored in English and political science at Barnard, but was advised to take some other courses—fine arts, economics, and anthropology. So it was that she found herself in the anthropology class of Dr.

Gladys Reichard. Hurston liked the subject. And when Reichard read Hurston's first term paper, she was so impressed that she showed it to a colleague at Columbia. That colleague was the famed anthropologist Franz Boas. Boas was impressed, too, and he invited Hurston to work with him in anthropology. She would have an opportunity to work with Dr. Reichard and another of Boas's students, Ruth Benedict, as well. Hurston decided she wanted to be an anthropologist and "thereby gave up my dream of leaning over a desk and explaining Addison and Steele to the sprouting generations."

Anthropology was a natural for Hurston. She had grown up steeped in the rich folklore of her people. Now, she realized, others wanted to hear and read the "good old lies," the stories and gossip she had listened to as a girl on the porch of Joe Clarke's store. There was nothing subtle about what was said on that porch, and Hurston loved overhearing it all. "There was open kindnesses, anger, hate, love, envy and its kinfolks, but all emotions were naked, and nakedly arrived at. . . .

"For me the store porch was the most interesting place that I could think of. I was not allowed to sit around there, naturally. But, I could and did drag my feet going in and out, whenever I was sent there for something, to allow

whatever was being said to hang in my ear. I would hear an occasional scrap of gossip in what to me was adult double talk, but which I understood at times." It was a rare opportunity for anyone. Hurston could relive those early, happy years in Eatonville and make it her work all at the same time.

Two weeks before her graduation from Barnard, Hurston was called to Boas's office. He had arranged for her to receive a fellowship from Carter Woodson's Association for the Study of Negro Life and History. Boas wanted her to spend six months in the field, beginning in Eatonville and working south to record songs, customs, tales, superstitions, lies, jokes, dances, and games. Hurston would begin in Florida because that state drew black people from all over the South. There she would find a cross section of the South. And by starting in her own backyard, she was surer of success in the beginning. There, "I was just Lucy Hurston's daughter, Zora."

Collecting folklore, Hurston discovered, was not as easy as it sounded. Part of the problem was that she was no longer "just Lucy Hurston's daughter." She was now quite polished by her years at Howard, Barnard, and Columbia. She had lost some of her country ways. "I knew where the material was all right. But, I went about asking,

Zora Neale Hurston in 1934, photographed by Carl Van Vechten. *Reproduced by permission of Carl Van Vechten Papers, Collection of American Literature, Beinecke Rare Book and Manuscript Library, Yale University.*

in carefully accented Barnardese, 'Pardon me, but do you know any folk-tales or folk-songs?' The men and women who had whole treasuries of material just seeping through their pores looked at me and shook their heads. No, they had never heard of anything like that around there. Maybe it was over in the next county." Hurston discovered her mistake and, with the help of a good, stern talking-to from Papa Franz, she found her way.

So Hurston did research. "Research," as she defined it, "is formalized curiosity. It is poking and prying with a purpose." Hurston used all her talents and resources in her fieldwork, including the poking and prying she had done as a little girl. And she wouldn't be content just collecting and writing reports. She produced a program of African-American spirituals and work songs that played at a theater in New York. Then she took her troupe to the National Folklore Festival in Saint Louis, Missouri; to Chicago; Washington, D.C.; and all over Florida. That same year she wrote her first novel, *Jonah's Gourd Vine*, about a black preacher who seems to most readers an awful lot like her father, Reverend John. The *New York Times* called it "the most vital and original novel about the American Negro that has yet been written by a member of the Negro race." The following year Hurston published her sec-

ond book, *Mules and Men*, a study of African-American folkways.

Hurston was especially interested in the work of her people. She visited men and women at work in sawmills, down in the phosphate mines, and out on the railroads. She watched the men spike down rails and then use long steel bars to straighten the track by prying and shaking it until all it needed was just a hair more to make it perfectly straight. The men moved together in perfect cadence on the command "Hank!" Here's what Hurston heard and saw:

Polk County. The clang of nine-pound hammers on railroad steel. The world must ride.

Hah! A rhythmic swing of the body, hammer falls, and another spike driven to the head in the tie.

Oh, Mobile! Hank!
Oh, Alabama! Hank!
Oh, Fort Myers! Hank!
Oh, in Florida! Hank!
Oh, let's shake it! Hank!
Oh, let's break it! Hank!
Oh, let's shake it! Hank!
Oh, just a hair! Hank!

The singing-liner cuts short his chant. The strawboss relaxes with a gesture of his hand. Another rail spiked down. Another offering to the soul of civilization whose other name is travel.

Part of collecting folklore is collecting dialects, the different ways people

Zora Neale Hurston collecting folklore in Eatonville, Flordia, in 1935. *Library of Congress.*

speak the same language. People in the South, in New England, in the Midwest, in Appalachia, and in Brooklyn all speak English, but all in different dialects. There are even different dialects in the South, in different states, in different towns. Hurston was interested in the varying African-American dialects. Each way of speech reflects the culture of the area. For instance, African-American dialect in Charleston, South Carolina, was shaped by African, Native American, and British speech. In New Orleans, the influences were African, Spanish, and French. In Thomasville, Georgia, they were African and British. Here's how Hurston

would record the sentence "They are going downtown" in each of these three places:

In Charleston: "De gwa downtown."
In New Orleans: "Dee gwon downtown."
In Thomasville: "Day goin downtown."

Hurston went to New Orleans to study the magic of hoodoo. She went on to the Bahamas, where the people speak English with a West African accent. Then her work took her to Mobile, Alabama, where she met a very special old man. Cudjo Lewis had been on the last boatload of slaves to land in the United States. This was back in 1859, and Kossola-O-Lo-Loo-Ay—that was his African name—was in 1929 the only African-American alive who had come over on a slave ship. Hurston found herself sitting and talking with him. "I found him a cheerful, poetical old gentleman in his late nineties, who could tell a good story. His interpretation of the story of Jonah was marvelous." Kossola also told Hurston the horrible story of how, at dawn, Dahoman women warriors attacked their city. They took all the able-bodied and beheaded everyone else, including the king. Kossola, who was nineteen, was marched to the coast in chains and taken by a slave trader. He recalled the ocean voyage and landing in Mobile, Alabama, where he began his life as a slave. "I lonely for my folks," Kossola told Hurston.

Through all of her fieldwork, Hurston kept writing books and articles. Her second novel, *Their Eyes Were Watching God*, was set in Eatonville. Her third, *Man of the Mountain*, is her retelling of the story of Moses, which was a favorite of African Americans. She wrote and produced another musical review based on the stories and songs she had collected. The show, called *The Great Day*, is about one day in a railroad work camp. She worked on another play, a folk comedy called *Mule Bone*, with the writer Langston Hughes. She became head of the drama department of the North Carolina College for Negroes and worked for Paramount Studios.

Hurston will always be remembered for her careful and loving collection of African-American folklore. Much of this folklore is gone now, forgotten, and Hurston's work, among others, preserves what we have left. But even more important is the message Hurston's life holds for young people today, especially African Americans. Writer Alice Walker, like so many African Americans, recalls the nourishment her writer's soul got from Hurston. Speaking at a celebration of Hurston's death, Walker said about her, "Zora Hurston's ash was diamond ash.

"Diamonds, you know, start out as carbon, or coal, deep in the folds of the earth. Over eons enormous pressure builds up and crushes the coal into diamonds, the hardest crystals known. Then some of us, like Zora, are crushed further, by the lies of enemies and the envious hostility of friends, by injustice, poverty and ill health, until all that is left is diamond ash. . . . Zora's diamond ash, her spirit, has been blowing across the planet on the winds of our delight, our excitement, our love. . . . Zora is us. That is why, reading her, we smile or cry when she shows us our face."

Alfred Kroeber

1876–1960   American anthropologist and linguist

Of Alfred Kroeber it was once said, "To date no one has written more wisely of mankind, or more understandingly of human culture." Certainly few had written as much: There are more than five hundred titles in his list of writings. He was an archaeologist, an anthropologist, and a linguist. He wrote with strength and grace. And he wrote about anything and everything that interested him—poetry and literature, cultures all over the world, kinship, the history of civilization, art, animal behavior, psychology, human nature, the social structure of societies, race, languages, and folklore. He devoted his life to one thing he valued above all else, "to free men intellectually."

Kroeber was born on June 11, 1876, in Hoboken, New Jersey. His father was Florence Martin Kroeber, who was born in Cologne, Germany, and was brought to America by his parents when he was ten years old. By the time Kroeber was born, his father had a thriving import business, specializing in European clocks. Kroeber grew up in New York City in a house full of beautiful timepieces. He played among tall floor clocks with their swinging pendulums, little animated cuckoo clocks, and French clocks under gleaming glass domes. He remembered, as a boy, delivering clocks around New York City for his father. Another thing he remembered about his father was his love of music and drama. Kroeber and his family often went to the theater and to Symphony Hall, and the children grew up loving music.

Kroeber's mother, Johanna Muller, was born in New York City. Her parents, too, were from Germany. "I was raised bilingual," Kroeber recalled, "English and German . . . the language of the household being German, of the street, English." Johanna attended private elementary and high schools in New York. Kroeber remembers her as a gentle person, but strong. He called her Mimi. She loved to listen to music, to read, and to be with people. Johanna was a happy person, always teasing and joking with her family. She was also a concerned person, always working in her own quiet way for good causes. Kroeber was her first child, the oldest of four. He had a brother, Edward, who died at the age of nineteen. And there were two sisters, Johanna, whom Kroeber called Yanchi, and Elsbeth, both of whom became teachers.

It has been suggested that a person who grows up bilingual is actually two people. Several anthropologists, especially, have pointed to their own bilingual upbringings as a factor that helped make them special people. "We all read German before English," Kroeber remembered, "and until Mimi's death we often used German in speaking of household things. Lots of family jokes almost have to stay untranslated. . . ." Speaking German was not just an accident of birth for Kroeber. They, like most German Americans, were proud

of their heritage and wanted their children to be proud, too. They saw to it that their children read the great German poets Goethe, Heine, and Schiller in German. Kroeber read Shakespeare for the first time in German. He recalls that the first entire book he read on his own was *Robinson Crusoe*, also in German. When Kroeber first went to school he had a German accent.

Kroeber began his schooling, at home with a tutor, when he was five. His tutor, Dr. Hans Bamberger, had an important influence on Kroeber, one that would affect his interests for years to come. Bamberger was the principal of the Workingmen's School, which had a special philosophy. He believed that the first thing children should learn is to observe the world around them. At an early age, also, children should begin using hand tools. Only later, Bamberger believed, should children be concerned with symbolic and abstract ideas. He encouraged Kroeber to sketch and to use carpenters' tools to make small woodworking projects. Together they built a little mechanical model of the solar system that showed the movements of the planets around the sun.

From the beginning, Kroeber's tutor put special emphasis on natural science. Kroeber made little mud-pie mountains that he then left outside on the windowsill. As the days went by, he could watch how the sun dried and cracked and the rains eroded these mountains. Kroeber and Dr. Bamberger wandered through Central Park collecting rocks, plants, and fungi. There was a microscope to look at these things closely, and soon the shelves of Kroeber's room began to fill with his specimen collection. He carefully prepared beetle, butterfly, and rock collections. He learned to prepare glass slides for his microscope. At a time when children were expected to live in the neat, very formal world of adults, Mimi was always understanding of her son's interests. The house was filled with cages for little creatures, aquariums full of fish, terrariums for frogs and lizards, Bunsen burners and chemistry laboratory equipment, and dissecting instruments. Kroeber was allowed the mess of learning and creative work.

Together he and Dr. Bamberger explored the world close up. When the two weren't out collecting or working in their home laboratory, they read together. Dr. Bamberger told Kroeber stories and read aloud from chronicles of ancient times. Their favorites were stories about Troy and the *Iliad* and the *Odyssey*. Kroeber got his first lessons in Greek from Dr. Bamberger, and with his mother he was learning French.

It was through his tutor that he met Carl Alsberg, who would become his lifelong friend. Carl, like Kroeber, also spoke German and English. He, too, was a student of Dr. Bamberger's, and soon the three of them began exploring together. The lives of the two boys complemented each other. They liked to visit each other's homes. Carl liked the controlled quietness of the Kroeber household. The Kroeber children, on the other hand, enjoyed the freedom they were allowed at the Alsbergs'. Much later, when Carl Alsberg became a renowned chemist, Kroeber wrote about him and their childhood: "A visit to the Alsbergs meant a roughhouse such as was never permitted at our home, with or without visitors; battles with brooms up and down the stairs, water fights in the attic, and a general piling on top of one another of the eight of us wherever we chose. Father Alsberg only smiled indulgently and Mother Alsberg rejoiced. The furniture was as shabby as comfortable, with no heirlooms or valuables to be broken. . . ."

Kroeber and Alsberg not only played, but they learned together. Alsberg later recalled those days: "I learned to read sitting on a park bench. On one side of me was Dr. Bamberger, a big man with a bristling red beard and gold-rimmed spectacles; on the other side Alfred, of whom I stood a little in awe. He could already read and he was tidy and contained—not like me." Perhaps more than any other of their adventures together, Alsberg always remembered their first geography lesson with Dr. Bamberger. "He took us to the center of the span of Brooklyn Bridge, then only a few years completed; our teacher took a compass and a map of New York harbor out of his pocket, spread the map out and explained north and south, east and west to us, and how to read a map. For most children—and adults, too, for that matter—north is up and south is down because that is the way maps are hung on walls—but not for us."

Exploring the out-of-doors with Dr. Bamberger and Alsberg continued until Kroeber was nine years old. Then he and Alsberg were sent to a private college preparatory school based on the model of German and French schools. Kroeber and Alsberg had learned so much from their tutoring that they were put in classes with boys three years older. But this formal, very serious school was nothing like the times they had spent with dear Dr. Bamberger. They had classes in Latin, Greek, and French; grammar, composition, literature, and history; mathematics, physics, and chemistry. The teachers, though good scholars, were humorless and stern.

Kroeber and Alsberg would find the fun part of learning on their own, after school and on weekends and holidays. With their friends and their younger brothers they organized what they named the Humboldt Scientific Society, after the great German scientist. Together, they explored the city and countryside around them the way they used to with Dr. Bamberger (who was pleased, no doubt, that now the boys were on their own). Alsberg described their meetings, or outings. "We went into the Bronx Park region which was then largely open country to collect beetles and butterflies, to an iron-smelting furnace where we collected fossils from the limestone used in smelting, to the Franklin zinc smelter where we collected . . . minerals, to the Palisades, to Snake Hill in the Jersey marshes, to such factories as would let us in. . . ." Later, when they got older, the boys' society took the shape of the learned societies of the day. They each wrote papers and then read their papers to the other members.

Kroeber's education continued in private schools. He attended the Gunnery, a private boarding school in Connecticut. Here he lived in the countryside for the first time, fishing, swimming, climbing the mountains, and in the winter ice-skating and tobogganing. Kroeber remembers discovering the seasons for the first time, reading them in the changes he saw in the trees. And it was here that he met another of his lifelong friends, Jim Rosenberg. Rosenberg, who was two years older than Kroeber, went on to Columbia College in 1891. Kroeber and Alsberg followed a year later. Kroeber was sixteen. At Columbia, he, Alsberg, and Rosenberg met a fourth friend, Joe Proskauer; they all would become inseparable. Later, each of them would make important contributions in the physical and social sciences.

His parents had intended to send Kroeber away to school, but his father's business began to fail, and the family had to give up expensive dreams. Kroeber went to Columbia because he could live at home. He found the classes not very challenging and the work too easy, and turned his energies to ingenious pranks. Jim Rosenberg remembers him as "an imp of mischief." Alsberg always felt that Kroeber was, of any of them, the least hampered by convention. He once painted some of the statues in Central Park blue and white, the colors of Columbia, and then brushed on red mustaches and hair. Kroeber later said he was protesting against the ugliness of the Victorian sculpture. He was caught and his father fined for his prank. (The paint was traced to the store where Kroeber had bought it.)

Kroeber had always loved literature and poetry, and so at Columbia he de-

cided to make literature his life. He took his B.A. and then, after a fifth year, his master's degree in literature. As a graduate student he taught literature and freshman English composition. It was also during this first graduate year that Kroeber discovered something about his interests. He had always been interested in history. But most of the history he encountered in school did not interest him because it was political history. The emphasis was always on important people and political events. At Columbia, a new kind of history was being taught, cultural history. This history was concerned with the whole of the human experience. Kroeber took an interest in this new approach to history. That was in 1896, and the date is significant for another reason. That was the year Franz Boas was appointed lecturer in anthropology at Columbia. Anthropology was a new field then, and Boas was one of the first in the whole country to be teaching courses.

Franz Boas, like Kroeber's father, was German-born. And like Kroeber, Boas's first interest was physical science—physics and geography. He had worked at the Royal Ethnographic Museum of Berlin before coming to America. Then he had gone to Baffin Land, up beyond the Arctic Circle, to study the folklore and language of the Inuit. Before coming to Columbia he had been

Alfred Kroeber as a young man. *Bancroft Library, University of California, Berkeley.*

appointed curator of the American Museum of Natural History.

It was only by chance that Kroeber decided to take a new course being offered at Columbia that year, Franz Boas's American Indian Languages. It was an unusual course. The seminar—Kroeber and two other young men—met with Boas around his dining-room table. Kroeber was so enchanted that he decided to study anthropology.

What attracted Kroeber to anthropology and Boas was linguistics. When he was a boy, he was interested in verbs in German and English. "I think it was in my first year of school, in my tenth year of age, in studying English grammar," Kroeber wrote later, "that I learned of 'irregular' or 'strong' verbs, and that most of these were contained in several 'classes' of forms, like sing-sang-sung, write-wrote-written, break-broke-broken. . . . This episode may illustrate a strong bent, a satisfaction in recognizing patterns, which seems to be at the root of my linguistic interests."

In this first class Boas's students studied the Chinook, Inuit, Klamath, and Salish languages. Later, Boas brought into class an Inuit woman from Labrador, Esther, who became Kroeber's first informant. She told stories in Inuit as Kroeber wrote them down phonetically. It was a skill he would use many times in his life when he came among native peoples.

Kroeber continued to study with Boas. The next semester, in addition to the language course, he took courses in statistics and physical anthropology. This semester the guests at the seminar were a group of Inuit—four men, one woman, and a ten-year-old boy brought back by the explorer Robert Peary. Using Esther as an interpreter, Kroeber put their myths and legends into writing and made lists of vocabulary words. He was appointed assistant in anthropology at Columbia and published his first article, containing the Inuit stories, in the *Journal of American Folklore*. That year, as well, Kroeber was awarded a fellowship in anthropology, which made possible his first fieldwork.

With the language experience in Boas's seminar, Kroeber was ready to begin work on his own. He spent a summer among the Arapaho Indians in Wyoming. After another academic year Kroeber spent the summer with the Arapaho and other nearby Plains Indians, the Ute, Shoshone, Bannock, and Atsina. He returned to write his doctoral dissertation—twenty-eight pages—on Arapaho art. After taking his doctoral examination, Kroeber became Boas's second Ph.D., and only the second anthropology Ph.D. in the United States.

Dr. Kroeber finished at Columbia, fired by Franz Boas's mission. There were languages out there, all over the world, spoken languages that had survived for thousands of years without one scratch of the pencil, stylus, or chisel. Now they were about to die with the deaths of their last speakers. Everywhere there were worlds, strange wonderful worlds and lifeways about to be destroyed, lost forever to the spread of civilization. Each one of these languages and cultures was precious, irreplaceable. They must be preserved and, if not saved, then at least recorded. Kroeber would go into the field with his notebook and pencil to record and save all that he could.

Finished with his academic work, Kroeber found himself heading westward, to San Francisco, to be the curator of the Museum of the California Academy of Sciences. He had worked under Boas at the American Museum of Natural History. He had learned to catalog and document artifacts and to preserve specimens in the laboratory. And he liked museum work. Perhaps it reminded him of his childhood adventures with Dr. Bamberger. Kroeber often made the point that anthropology had grown up in museums long before it was taught at the university.

The museum had a small collection, and very soon Kroeber had gotten everything in order. He asked the director for permission to travel northward up the coast, to where he knew there were still Indians. The answer was yes. Kroeber received one hundred dollars to pay for travel—train, stagecoach, and horses rented at livery stables—artifacts for the collection, and informants' fees.

For Kroeber, California was an anthropologist's dream. Within this one state were more different languages than any other place of the same size anywhere in the country. Among them were many languages that had not yet been classified or recorded. But time was running out. Loggers were already cutting into the coastal redwoods and farther inland to Indian lands. Many Indians had been killed in the Spanish-Mexican invasion of California. Many who had survived those years were killed by white settlers. They had been intruded upon, their lands taken, and their lifeways disrupted beyond any hope of saving. Still, Kroeber hoped to work with the few Indians still living on their ancestral lands. He would find the last remaining speakers of the ancient languages and record their stories.

So Kroeber headed for the mouth of the Klamath River, almost as far north as you can get on the California coast. He would live like the Indians whose lives he would record. His wife and

biographer, psychologist Theodora Kroeber, describes that first journey into Indian country.

A salmon cannery at Rekwoi [Requa today] was working to capacity when Kroeber arrived. . . . He stayed at first at the small hotel which housed the cannery workers, but within a few days he had outfitted himself with two army blankets, a coffee pot, fry pan and stew kettle, a small axe and a machette, lacking only the flat gold-washing pan to have looked like another "prospector." He was now free to build his fire and camp beside the open ocean or on one of the splayed banks of the river mouth, or to go upriver into its gorge. The bounty of the cold Pacific was his: surf fish, mussels, crabs, clams, with salmon from the river. Along the shore of the sea and on the gravelly spits beside the river and up the terraced sides of the river canyon were Indian villages and living Indians. They spoke a language which intrigued him and they lived according to an aristocratic formalized mode which caught his imagination.

Over the next few years, Kroeber and his colleagues would complete much of the work yet to do. On that first trip he had lived among the Yurok Indians of the lower Klamath River. He would do fieldwork with both them and the Mohave Indians, another of his interests, for the rest of his life. Kroeber was invited to be an instructor in the new Department of Anthropology at the University of California at Berkeley. There would also be a new Museum of Anthropology, which Kroeber would help set up.

Kroeber traveled widely to do his fieldwork. His studies took him all over California, but also outside of the state. He conducted anthropological expeditions to New Mexico, the Philippines, Mexico, and Peru. He did archaeology as well as anthropology and linguistics. The titles of his many books show his broad interests. Among them are *Basket Designs of the Indians of Northwestern California*, *The Chumash and Costanoan Languages*, *Arapaho Dialects*, *Peoples of the Philippines*, and, perhaps, his most famous, *Handbook of Indians of California*. Always mindful of the needs of students in the new field, Kroeber also wrote a textbook, *Anthropology*, in which he summarized all the important anthropological discoveries made to date (1925). He wrote on *The Nature of Culture* and "Sign and Symbol in Bee Communication." His books were known for their beautiful writing style as well as their scholarship.

If he had to choose a favorite episode in his life, Kroeber would probably choose the adventure that began with his reading of a San Francisco newspaper in August 1911. The headlines and articles reported that an Indian, naked, emaciated with hunger, and lost, had wandered onto a ranch near Oroville in northern California. Kroeber immediately called the sheriff. Yes, the story was true, he was told. Not knowing what else to do with the man and unable to understand his language, the sheriff had put him in jail.

The next day Kroeber's colleague Professor T. T. Waterman was on his way to the isolated little town on the Feather River. Waterman was able to talk to the tired, dazed, and frightened wild man and was able to understand him as well. He was a Yana Indian.

Kroeber got busy making arrangements. In a few days Waterman and the Indian were on their way to San Francisco. The staff of the Museum of the California Academy of Sciences had furnished a room for him. They first made him comfortable and reassured him over and over that they would protect him and care for him. The whole staff began learning Yani, the Indian's dialect. Kroeber decided to give the Indian a name. He knew from his studies of California Indians that it would be taboo for the Indian to tell his personal, private name to strangers. Kroeber chose the name Ishi, "one of the people."

Ishi was the last of his people. There was no one left but him. His family

Ishi in August 1911. *From* Ishi in Two Worlds
*by Theodora Kroeber. (Berkeley: University
of California Press, 1962.)*

and countless other Indians had been
shot, hanged, sold as slaves, or driven
off their lands by white people in search
of gold. For forty years, since he had
been a boy of ten, Ishi and a handful
of his people had hidden from the
whites, frightened, always fearful they
might be found and killed. Eventually
all of Ishi's family died, and for three
years he had been alone. He was alone
without another person who spoke his
language. He was alone without his family and friends. He continued living as
his people had lived for generations and
generations, fishing with a harpoon he
made himself, hunting with his own
bow and arrows and sling.

Kroeber and Ishi became friends. Often Kroeber would be sitting in his office and from next door would come
the sounds of tiny flakes of glass dropping to the floor. Looking in, Kroeber
would see Ishi fashioning an arrowhead
from a piece of shiny, black volcanic
glass. The glass, called obsidian, was
gathered by the Yana from the slopes
of Lassen Peak. Kroeber would sit down
next to Ishi and watch how he pressed
his deer-antler chipper against the
piece of glass, releasing a flake. In a
short time Ishi would have a beautiful
arrowhead or spearhead, made just as
he had learned how long ago as a boy.
He would take Kroeber back to the wilderness with him, to swim in the cold

streams and walk over the trails Ishi's people had used since the beginning of time.

Ishi was the last of the hunter-gatherers, the last one of his tribe to know the old ways. "He was also a remarkable human being," Theodora Kroeber wrote in her book *Ishi in Two Worlds*. She wrote this beautiful story because she knew Kroeber couldn't, wouldn't ever write it. He was too close to Ishi. Ishi amazed everyone with the way he became accustomed to his new life, so different from his traditional one. "However fearful and timid he was in the strange world where he found himself, Ishi never lost the sense of his own identity. He always knew who he was: a well-born Yana to whom belonged a land and Gods and a Way of Life. These were truths learned in childhood; one lived by them and according to them and at the end one would travel the trail to the west out of the white man's world to the Yana Land of the Dead, there to rejoin one's family and friends and ancestors."

A very few years later Ishi was dead of a white man's disease, tuberculosis. His body was cremated according to the custom of his people. Kroeber was away at the time and could not be there to attend to the last rituals for his friend. But Kroeber would never forget what Ishi, his gift from the wilderness, had taught him. It was more, much more, than just how to make arrowheads, use a fire drill, dig roots from the ground, and speak Yani. Ishi taught Kroeber the Yana lessons of life itself.

Austen Henry Layard

1817–1894   French-born English traveler and adventurer who uncovered the palaces and treasures of Nimrud

The quest of a lifetime began at dusk. It was April 1840, and Austen Henry Layard, traveling south toward Baghdad, came upon a splendid sight which he later described in *Ninevah and Its Remains*. "As I descended the Tigris on a raft, I again saw the ruins of Nimroud, and had a better opportunity of examining them. It was evening as we approached the spot. The spring rains had clothed the mound with the richest verdure and the fertile meadows, which stretched around it, were covered with flowers of every hue. Amidst this luxuriant vegetation were partly concealed a few fragments of bricks, pottery and alabaster, upon which might be traced the well-defined wedges of the cuneiform character."

What Layard had found written in clay and stone was the ancient script of people who lived five thousand years ago. The wedge-shaped marks in clay had recently been deciphered for the first time (see the chapter on Georg Friedrich Grotefend). And they were Layard's clue that he was near, perhaps actually standing on, the ancient kingdom of Nimrud. He had read about this place in the Bible, in the Book of Genesis, and about its great king, Nimrod: "He began to be a mighty one in the earth. He was a mighty hunter before the Lord: wherefore it is said, Even as Nimrod the mighty hunter before the Lord. And the beginning of his kingdom was Babel, and Erech, and Accad, and Calneh, in the land of Shinar. Out of that land went forth Asshur, and builded Nineveh. . . ." Now the young explorer was standing in the twilight, looking out over the plains of Shinar, and he made himself a promise: "My curiosity had been greatly excited, and from that time I formed the design of thoroughly examining, whenever it might be in my power, these singular ruins."

Layard was born in Paris on March 5, 1817. His father, Henry Peter Layard, was a retired British colonial official, and his mother, Marianne Austen, Henry Peter's childhood sweetheart. The boy's earliest memory was of, at age three, being at the Paris zoological gardens, his nursemaid frozen in horror and his infant brother, Frederick, screaming in terror as he put his arms around and hugged a large lion cub. He recalls forming friendships, many of which his family were certain would be fatal, with all kinds of creatures. The boy was originally baptized Henry, but his name was changed to Austen later to honor and please an uncle. As a young man he chose once again the name Henry, which was how he was known by his friends throughout his life.

Layard attended schools for a short time in England, France, and Italy, but remembered later in his autobiography that he learned nothing. He was, in fact, a terror. At Moulins, his school in France, he once threw an inkwell at the teacher, which missed his head and crashed instead against the blackboard. He was beaten with a large wooden ruler, locked into the cellar, and allowed only watery green soup for twenty-four hours. Nor was Layard popular with the other students. They were Catholic and hated him because he was both English and Protestant. They beat him up regularly, so Layard learned more about fighting, punching faces, and kicking shins than anything else. Wherever there was trouble, Layard was part of it. He once bought gunpowder, which he fired in a friend's toy cannon, nearly blowing up both of them.

Layard's parents finally removed him from Moulins when they were told by the headmaster that their eight-year-old was disrupting the entire school. Even as a child, Layard was perceptive about what was happening to him. Because his parents did not have money to send him to a college or university, he felt, the teachers ignored his talents and gave their attention to more fortunate children who would be going on to higher education.

Layard's mother, Marianne, was well read and it was she who provided him with much of his education at home. The family dinner table was a gathering place for artists, poets, writers, and travelers from whom he heard tales of wondrous places. Among the regular visitors to the Layard home were the young writer (and future prime minister) Benjamin Disraeli and E. J. Trelawney, friend of the poet Byron.

Layard's father was interested in Italian painting and often took him along when he visited art museums and galleries. "He took pleasure," Layard later wrote, "in pointing out to me the beauties of the works of the great Masters and in teaching me how to distinguish them by their peculiar style or 'manner.'" While living in Florence, Italy, Layard became so familiar with many of the churches, buildings, and pictures in the galleries that, at the age of eight, he was sometimes a guide to visitors. Whenever he saw a painting by a Florentine painter he surprised his father by being able to make a good guess who the artist was.

One of Layard's childhood friends in Florence was a renowned artist, Seymour Kirkup, who often invited the boy to visit his studio. Kirkup enjoyed Layard's company and told him stories about the history of the city and taught him drawing and painting. So important was this friendship that Layard decided as a youngster that he wanted to be a painter, to make it his profession. He took lessons for only a short while. He loved drawing and during summer holidays would make precise little pencil sketches of thatched-roof cottages and church towers. He wasn't serious about art, no more than he was serious about any one thing at this age, but later in his life his drawing skills would stand him in good stead. As much as he, too, loved art, Layard's father counseled his son to find a more profitable profession.

Layard, who did not like school, loved reading and learning. At a young age he learned to speak French and Italian as well as his native English. While in Italy he learned Latin, and then, from the father of a childhood friend, Greek. One of his greatest joys, when he and his family were living in London, was visiting the British Museum, peering for hours into cases filled with wondrous things from worlds long ago, like cylinder seals and clay tablets covered with cuneiform characters. Another great joy was wandering around the city and poking through dusty, worn volumes in used-book shops and street stalls, looking for some treasure. Whenever he had a few coins he would spend it on a beautiful secondhand book or perhaps an old faded and tattered print. At home his father read to him the poets and playwrights of Elizabethan England—Spenser, Shakespeare, and Ben Jonson. His father encouraged him to take books from the shelves of the family library and read about what interested him. On his own he read all of his father's books on Italian history and still found time for his favorites, the novels of Walter Scott.

But there was one book more than any other that fired his imagination: the *Arabian Nights*. He remembered lying for hours on the marble floor of his father's library reading and rereading his favorites of the one thousand and one stories. He read the stories in French, for they had not yet been translated into English. "My imagination was so much excited by it that I thought and dreamed of little else but 'jins' and 'ghouls' and fairies and lovely princesses, until I believed in their existence. . . ." He dreamed of traveling to faraway places, to the world of Sinbad, to the exotic settings of Scheherazade.

Young Layard could not imagine he would ever get to travel around the world to the places he dreamed of, but still he dreamed. He, unlike most of the wealthier children in his school, would not go on to university, but to work. So, when he was sixteen, he was sent to be an apprentice to the law in his uncle Benjamin Austen's office. He was to be a solicitor, an attorney, like his uncle, and he had no choice in the matter—it was what his parents wished. Now he was expected to spend his time reading dreary books on the laws of England. But still he dreamed, and kept hidden a book or two on travel and his-

tory that, like a sly schoolboy, he'd read when his uncle wasn't watching him. For five years he suffered hunger, dampness, and winters in a dingy gray back room of a run-down lodging house. His parents sent him what little money they could, and his uncle was indifferent to him. If he bought books, even for pennies, he did not eat, and often his choice was not to eat. His only joys now were his reading, which his uncle constantly condemned as frivolous, and his flute, which he had learned to play in school.

In the Austen home, as in the Layards', there was a tradition of entertaining artists and writers. Layard would never forget bright moments on Sundays when he might be invited to the Austens' for dinner or to the home of Henry Crabb Robinson, a successful attorney who had befriended him, for breakfast. He could eat, perhaps more food than he had eaten all week, and he could meet interesting people. It was at these Sunday gatherings that he listened and talked to famous travelers, such as the painters J. M. W. Turner and Charles Lock Eastlake and the great poet William Wordsworth. Layard later recalled England's poet laureate as a "venerable and stately" man, but also remembered that he was very kind to the unknown young man who stood before him in awe and asked what must have seemed like so many foolish questions.

Layard enjoyed being with these brilliant men, listening to their ideas. But most important, he was beginning to find himself by meeting other men who enjoyed reading what he enjoyed reading and talking about things that interested him. When he met Benjamin Disraeli once again, he found out a secret about the great writer, later to become Britain's prime minister: Disraeli had also been an apprentice to the law with Uncle Austen and had also found it dreadfully boring. He, too, had secreted his favorite books in the office, read them when he was supposed to be studying books of law, and had been caught at it and scolded by Uncle Austen.

In spite of everything, Layard completed his work. And then events at once distressing and wonderful happened. Uncle Austen, disappointed by Layard's attitude, refused to accept him as a partner as he had promised. Layard felt that he had failed, but worse, he was treated like a failure by his aunt and uncle. He was no longer welcome at the Sunday dinners. But then, at this very time in his life, his uncle Charles Layard appeared, having just returned from Ceylon, an island off the southern coast of India (now Sri Lanka). His uncle invited Layard to return to Ceylon with

him and find work there. Unlike Uncle Austen, Charles Layard encouraged the young man to find himself and the life he would like. He even introduced his nephew to a man with whom he thought Layard would enjoy traveling. Layard and Edward Mitford took to one another immediately. The older, more experienced traveler offered Layard the promise of fulfilling his childhood dreams. Now he could go to Asia and India, to Persia and, perhaps, even to Baghdad, the land of Scheherazade.

Excited about his upcoming journey, Layard found out as much as he could about the lands through which he would be traveling. He and Mitford would travel overland from England, eastward across Europe and central Asia, and then down through India to Ceylon. It should be remembered that this was 1839, and Layard was now twenty-two years old. Little was known about central Asia. Only a handful of European adventurers had ever made the trip, and even though Mitford and Layard were experienced travelers, it was considered difficult and very dangerous. Layard sought out a number of travelers who had been to the places he and Mitford would be going. He reread books that had thrilled him as a boy, like *The Persian Adventurer* by Baillie-Fraser. Now he read with the heightened interest of one who was really going to the places described in those books. He consulted the Royal Geographical Society, which suggested routes and asked, in turn, that he report to them on what he found. Layard and Mitford would be traveling paths through central Asia unknown to outsiders. The journey across eastern Europe and into central Asia would require an armed escort. Much of the way would be made on horseback (and Layard had never been on a horse) and would take many months, maybe even a year. He had never traveled anywhere except in the relative comfort of Europe. But he was resolved, and in July 1839 the two set out on their journey. At the suggestion of the British ambassador to the court of the shah, they would take a mysterious route through Persia. The armies of Alexander the Great had once traveled through this region. But that had been over two thousand years ago, and no European had ever been there since. It was that journey with which we began this story, when Layard saw for the first time the ancient lands where once stood great cities he had read about—Nineveh, Nimrud, Kish, Baghdad.

Layard prepared well before leaving. He read whatever he could find on the ancient kingdoms and peoples described by the Greek historians and the Bible. He read what little was then available on cuneiform and brushed up on the bit of Persian he had learned as a boy. In his reading Layard came across a report by Major Henry Rawlinson, a former military adviser in Persia (who later would continue Grotefend's work on deciphering cuneiform). Rawlinson told Layard of rumors he had heard of the remains of the ancient city called Shushan in the Bible, the Shushan of Esther and the prophet Daniel. Rawlinson had been unable to reach the ruins, and so Layard vowed that he would find Shushan if it was at all possible.

Layard never made it to India or Ceylon; not on that trip anyway. So captivated was he by the wildness of Persia and his dreams of discovering the kingdoms of ancient Mesopotamia that, when he arrived there, he decided to stay. While in Persia he met Sir Stratford Canning, the British ambassador to Istanbul, Turkey. It is a longer, more complicated story—Canning was actually employing Layard as a kind of spy— but the short of it interests us most. Canning offered to finance and help Layard set up a trial archaeological excavation. The dream had come true at last. No longer would Layard be content with just reading history; now he would be digging down into the past himself.

So Layard stood on a sandy, flat plain bounded by the Tigris and Euphrates

A watercolor painting of Austen Henry Layard in Persian dress. *Object #1976–9–259. Department of Western Asiatic Antiquities, Copyright © British Museum, London.*

rivers. Here and there the flatness was broken only by tells, or mounds. Today this place is called Iraq, and it was here, archaeologists believe, that civilization was born. It is a land of the Bible, known in the Old Testament as *Aramnaharaim,* "the land between the two rivers." The Greeks called it Mesopotamia, which means basically the same thing. And it is here where archaeologists would find traces of the first cities in history, some going back perhaps seven thousand years. In those days, the Assyrian kings moved the capital of their powerful kingdoms up and down along the banks of the rivers. One of the earliest was Ashur, then Nimrud (called Calah in the Bible), and then Nineveh. No one had seen these cities for thousands of years, and when Layard was a boy they were myths.

The site Layard chose to excavate was what he believed to be Nineveh. And from the first moment he arrived on the site he was finding incredible objects. "The eye wandered over a parched and barren waste, across which occasionally swept the whirlwind, dragging with it a cloud of sand. . . . Twenty minutes' walk brought us to the principal mound. The absence of all vegetation enabled me to examine the remains with which it was covered. Broken pottery and fragments of bricks, both inscribed with the cuneiform char-

acter, were strewed on all sides." Later his Arab workmen brought him a large, beautiful fragment of bas-relief. "Convinced from this discovery that sculptured remains must still exist in some part of the mound, I sought for a place where excavations might be commenced with a prospect of success."

Fortunately for us, Layard left detailed accounts of his work and discoveries. His *Nineveh and Its Remains* was a best-seller in its day (1849) and is beautifully written and illustrated. It's also quite readable, once you get used to nineteenth-century English. But should you choose to read it—and it is a great adventure story—you should know that it contains one not-so-slight error. Layard, you see, wasn't in Nineveh, as he had thought. Later work showed that he was actually excavating Nimrud. But he could not have known any better. One of the inscriptions he found, however, would reveal the name of the site in a few years, when the cuneiform could be deciphered. It was a history of the king Assurnasirpal, and it told what had happened to Nimrud, or Calah: "The former city of Calah, which Shalmaneser, king of Assyria, a prince who lived before me, had built, that city had fallen into ruins and layed prostrate. That city I built anew, and the peoples who my hand had conquered, from the lands which I had brought under my sway . . . I took and settled them therein."

Layard's crew would seem hopelessly small compared to the hundreds that would be employed in later excavations. He began work with six men, but within hours they were already uncovering important finds. Layard's method—the standard technique of the day—was to dig trenches at various places through the mound. Since trenching with hand shovels is very slow work, success often depends on the archaeologist's eye. Layard must have read his mound quite well, because his first trench revealed ten alabaster slabs covered with inscriptions and pictures carved in relief. He had discovered a palace, the size of which he could scarcely believe. "I had satisfied myself beyond a doubt that it was the most ancient building yet explored in Assyria. . . . There were now so many outlets and entrances, that I had no trouble in finding new rooms and halls—one chamber leading into another. By the end of the month of April I had explored almost the whole building; and had opened twenty-eight chambers cased with alabaster slabs."

He describes for us how painstaking the work became with the discovery of some beautiful ivory ornaments: "These ivories, when uncovered, adhered so firmly to the soil . . . that I had the greatest difficulty extracting

them, even in fragments. I spent hours lying on the ground, separating them with a penknife. . . ." Layard had no money to hire an artist, so he fell back on those few drawing lessons he had enjoyed years ago as a boy. "I was able to draw a few of the ornaments, in which the colors chiefly distinguishable were red, blue, black and white."

The work continued with new finds coming to light every day. Layard recalled one especially exciting day. The workmen had exposed the upper part of a sculpture so awesome that they immediately stopped work and galloped off on horseback to Layard's camp to have him come see what they had found. "The Arabs withdrew the screen they had hastily constructed, and disclosed an enormous human head sculptured in full out of the alabaster of the country. They had uncovered the upper part of a figure, the remainder of which was still buried in the earth. I saw at once that the head must belong to a winged lion or bull. . . ."

Something about the head was terrifying. "This gigantic head, blanched with age," Layard wrote, "rising from the bowels of the earth, might well have belonged to one of those fearful beings which are pictured in the traditions of the country as appearing to mortals, slowly ascending from the regions below. One of the workmen, on catching

An engraving depicts the lowering of a great winged bull from a wall at one of Layard's excavation sites. *Mary Evans Picture Library, London.*

the first glimpse of the monster, had thrown down his basket and run off towards Mosul as fast as his legs could carry him." Eventually Layard's men found thirteen pairs of huge winged lions and hundreds more smaller wondrous objects. Most important, though, were the inscriptions. Later, when they were deciphered, they told the story of this place. Layard and his small team of Arab workmen had found the palace of the great king Assurnasirpal II.

The pages of *Nineveh and Its Remains* are filled with detailed drawings of the finds and Layard's descriptions of the work. But he goes beyond just listing

and describing. He gives his reader a sense of what these places must have been like. He helps us see and feel what it was like to be in a place that was once magnificent and imposing but is now only ruins and rubble. His description of the palace at Nimrud, for instance, asks the reader to imagine being a stranger who enters for the first time.

He was ushered in through the portal guarded by the colossal lions or bulls of white alabaster. In the first hall he found himself surrounded by the sculptured records of the empire. Battles, sieges, triumphs, the exploits of the chase, the ceremonies of religion, were portrayed on the walls, sculptured in alabaster, and painted in gorgeous colors. Under each picture were engraved in characters filled up with bright copper, inscriptions describing the scenes represented.

The stranger trod on alabaster slabs, each bearing an inscription, recording the titles, genealogy and achievements of the great king. Several doorways, formed by gigantic winged lions or bulls, or by the figures of guardian deities, led into other apartments, which again opened into more distant halls. . . . Square openings in the ceilings of the chambers admitted the light of day. A pleasing shadow was thrown over the sculptured walls, and gave a majestic expression to the human features of the colossal forms which guarded the entrances. Through these openings was seen the bright blue of an eastern sky, enclosed in a frame on which were painted, in vivid colors, the winged circle, in the midst of elegant ornaments, and the graceful forms of ideal animals.

Later generations of archaeologists have sometimes been critical of Layard's work. Though it's true that Layard, like all archaeologists of his day, was interested mostly in beautiful things for museum collections, his writings were a different matter. His interest was that of a collector. But Layard's writings reveal a man who, even if not experienced and well trained, was careful and observant.

We must remember that archaeology in the 1840s was not yet the science it is today, and many techniques were simply not known then. Layard had to invent techniques of excavation as he went along. Many things he did were being done for the first time. He made mistakes, even serious mistakes, but that is usually the price of being a pioneer in a new field. He once wrote, "I shall be well satisfied . . . if I have succeeded in an attempt to add a page to the history of mankind, by restoring a part of the lost annals of Assyria." He has done that and more. In his two books, *Nineveh and Its Remains* and *Nineveh and Babylon*, Layard wrote the beginning chapters of the science of modern archaeology and the study of Assyrian history.

Louis S. B. Leakey

1903–1972   English anthropologist, archaeologist, and paleontologist

Louis S(eymour) B(azett) Leakey was born in Kabete, Kenya, about ten miles from Nairobi, on August 7, 1903. Leakey was British, but he was born and grew up in Africa, because it was to Kenya that his missionary parents had been sent just the year before. They were the first members of their church to work among the Kikuyu, Kenya's largest tribe. Kenya would be Leakey's home, and the African people his closest friends. He would spend most of his life and do his most important work here. Sixty-nine years later he would be brought back to the place of his birth and buried alongside his parents in African soil.

During this one life span the history of human evolution was completely rewritten, and it was this extraordinary man who wrote most of the new chapters. At the time of Leakey's birth, human history was thought to have begun somewhere in Asia, little more than a hundred thousand years ago. By the time he died, Africa was discovered to be the birthplace of humanity, and the date had been pushed back millions of years.

Leakey inherited his dedication and devotion to Africa from his parents. His father, the Reverend Harry Leakey, was born in France. Harry Leakey began his education in Paris and was then sent to school in England. The family was poor, and by the time he was sixteen, he was earning his keep by teaching French at a grammar school. He went on to a theological college and was ordained a minister. Earlier, when

129

he was twelve, he had met Mary Bazett, who became a missionary in Africa on her own. She was one of thirteen children and, from an early age, felt called to missionary work. She and three of her sisters—all under the age of twenty-four—sailed for three exhausting months around the Cape of Good Hope and then up the east coast of Africa to Mombasa, Kenya. They were the first unmarried white women to land there. Mary Bazett returned to England from her mission. Soon after, she and the Reverend Leakey were married and returned to Africa together, this time to the village of Kabete in Kenya.

Mary Leakey had learned Swahili her first time in Africa and so taught it in the school her husband set up for Kikuyu children. The Reverend Leakey taught them carpentry. At first only the boys and men came to the classes—the women were not allowed by their parents and husbands to go to school—but then some of the young girls began to attend. Mary Leakey started a primary school for girls. Only a few came at first, but eventually more and more students showed up. If you visit the site of the old mission, you will find there now the Mary Leakey Girls' Secondary School. Today, Mary Bazett Leakey is remembered as one of the pioneers of women's education in Kenya.

Leakey was born in his parents' mud-walled, thatched-roof bungalow in a Kikuyu village. Their house was built of the same materials the villagers used for their dwellings. Leakey was quite a curiosity. He was the first European baby the Kikuyu had ever seen, and everyone within walking distance came to see the white infant. One day the tribal elders gathered solemnly around the baby in his basket and all spat on him. It was a sign of trust, Leakey later explained in an article by Melvin M. Payne in *National Geographic*. "The Kikuyu believe that to possess a part of another person, a fingernail, a lock of his hair, even his spittle gives one the power to work deadly black magic against him. Symbolically, the elders were putting their lives in my hands. The elders," Leakey added with a smile, "made me the best-washed baby in East Africa."

It was just after Leakey's appearance that his father began his translation project. The Reverend Leakey was the first to translate the Bible into Kikiyu. In preparation for his translation, he taught one of his students, Stefano, to speak and read English. Stefano, in turn, taught the Reverend Leakey to speak Kikuyu and to help him create a written language based on the Kikuyu sounds. Stefano learned the Bible almost by heart in English and so was able to help with the translation.

With Stefano's teaching, Leakey and his younger sisters became bilingual. Then their father started them on learning French. He insisted that the family speak French at meals and speak English only on Sundays. When Leakey's youngest brother, Douglas, was born, his mother and father arranged for a Kikuyu woman to look after him. The nurse told the children African folktales, which Leakey learned by heart and, later, told to his own children.

Leakey loved animals from the time he was a youngster. His love of wildlife came, he always said, from his father. As a boy the Reverend Leakey had spent many pleasant hours in the Paris zoo. He and his six brothers and sisters got into the zoo free whenever they wished because his father—Leakey's grandfather—had published a book on birds and was a lifelong member of the Zoological Society of London. The Leakey children were treated often to visits to the Nairobi National Park. At home, Leakey remembered the aviary his father built and that there were always lots of pets—tree hyraxes, serval cats, bush babies, monkeys, genets, and even small bucks.

When Leakey was about ten, his father engaged a governess, Miss Broome, who tutored the children. The Reverend Leakey chose her especially because she was also a keen naturalist.

She would take the children on walks to search for birds' nests and collect butterflies. Leakey remembered fondly how they would go for nature walks through the forest and observe animals. His favorite walk was to some waterfalls that could be reached only by crossing a stream on slippery, water-polished stones. It was on these walks that Leakey first found and collected stone arrowheads and tools. It was, he remembers, the earliest stirrings of his interest in archaeology and paleontology.

Leakey grew up a Kikuyu. He was fluent in Kikuyu and another local language, Kiswahili, as well. He made the language so much his own that he actually thought and dreamed in Kikuyu. His only playmates, besides his brother and sister, were the children of the village. They taught him their games. He, in turn, taught them how to play the English game of rugby, and organized his Kikuyu friends into barefoot soccer teams. Much of their play was really work. Kikuyu children were given more responsibilities at an earlier age than European children. So Leakey would help his young friends herd their goats. Meanwhile, their sisters would be helping their mothers with gathering food, planting, cooking, and looking after their little brothers and sisters.

Leakey was accepted by the Kikuyu

as one of their own. At night he sat with the elder tribesmen around the fire in front of their huts and heard the ancient stories of Africa. No one knew how old the stories were. They had been passed from generation to generation, the elders telling the children. Now the stories had reached Leakey's generation. The elders shared with him the rules, customs, and lore of the tribe and instructed the children on their responsibilities as they grew up. From the elders, also, he was given his Kikuyu name, Wakaruigi, which means "son of the sparrow hawk."

Leakey learned all he could from his Kikuyu extended family. He even built himself a hut, smaller than but otherwise just like the ones his Kikuyu friends lived in. Actually, he built several, each one larger than the other, using the same materials and methods used to build the other huts in the village. Eventually, when he was fourteen, he had built a two-room house of mud and woven sticks. One room he made his bedroom and in the other he put his natural history and archaeology collections. Leakey's parents encouraged his interests and sometimes even let him sleep in his hut and cook over his own fire.

At thirteen Leakey became certain of his life's work—as certain as a boy of thirteen can be. "I had almost made up my mind to make the study of birds of Africa my life's hobby if not my life's work." A book changed his mind. "A Cousin in England sent me as a Christmas present a book called *Days Before History* by H. R. Hall, which was a simple story of the Stone Age. I read and re-read this, and each time I did so I was fired afresh with the desire to find Stone Age tools and Stone Age man in East Africa."

Leakey searched the land he knew so intimately, but he could not find any flint tools. The reason, he soon discovered, was that Stone Age Africans didn't make tools of flint. "I went on searching in Kenya," he explained in *Adam's Ancestors*, "and one day I found a fine piece of shiny black stone looking for all the world like glass, but obviously worked into an arrow-head. I found that this shiny black stone was common in the district, and soon started collecting every piece I could lay my hands on, keeping all, for fear that in my ignorance of what was and was not humanly worked, I might throw away some precious piece." Later, he took his collection to the British Museum and was shown how to tell which had been fashioned by human hands.

Turning thirteen was a special event in a Kikuyu boy's life: This was the age at which he was initiated into manhood. When Leakey turned thirteen, he was invited to be initiated along with his friends in his age group, the Mukanda. He took part in ceremonies that made him a member of the Kikuyu tribe, a junior warrior. His Kikuyu "brothers" taught him to be an expert hunter. He practiced by throwing his spear through a small rolling hoop made of twigs. He learned to make snares. An old hunter, Joshua, taught him how to stalk wild game. From Joshua, Leakey learned the habits, the calls, and the tracks of every animal around.

The Kikuyu hunted with weapons like short spears, bows and arrows, and clubs, which required the hunter to get up very close. Leakey learned to creep up so quietly that he could get close enough to an animal to reach out and touch it with his hand. He learned to stalk and catch an animal with his bare hands. By moving in just the right way, the animal sees the hunter as a small tree, or a bush, or maybe doesn't notice him at all. Leakey was taught to hide his hands at his sides as he approached an animal—to wild creatures hands mean humans, danger, death.

Leakey used these lessons throughout his life. Later, when he became famous for what he called "Leakey's luck," he attributed it to things he had learned as a child. What were the most important things he learned during his Kikuyu childhood?

Two things. Patience—especially patience—and observation. In Africa survival depends on your reaction to irregularities in your surroundings. A torn leaf, a paw print, a bush that rustles when there is no breeze, a sudden quiet— these are the signals that spell the difference between life and death.

The same recognition of something different—a glint of white in the face of a cliff, an odd-shaped pebble, a tiny fragment of bone—leads to the discovery of fossils.

And patience. I can still hear the Kikuyu elders telling the boys of my age over and over: "Be patient, be careful, don't hurry. Try again and again and again."

I remember when Mary discovered the 25,000,000-year-old skull of *Proconsul. . . .* We had combed that particular site at least seven times—both of us— without results. But we kept going back, and on the eighth try, Mary found it.

To be a successful fossil hunter, then, one must be patient and observant. "My Kikuyu training taught me this: if you have reason to believe that something should be in a given spot but you don't find it, you must not conclude that it isn't there. Rather, you must conclude that your powers of observation are faulty."

Leakey and the men of the Mukanda age group remained friends their whole lives. One member, Heslon Mukiri, later worked with Leakey on several of his excavations and shared credit for many of his important finds. To his Kikuyu brother, Leakey entrusted his most important finds. On one expedition Heslon found a hominid tooth in a fragment of lower jaw embedded in a block of limestone.

Whenever Leakey returned to Kabete it was always like coming home. He was a part of Africa, and Africa was a big part of him. Koinange, a tribal chief who knew Leakey most of his life, said of him: "We call him the black man with a white face, because he is more of an African than a European."

Leakey's African boyhood was interrupted when, at sixteen, he started school in England. Up until then he had had no formal schooling, but his Kikuyu friends and elders and his beloved tutor Miss Broome had given Leakey much of what he would need for the rest of his life. From her he had learned several subjects, including mathematics, French, and Latin. Most important, though, she had instilled in him the love of learning. It must have made her especially proud when, after she had to leave the family, Leakey and his sisters continued teaching themselves with the help of their father. Leakey even taught in his father's school.

When Leakey entered Weymouth College in England he was in for a shock. He had been free to explore and learn on his own. He had been a leader among his Kikuyu friends. His best friend, like many of the young tribesmen, was about to be married. Leakey had even built his own hut and spent a lot of time alone there. Now he was at school. He had to have passes to go here or there. There were strict times to be in bed at night. The rules seemed so absurd and the students so utterly childish. Still, Leakey persevered, graduated, and went on to Saint John's College, Cambridge.

There's a story Leakey enjoyed telling about getting into Cambridge. Among the requirements was that he have a knowledge of two *modern* languages. He proposed French and Kikuyu. Kikuyu would not be allowed, the authorities argued, because it was not a written language and had no literature. Not so, Leakey argued; Kikuyu could be written and it had a literature—his own father had translated the Bible into Kikuyu. Leakey had them. Besides, the language was spoken by half a million people. The authorities had to agree to accept his two modern languages by their own rules (though they quickly changed them so such a thing wouldn't happen again).

There's a second chapter to this story:

There was no one at Cambridge qualified to examine Leakey at the end of the year. So they sent a letter to the University of London requesting two examiners who could speak Kikuyu. Imagine the shock when the reply arrived with the names of only two people, apparently, in all of Britain qualified to give an examination in Kikuyu: G. Gordon Dennis, a retired missionary, and Louis S. B. Leakey!

Leakey's studies at Cambridge were ended, at least temporarily, by a rugby injury that left him with terrible headaches. The cure, the doctor told him, was to give up his studies, leave Cambridge, and spend a year in the open air. Leakey turned his disappointment into an opportunity. He found out that the British Museum was looking for someone with African experience to assist Dr. William Edmund Cutler on a fossil-hunting expedition in Tanganyika (now Tanzania). Cutler was famous for his dinosaur finds in Canada. But he had never been to Africa. Leakey applied and got the job. He would oversee the workers, whose language, Swahili, he knew. And he would collect small animals and birds for the museum, using skills he had learned from his Kikuyu friends.

From this first expedition Leakey learned a lot of skills and techniques that he would use the rest of his life.

Looking for hominid fossils is no different from looking for dinosaur fossils. He learned to first expose the fossil bones with small tools, picks, and brushes. Then, because the fossils were crumbly, they would be hardened with a coat of shellac. Finally, they would be covered with a thick coating of plaster of Paris to protect them in shipment. Leakey celebrated his twenty-first birthday in his beloved Africa, doing what he had dreamed of doing as far back as he could remember.

Leakey spent the next ten years conducting his own fossil hunts in East Africa. He also completed his studies in anthropology and archaeology at Cambridge and found time to lecture and do research. The professors at Cambridge considered his search in East Africa a waste of time. "If you really want to spend your life studying early man," he was told, "do it in Asia." At that time the oldest human fossil remains had been found in Asia—Java Man and Peking Man. It was believed, then, that the birthplace of humankind would be found somewhere in Asia, so this is where everyone was searching. Still, Leakey insisted on searching in Africa. "Even then," he recalled years later, "I believed Darwin's theory: that the mystery of man's past would be unraveled here in Africa." Leakey reasoned that there must have been

Mary and Louis Leakey digging for bits of bone of prehistoric man in Tanzania. *UPI/Bettmann.*

cultures in Africa as old as, if not older than, those found in the rest of the world. "I argued to myself," he wrote in *Adam's Ancestors,* "that if only I could find the right places in which to search, I must be able to find this oldest culture in East Africa too." That's exactly what he did.

Leakey and his wife, Mary Nicol Leakey, and, eventually, their three children—Jonathan, Richard, and Philip ("the finest Land-Rover driver in East Africa," his father called him)—would spend the rest of their lives searching for clues to human evolution. Several times "Leakey's luck" seemed to be at work. Once he stepped out into midair, about to tumble down the face of a hidden fifty-foot cliff. As he went over, Leakey clutched at some branches, saved himself, and managed to get back up onto safe ground. It was only then that he caught sight of something sticking out from the face of the cliff. Down on his hands and knees, peering over the edge, Leakey saw a stone ax embedded in the soil. When he had finished excavating the site, he had discovered the first habitation of "hand-ax man," who lived about 200 thousand years ago.

He had also unearthed over two thousand tools chipped from obsidian, volcanic glass. His theory about human origins in Africa was affirmed. You can visit this site today at a place called Kariandusi, in Kenya. It's been turned into an open-air museum where you can see the excavations, with the fossils and tools lying just as Leakey found them.

Leakey's luck held. Studying the axes he found at Kariandusi, he thought he had seen something like them before. He had. Similar axes had been found in 1913 by a German geologist at a place called Olduvai Gorge. Leakey would go there. "Olduvai was all but inaccessible. It required seven solid days to reach it from Nairobi." But the trip proved worthwhile for Leakey. "Within eight hours of getting there, I'd found hand axes." Leakey would return often to Olduvai, a place he called a "treasure house" of fossils.

Over the years that followed, he and Mary made many important finds. Together they uncovered the almost complete skull of a creature called *Proconsul*, who lived 25 million years ago. *Proconsul africanus* was not human, but Leakey believed it might have been a common ancestor of both humans and apes, near to the point where the two species branched off. Soon they had found another ancestor, *Kenyapithice-*

cus, who lived 14 million years ago and whose small canine teeth were like those of humans.

Returning to Olduvai, the Leakeys continued the search for the earliest human. It was there that Mary found *Zinjanthropus*, "East African Man" (see the chapter on Mary Nicol Leakey). Zinj, as they called him, might be an important link in the long chain of human evolution. He stood about five feet tall, but had a brain only about half the size of a modern human. Most important, Zinj walked upright like humans, not on his feet and hands like the apes. Leakey later came to the conclusion that *Zinjanthropus* might not have been in the mainstream of human evolution. Instead he might have been a member of a race that branched off and eventually came to a dead end.

Later Leakey found the fossils of another creature, *Homo habilis*, "human with ability," a small-brained creature who lived in East Africa at the same time as *Zinjanthropus*—600,000 to 1,750,000 years ago. What's important about *Homo habilis* is that it made tools and, therefore, may be more directly related to modern humans.

By now archaeology had become a family activity for the Leakeys. Both Jonathan and Richard worked on and graduated from their parents' Olduvai team. Jonathan found other *Homo ha-*

Dr. Leakey with the skull thought at the time to be that of "Zinjanthropus." *UPI/Bettmann.*

bilis fossils, a jaw and teeth. Later, Richard found a lower jaw for *Zinjanthropus,* thus completing the fossil skull found by his mother.

You might be wondering, as you read, how it is that archaeologists can know so much about a creature from stones and a few bits of fossil bone millions of years old. To Leakey, the prob-lem had always been a simple one. To understand the habits of humans or near-humans, he needed only to look at himself and modern humans. Leakey relied a lot on experiments in addition to the fossil evidence. That, for instance, was how he knew what *Zinjanthropus* ate. "Where we find such big molars," he pointed out, "we can be reasonably certain that the owner fed on coarse vegetation. Yet we know from broken bones strewn on the 'living floor'—that is the actual site where *Zinjanthropus* made his rude home— that he ate small animals, and the young of the giant beasts he perhaps could not hope to kill as adults." What's more, Leakey guessed that Zinj must have used stone tools to cut its meat because its front teeth were too small to have torn into the skin and fur of even a small animal. But how could he make such a guess? Well, he tried it. His own teeth, he realized, were about the same size and shape as Zinj's, and Leakey found that he could not tear the furry skin of a rabbit with his hands or his teeth.

Although the importance of Leakey's many finds are not disputed, there is a lot of discussion and disagreement about his interpretations. This happens because scientific inquiry and discovery always lead to new ideas. For this reason, there are almost as many theories about *Zinjanthropus* and *Homo habilis* and other finds as there are archaeologists and paleontologists.

Leakey was never angered about the questioning. It was, he understood, the result of paleontologists having so little evidence to work with. "Theories on prehistory and early man constantly change as new evidence comes to light.

A single find such as *Homo habilis* can upset long-held—and reluctantly discarded—concepts . . . and the necessity for filling in blank spaces extending through thousands of years all contribute to a divergence of interpretations. But this is all we have to work with; we must make the best of it within the limited range of our present knowledge and experience."

This has been the story of Leakey's search for understanding the distant past. But he was not content with just looking back. Leakey's reverence for the natural world was part of him his whole life. He was saddened by the destruction of the forests and wildlife caused by the encroachment of Europeans in Africa. His deep concern for the animals—the slaughtering of herds, their dislocation and rapid extinction— troubled him so that he had to call the attention of the world to their plight. He spoke and worked for setting aside game preserves in Africa, and he helped found Kenya's national park system. In his later years, especially, Leakey would often share with friends his concerns about problems today—over-population, pollution, overcrowded cities, and violence. And his friends remember him saying, "I have become more and more concerned not only with man's past but also with his present and future."

Mary Nicol Leakey

1913–   English artist, archaeologist, and paleontologist

The Land Rover roared across the African plain, bouncing and rattling over the rough, rocky ground, a great cloud of sand and dust billowing behind. Mary Nicol Leakey pressed the gas pedal to the floor until she was almost flying over the desert. Just ahead were the tents of the camp she had left earlier in the morning. In one of the tents, Leakey's husband, Louis, leaped up, alarmed, still groggy from the flu and a headache that had kept him from leaving camp with Leakey.

The Leakeys had spent many seasons here at Olduvai Gorge. Their careful work had unearthed thousands of fossils and stone tools. Every day for months now, they had gotten up and had tea and some breakfast. Then they had loaded water and the dalmatians, Sally and Victoria, into the back of the Land

Rover and driven out to a rocky, eroded hillside. Once at the site they would spend the day on their hands and knees under the hot sun, sifting through the sand and crumbled rock with their hands and a small trowel. Their eyes were alert for the tiniest traces—a bit of chipped rock, a splinter of bone—evidence of early humans.

Louis Leakey shaded his eyes with his hands and watched the fast-approaching Land Rover. What was wrong? He had never seen his wife drive this recklessly before. Had she been stung by a scorpion? Maybe she had been bitten by a snake that had somehow gotten by the dogs. He waited anxiously. The Land Rover skidded to a stop, and above the noise of the engine came Leakey's voice shouting something to him. "I've got him! I've got him!" Louis understood instantly. He jumped into the car, his headache forgotten now, and together they roared out of camp, back in the direction from which Leakey had come.

As they drove at full speed, Leakey related to her husband what had happened. There was plenty of exposed material in the rock where she began creeping slowly and methodically up the hillside. (The rains that erode the surfaces of gorges are a great help to archaeologists.) "But one scrap of bone that caught and held my eye was not lying loose on the surface but projecting from beneath," she recalled in her book *Disclosing the Past.* "It seemed to be part of a skull, including a mastoid process (the bony projection below the ear). It had a hominid look, but the bones seemed enormously thick— too thick, surely. I carefully brushed away a little of the deposit, and then I could see parts of two large teeth in place in the upper jaw. They *were* hominid. It was a hominid skull, apparently *in situ* [in place], and there was a lot of it there." At that point, Leakey knew she had found "him," the fossil evidence they had been looking for for twenty-eight years. She covered up the fossils, made a small cairn—a pile of rocks to mark the spot—and sped back to get Louis.

Now they were back at the site, scrambling up the hill to Leakey's find.

She was right. The teeth were molars, about twice as big as the molars of a modern human, but Louis recognized them instantly as hominid. "I turned to look at Mary and we almost cried for sheer joy, each seized by the terrific emotion that comes rarely in life. After all our hoping and hardship and sacrifice, at last we had reached our goal— we had discovered the world's earliest known human."

Leakey's discovery seems like luck, one of those accidents by now familiar to us in stories of discovery. In a way it was. But there's a lot more to it than that. First of all, Leakey was in the right place. She and Louis knew, from past experiences at this site, that if they were going to find an early human, it would probably be here. But most revealing was her firm confidence. She instantly recognized the fossils as being a jaw and teeth. And then she made a sound guess that they were hominid. That wasn't just luck. That came from years of study and experience. Leakey's training, her reading and research, her observation skills, all together made her discovery—and others that followed— possible.

Mary Douglas Nicol was born on February 6, 1913, in London, England. Her father, Erskine Edward Nicol, was a landscape painter, as his father had been before him. Nicol became a talented artist, too, and feels her talent must have come directly from her father and grandfather. "I never had any formal instruction," she wrote in her autobiography, *Disclosing the Past*, "but took to it naturally and with pleasure on my own initiative, from the age of about ten." She apparently inherited her interest in archaeology as well. One of her ancestors who lived in the eighteenth century, John Frere, was an archaeologist before there really was such a thing. His son, John Hookham Frere, was the first to recognize peculiar stones found around England to be Stone Age tools and weapons.

Erskine Nicol went to Egypt to paint. He spent four years there living with a Bedouin tribe. It was in Egypt that he met and married Cecilia Marion Frere. Nicol's mother was an amateur painter who was always deeply interested in art. She had studied art as a young woman living in Florence, Italy. After they were married, Nicol's parents lived on a houseboat on the Nile. Nicol might have been born in Egypt, but her parents decided to return to England for her birth.

Nicol grew up around archaeology. "My father took a deep interest in Egyptology and the archaeological work that was going on around him. He was fascinated by Egyptian mummies and by the rich objects from royal burials." One of Erskine's closest friends in Egypt was a young man named Howard Carter, who was then working for the Egypt Exploration Society as a draftsman, drawing beautiful likenesses of the objects being found in excavations. Occasionally, when he had a question about his work, Carter would ask his friend Erskine for help. A few years later Carter became the foremost Egyptologist of his day, having discovered Tutankhamen's tomb. Nicol remembers his visits to their house in England.

Nicol's earliest memories are of Italy. Her parents frequently went there and to Switzerland to paint, and she always went with them. "It was during [a] stay in Italy that I had my first reading lesson, when my father decided it was time I learned to read. And so it was, for I was seven or eight at the time. He started me straight off on *Alice in Wonderland* and *Robinson Crusoe*. This strategy paid off, fortunately: I picked up the idea quickly and from that time I read eagerly any book I could get my hands on." Later, Nicol and her family moved to France, where she attended school with French children and easily became fluent in her new everyday language.

It was in France as a girl that she first discovered archaeology. Her father visited as many sites of cave art as he could, and always took her with him. She especially liked Cap Blanc, where people hundreds of thousands of years ago had sculpted horses into the walls of the cave. "I was much impressed by these, and my father even more so. I liked the animal engravings even better than the paintings because I had sharp eyes and was often first to decipher them when they were hard to see, being very often superimposed one on another."

Nicol's parents always traveled together. Her mother had also learned French as a girl and now was the family's interpreter on their various outings. They would visit a little archaeological museum, whose caretaker, Elie Peyrony, a prehistorian, befriended the Nicols. Nicol remembers him fondly: "I suppose it was in his museum that I first became aware of the finely shaped flint tools and the beautiful decorated bone points and harpoons that came from the rock shelters."

Peyrony was excavating a site nearby, and he invited Nicol and her father to come and watch the digging. Nicol later recalled with horror how terrible Peyrony's techniques were. Still the experience was "powerfully and magically exciting because my father and I could, with M. Peyrony's apparent acceptance, search through his spoil heaps and find rich treasure; treasure we could take home and keep. My father started it, with his love of objects, but

I was only a short distance behind and soon became the chief collector." Even then, Nicol was beginning to think like an archaeologist. "I did make some rudimentary classification of my collection for purposes of sorting, and I remember wondering about the ages of the pieces, and the world of their makers."

There would be other archaeologists in Nicol's childhood. A few years later, she met the Abbé Lemozi, another amateur archaeologist. The Abbé knew all the local archaeological sites in detail. He had discovered some amazing prehistoric paintings in a nearby cave. Even then Nicol realized that the Abbé was a highly competent archaeologist. One day he took her and her mother to explore the cave. They had to crawl a very long way, carrying lamps, through low, narrow passages. Soon they entered a huge underground chamber whose walls were covered with magnificent paintings. Seeing those paintings, Nicol remembered years later, had a profound effect on her. "The Abbé kindled my interest in prehistory and also gave me a very sound groundwork in excavating. After that I don't think I ever really wanted to do anything else."

It was in the midst of this great adventure that tragedy struck. Nicol was very close to her father; they shared many interests. But when he suddenly became painfully ill, her life changed. Their friend the Abbé took care of him. Her father, deep in his own suffering and pain, dropped out of his daughter's life. Nicol treated her sadness by taking long walks out into the countryside, taking comfort in the sight of animals in their natural settings. She became a skilled observer of nature and learned to watch the shiest of animals close up without disturbing them. And then, it was all over so quickly. "I was barely thirteen, and I had just lost forever the best person in the world."

Nicol and her mother returned to London, where they set about starting a new life. Nicol was enrolled in a convent school, but she was not happy there. Her real-life experiences and all the interesting people she had met made school seem childish, "wholly unconnected with the realities of life," as she put it. One day she pretended to have a seizure in class, using soap to make it appear she was frothing at the mouth. Then she deliberately caused an explosion during a chemistry lesson. There was, she suspected, between her mother and the mother superior "some thin-lipped stuff about 'Dear Mary is such a high-spirited girl.'" After a second explosion, "even my mother gave up on convents. At least I ended my school career with a bit of a bang." Nicol and her mother sat down to discuss what would happen next.

It was now clear to Nicol and her mother "that schools and I were an impossible combination." She had kept up her drawing all along, so it was possible she might follow in her father's footsteps. Another alternative was for her to take up archaeology seriously. "In my own mind," she recalls, "there was never much question that the latter was the right choice." But how could she become an archaeologist? Professional archaeologists had to have a university education and degrees—several. "I had never passed a single school exam, and clearly never would, and there was accordingly no way in which I could become a candidate for entrance to any university to study archaeology or anything else." Her mother even arranged an interview with a professor at Oxford. But he made it very clear that she would never be accepted there. That was the first and last time she was at Oxford, or any university for that matter (until 1981; but more about that later).

These pages are filled with the stories of great archaeologists who had little if any schooling (see the story of Nicol's father's friend, Howard Carter). Nicol would find a way, for, like these other archaeologists, she was spunky and resourceful. She joined the London Gliding Club, of which she was the youngest member, and the only unmarried female member. She began attending lectures in geology and archaeology, and among her lecturers was R. E. M. Wheeler (later Sir Mortimer Wheeler). But the lectures weren't enough—Nicol's mind was set on *field* archaeology. "If I were to become an archaeologist it was also absolutely essential to gather field experience."

Nicol began writing letters to anyone she heard of who was excavating. Mostly she received polite refusals. But then she received an offer with a familiar name. Just after the explosive end of her convent education, she had visited an important Stone Age site at a place called Windmill Hill. What was so exciting to her was that there were excavations going on. Her mother found out that Alexander Keiller was in charge and sent a note to ask if she and her daughter might meet the staff and talk with them about their work. So it was that Nicol got to meet Alexander Keiller and his sister-in-law, Dorothy Liddell. Liddell was well known in the study of English archaeology, and *she* was actually directing the digging. This was a new experience for Nicol. "Perhaps when I met Miss Liddell this first time I absorbed there and then the notion that a career in archaeology was certainly open to a woman."

The letter of acceptance Nicol now held in her hand was from none other than Dorothy Liddell. In the summer of 1930 Nicol went off to dig. For the next four years she would be one of Liddell's two chief assistants at Hembury, an early Stone Age site in Britain. "The work was always interesting, and had its moments of excitement—like the time I was working on the entrance, and its cobbled causeway came to light." Nicol grew to like and admire her mentor. And Liddell had tremendous confidence in Nicol. She asked Nicol if she would, between field seasons, make drawings of the finds, including flints, which Nicol knew so well. This was the first time Nicol had ever drawn stone tools for publication.

Those first drawings would be even more important to Nicol than she could guess. They were seen and admired by another archaeologist, Dr. Gertrude Caton-Thompson. She asked Nicol to draw the stone tools from her excavations in Egypt, for her new book. Nicol was honored. And she was to have, as well, a lifelong friend. Caton-Thompson treated Nicol from the beginning as an equal, a colleague, and always said that it was Nicol who was doing the favor. The appreciation of her illustration skills renewed Nicol's confidence in herself and gave her new ideas about the direction of her career. But she still had no idea just where her drawings were taking her.

When next Nicol heard from Caton-Thompson, she was being invited to a dinner party. The party was in honor of Louis Leakey, who was lecturing at the Royal Anthropological Institute. Mary Nicol and Louis Leakey met, and in the course of their conversation, he asked if she would do the drawings for his new book, *Adam's Ancestors*. Over the next few months, they would collaborate on the drawings for this book and begin work on drawings for other projects as well. They would also become partners in archaeology and companions in life, and soon would be married.

Nicol was now an archaeologist. She continued her work in England, where she was now supervising her first dig, this time with another archaeologist, Kenneth Oakley. It turned out to be a perfect partnership. He had little training in archaeological excavation. She was by now an experienced excavator but had little of Oakley's specialized knowledge of prehistory. Their skills complemented one another perfectly. From this dig would also come Nicol's first publication, an article about their work.

This would be Nicol's last dig in England. In a few weeks she would leave England for Africa, to join Louis Leakey in Tanzania. And then she would see Olduvai Gorge for the first time, "a view that has since come to mean more to me than any other in the world."

There were two Marys in Africa, and for many years the world knew only one of them. There was Mary Nicol, the experienced, accomplished archaeologist becoming known for her work in Britain. And then there was Mary Leakey, who was now thought of as Louis Leakey's wife and assistant. Mary's identity and her work were eclipsed by the presence of her more famous husband. Yet, from the very beginning, Mary Leakey was making important discoveries of her own. It was not until the death of her famous husband in 1972 that Mary Leakey was fully recognized for her individual accomplishments.

Soon after arriving in Africa, Mary Leakey was doing important excavations. While Louis Leakey was finishing up one of his projects, she began digging at Hyrax Hill—named for the little animals that lived in the crevices between the rocks—north of Nairobi in Kenya. There, near the base of the hill, she found a Neolithic settlement of stone-walled houses and a cemetery with nineteen burial mounds. She found stone tools chipped from obsidian, shiny black and green glass that flows from volcanoes. At another settlement she found things made of iron, evidence of the beginnings of the Iron Age. She also found sets of cup marks ground into the rocks, which were used for a game played with little stone counters. She discovered that the game of *bau*, which is still played by adults and children in Africa today, goes all the way back into the prehistoric past.

Here, too, Mary Leakey found a place in nature such as she had enjoyed as a girl. From Hyrax Hill she had a magnificent view across a lake. To this lake came flocks of flamingos, well over two million of them at certain times of the year. She always took time from her work to watch them, "fringing the shallow soda lake with a broad irregular band of pink, paler when the sun was high and deepening to a rose colour in the rich evening light when the grassland turned golden."

During World War II, Louis Leakey left his field research to work for British intelligence. Mary Leakey, however, continued working on some of their projects on her own, taking time out for the births of two of their children, Jonathan and Richard (see the chapter on Richard Leakey).

Mary Leakey now had two careers. "I quite liked having a baby," she recalled when her children were grown, "but I had no intention of allowing motherhood to disrupt my work as an archaeologist." She often had her children with her when she dug at a place called Olorgesailie, where she found another Stone Age settlement. "It was an extraordinary site: the implements ran into hundreds and lay in close concentration . . . looking as if they had only just been abandoned by their makers."

After the war, Mary and Louis Leakey returned to their fieldwork together, but also continued to work independently. In 1948 Mary Leakey discovered some "interesting looking bone fragments." Eventually she found enough bone fragments to reconstruct the skull and upper and lower jaws of an apelike creature. "Back at camp, working for long hours, I set myself to fit together the 30 or more separate pieces of the skull. Once I dropped a tiny piece into the dust on the tent floor—only a crumb of bone, but a vital link in joining two larger pieces. It took ages to find, but we got it. At last the task was done. . . ." *Proconsul africanus*, as it was called, was not a hominid, but then it wasn't an ape either. *Proconsul* was clearly not the link in human evolution the Leakeys were hoping to find. But the skull did turn out to be one of the oldest and most important finds in Africa to that date. The search would continue for even older evidence of human evolution.

Political turmoil in Kenya in the 1950s caused another temporary interruption to the Leakeys' work. But it gave Mary Leakey a chance to work on a project she had long had in mind. She had once visited a Stone Age site in Tanzania with thousands of rock paintings. She had hoped someday to record the paintings and publish her drawings in a book. Now she had the time. She carefully traced some sixteen hundred of the paintings onto sheets of clear cellophane. Then she transferred the drawings, reduced to a smaller scale, onto drawing paper. She chose gray and buff papers to simulate the rocks on which the figures had been painted. She mixed poster paints to get the same reds, blacks, yellows, whites, and oranges the Stone Age artists had used. They had made their paints by grinding rocks into powder and then mixing in grease. The beauty of the paintings made her work a joy. But more important, she got new insights into life long ago. Now "it was possible to get a glimpse of the Late Stone Age people themselves, and of incidents in their lives. There were details like clothing, hair styles and the fragile objects that hardly ever survive for the archaeologist—musical instruments, bows and arrows, and body ornaments depicted as they were worn." For years, Mary Leakey had been concentrating on bones, stones, and cemeteries. The change felt good. "No amounts of stone and bone could yield the kinds of information that the paintings gave so freely. . . . Here were scenes of life of men and women hunting, dancing, singing and playing music." She found joy in all the paintings

of animals—elephants, antelopes, white rhinos at full gallop, zebras, giraffes, lions, ostriches, and snakes. Her drawings were turned into a beautiful book called *Africa's Vanishing Art*.

Mary Leakey's next great discovery was the one that opened this chapter. After finding the large hominid jaw and teeth that morning, Louis and Mary Leakey sifted through tons of rock and soil until eventually they found over four hundred bone fragments. It took months to fit all the fragments together like a three-dimensional jigsaw puzzle. "To the non-scientist the procedure seems agonizingly slow and endless," Louis Leakey explained to an interviewer. "And it is true that Mary and I have spent more of our lives on our hands and knees than on our feet." When they were finished, though, they were able to look for the first time into the face of *Zinjanthropus*, at that time the oldest hominid ever found, dating back 1.75 million years.

Any one of Mary Leakey's finds would have given purpose to a lifetime of work. But in 1978 she came upon what she considered the most significant of all her finds. She stumbled upon a trail, some twenty-three meters (about seventy-five feet) long, with what seemed like hominid footprints. Archaeologists had been finding animal footprints for some time, but if these prints turned out to be hominid, then it would be the first time ever. The prints survived so long because they had been left in soft volcanic ash, which then hardened and filled in with sand. Mary Leakey called on Dr. Louise Robbins of the University of North Carolina, who was an expert on footprints. Dr. Robbins agreed the prints were hominid. They were, Mary Leakey observed, "so sharp that they could have been left this morning." The prints had been made 3.6 million years earlier.

Mary Leakey's guess was that the footprints were made by two adults and a child. She liked to think that they were the prints of a long-ago family—a man, a woman, and a youngster. In some places two of the prints were superimposed, one on top of the other. The smaller of the two adults, she guessed, must deliberately have stepped into the soft footprints left by the larger one, as if in play. Mary Leakey was touched by the humanness of the prints. She carefully followed the path of the family, especially the footprints that she thought of as the mother's. "At one point, and you need not be an expert tracker to discern this, she stops, pauses, turns to the left to glance at some possible threat or irregularity, and then continues to the north."

There was another important discovery here. The family was bipedal, walking upright on two legs. But nowhere

Mary Leakey working at Olduvai Gorge. *The National Museums of Kenya.*

in excavations of sites this old were tools ever found. The two facts, side by side, suggested to Mary Leakey that hominids walked upright *before* they learned to make tools. In fact walking upright was a necessary first step. "This unique ability to walk upright," she concluded, "freed the hands for myriad possibilities—carrying, toolmaking, intricate manipulation. From this single development, in fact, stems all modern technology. Somewhat oversimplified, the formula holds that this new freedom of forelimbs posed a challenge. The brain expanded to meet it. And mankind was formed."

In June 1981 Mary Leakey found herself in a most unexpected place, at a special ceremony, standing before the chancellor of Oxford University. "She is not content with finding bones," he told the gathering of scholars. "She also hunts footprints in the manner immortalized by Winnie-the-Pooh and Piglet. . . . She is a descendant, wife, and mother of anthropologists. . . .

She joined this profession because of her remarkable skill in drawing . . . [and] I must finally reveal something which will encourage many people and be a salutary lesson to us in the universities: Dr. Leakey has already two honorary degrees; she has great skill in an academic discipline; but she never went through any university course. I present Mary Douglas Leakey, a Fellow of the British Academy, for admission to the honorary degree of Doctor of Letters."

Richard Leakey

1944–   Kenyan paleoanthropologist and archaeologist

"People say that the white man has no future in Kenya," Richard Leakey once remarked. "That's rubbish. But if he has a white face, he must have a black mind." Richard Leakey, like his famous father, Louis S. B. Leakey, is that sort of man. He is white. He grew up in Kenya working alongside his paleontologist parents and living with the people. He speaks the languages and considers himself Kenyan. He has also inherited what his father and mother, Mary Nicol Leakey, called Leakey's luck. Like them, he has devoted his life to furthering our understanding human evolution.

During the 1960s and 1970s Richard Leakey hunted fossils at Lake Turkana in northern Kenya. His finds suggest that the beginnings of our humanness go back twice as far into the past as was previously thought. Before his finds, the earliest hominid remains were about 1.75 million years old. But the fossils Richard Leakey has uncovered and reconstructed suggest that intelligent human beings made their homes on the shores of the lake some 3 million years ago. They lived and hunted in groups and made stone tools. And they probably lived alongside other early humans, similar to the ones Louis and Mary Leakey had discovered at Olduvai Gorge. Richard Leakey believes that their coexistence was a peaceful one.

Richard Erskine Frere Leakey was born at the Nairobi Hospital in Kenya on December 19, 1944. (Accounts of his parents, Louis S. B. and Mary Nicol

Leakey, are also told in this book.) When Richard Leakey was born, the family, including his older brother, Jonathan, lived at the Coryndon Museum in Nairobi. His father was then curator of the museum. Later, largely because of his father's efforts, the small building with its two galleries became the National Museum of Kenya.

"Before I was sent to school," Richard Leakey recalls in *One Life: An Autobiography*, "I was fortunate in spending a lot of time out-of-doors. Both my parents believed strongly in taking children along on their field trips—if it was possible. Among my earliest recollections, are long bumpy journeys over very rough and dusty roads." Richard Leakey became a part of the African countryside and it became a part of him. "I am quite sure that my very early exposure to the African bush had a major influence on me. To this day, I love to spend time in the wild desolate places. . . ." The love of desolate places is a must for anyone wanting to be a paleontologist.

What Richard and Jonathan Leakey thought of as play was actually early scientific training. Richard Leakey remembers when the two of them used to make plaster-of-paris casts of fish.

The technique was quite simple and great fun. A fish . . . was laid to rest on a bed of sand in a suitable container—often one of my mother's baking dishes. The sand was built up to provide a perfect line so that exactly half the fish was buried, and half exposed. We poured molten wax over the fish giving it a coat at least a quarter of an inch thick. Once the wax had cooled and hardened, the dish was turned over, the sand washed away and the fish extracted from the wax mould. Freshly mixed plaster of Paris was then poured into the mould and allowed to harden for several hours. The whole thing was then placed in a container of boiling water to melt the wax, and the plaster fish was extracted. When the water cooled the wax was re-used for the next cast.

Richard and Jonathan Leakey's "great fun" had been a very advanced method of preserving fossils some thirty years earlier, a technique their father learned in the field collecting dinosaur bones.

Richard Leakey remembers his parents' preparations for their field trips when he was a child. They were—though he didn't realize it then—training and experience for trips he would make on his own later. "The visits to Lake Victoria, each lasting a month, were particularly exciting. For several weeks before setting off, we all felt we were preparing for an adventure. Lists were made, remade and discussed. Supplies were assembled and packed into rugged wooden boxes. Plans were

Young Richard Leakey at Olduvai Gorge. *The National Museums of Kenya.*

made, and on the day of departure we would be awake long before dawn. . . . Mother and Father sat in the front and we children (my brothers Jonathan and Philip and various friends) were bundled in atop the rest of the luggage. . . . Father always liked an early start and usually by sunrise we were well on our way."

Like his father before him, Richard Leakey played with and learned from the local children. Sometimes he would go off with his older brother to hunt for additions to Jonathan's collection of bird skins and eggs. But often their arrival at their father and mother's site brought visitors. "The many local children," Richard Leakey recalls of those fun times, "would gather to watch these strange people at work so that sometimes we would get to play with children of our own age. I remember being taught to make model canoes and boats from reeds, sticking each reed to the next by driving long acacia thorns into it much as you would use nails to join planks. The creativity of the local children was infinite."

It was during another one of his days in the field that Richard Leakey was witness to one of the great scientific finds of all time. The details of the discovery are told in Mary Leakey's story elsewhere in this book. But it's interesting to hear her son's impressions of that morning.

My mother found a remarkable complete fossil skull and a jaw of a primitive ape; the first such skull to be found. No other skulls of this creature have been found since and it ranks as one of the most important finds ever made by my mother in her long and successful career. Although I was only four years old I still have a vivid picture of the site, which was on a small stony hill, quite close to a gnarled and virtually leafless tree. I remember the tree because the excavations took a number of days to complete, and during this time I had no option but to amuse myself as my parents worked. The only available shade was some way off from the digging where I felt very isolated. How I wished that the wretched little tree could have had some leaves so that I might have a place to play near the spot where my parents were clearly having such a good time!

As you might expect, Richard Leakey's boredom soon got to his parents. That's what happened one day when he was six. His parents were intent on some particularly delicate work. And they had made it clear to him that he

was not to get in their way or distract them. He began complaining aloud that he was hot, and bored, and thirsty. "What time is it?" and "What can I do?" and "When will we eat lunch?" he whined over and over. Finally his father, run out of patience, barked at him, "Go find your own bone and dig it up!"

Now, the hillside where the Leakeys worked was covered with countless fragments of bone. Most of them could be dug up without any loss to science and, besides, Richard Leakey now had permission to dig.

So, I moved off to look for my bone—at least I had something to do! I had only gone about 30 feet from my parents when I found a small scrap of brown-coloured fossil bone showing on the surface of the site. I had my own dental picks and small brush and I set to work, probably with some reluctance.

It proved riveting. My bone quickly showed signs of being large, well embedded in the sediment and, more important, the shiny enamel surfaces of some teeth quickly appeared after my initial scraping and brushing. What was it? I became engrossed and was soon entirely oblivious of the heat and flies for the first time that day. This is now a common sensation but then it was my first experience of the incomparable thrill of uncovering something that has lain buried for hundreds of thousands of years.

My prolonged silence soon aroused my

parents' curiosity. . . . My father came over and was instantly alert. I was happily uncovering a complete jaw of an extinct species of giant pig, the first such complete specimen to have been found!

When he wasn't in the field with his parents, Richard Leakey was attending primary and secondary school in Nairobi. He found the traditional British boys' school terrifying and useless. From the very beginning he stood up for his moral principles. From his parents he had learned to despise the treatment of black Africans by white colonists. Like his father, too, Richard Leakey's close friendships with Kenyan boys taught him personally the injustice of one race suppressing another. He had the bravery to condemn white supremacy among the sons of white colonists. For this he was punished by the boys, bullied constantly, even locked in a cage and spat and urinated on. He was not helped by the teachers or headmaster, because they, too, despised this boy who spoke up in defense of his black Kenyan brothers. "I was called a nigger lover, a Kaffir lover, but I was quite happy to be ostracized."

Richard Leakey did well enough at school, but not as well as was necessary to get into a university. About this he was pleased, for school had always been unpleasant for him. And besides, now he could spend all his time riding

horses, exploring the bush, and tracking wild animals as he loved to do. Then it happened that he was invited to drive for a photographer, Des Bartlett, who was filming wildlife in Africa and also documenting Louis and Mary Leakey's excavations. Now Richard Leakey could do what he had always done—he had driven the Land Rover since he was fourteen, illegally—and get paid for it. He could spend his days driving through the countryside he loved and assist Des Bartlett with his filming. Together they headed for the Serengeti to film elephants, lions, giraffes, and all the other animals Richard Leakey had grown up with as a child. They stopped at Olduvai Gorge along the way to visit and to film the Leakeys at work.

Richard Leakey was now seventeen and had no intention of entering his father's profession. In fact, he could not imagine anything less exciting than spending his life digging in the hot sun. "There was no doubt in my mind that I should avoid at all costs an academic life and, in particular, I was determined to distance myself from my parents and their work on fossils and prehistory, largely because I wanted to be my own man."

But Richard Leakey had an idea. It was 1961, and Kenya and Tanzania were suffering the effects of a long drought. Animals were dying in large numbers. Richard Leakey was opposed to hunting and killing, but now he had a source of dead animals of all species. He would collect the carcasses and boil them in a huge pot until all the meat fell away from the bones. Then he would bleach the bones with hydrogen peroxide and leave them to dry and whiten in the sun. Finally he would carefully label each bone and sell the complete skeletons to universities and museums around the world.

Richard Leakey, it seems, could not help doing things that taught him what few people knew. Like his earlier fossil discovery, he had no idea of the significance of what he was doing. "The work taught me a great deal about the comparative shapes of bones of different mammals and I was not long in becoming quite proficient at identifying the various species on the basis of individual bones, although at the time I had no inkling of how important this skill was to become only a few years later."

Richard Leakey would have more adventures. When the *National Geographic* team visiting his parents at Olduvai needed an experienced driver, he helped out by acting as guide. He took some of the magazine's staff on tours of East Africa and soon, when he had his own Land Rover, became a safari guide. He set up his own company and began earning a living on his fees. Later he got his pilot's license.

But Richard Leakey was not happy with taking people on safari. He grew tired of his role, as he put it, as "white hunter," and tired as well of being a servant. His mind was always open to a new idea, though he wasn't always quite sure what it might be until it just happened. And then it happened. It wasn't a new idea, really, but an old, lingering one. He was flying to Olduvai. "On the way I saw some exposed sedimentary deposits along the western shore of Lake Natron. These fascinated me because they looked very similar to those at Olduvai, although on a much smaller scale."

Richard Leakey's autobiography, *One Life*, includes a chapter titled "Out of My Father's Shadow." Richard Leakey had to deal with his father's fame and his prominence in the world of archaeology. When a parent is famous in a certain field, it's unlikely a child will enter the same field and have to compete. But Richard Leakey had achieved his goal; he had become his "own man." And now, it seems, he could admit to himself what it was he loved doing, what he had always loved to do. Perhaps it was his experience discovering the extinct giant pig. Maybe it was the joy he saw his parents taking in their work. Perhaps it was the magic of Africa and the lure of finding the remains of ancient apes and humans. Whatever the reason, Richard Leakey became a paleontologist almost without giving it a second thought.

The expedition team that went to Lake Natron consisted of Richard Leakey, his younger brother, Philip, and Glynn Isaac, an experienced and well-known archaeologist. Isaac was included because he was Richard Leakey's close friend, but also because Louis Leakey had suggested that his son take along a professional with academic training. Richard Leakey also brought along six Kenyan workers, including his friend Kamoya Kimeu.

In a matter of days, Richard Leakey demonstrated that he had brought with him Leakey's luck. He tells in his autobiography what happened: He had been in Nairobi trying to find a plane. It was important, he told the pilot, who wasn't able to take him until another day. That would be too late, he pleaded—"a member of expedition" had gotten lost and he needed a plane to carry out an "emergency search." Once they were in the air, Richard Leakey explained to the pilot who they were looking for—it was Ben, his dog.

"It was while I was away in Nairobi that the excitement began at Lake Natron. Kamoya discovered a complete lower jaw of *Zinjanthropus* projecting from a cliff face just a few feet from where I had myself been searching be-fore my trip back to Nairobi. What a moment it was!" What they had found was the only known lower jaw of the species whose fossil skull Mary Leakey had found at Olduvai. "I contacted my parents at Olduvai by radio the next day, and flew there to collect them. . . ." By now Zinj's name had been changed to *Australopithecus* (it was not a new species as the Leakeys had originally thought, but similar to others that had already been found). And it was known to have lived 1,750,000 years ago.

Richard Leakey's team continued to find evidence of early humans at Lake Natron, including stone chopping tools. These proved to be similar to the tools his parents had found at Olduvai and, therefore, were about the same age. Richard Leakey's find brought support from the National Geographic Society for another expedition to Lake Turkana. The lake, which is in a large valley, looked to Richard Leakey's experienced eye to be a good place to dig. And he was right again. The team found the shore littered with bones of animals, some of which lived 4 million years ago. "And I was sure that where large herds of animals lived, man's ancestors also lived, hunting them for food." Later he found three more jaw fragments of *Australopithecus*, proof that near-humans had lived by the lake.

Richard Leakey at Koobi-Fora. *The National Museums of Kenya.*

The next year Richard Leakey and his "Hominid Gang" returned to Lake Turkana, this time to a place called Koobi Fora. It was to be the scene of another famous Leakey accident. One of the camels, named George, tired, stopped, and refused to go on. The team, including Richard Leakey's wife, Maeve Epps Leakey, decided to take advantage of the unplanned rest and explore a nearby dry streambed. Richard Leakey explains what happened then. "I was leading, several paces ahead of Maeve, when to my astonish-

ment I saw an *Australopithecus* face looking at me from a distance of about fifteen feet. I instantly recognized what turned out to be a complete fossil skull lying on the sand.

"You can imagine our feelings. The skull was readily recognizable because it was remarkably similar to 'Zinj,' the *Australopithecus boisei* skull found by my mother at Olduvai in 1959, almost ten years to the day before our discovery." What was so amazing to Richard and Maeve Leakey was that the skull Mary Leakey had found had been the only one known. What's more, it had been broken in so many fragments that it had taken several weeks to put it together again. "Yet here were we, staring at a complete skull in the bed of a sand river. . . . It is the only time that a discovery has left me truly breathless." The next day Richard Leakey took the skull to show to his mother. "It is difficult to describe the surprise and the delight of everyone when I carefully lifted the complete skull from its box and placed it gently in my mother's hands. It was the sort of moment in one's life that can never be forgotten. I had as much pleasure from my mother's reaction as I had from finding the skull itself!"

Perhaps even more important than the skull was what Richard Leakey found in association with it. Nearby he and his team found stone tools. They also found broken antelope bones, broken so that a person could eat the marrow inside. The stone tools and bones were found to be 2,600,000 years old. Even though the tools and bones were close to the skull, Richard Leakey did not believe they belonged to the creature whose skull they found. Louis Leakey had done an experiment proving that *Australopithecus* was a vegetarian, who, Richard Leakey guessed, "would have little need to devise cutting tools." Like his father, he believed there was

another hominid around at the same time as *Australopithecus*. It was this yet-undiscovered creature who ate meat. It must have made the tools and eaten the antelope. And it coexisted with *Australopithecus*.

Richard Leakey's next discovery proved their theory correct. Returning to lake Turkana a year later, he and his team found the evidence they had been looking for: a fossil skull that revealed a large-brained ape-human, whom the Leakeys called *Homo habilis*. The next year, Richard Leakey's assistant, Bernard Ngeneo, found even more support for the theory: a shattered cranium—not human, but more advanced than an ape. The bones were found in a deposit that had been dated to 2,600,000 years ago.

Ngeneo's story is interesting. He had come along with the expedition to work in the camp kitchen. One day he asked Richard Leakey if he could see the area where the scientists were working. So Richard Leakey took him to the site. He momentarily turned his attention away from Ngeneo, and then it happened. "Bernard wandered off and found an australopithecine thigh bone which was lying only 100 yards from where Glynn and his team had been working for almost two months! Needless to say, this earned Bernard a place on the expedition's prospecting team. . . . During the subsequent years he found a number of important specimens."

What Ngeneo found was eventually designated 1470 (named for its registration number at the National Museum of Kenya). The search for more pieces of the skull began immediately. Over the next six weeks, Maeve Epps Leakey and Dr. Bernard Wood, an anatomist, pieced together some 150 pieces of fossil bone—some no bigger than a fingernail. "Maeve carefully washed the fragments and laid them out in a wooden tray to dry in the sun and before long we were ready to begin to find which pieces could be joined to others. In no time at all, several of the bigger pieces fitted together and we realized that the fossil skull had been large, certainly larger than the small-brained *Australopithecus* such as we had found in 1969 and 1970."

And what was so important about 1470? The large cranium meant this newly discovered creature had a bigger brain, 800 cubic centimeters—not as big as a modern human, about 1,500 cubic centimeters, but large. "This was fantastic new information," Richard Leakey reported. "We now had an early fossil human skull with a brain size considerably larger than anything that had been found before of similar antiquity. Also, we had found some limb bones. . . . The whole shape of the brain case is remarkably reminiscent of modern man." What's more, the thigh bones, he reported, were "practically indistinguishable from the same bones of modern man." The date of this find was 2,500,000 years ago. Richard Leakey now had the hominid who was more advanced than but nevertheless lived alongside *Australopithecus*.

Discussion of 1470 continues, and Richard Leakey continues to make new discoveries. Each adds new insights into the beginnings and evolution of humans. But Richard Leakey, like his mother and father, has other reasons to dig. "It's not just the old bones we're interested in. It's important to know if our earliest ancestors were decent, cooperative creatures instead of killer apes. If we push back our knowledge of the past, it might give us some understanding about our future and ourselves."

Robert Harry Lowie

1883–1957   American ethnologist

"When I was a boy of eight or nine in Vienna, I got hold of an abridged version of the Leatherstocking saga," Robert Harry Lowie tells us in his autobiography, *Robert H. Lowie, Ethnologist: A Personal Record.* "An older cousin and I also steeped ourselves in a series of *Indianerbüchel* . . . paperbound booklets about adventures among the Redskins. As a consequence, we were fired with admiration for the Comanche tribe and firmly resolved to emigrate to the Far West in order to aid that valiant people against the villainous Apache." As it turned out, Lowie's family emigrated to New York just a year or two later. And when he was older, Lowie did travel to the Far West, to California. But it wasn't as a Comanche warrior that he crossed the plains. Lowie grew up to be one

of the world's great scholars of American Indian lifeways.

Lowie was born on June 12, 1883, in Vienna, Austria. His father, Samuel Lowie, a businessman, was born in Budapest, Hungary; his mother, Ernestine Kuhn, was born in Vienna. Her father was a physician and a classical scholar. Lowie was closer to his mother and his younger sister, Risa, than to his father. He remembered his father as a quiet, retiring man, burdened by problems with his business. But his mother was just the opposite. Outgoing and cheerful, she was also a gifted musician who enlivened his childhood. It was her he always remembered best. It was his mother and father's Viennese style and character that shaped his personality for the rest of his life.

As a youth Lowie loved to travel. It

wasn't that he did much of it when he was young, but he dreamed of visiting mysterious foreign places. He remembered finding a place on the map and then "feeling an almost overpowering urge to drop whatever I was doing and rush off to visit it. In my grandfather's library in Vienna I had read the story of Alexander von Humboldt's researches in South America, also accounts of David Livingstone's missionary labors, and of Paul du Chaillu's journeys to the haunts of pygmies and gorillas. In my childhood Sir Henry M. Stanley's name [an early explorer of Africa] was on everyone's lips, and as a birthday gift I received juvenile versions of Emin Pasha's and Hermann von Wissmann's travels."

Finally, at ten, Lowie got his wish. Before the family emigrated to America, they made a farewell excursion to Budapest to visit his father's family. Then there was the exciting journey from Vienna to the port at Hamburg, followed by the voyage by ship to New York City. "During this period," he wrote in his autobiography, "I kept a diary that reflects my passionate interest in travel." When the family traveling stopped, Lowie created adventures of his own, just for the excitement of going somewhere. "Wistfully I would sometimes cross the Hudson on the Fort Lee ferry, and then take the Hacken-

sack trolley as far as it went, in order to visit at least another state; a week in the Catskills seemed like a sojourn in a far country."

Lowie attended school in Vienna until his family emigrated to America. He attended Public School 83 and continued up through the grades in the New York City school system. Even as a child Lowie was an anthropologist, always comparing his new life to the one in Austria. He recalled how different life was at P.S. 83. "We each had an assigned seat in which we could keep our books and papers, so we did not need to carry everything home with us every night in the knapsack that is [so much a part of] European education. We did not get report cards in those days, although one fellow pupil had heard of such a thing as a 'stifficate,' for the meaning of which I searched through a dictionary in vain. As strange as anything were the teachers; except in the two higher grades of grammar school they were all women!"

After graduating from high school, Lowie went on to the City College of New York, graduating with a B.A. degree at eighteen. At first, he was interested in classical studies—he loved Latin and Greek. He was good in languages. Lowie received the Claflin Medal for his work in Greek and the Serena Mason Carnes Prize for his

Spanish skills. Then he found that most of his friends were becoming scientists. He spent his spare time reading about general science and botany and collecting leaves in Central Park. At one point he thought he might study biology and chemistry. "But it soon became clear," he wrote later, "that I lacked the manual skills required of a professional chemist."

Like many early anthropologists, Lowie discovered the field accidentally. He was looking through a course catalog for Columbia University and came across the name Franz Boas. Although he didn't know of Boas, Lowie was impressed with his qualifications and found his biographical sketch fascinating. "So we decided that I should major in anthropology, while taking psychology as my minor; and I enrolled, accordingly, in the fall of the year." His first two courses were with Boas, one on statistics and the other on North American Indian languages. Lowie later realized that his decision to study Indians had a lot to do with his boyhood reading, which he still recalled vividly.

Lowie found the courses too difficult: "The work on languages was good fun, but rather too advanced for me at that stage, while the discussion of statistics left me in a state of utter befuddlement. It was only by taking it all over again in my second year that I gained some

glimmerings of understanding." Later, when Lowie had students of his own, he understood what had happened. Anthropology was such a new field then that no one knew how to teach it. There was no clear idea of what a Ph.D. program should include or how it should be taught. There were not yet any textbooks on anthropology. Lowie remembered Professor Boas's teaching as the sink-or-swim method. He put his students to work on anthropological research, leaving them on their own to work out how and what they would study. If they did well, they received a degree.

Lowie was one of the several anthropologists of the time who also studied psychology. It was a field from which many anthropologists came. And it proved valuable in fieldwork and understanding human behavior. Later, Lowie would use his understanding of psychology in his work on religion. Lowie also studied Latin American history and archaeology. He took seminars on American Indian languages and attended lectures on Chinese and Japanese civilization. He worked as a volunteer at the American Museum of Natural History in New York City.

Lowie was also working to make money for his education. He taught in the New York City public schools—fourth grade—and earned extra money teaching evening adult classes in German. Still, he found time to write. His first published work was an article he wrote as a student on the American poet Edgar Allan Poe, which was published in *New Yorker Review*. With all this Lowie completed his graduate work and received his Ph.D. in just four years.

During his first three years of studying, Lowie did no fieldwork. That was not unusual. Many anthropologists did not have their first practical experience in the field until after they received their doctorate. The methods that would be needed were not taught in any course. "I gathered," Lowie wrote, "that ethnologists practiced a mysterious something called 'field work.'" Lowie was anxious to work in the field. He likened his inexperience to a chemist who had never done experiments in a laboratory. But how one got out into the field, especially when one was a student working day and night to pay for his schooling, was even more of a mystery. Lowie soon had an answer to his wondering. "The solution came unexpectedly one day when [his professor Clark] Wissler asked me whether I should care to go to the Lemhi Shoshone in central Idaho. I knew nothing about them, not even that they were closely related in speech to those heroic Comanche who had thrilled me as a boy. However, I jumped at the chance

offered and prepared, as well as I could. . . ."

Preparing oneself was not as easy in Lowie's day as it seems now. It was not just a matter of stopping by the library. This was 1906. Very little was known or had been written about Native Americans. About the Shoshonean tribes Lowie was to study, almost nothing was known. What little there was could be found in the journals of explorers and fur traders like John Frémont, Alexander Ross, and Jedediah Smith. Professor Wissler referred Lowie to the *Original Journals* of the explorers Meriwether Lewis and William Clark. Nothing had been written about the Lemhi territory since Lewis and Clark had been there—a century earlier. Their excellent journals would not be much help to Lowie. "The great explorers were doubtless excellent observers, but their stay with the Shoshone was brief; and although their notes on externals were good, they recorded little indeed on religious and social life."

Finding anything to read on the Indians of the Lemhi territory was difficult enough. Getting there would be even harder. Lowie described what it was like in those days for a young anthropologist to get to Indian territory. "Some Indian reservations were indeed traversed by a main railroad line, but many were to be reached only by changing to a branch line, possibly with narrow-gauge tracks; and after getting to this station, the traveler might still have a journey of fifty or a hundred miles by horse-stage ahead of him." It took Lowie thirty-eight hours to travel by train just from New York City to Chicago. What's more, the Lemhi Indians had been on the move; just where, there was no way of knowing for sure. So Lowie faced the possibility of traveling for weeks only to find that the people had moved on to somewhere else.

It was not a good beginning. Lowie seems to have asked all the wrong questions at the wrong time. But he was there to learn how, and soon he met a young man who offered to help him. From Lowie's description, we learn something about methods of field studies in the early days. "Fortunately the lad who interpreted for me knew what was wrong. He took me aside and asked whether I could meet him on the following day at an aged aunt's, who was living at Inkom, about ten miles away. He felt that in the bosom of her family the aunt was sure to 'open up.' There turned out to be no morning train to Inkom, so I walked all the way. The old lady proved agreeable, and so at last I was able to take down my first text in an aboriginal [Native American] tongue. My phonetics were terrible, but I did get a fairly complete version of an animal tale widely known among the Indians of the Great Basin and California."

Nothing Lowie studied at Columbia had prepared him for this adventure. Certainly growing up in Vienna and New York City was no preparation for what was to come. He traveled by train from Pocatello, Idaho, to Red Rock, Montana. He then rode a stagecoach for two days and finally reached Lemhi, Idaho. In all, the few miles from Pocatello to Lemhi took as long as the thousands of miles from New York City to Pocatello.

Lowie had reached the Shoshone, but his transportation problems were not over. "One of my first worries was how to get about the reservation, because the Indians lived widely scattered instead of being settled in a village near the Agency. A few of them could be reached afoot, but they were not the most promising informants. I therefore learned to straddle a horse and after a while managed to ride several miles at a time, though not with ease, let alone elegance."

Lowie's autobiography reveals that he had an important trait for an anthropologist—a sense of humor. For instance there was the time he realized that the Indians were also observing him. "Little escaped the attention of the Lemhi. First they named me Four-eyes because of my spectacles. A little later my hirsute [hairy] forearms and chest earned me the sobriquet of Bear-white-man; and on appearing one day with a visored cap, I was promptly dubbed Night-hawk-lies-down, because the projecting part of my headgear was supposed to suggest the posture of that bird at rest."

All the time Lowie was observing the Indians, he was having to learn their language as well. There were no grammar or conversation books for Shoshone. So there was no way for even a gifted linguist like Lowie to learn the language before setting out for Idaho. He could use an interpreter, and he did, at least in the beginning. But there were very few Indians in those days who spoke English, at least not as well as he needed. And, besides, Lowie believed that an ethnologist should learn the languages of the people he was studying. To him, though, learning a language did not mean learning just enough to get by. What he meant by learning a language was mastering it, speaking it as well as he spoke English.

Native American languages are extremely difficult for English speakers. And there are a great many of them, hundreds and hundreds just in North America. But Lowie realized that Indian culture was being destroyed, and with it would surely go the native lan-

guages. Even he probably had no idea what precious little time was left. So he set about learning as much of the Shoshone language as he could. He recalled one of his lessons. "Once the chief's son enigmatically pointed at me and began gesticulating vigorously, lowering and raising both hands. Finally, he translated: 'You, how much snow?' I was as bewildered as before, though it turned out to be the standard sign language for asking my age—how many winters had I seen. The movements of the hands indicated the falling of rain or snow."

After his return from Idaho, Lowie was appointed assistant curator at the American Museum of Natural History, where he had worked as a volunteer. The director, Professor Wissler, began sending him to do fieldwork among other Indian families. He was particularly interested in the Blackfoot Indians, and so Lowie's next journey was to southern Alberta, Canada, the home of the Northern Blackfoot.

It was not until he arrived that Lowie discovered he had a problem. Problem solving is another important skill for an anthropologist. Lowie had been told about an experienced interpreter named Rex. He was the only one who spoke English as fluently as Lowie needed. But at that very time, the Blackfoot Indians were angry with the white authorities. And if Lowie had gone to find Rex, the Indians would have hidden him and refused to help. Lowie's problem was how to get Rex to come to him. And he had a great idea.

Lowie had read a book by an English anthropologist about games similar to cat's cradle that are played by people all over the world. The Inuit and many other people play such games. To play, you take a loop of string and make all sorts of complicated string figures on your fingers. The string loops between and around and through the fingers, back and forth between the hands to make a beautiful, intricate spiderweb. Some people used their teeth and their toes to make special figures. And sometimes they passed the figure from one pair of hands to another. The designs were believed to have magical powers. Some years before, Lowie had mastered several of the figures. And now he found a use for his skill at cat's cradle. "I began strolling through the camp, developing different figures with a piece of string while apparently looking neither right nor left. The Blackfoot came out of their tipis, staring at me in rapt attention, and finally themselves summoned Rex to discover the meaning of my strange antics. Thus I obtained an interpreter for my week's stay."

Lowie wished he could have stayed longer. He was fascinated by the Blackfoot. Perhaps more than any other tribe, their culture was still intact. "There was much to be seen during that week's celebrations," he would remember the rest of his life.

All the display of colorful aboriginal living which I had so sorely missed among the Lemhi was now spread out before my eyes. Never again have I seen so close an approximation to what life within an old Plains camp circle must have been like; nowhere again have I seen so many painted lodges. I recall particularly one with the figure of a snake coiled around the tent cover. . . . Gifts were being passed back and forth lavishly, reminding me of what I had read about the potlatches of Northwest Coast Indians. I witnessed a round dance like the one I had joined in at Lemhi, except that the men did not clasp their partner's shoulders. Men alone performed the "Grass" dance, some of them naked except for breechclouts, moccasins, and ornaments, others in buckskin shirts and fringed leggings. Without understanding it, I even stumbled upon part of a sacred ceremony, in which the twenty members of a woman's society constructed a lodge for their ritual.

Lowie reluctantly left the Blackfoot for his next assignment. He was off to Morley, Alberta, for a seven-weeks' stay among the Stoney Assiniboine. They,

Robert H. Lowie. *From* Robert H. Lowie: A Personal Record. *(Berkeley: University of California Press, 1959.)*

too, were scattered over the land, and so Lowie traveled on horseback and camped out in a tent next to his interpreter and his family. "My horsemanship greatly improved on the rocky trails of the Stoney reserve. . . ."

He then got his orders for the season's last stop. Lowie was to move on to southern Montana and a visit with the Crow Indians. He was to be there only a month, but it was to become the focus of his life's work. "From the very start

of my stay with the Crow I was delighted. . . . there were plenty of men in their thirties and forties who had been to eastern schools, spoke excellent English, yet retained contact with their own people and with ancient customs. Some of them took pride in wearing their hair long and braided, while adorning their persons with native decorations. . . . As for the older generation, from which I naturally recruited my chief informants, all of them had lived the old life of buffalo hunters and warriors. They proudly showed me the scars of arrowpoints on their bodies. . . ."

Today we can reach any Indian reservation in hours by jet plane and car. So we must take a moment to remember what it was like in the days when Lowie was a young anthropologist. Only a few decades had passed since the days of the frontier. It was still a wild and beautiful place untouched by human hands. There were no big cities and only a few towns and Indian villages scattered here and there on the vast plains. As Lowie discovered, many of the Native American elders grew up and were adults in the days before the coming of white settlers, when the Indians were free. He loved these people, their spirit and their energy, and it comes as no surprise that he chose to spend his life studying them.

Lowie spent more time living and doing fieldwork among the American Indians than any other anthropologist then or since. In addition to the Shoshone, Assiniboine, Northern Blackfoot, and Crow, he lived among many other groups. He visited, studied, and wrote about the Chipewyans of Alberta, the Hidatsa of North Dakota, the Southern Ute of Colorado. He knew the Paiute of Nevada and Utah, the Washo of Nevada and California, and the Hopi of Arizona. All the time he knew he was fulfilling his childhood dream, to live among the Indian nations on the Great Plains. Many times during these years, he would think back to those children's books in German in which he first read about the lifeways of the "Redskins."

Lowie would return to the Crow on his own again and again. They became, as anthopologists think of them, "his" people. He learned their language well enough to understand much of what he heard and to pose the questions he wanted to ask. It was this understanding of the language and Lowie's sense of community with the Crow people that made his studies so rich.

Lowie always felt that the Indians taught him about the world and about life. One of the stories he told is of the lesson he learned from a young Indian. He had come to Lodge Grass to see a dance that night. While he was waiting for the dance to begin, a young Crow came up and began talking to him. Wolf-lies-down spoke "fair English," Lowie later recalled. The young man asked him amiably why he was visiting, wondering if Lowie was there to buy horses from the reservation. Lowie thought about how he used to word answers to children who spoke English as this young man did. "So I answered somewhat as follows: 'Well, I am here

A photograph taken by Robert Lowie of a Hopi dance. *Department of Library Services, American Museum of Natural History (Neg. No. 283608).*

to talk with your old men to find out how they used to hunt and play and dance. I want to hear them tell the stories of ancient times . . .' But at this point young Wolf-lies-down, who had never been off the reservation, interrupted me with, 'Oh, I see, you're an ethnologist!'"

A "marginal man" was the way Lowie often described himself. It meant that he was not quite a part of his society, that he lived at the edges. He grew up in the United States. But he grew up in a German family where only German was spoken, and in a largely Ger-

man neighborhood. He spoke fluent German, his mother tongue, but he also spoke perfect English. He wasn't German, but then, he wasn't American either. He found that a lot of Americans were like him. In New Mexico, for instance, he knew of people born and raised in the United States who spoke only Spanish. Another example were the cities of Milwaukee, Wisconsin, and Cincinnati, Ohio. There he had met American-born people who spoke only German.

Lowie often wondered if this marginal quality of his life made him a better traveler and anthropologist. It may be easier for people like him to fit in, wherever they might be. The bilingual person is forever a split person. "The 'marginal man,'" Lowie observed, "starts with at least two modes of thinking and acting. . . ." Such a person would be more aware of differences in other people, Native Americans for instance, than people who live always in one way. For this reason, he felt, bilingual, marginal people would perhaps make more perceptive observers and anthropologists.

There was one story, more than any other, that Lowie liked to tell. It is the way he wanted always to be remembered. He was sitting in a little restaurant near the reservation, and he overheard two Indians speaking in Crow. "You see that white man over there?" one of them asked the other, nodding toward Lowie. "He looks like any other white man, but when he comes to the campfire, you'd never know him from an Indian."

So it was that the little boy who read the Leatherstocking Tales and dreamed of being a Comanche warrior grew up to become the world's foremost authority on the Plains Indians.

Max Mallowan

1904–1978   Excavator of the biblical city of Nimrud

"When did we first think of digging at Nimrud?" wrote Max Mallowan in his autobiography, *Mallowan's Memoirs.* "I hardly know the answer, but when I look back it seems that the plan had begun to take shape in my mind a long time ago." Max Mallowan first saw the site of the ancient city when he was a young man, just twenty-one years old. He had come as an assistant to the archaeologist Sir Charles Leonard Woolley, who was then excavating the city of Ur.

After the end of my first season, in March 1926, I drove northwards, excited at the prospect of seeing the upper reaches of the Tigris in the spring. In those days we used to travel in the earliest known type of Ford, which was as good as a mule on rough ground. It cost us sixteen

Turkish gold pounds to go from Baghdad to Alexandretta through Mosul and the Sinjar, a three-day journey. I remember an old man telling us that it had taken him just three months by caravan forty years before. But it was on that drive to the north . . . that I had my first glimpse of a country that seemed like an archaeologist's paradise.

Mallowan was not the discoverer of Nimrud, nor was Woolley. Both men were continuing the work of Austen Henry Layard, who had first explored the site and unearthed the ancient city nearly a century before. Layard had done a remarkable excavation for his time. But there was still much for archaeologists to do. Better excavation techniques and new knowledge gotten from other sites brought archaeologists back again and again. Mallowan would return for another dig thirty years later, this time as director of his own well-staffed expedition.

Why does someone dig in the ground to find what's left of cities thousands of years old? It can be enjoyable work and provides an opportunity to live in interesting places around the world. There's the excitement of new discoveries, and so much to learn. Ancient languages and the faces of people who lived long ago appear as if by magic out of the sands. Most archaeologists would agree that any one of these would be reason enough to pursue their profession. And they'd say that there are so many questions that need to be answered.

That's how it began for Mallowan, with questions. What was it like living in the days of the Old Testament? What were cities like, and how were they changing? And the great city King Sargon built at Khorsabad—why was it never finished? Why was it abandoned when he died in 705 B.C.? How did the style of pottery, jewelry, tools, and furniture change? What influence did Assyria have on the arts and crafts of its neighbors? What was the basis of the Assyrian economy? "The answers to many of these questions," Mallowan wrote, "presented a challenge, an invitation to the digger."

Mallowan was born on May 6, 1904, in London, England. His father, Frederick, was Austrian and had been an officer in the Emperor's Horse Artillery. Frederick Mallowan left Austria and went to London, where he became a chemist. Mallowan's mother, Marthe Duvivier, was born in Paris. "Mother devoured romantic novels and all the classics and wrote poetry of a lyrical kind, some of which had, I believe, merit and was published in high-brow reviews. . . . She lectured on the arts with verve and style and had the love of language that comes naturally with the Latin temperament. . . . 'Ah, you boys,' she used to say, 'you have no go,' when all we wanted was to be left in peace."

Mallowan recalls that his first adventure in archaeology came when he was four years old. "There was a small garden with a brick wall at the end of it and here I made my earliest excavations and still have a picture of the Victorian china sherds recovered deep from the jet black soil." When he was eight Mallowan attended Rokeby preparatory school. "I was immediately taught the rudiments of Greek by a lady named Miss Vines who wore a large straw hat decorated with grapes. She imparted to me an early love for the language from which I have had nothing but enjoyment." Mallowan also enjoyed playing cricket. From there he went on to secondary school at Lancing, where he had among his friends the writer and poet Robert Graves and another writer, Evelyn Waugh.

In his autobiography, Mallowan says little about his schoolwork, with one exception—writing. If you read his later archaeological reports, like his three-volume *Nimrud and Its Remains*, you're in for a surprise. His writing is lively and the story of his work at Nimrud, though scholarly, unfolds like an adventure story. He would probably give credit for his writing skill to his favorite teacher, J. F. Roxburgh. Mallowan always remembered him fondly: "Roxburgh who also loved English literature and good writing made us think about language, and his marginal comments on our essays were always thought-provoking. Frequent abbreviations would appear in the margin such as CCC which meant *cliché, cant, or commonplace*. He was constantly pushing and probing to extract a spark of originality. . . ."

From Lancing, Mallowan went on to Oxford. It seems that even from his first year he was thinking of himself as an archaeologist. Among his favorite tutors were Stanley Casson, archaeologist and historian of ancient Greece, and Gilbert Murray, who lectured on Greek poetry. Mallowan studied Latin poets as well. And one class he espe-cially looked forward to each week was on Greek sculpture. "For this subject I had some understanding, as this was for me a prelude to archaeology. Percy Gardner, a tall upstanding figure, lectured in a frock coat and winged collar of a type which must have gone back to the 1860s." Gardner insisted that his students study at the British Museum and take the guided lectures. It was here that Mallowan began to imagine himself as an adult. "These tours of the British Museum provided an incentive for taking up an archaeological career, and when I heard Percy Gardner lecture on the Hermes of Praxiteles I reflected on how wonderful it would have been to be present at the time of its discovery in the Temple at Olympia and thereafter thought of all sculpture in its original setting."

Mallowan must have wondered how he would become an archaeologist. But as so often happens, the turning point in his life was something of a happy accident. He had just finished his examinations the day before and on a warm summer morning was out for a walk on campus. By chance he ran into the dean of the college, a distinguished theologian. "'Mallowan,' he said, 'what plans have you for the future?'

"'I fear,' I replied, 'that I may be condemned either to enter the Indian Civil Service or pursue the Law.'

"'And what do you really want to do?'

Part of the excavation at Ur, built about 2100 B.C. *Department of Western Asiatic Antiquities, Copyright © British Museum, London.*

"'Just one thing,' I said—'Archaeology, to which I have been attracted by hearing Percy Gardner talk about the discoveries at Olympia. I want to go to the East and look for things there.'

"'Go and see the Warden,' he said, 'he may help you.'"

Mallowan went immediately to the warden's office, not realizing how quickly his hopes would come true. "Warden Fisher kindly gave me a letter of introduction to the well-known Orientalist D. G. Hogarth, then keeper of the Ashmolean Museum, who that very morning had received and indeed had spread on his desk a letter from Woolley asking for an assistant to help

him at Ur of the Chaldees—that was in 1925."

Mallowan met Woolley and was soon invited to join the famous archaeologist's staff. He also met, and apparently impressed, Katharine Keeling, soon to become Lady Woolley. That was the acid test! But Woolley was especially impressed to hear how, when visiting the British Museum, Mallowan had bought and read Woolley's first report on Ur. Here was a young university graduate speaking knowingly about the discovery of the Temple of the Moon God. It could not but have touched Woolley's heart.

So it was that Mallowan and Woolley

traveled by boat and overland to Baghdad and from there to Ur. Mallowan had no experience in archaeology—save the small digs for potsherds in his childhood garden. His job would be general field assistant and he would be taught the job by Woolley as he went along. "In addition, I was expected to learn Arabic and become reasonably proficient at the spoken language. I was never a good linguist, but by dint of keeping Van Ess's grammar in my pocket for several years on end I became tolerably competent in the speaking and understanding of it." Another of his duties was to keep up the paybook. And he was also the medical officer, tending to the workers at the end of the day.

All of this was no small responsibility. Woolley employed about two hundred and fifty men. The men were organized into gangs. In each gang were a pickman; a spademan; and four, five, or six basketmen, depending on how far the soil had to be carried. Mallowan guessed that over the twelve years of excavation these workmen carried in baskets hundreds of thousands of tons of soil from the site. They worked from sunrise to sunset, with half an hour for breakfast and an hour for lunch. Mallowan was responsible for overseeing the whole operation. At the end of each season Mallowan also became chief packer of the antiquities. The task of packing forty to fifty crates was a delicate one. He accompanied the valuable cargo on the train to Basra and then to the docks, where he watched it being loaded on a steamer for the long journey to England. By the end of his six years with Woolley, Mallowan was an expert archaeologist. He had been trained by the very best there was.

When his work with Woolley was done, Mallowan was invited to Nineveh, a site north of Ur on the Tigris. He would be assisting Dr. Campbell Thompson in digging a pit down through the great mound until they reached prehistoric times. His work at Nineveh would be exactly the kind of digging he had done for Woolley. But there the similarity would end. His work in the south had been in Babylonia. Now he would be learning about the people of Assyria, a very different culture. Babylonian life was scholarly, religious, and placid, agricultural, and self-sufficient in grain. A network of canals had been dug through the countryside for irrigation. This self-sufficiency turned the country inward on itself. Assyria was not so self-sufficient, nor was it as peaceful. The cities were constantly under attack by people from the nearby mountains. To survive, Assyria was in a constant state of defense, permanently at arms. The result was that the Assyrians became a nation of warriors. Mallowan, then, expected to find evidence of this very different kind of society.

Dr. Thompson was most interested in finding tablets and was not as accomplished an archaeologist as Woolley. For Mallowan, then, this was an opportunity to try out all the techniques he had learned. He found five different strata, or levels of settlement. The bottom, or oldest level, he called Ninevite I and the top, or most recent level, Ninevite V. And he figured that the bottom level dated to about 6,000 B.C. and the topmost level 3,000 B.C.

"The stratum which contained Ninevite V was about twelve feet deep and of extraordinary interest." For Mallowan this was one of the most exciting excavations. "It consisted of the debris of ruined mud-brick houses which were partly filled with windblown sand, showing that they had been open and deserted for a time after their abandonment. This stratum contained a remarkable painted pottery which has never been found elsewhere in such profusion, and before this time had hardly appeared at all."

With all this experience Mallowan was now feeling ready to do a dig of his own. He was twenty-eight and already one of the most experienced—and certainly best trained—archaeologists of his day. He asked the British

Max Mallowan *(left)* with his wife, Agatha Christie, and Sir Leonard Woolley. *From Mallowan's Memoirs by Max Mallowan. (London: Collins, 1977.)*

Museum to sponsor him, and to his great joy was accepted. It would be a small expedition. The staff would include himself and John Rose, a friend and architect who had worked with Woolley at Ur. Mallowan would also include on his staff his wife, Agatha. They had worked together almost every season since their marriage—they had been introduced by the Woolleys—but she was not known as an archaeologist. She was Agatha Christie, the mystery writer, who is perhaps best known for her character Hercule Poirot, a brilliant detective in the tradition of Sherlock Holmes. Her most famous book is probably *Murder on the Orient Express,* though her millions of readers all have their own favorite.

Even a small excavation and small staff were to take some doing. Mallowan was now discovering what it was to be in charge, and he liked it. "I was ready to conduct a dig of my own and the prospect of having a first independent command wholly free of servitude to others, however pleasant that might have been, was bliss, for I have never shirked responsibility." Raising money turned out to be the easiest part. Then there were travel arrangements to take care of. Mallowan would need a permit to dig from the director of antiquities in Baghdad. Then they would have to find the owner of the land to get his permission and to arrange to rent the site. But there was more to it than that. They needed not only the owner's permission, but also that of the holder of the mortgage. It turned out there were no fewer than fourteen mortgages on the site, and the number seemed to be increasing daily. Eventually they had a contract. Now it was time to find a house out of which to work. Finally, they had recruited workers and could begin work. "It was pleasant," Mallowan later recalled of his first expedition, "to be able at last to order the men to

dig exactly where one wished without further consultation."

Their little mound was called Tepe Reshwa, near the village of Arpachiyah. The first few weeks were disappointing and they began wondering if the sight they had chosen was a dud. "We soon discovered we were wrong. In a few weeks' time both the architectural discoveries and the small finds proved to be of the most exciting character." They found an ancient cemetery, the graves filled with beautiful pottery. "Some of the larger bowls were decorated with big broad sweeping bands on the inside, great swathes around the bowl, a strange and rather attractive design which I have never seen elsewhere."

The work at Arpachiyah became more intriguing by the day. They discovered some remarkable buildings, of a type previously unknown in that part of the world. The buildings—which Mallowan and Rose thought might be shrines—were round with domes. There were ten of these circular buildings, the largest thirty-one feet across and over thirty feet high. "If these handsome domed buildings were indeed shrines, to whom were they dedicated?" Mallowan asked himself. "To that question I think we know the answer, because in association with many of them were found numerous specimens in clay and just a few in stone of a figure that we called the 'Mother Goddess.'"

In the annals of archaeology this first independent dig of Mallowan's is not as important as some. But to Mallowan it was very important. "Since Arpachiyah," he wrote at the end of his career, "I have led many other expeditions or have been closely connected with them in the Orient over a period of 50 years, but this, my first independent dig in which Agatha and John Rose alone took a main share, stands out as the happiest and most rewarding: it opened a new and enthralling chapter and will for ever stand as a milestone on the long road of prehistory."

Mallowan went on to organize other digs of his own. He moved on to other parts of Mesopotamia, to present-day Syria. Here he hoped to find tablets inscribed in cuneiform. Very few tablets containing the writing of ancient Sumer had been found in Syria. Mallowan was excited by the possibilities. "To me the prospect of filling in blank pages of history was a powerful incentive as it always has been throughout my professional life." It was now 1934, and Mallowan and Christie were on their way to Syria. Archaeology was changing in many ways, and one of them was the use of motor vehicles. Rather than just going out and buying a four-wheel drive as an expedition would today, it was in those days an adventure that Mallowan afterward remembered with a smile.

"Our first and most difficult task in Beirut, was to obtain a vehicle suitable for the rough ground over which we intended making our survey and as nothing immediate was available we had to obtain a four-cylinder Ford with a very sturdy engine for the sum, as far as I remember, of not more than £150. For a little money in a local workshop, we had the chassis built very high, and rather top heavy, but the best that could be done in Beirut. It was painted lavender blue, and on account of its height and dignity, indeed majesty, we rather impertinently nicknamed it 'Queen Mary.'"

Mallowan's next dig was at Chagar Bazar in Syria. Here he unearthed architectural remains, including more of the domed buildings. The excavators found unusual painted pottery, clay figures of humans, and the first evidence of ironwork. There was beautiful copper and silver jewelry. But with all these wonderful things, Mallowan was most interested in a tiny copper bead. It had been found at a great depth, in a layer from one of the earliest periods. This seemingly insignificant find was actually one of the most important of the dig: evidence of the beginnings of metallurgy.

Mallowan was now finding pottery in many different colors and designs. This was significant, too. The potters, he realized, had begun to experiment with their kilns. They had been learning to adjust the hotness of their fires. What's more, he could tell, they had been trying out different kinds of pigments. They had found that a little red pigment on the bowl turned out red in the firing. But if they put it on thicker and made the fire hotter, the pigment turned black. They had found a cream-colored slip that, when brushed onto the pot and then fired, turned a rich apricot color.

Mallowan intended to continue his work in Iraq and Syria. His plans were interrupted, however, by World War II. He returned to London, anxious to play some role in the war, only to find, at first, that no one could decide how to use a man whose only skill seemed to be digging in the sand. Eventually he did serve as an intelligence officer with the Royal Air Force in North Africa. Mallowan returned to England after the war to spend two years writing his book on the excavations at Brak and Chagar Bazar. He was then appointed to the faculty of the Institute of Archaeology at the University of London.

During his years at the institute Mallowan enjoyed his teaching. He influenced the lives of many young people, some of whom would join a new genera-tion of accomplished archaeologists. Mallowan recalled with agony the dry lectures of his childhood, and put all his energies and sense of humor into his teaching. In a time when most professors simply lectured, Mallowan made a point to involve his students, to include them in discussions and make them a part of the class. "Above all I found teaching a two-way traffic, for the pupil, although the receiving instrument, is a sounding board and must reverberate on the master." He liked knowing his students, and often spent a lot of time with a student who was considered a dullard by other teachers. He preferred small classes. "Seminars and the time devoted to a single pupil, are obviously a better way of exchanging knowledge than lectures. In classes that were not too large, I invited listeners to interrupt whenever they wished." While he taught, Mallowan also spent seasons in the field. It was during these years that he set out on his most famous discovery.

"There were four ancient Assyrian capitals which I might have chosen to excavate in Iraq—Nineveh, Nimrud, Ashur and Khorsabad." Mallowan considered the possibilities of each site. But for lots of reasons—some technical, some emotional—he decided against all but one. For him Nimrud offered more than any other site in Assyria. When Mallowan wrote about Nimrud,

The remains of the outer wall of Nimrud can be seen in the background of this photograph. *Department of Western Asiatic Antiquities, Copyright © British Museum, London.*

though, it was clear that his interests were more than scholarly. Nimrud touched his heart. "To many travellers there is no more romantic spot than Nimrud, where forty years ago the bearded heads of protective stone *Ia-massu*, half man, half beast, stuck out of the ground outside the gates of the ancient palaces, the last of the faithful servants that guarded the warrior priest kings of Assyria. This is my memory of it as I first saw the place after my first season's work with Leonard Woolley at Ur of the Chaldees on the barren steppe of southern Babylonia. Here I realized was an archaeological paradise where one day after I had done my apprenticeship, I might be privileged to enter."

In 1949 Mallowan requested permission to dig at Nimrud. It was a very special year, an anniversary. "This was an appropriate time for making the request because exactly a century had lapsed since the beginning of Layard's excavations on the same spot." Permission was granted him. Mallowan assembled his team. There was his wife, who had helped him now for years. She would do much of the photography.

Then there was Mahmud, who had gotten his doctorate in Oriental languages in Berlin and loved his teaching at the University of Baghdad. And there was Robert Hamilton, who spoke Arabic beautifully; he was a surveyor and a gifted artist, who would keep the architectural record of the dig. They would recruit in all about seventy workers. Mallowan chose carefully. "Some of my recruits had been among my workers at Nineveh and Arpachiyah and referred to Agatha as their aunt."

Nimrud was an immense city, built by two great kings—Ashurnasirpal II and his son, Shalmaneser III. Their rule spanned sixty years (883–824 B.C.), and in that time they built a strong empire. At one time Nimrud had a population of 100,000. Layard had found wondrous things here, but, in all his digging, not one clay tablet inscribed with cuneiform. This would be one of Mallowan's most important objectives. "It seemed incredible to me that so large a city could have been devoid of economic, business, historical and literary texts. I would have staked my life that in the end we would find all these things, and find them we did."

Mallowan began where Layard had left off. His pick-and-spademen found many beautiful relics, including ivory carvings of horses, gazelles, figures of men and women—which he was especially hoping to find. They found immense buildings—palaces and temples—as well as private houses. They found spears and golden jewelry, amulets, cylinder seals, and even an ancient safety pin. They found the kings' throne and monuments on which were recorded the histories of the kings. And they did find tablets and inscriptions. But Mallowan came away from Nimrud with more than artifacts or even knowledge. As with his other digs, he recalled most fondly the experience itself. Perhaps that was for him the most important thing.

"Now that we must take leave of this site," he wrote at the end of his beautiful book *Nimrud and Its Remains*, "we can recall with joy the carefree days when we set out in 1949 with the glorious prospects of discovery. The mound of Nimrud was untenanted then, as it had been a hundred years earlier, except for a few humble shepherds. We worked untroubled and little known, on the green swards, gazing with joy over the meadows to the Tigris and the hills of Kurdistan where lay the bones of countless generations of men who had ventured forth, in war and in peace, from the home town where we still remembered them."

Margaret Mead

1901–1978 American anthropologist

"I have spent most of my life studying the lives of other peoples, faraway peoples, so that Americans might better understand themselves." Margaret Mead was an anthropologist, and in that one sentence she sums up her life's work. Her interest was people, all kinds of people, all over the world. She was curious about how they relate to one another—babies and adults, adolescents and elders—and to the place in which they live. One of the things anthropologists do is visit and observe people alive today whose lifeways are perhaps thousands of years old. In this way, anthropologists can help us understand where our customs came from and how they have changed over the years. Most important, anthropologists help us understand how it is that people can be very different but in some ways are all alike.

Mead was especially interested in children. She observed the relationship between parents and children in many old cultures and in present-day cultures as well. Her purpose was to learn something about how families are different in different cultures and how they are similar. She once made a film that shows how she and other anthropologists work. The film is called *Four Families*, and to make it she took a cameraman into one home in each of four countries—India, France, Japan, and Canada. In each home she watched the same events: children and parents together at the evening meal and children being bathed. The films are so real that the viewer feels like a member of the family. The families go about their daily lives almost as if the camera weren't there. By watching the same events in the four homes side by side, it's easy to compare the same rituals in four cultures. Observing carefully, we realize that although the cultures seem very different, the relationships between the parents and their children are familiar to all of us.

Mead was, in her day, the foremost woman anthropologist. She is responsible, perhaps more than any other person, for interesting young people in becoming anthropologists, especially young women. In her time it was unusual for a woman to be traveling around the world alone, living among people in places like Bali, Samoa, and New Guinea. Once, when she was a student, Mead was told by one of her professors that it would be best if she stayed home and had children instead of going off to islands in the South Seas to study adolescent girls. She wrote the professor this poem as her answer:

Measure your thread and cut it
To suit your little seam,
Stitch the garment tightly, tightly,
And leave no room for dream.
· · · · · · · · · · · ·
Head down! Be not caught looking
Where the restless wild geese fly.

Eventually Mead would have a child, but as a young woman she was curious about the world around her and wanted, in her own way, to make some sense of it. She was one of the first women to work by herself in the field and to study people while actually living with them for some time. Chances are, if you study anthropology, you'll read one of her books, such as *Coming of Age in Samoa, Growing Up in New Guinea,* or *Family.*

Mead's life was not typical for a woman of her times and neither was her childhood. She was born on December 18, 1901, in Philadelphia, Pennsylvania. Her father, Edward Sherwood Mead, was a professor of economics at the University of Pennsylvania. Her mother, Emily Fogg Mead, was a sociologist, who was finishing up her college work at Wellesley and Bryn Mawr when Mead was a little girl. But Emily Mead was not just a scholar. Mead recalled her mother's concern for others and her sense of responsibility in a harsh world. The daughter would grow up sharing her mother's values. "She . . . felt it was important to continue her own intellectual life and to be a responsible citizen in a world in which there were many wrongs—wrongs to the poor and downtrodden, to foreigners, to Negroes, to women—that had to be set right," Margaret Mead recalls in her book *Blackberry Winter.* Emily Mead unknowingly introduced her daughter to the work of anthropology through her research in sociology. "My first experience of field work," Mead remembers, "was through my mother's work among the Italians living in Hammonton, New Jersey, where we had moved in 1902 so that she could study them."

Mead's first memories were of moving frequently. She might live in Philadelphia when her father was teaching and then live on a farm for the summer. However often the family moved, they always returned to their home in Hammonton. Mead remembers how each move brought her a special kind of joy. Each new place was an adventure. "All the other houses were strange—houses that had to be made our own as quickly as possible so that they no longer would be strange. This did not mean that they were frightening, but only that we had to learn every nook and corner, for otherwise it was hard to play hide-and-go-seek." In this way, Mead's childhood was a picture of what her life would become. "Going away, knowing that I shall return to the same place and the same people—this is the way my life has always been."

With all her travels Mead became a citizen of the world. "For me," she wrote in her autobiography, *Blackberry Winter*, "moving and staying at home, traveling and arriving, are all of a piece. The world is full of homes in which I have lived for a day, a month, a year, or much longer. How much I care about

a home is not measured by the length of time I have lived there. . . . Home, I learned, can be anywhere you make it. Home is also a place to which you come back again and again."

Perhaps the most important adult in Mead's childhood was her father's mother, Martha Ramsay Mead. Grandma Mead had lived with the family from the time her son married until she died in 1927. Like most grandmothers she was more lenient than parents are and, as Mead remembers her, more affectionate. Soon a very special relationship developed between grandmother and granddaughter. "She sat at the center of our household. Her room—and my mother always saw to it that she had the best room, spacious and sunny, with a fireplace if possible— was the place to which we immediately went when we came in from playing or home from school." Grandma Mead was an enchanting storyteller. She read Latin, did many things with her hands, and helped Mead with her studies in school.

Grandma Mead had taught school when she was a young girl, at a time when it was unusual for a girl so young to be a teacher. She and Mead's grandfather went to college together, and he became a school superintendent. It was from her grandmother that Mead learned about the world, more than from school. She learned algebra when she was very young. "On some days she gave me a set of plants to analyze; on others, she gave me a description and sent me out to the woods and meadows to collect examples, say, of the 'mint family'. . . . The result was that . . . I learned to observe the world around me and to note what I saw— to observe flowers and children and baby chicks." Before she was eight years old, Mead was taking notes on the behavior of young children in her neighborhood.

Grandma Mead taught her granddaughter about life. She was, in her time, a pioneer in child psychology, and understood ideas that would not be generally recognized for years to come. She had an understanding of childhood few people had then. In many ways she set the direction of her granddaughter's future. For one thing, she was aware of the difference between the way boys and girls grew up. She understood that boys were more vulnerable than girls of the same age and needed more patience as well. And in many ways she let Mead know that she could do anything she wanted to do. "Grandma had no sense at all of ever having been handicapped by being a woman."

Mead's grandmother had gotten her to look around at the world in a way that was different from the way most children (and adults) saw it. Mead was

becoming an observer, trained to see similarities and differences in people. Like many children she wondered, sometimes worried about, whether her family was "normal." "From my earliest childhood I compared my own family with the kinds of families I heard about, learned about in songs, and read about in books. I thought seriously about the ways our family resembled other families, real and fictional, and sometimes sadly about the ways we did not fit into the expected pattern. . . . Tracing old patterns was something I began to do very early, as I noted family resemblances—who in the next generation had the eyes or the nose or the curling hair or the sharp wit of some member of the generation before.

"Some years we went to school. Other years we stayed at home and Grandma taught us. That is one way of describing my schooling." Mead attended elementary and high school on and off, including various schools run by the Society of Friends (Quakers). In high school she wished to be a painter. Then she found out that to be a painter she would have to go to an art school rather than a university, and she changed her mind. "For me, not to go to college was, in a sense, not to become a full human being."

When she entered DePauw University, in Greencastle, Indiana, at seventeen, she majored in English. Mead loved to write. She had written poetry and even begun a novel. She enjoyed corresponding with pen pals. But she discovered that at DePauw she was an outcast because of her eastern upbringing. She enjoyed her classes well enough, but she longed to return to the part of the country in which she felt comfortable and at home. In 1920, then, after spending a year at DePauw, she entered Barnard, the women's college of Columbia University.

It was at Barnard that Mead would find her life's work. She had switched her major to psychology; her parents had reared her to be a social scientist in bent and attitude. She had all but decided to become a psychologist, when she found herself in a class taught by Franz Boas. She also met Boas's teaching assistant, Ruth Benedict, who invited Mead to her graduate seminar. Soon Mead and Benedict became close friends. "By the end of the first term, I had decided to attend everything Boas taught." Mead had a decision to make, and she confided in Benedict. She had already begun her master's essay in psychology. She had been thinking of going on in sociology, her mother's field. She asked Benedict what to do, and her answer was straightforward: "Professor Boas and I have nothing to offer but an opportunity to do work that mat-

ters." It was all that needed to be said. "That settled it for me," Mead remembered later. "Anthropology had to be done *now*. Other things could wait."

Mead continued her graduate work in anthropology with "Papa Franz," as his students called him. She had done a paper for him on Polynesia and had become interested in the peoples who lived on the islands in the South Pacific. Mead's work so much impressed Boas that he offered to help her apply for a grant that would enable her to do fieldwork. But when she proposed to Boas that she do her fieldwork in Polynesia, he said no, it was too dangerous. Mead was insistent, and Boas finally agreed to let her go on one condition—that she choose an island at which ships stopped regularly. She decided on Samoa because it was less spoiled than the other islands and because a steamship stopped there every three weeks. She received her grant from the National Research Council and now she would spend her summer preparing for her first visit to Samoa.

A sense of urgency gripped her as she began her work. "Even in remote parts of the world ways of life about which nothing was known were vanishing before the onslaught of modern civilization. The work of recording these unknown ways of life had to be done now—*now*—or they would be lost forever. . . . I was determined to go to the field, not at some leisurely chosen later date, but immediately—as soon as I had completed the necessary preliminary steps."

But how do you "record" ways of life? Mead didn't know; she knew very little about fieldwork. In none of her seminars had fieldwork been discussed. Her education was all about theory. She had read other anthropologists' reports from the field, but she had not had any opportunity to practice, to work under the supervision of an experienced fieldworker as anthropology students do today. She knew nothing of the day-to-day fieldwork of other anthropologists.

Besides the research problems, there were other, more basic, questions. How would she arrange travel? Where would she live? What about food and supplies, equipment? What medicines were needed? What kind of clothing should she take? How would she handle the isolation, the loneliness? And what about language? No one knew conversational Samoan, except a few missionaries and their children. There were no Samoan language books in the bookstores, or in the library, for that matter. The way fieldwork had been approached since the earliest days of anthropology had not changed: Give students a good theoretical background, and then send them off to live among

people in a far-off corner of the globe, and somehow they'll work everything out for themselves. "If young field workers," she observed, "do not give up in despair, go mad, ruin their health, or die, they do, after a fashion, become anthropologists." That's what Mead would do.

"And so I arrived in Samoa." Mead knew for certain only that she was in Pago Pago. What would happen next was anyone's guess. She had brought with her only a few things—cotton dresses, spare glasses, a flashlight, a camera, pencils and notebooks, and a portable typewriter.

Eventually she made it to the village of a Samoan woman whom she had met in Honolulu on her way over. Arrangements had been made for her to stay there. She moved into the household of the chief and began wearing the saronglike native women's dress. All the time she had been practicing the few words and phrases she knew on children that she met. She learned to appreciate Samoan food. But one custom, especially, made her uncomfortable. As the guest she would be served first. Then the whole family would watch her eat until she had finished. Only then would they begin to eat. She had a hard time sitting cross-legged as the Samoans did, but soon she got used to that too. "Day after day I grew easier in the language, sat more correctly, and suffered less pain in my legs. In the evenings there was dancing and I had my first dancing lessons.

"It was a beautiful village with its swept plaza and tall, round, thatched guesthouses against the pillars of which the chiefs sat on formal occasions. I learned to recognize the leaves and plants used for weaving mats and making tapa [cloth]. I learned how to relate to the other people in terms of their rank and how to reply in terms of the rank they accorded me." This first visit was a kind of practice for Mead and a way to accustom herself to Samoan ways. Her work would not be done here, but on another island, Tau, where she would spend the next nine months.

Mead's plan, which she had worked out with Professor Boas, was to study adolescent girls. Specifically, she wanted to find out how adolescent girls reacted to the restraints put on their behavior as they got older. In most societies children are allowed a lot of freedom—allowed to behave like children. Then as they get older, restraints are put on their behavior and they are expected to be more responsible. This was the 1920s, and in the United States the rebellion of adolescents against their parents was being written and talked about for the first time. Did this rebellion also happen, Boas and Mead wondered, in native cultures? Or was it just in modern, industrial societies like the United States and Europe that young people acted this way? Was it because modern cultures demanded more conformity? American adolescents expressed their rebellion with sullenness and sometimes outbursts of anger. Was this the way adolescents acted in other cultures?

Boas was also interested in other behavior he had observed, "the excessive bashfulness of girls in primitive society. I do not know whether you will find it there," he wrote to Mead in Samoa. "It is characteristic of Indian girls of most tribes, and often not only in their relations to outsiders, but frequently within the narrow circle of the family. They are often afraid to talk and are very retiring before older people." These were a few of the issues Mead hoped to study in Samoa.

Mead set herself up in the village on Tau. She would have a Samoan house to use as her "office," a place to interview girls. She was assigned a girl who would be her constant companion—the culture did not allow women to live alone in the village. She found the girls of the village eager to talk with her, filling her house all hours of the day and night. She interviewed each girl alone, and spent time wandering about the village, observing the children's

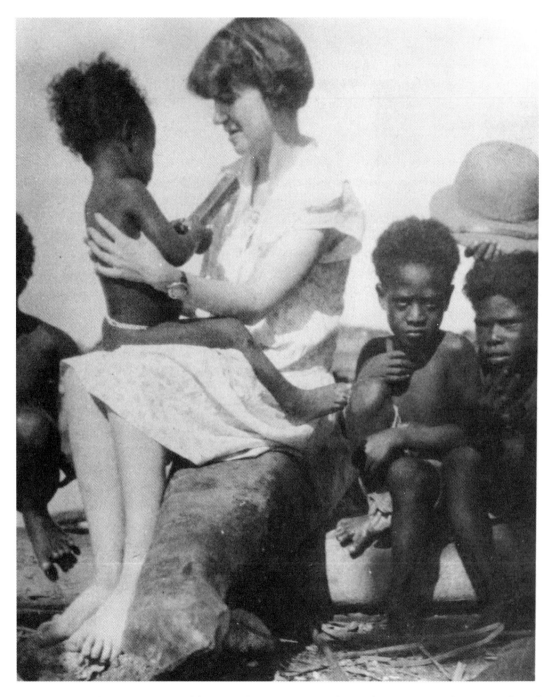

Margaret Mead with Manus children Ponkiau, Bopau, and Tchokal. *Institute for Intercultural Studies, Inc., New York, NY. Photograph from the Collections of the Library of Congress.*

lives. She would go out on fishing trips or sit for hours watching a woman weaving. All the time she was observing, taking notes mentally or on paper. Eventually she had a census of the whole village and understood the background and kinship of all the girls she was studying.

Tau was becoming another of Mead's many homes. "The pleasantest time of the day here is sunset," she wrote to her friend Ruth Benedict. "Then accompanied by some fifteen girls and little children I walk through the village to the end of Siufaga, where we stand on an iron bound point and watch the waves splash us in the face, while the sun goes down over the sea and at the same time behind the cocoanut covered hills." Every event of the day was to be observed carefully, for each gave Mead more information about the people. "They dance for me a great deal; they love it and it is an excellent index to temperament as the dance is so individualistic. . . ." Later, when Mead returned to Tau for a visit, she was remembered with fondness. "My adopted family comforted me, and I realized that they would gladly have cared for me for the rest of my life."

Mead returned to New York to work on a book and to take up her duties as assistant curator of ethnology at the American Museum of Natural History.

Whenever she taught and trained young anthropologists, her first experiences in Samoa were always remembered. She was especially intent on making sure that a new generation of anthropologists would not have to suffer the old system that denied them practical training. "I try to work against it by giving students a chance to work over my own field preparations and notes, by encouraging them to work at photography, and by creating field situations for my class, in which they have to work out a real problem and face up to the difficulties of an actual situation in which there are unknown elements. For only in this way can they find out what kind of recording they do well—or very badly—or how they react when they discover they have missed a clue or have forgotten to take the lens cap off the camera for a critical picture."

Mead returned to the South Pacific to continue her investigations with other peoples. She lived with the Manus tribe of the Admiralty Islands. From her experiences came the books *Growing Up in New Guinea* and *Social Organizations of Manu'a*. Her third field trip, this time in America, was to study an American Indian tribe, which she called "the Antlers" to protect their privacy. She would return to New Guinea again, and then begin her longest adventure, three years in Bali.

Mead was appreciated as a writer as well as an anthropologist. Some of her books, like *Coming of Age in Samoa* and *Male and Female*, became best-sellers. Her book *Balinese Character: A Photographic Analysis* is an example of the pioneering use of photography to describe a culture and a people. She always wrote with humor and humanity and was best at looking at people in a way that others hadn't. She took a critical look at her own culture in a book called *And Keep Your Powder Dry: An Anthropologist Looks at America*. In this book she helped Americans see their own culture more clearly by setting it against the background of seven other cultures she had studied.

Mead had all along been looking at different cultures to answer the question that most interested her: How was it that the behavior of boys and girls was different? By then scientists were certain that the differences did not come with each child at birth, as it seemed, but were actually learned. Mead was quite certain of this. Boys and girls behaved differently because society expected them to be different. "Differences in sex as they are known to-day," she concluded after several of her studies, "are based on the bringing up by the mother." What Mead discov-

ered was that mothers encouraged daughters to behave like them, but taught sons to be different.

Most anthropologists are content to be observers and reporters. But Mead had hopes for a new generation of children. She worked as hard to shape that new generation as she did to analyze the older ones. She spoke at many conferences on children and child study. Her concern for education led her to the study and the book *The School in American Culture*. She was sympathetic toward teachers. Their problem, she said, was having to keep pace with children in a rapidly changing world. She had ideas, too, about how to help children feel comfortable in this changing world. We should, she advised mothers, "teach our children to nest in the gale, to have the habit of adjusting, to be pleased when they do adjust." To Mead, that meant "being able to be at home anywhere in the world, in any house, in any time band, eating any different kind of food, learning new languages as needed, never afraid of the new, sad to leave anywhere where one has been at home for a few days, but glad to go forward."

Mead was this kind of a child. She touched the lives of countless people—her students, the readers of her books, the families she lived with, the children she interviewed, other anthropologists

Margaret Mead holds two examples of art she brought back after a seven-month visit to a Manus village. *UPI/Bettmann.*

around the world. "Anthropology had attracted Mead in the first place," Jane Howard, one of her biographers, wrote, "because its borders are so flexible, but even it could not contain her. Nothing could. She made her own rules and lived many lives. She rushed across oceans and continents, time zones and networks and disciplines, knocking down barriers and redefining boundaries."

Elsie Clews Parsons

1875–1941   American sociologist, anthropologist, and folklorist

President Theodore Roosevelt and Judge Learned Hand, one of America's most distinguished jurists, were among her closest friends. Her husband, Representative Herbert Parsons, was a United States congressman from the state of New York. She wrote important studies on American Indians, people of the West Indies, and African Americans. Her work was greatly respected by anthropologists and sociologists all over the world. She was the first woman ever elected president of the American Anthropological Association. But most Americans who read her books or read about her in the newspapers did not like Elsie Clews Parsons. Her most famous book, *The Family*, and her ideas were denounced as "disgusting," "strange and impossible," "indecent," "revolutionary," "absurd," and having "the morality of the barnyard."

That was in 1906. Today, Parson's ideas, while still not for everyone, are widely accepted. In fact, were *The Family* published today, it would seem terribly dated. Parsons was very much ahead of her time. Much of what she suggested then has become customary now. But she shocked American sensibilities in several ways. As anthropologists often do, she made us look at and talk about behavior people preferred to put out of mind. And she was a woman. That fact was probably more important than anything else. For years men had been writing frankly about sexual behavior and relationships. But Americans could not tolerate a woman writing about such things. One of Parsons' greatest contributions was to pave the way for future generations of American women anthropologists.

She was born in New York City on November 27, 1875. Her mother, Lucy Madison Worthington, had been born in Kentucky and grew up in Keokuk, Iowa. She met her husband, Elsie's father, at a ball given by President Ulysses S. Grant at the White House. Henry Clews had been born in Staffordshire, England, and at fourteen he visited New York and decided to stay in the United States. He became a successful banker, and by the time Elsie was born the family was quite wealthy.

From her youngest years Parsons was an independent thinker. As much as she loved her father, she did not accept his social ideas. Henry Clews's philosophy of life was then called social Darwinism. He believed in the survival of the fittest, in business and in life. Those with the most intelligence and talent naturally rose to the top. They were the survivors. It was nature's way, he would argue. The poor and unfortunate were unfit and, therefore, should not survive. Parsons also rebelled against her father's disdain for scholarship. He considered a college education useless. "In many instances," he once said, education was "not only a hindrance, but absolutely fatal to success." By *success* Henry Clews meant business success.

Her father's attitude toward education actually worked in her favor. He saw no sense for a man to be educated, but a woman—well, she had nothing better to do anyway. So he encouraged his daughter's quest for learning. Henry Clews objected to women's suffrage; indeed, women, in his view, had no place in public life or the practical world. So the impractical world of scholarship was, to him, the perfect place for an intelligent, energetic woman like his daughter.

Her mother gave her little encouragement. She was a very social woman, whose only interests, Parsons once said, were clothes and planning parties. Parsons liked her mother's cheerfulness but was angered by her narrow-mindedness. Lucy Clews simply could not understand her daughter. She described her once as an "unusual" child and was always puzzled that her daughter had "no special longing for material things." Parsons recalled her mother objecting to her playing with little boys in the park because it was unladylike. Later she insisted on reading any letters her daughter wrote to young men. Parsons also recalled having to wear a veil and gloves whenever they went out, and taking them off whenever her mother's back was turned. She was constantly nagged by her mother about showing "proper manners" and reminded about lowering her voice and being more careful about her dress. They disagreed over her going to college. Lucy Clews felt such "work" was selfish and unhealthy for a girl, and tried to discourage her daughter from reading and studying. She always kept hoping for things that would distract her daughter's attention from reading poetry and Greek philosophy and history. "Mama told me with earnest emphasis," Parsons remembered, "that the best thing that could happen to me was 'to fall desperately in love.'"

Parsons rebelled against her mother by becoming all the more independent. She entered Barnard, a newly founded women's college, when she was eighteen. There she excelled in her academic studies—zoology, sociology, economics, Greek, American history, philosophy, and education. Already Parsons was interested in social issues. She wrote an essay questioning why children were not being taught at home and at school to think on their own. She had seen in her own life how parents pushed children always to conform, to be like everyone else. Children, she argued, should instead be encouraged to have their own ideas, to think independently. It was in her last year at Barnard that Parsons read about new courses in sociology to be offered at Columbia University that would cover subjects that interested her—family and divorce, poverty and crime.

After graduating from Barnard, Parsons went on to Columbia for an M.A. in sociology. What was unusual about her research was that it was based on fieldwork. At that time, few students actually went out to do their own investigations on their subjects. Parsons visited families in the tenements and based her study on the case histories of 787 people on relief. Professor Franklin H. Giddings, chairman of the sociology department, liked her work and awarded her a fellowship.

Now she would enjoy a rare opportunity for a woman. She would be responsible for Giddings's undergraduate students at Barnard. She would teach an important course. "I am also to develop it along my own lines more or less," she wrote her friend Herbert Parsons. "I think it will be pretty good fun and very useful work too." She taught courses on the family for the next three years. Her work was good, and she was appointed a lecturer in sociology at Barnard College. At twenty-four she completed her doctorate. That same year she married Herbert Parsons.

Herbert Parsons, like Elsie Parsons's parents, had a hard time understanding the woman he loved. His habits and ideas were more conventional than

An early photograph of Elsie Clews Parsons. *Schlesinger Library, Radcliffe College.*

hers, but he was known for his high ideals and principles. They shared a political and social philosophy, one of fairness for all people. Herbert Parsons was elected to Congress and was known throughout his career for his integrity. Teddy Roosevelt respected him greatly and wrote about him in a letter to Parsons, "He has combined strength with decency in a way which makes him a mighty useful public servant."

As Herbert Parsons surely knew, his wife had definite ideas about the institution of marriage—and any other institution, for that matter. She disliked anything that was done just because it was customary. She refused to wear a hat when all women were expected to wear hats because it was "fashionable." She would often sit and talk with the men after a dinner. (Men and women in those days kept strictly to themselves socially.) She wore sandals on Park Avenue, a fancy, proper street in New York City. And she insisted on wearing, from head to foot, her favorite color—orange! Parsons did not believe in organized religion or its rituals, like weddings and funerals. She was also a pacifist, opposed to war.

Parsons's children rejected her values, just as she had her parents'. When her daughter, Lissa, was a teenager, she was embarrassed by her mother. She once described her in a writing assignment at school as someone "rather tall" who liked to write books and "go without clothes." Lissa was embarrassed by the way her mother dressed, that she had black friends, and lived with Indians on her field trips. Lissa would ask her mother not to appear when her friends came to visit. Parsons remained good-natured about it. She understood that Lissa was going through just what she had as a child, and so mother and daughter remained friends.

Most difficult for Parsons's parents, her husband, and her daughter to accept was that Parsons was, long before most people knew what the word meant, an outspoken feminist. Once her mother asked peevishly, "What *is* feminism?" Parsons tried to answer in a way her mother would understand. "When I would play with the little boys in Bryant Park although you said it was rough and unladylike, that was feminism. When I took off my veil or gloves whenever your back was turned or when I stayed in my room two days rather than put on stays, that was feminism. When I got out of paying calls to go riding and sailing, that was feminism. When I would go to college in spite of all your protests, that was feminism. When I kept to regular hours of work in spite of protests that I was selfish, that was feminism. When I had a baby when I wanted one, in spite of protests that I was not selfish enough, that was feminism."

Still her mother did not understand. To her, Parsons's behavior was just the thoughtless acts of a "rebellious daughter." But for Parsons, feminism meant social freedom for women. And that was part of her larger quest for social freedom for everyone. It was clear to Parsons that if any one group of people is not free—women, blacks, the poor—then no one is free. That's why she had a lifelong interest in African Americans and their search for acceptance and freedom. The United States could never be a free country, she believed, as long as there were Americans who were not free.

Anthropologists study other cultures for many reasons. For some it is a personal search. Understanding the behavior of others helps us to understand our own behavior. Watching the relationships between people in another culture helps us to see what's going on in our own. Lucy Clews was an example of why anthropology is necessary. She could not see that women in the United States were not free. She could not imagine her life as being any other way than the way it was. But suppose she read about another culture, somewhere far away, in which the women were not free: a place where men, but not women, were educated. A place

where men wore clothes that allowed them free movement, but women wore strange clothes that bound and hobbled them. A place where women must know their place, which was only with other women. Then she would probably have said, "Well, obviously, *those* women are not free." The anthropologist's answer is: "You *are* one of those women. Don't you see?"

Parsons wrote several books on women. In *The Old Fashioned Woman* (1913) she described women's lives in other societies. But she was really speaking to American women. She showed what happens whenever a person's behavior is restricted: that person is never able to grow to her or his full potential. What's more, the people who impose the rules are as trapped and enslaved as those who must bend to them.

In another book, *Fear and Conventionality*, Parsons showed how we can become trapped in a vicious cycle. Humans fear change. So to keep from having to change, we set up a system of rules. Everyone is forced to conform to the rules. We conform because we fear what will happen to us if we don't. Some rules are good; they help us to live together. But others are not, if their purpose is to keep some people in line. When they are enforced too strictly, they cannot be changed. And if rules cannot be changed, then we are trapped and our culture cannot grow and adapt.

In *Social Rule* Parsons made us face up to how much of our energies are spent ruling and controlling others. In all her books her way was not to judge or make readers feel ashamed. She did not argue loudly, but confidently and precisely. She respected our ability to make up our own minds. But she wanted us to see clearly what was really happening and how it all affected our lives.

Parsons was bringing these ideas out into the open for the first time in the United States, which took courage. It was taboo, forbidden, to talk openly about very personal things; it was especially forbidden for a woman to do so. So Parsons had to use a man's name, "John Main," in order to get her books published. In this way, she deliberately forced us to look at ourselves. She suffered cruel criticism for her efforts. Critics—clergymen, college and university presidents, professors, women as well as men—attacked her personally. Americans have always had problems facing up to what really happens here. So when Parsons held up our lives to us, it was like looking into a mirror. We not only didn't like what we were seeing in ourselves, but we hated her for showing us.

Parsons didn't care about the attacks.

She knew that such denial was the first step toward the changes to come. She was concerned that her parents and husband and children not suffer because of her. Her willingness to say the unspeakable, to bring the hidden out into the open, changed our ways of thinking. She was the first, and now other women and men—whose stories are elsewhere in this book—could follow more easily.

Parsons's understanding of American culture was clearer because of her travels elsewhere. Remember, this was the early 1900s, and not many people had traveled very widely. It was a time before there were planes to fly to faraway places, and few people owned cars. Most Americans had never been more than a few miles from home. Many people lived their entire lives from birth to death in the same small town. People raised their children in the same neighborhood of a big city in which they had grown up. Children played in the same streets and went to the same schools, churches, and synagogues as their parents and even their grandparents had before them. There was simply no way to get another perspective on life, to see it from another angle.

Parsons was fortunate enough to have visited many cultures. When she was a young woman she went to Canada, Europe, Africa, Asia, and Latin America. She traveled to Greece, Egypt, the

Philippines, to every part of the United States, to the Caribbean, Mexico, Guatemala, and Ecuador. She didn't go to the fashionable places where most well-to-do Americans went. She went to out-of-the-way places to be among the common folk. Her travels were not just vacations. Each trip was a chance to observe other people and other lifeways.

When she was about forty, Parsons discovered anthropology. The problems were similar to those of sociology. But what she liked about anthropology was the methods that had been developed over the years to study cultures. Unlike sociologists in those days, anthropologists went into the field and carefully observed, perhaps for years. They often lived among their subjects. And their writing and conclusions were always based on factual observations. The cause of her changing fields was her travels through the Southwest and her first visit to a pueblo. She became fascinated with the religion of the Pueblo people and the structure of their culture.

Parsons later wrote about that day she discovered the beauty and mystery of the Southwest. She had met an ex-schoolteacher who was now a rancher, Clara True. True supplied Parsons with a horse and an Indian boy, Santiago, as guide, and they rode in every which

direction to explore the New Mexico countryside. "There was a scramble up the canyon by steep cross-cuts known to the boy and then across the table-lands a long stretch of delightful, easy riding—by this time I was more at home in the Mexican saddle and my knees began to have grip in them." Parsons found the ruins of an ancient pueblo. "I wandered in and out of the skeleton of that partly excavated town in the edge of the mesa, above the cave rooms below, and as I examined the wall niches and hearths, the lintels and passages I tried to reconstruct the past. . . ."

Parsons returned to the ruins with Santiago, intent on digging. She found some bits of pottery and some intriguing little sticks. Each was as long as her palm, painted black, and decorated with feathers bound onto the sticks. "Feathers in the open don't last for centuries, these were not from the cliff dwellers. 'How did these get here,' I asked Santiago. 'Don't know,' he answered, but there was an indifference in the manner of that answer that suggested that he *did* know."

That experience was very important to Parsons. "One thing at least I learned on this trip, I thought as we rode back to the ranch—what interests me most. Not the artifacts we've dug up or the construction of that chamber . . . none of these, but the comment of Santiago, more particularly his unspoken comment. I am more curious about what he would not tell me and why he would not tell. . . . It is interesting to reconstruct the culture of the ancient town builders, but it is still more interesting to study the minds and ways of their descendants."

For much of the rest of her life Parsons continued studying Native American lifeways. She first went to Zuñi, New Mexico, in 1915. It was a time, she realized, when American Indian culture was at a crossroads. Many of the old customs were dying or, worse, were already lost forever. The elders who remembered the old ways were dying too. White, European culture had all but destroyed Indian ways. Parsons, like many anthropologists, felt it her life's mission to record as much of Indian life as she could. She knew she could not save the old ways—it was already too late for that. But she hoped that, by writing down the stories of the elders, she could at least keep it all from being forgotten.

That trip to Zuñi was the beginning of a lifetime of work. Over the next quarter of a century Parsons returned many times to the pueblos. She visited Laguna, and later returned with her teacher, Professor Boas. She lived at the Tanoan pueblos along the Rio Grande. She worked among the Pima

of Arizona, the Kiowa and Caddo in Oklahoma, and the Cahita of Sonora, California. Much had been written about these people, but it was all badly organized and disconnected. Parsons created a clearer picture of Indian lifeways. And in so doing she also developed study methods that are still being used today.

She was especially interested in the origins of custom and ritual. After many years living among different Native American tribes, she began to see certain similarities. How was it that peoples who spoke different languages and seemed to be different had similar rituals? It must have been, she reasoned, because the customs came from long ago, from an earlier culture. Because the later cultures developed from this earlier, unknown one, they each kept some of the old ways. Parsons called these *antecedents*, from earlier times.

Much of American Indian history was influenced by the Spanish who settled the Southwest. Historians and anthropologists already knew this. But Parsons was the first to understand how much the Spanish influenced pueblo culture. She found similarities between Indian and Spanish witchcraft. She recognized Spanish influences in the Hopi kachina dances. (Some of the characters in the Hopi dances—the clowns and other masked figures—are very similar to fig-

A painting depicts a Native American ritual, the Ceremony of the Corn Fathers. The Town Fathers sit singing behind the altar while the seven Corn chiefs pray. Women members of the Medicine Society are seated along the wall. Isleta Painting #78 by Joe B. Lente, April 1939. *American Philosophical Society.*

ures in old Spanish dances.) When she looked at the Aztec culture in Mexico and then at the Pueblos, she again saw similar customs. That's because, she suggested, there were Spanish antecedents long ago in both cultures.

Parsons's interest in the origins of customs brought her to the study of folklore. The stories that people tell serve many purposes. In cultures without writing they are the way people pass on their heritage from generation to generation. In these stories, also, are lessons and rules to live by. Many of our folktales are meant to be lessons. They tell what terrible things happen to young people when they are "bad" and how they are rewarded for being "good." Another thing we learn from folktales is how people used to think a long time ago. They are like the artifacts archaeologists dig out of the ground, only folktales are thought artifacts. Folktales are left over from hundreds, often thousands, of years ago. And they tell us about life in those times. These were some of Parsons's reasons for being interested in folklore.

Anthropology includes folklore. Instead of writing reports on what they see happening, folklorists copy down word for word the stories people tell and the songs they sing. They not only write down the words, but they spell them just the way they are spoken. This spoken form of a language is called the vernacular. And the different ways people speak a language are called dialects. Black people who come from different places—for instance, Africa or the Caribbean—speak English, but in different dialects.

Dialects tell us not only where people originally came from, but also where they might have stopped along the way. So when Parsons recorded Indian and African-American folktales, she wrote them down exactly as her storytellers told them. Over several years she collected African-American folklore from Cape Verde Islanders in New England and south from Virginia to Florida. She also recorded black folklore from Haiti, Santo Domingo, the Bahamas, Bermuda, and Barbados. In her notes were tales, riddles, games, and songs her informants told her. She liked the natural feelings expressed in the words and music. These she published in a book called *Folk-Lore of the Antilles, French and English*.

Parsons enjoyed her fieldwork. Often she would be invited into a black family's home and spend hours visiting with them. Sometimes there would be three generations in the room with her and all their many friends. She would start by telling stories and riddles she knew. There would be much laughter, and then, one by one, everyone would begin telling their favorite riddles. The warm informality made it more like a family gathering than work for Parsons. Soon the storytelling would begin, and go on and on and on.

Children and their stories also interested Parsons. She visited many black schools, like the Summerfield Colored School in Sanford, North Carolina. She would tell the children what she was up to and then read a sample of the many tales she had collected. The students would write tales they knew and read them to Parsons, who awarded prizes to the best stories. It pleased her that she was also helping the children. Her interest in their folklore made them proud of their own culture. And it was a chance for them to become real writers. It was certainly a most unusual lesson, and it's unlikely the children would ever forget the day Elsie Clews Parsons, the storytelling lady, visited their class.

Hortense Powdermaker

1900–1970   American anthropologist

Hortense Powdermaker, along with Elsie Clews Parsons and Ruth Benedict, opened the field of anthropology to women. None of them started out to be anthropologists. Anthropology was a new field then. It was not offered as a major in most undergraduate colleges when they were young. Both Parsons and Benedict began as sociologists, and Powdermaker majored in history. In some ways, their early years were similar. Each woman discovered anthropology later in her life. And for each woman, the choosing of anthropology as a career came out of childhood experiences. Studying other cultures helped them to understand their own lives. And they, in turn, were able to help us understand ourselves better. Powdermaker, Parsons, and Benedict pioneered what was to become a new field for a new century. Each developed new methods, which would become the methods for generations of anthropologists to come.

Powdermaker was born in Philadelphia, Pennsylvania, on December 24, 1900. Her mother was Minnie Jacoby, and her father, Louis Powdermaker, was a businessman. As far back as she could remember, Powdermaker did not feel a part of her family. She recalled in *Stranger and Friend: The Way of an Anthropologist*: "As a child, I did not accept the norms of my upper-middle- and middle-class German Jewish background (a paternal grandmother was English Jewish). I was second generation born in the United States." It was the business interests of all the men in the family that Powdermaker could not relate to. For much of her childhood she found herself "rebelling against the business values and the social snobbery. At the age of fourteen, after visiting an uncle and aunt, I wrote a poem called 'Things,' expressing scorn for the stress on acquiring and taking care of material things."

Powdermaker's family moved to Baltimore, Maryland, where she attended Western High School. School became her life. Her favorite subjects were literature, history, and Latin. Literature was where she lived. "I read omnivorously, and the fictional worlds created by Romain Rolland, Hawthorne, Dostoevski, Thackeray, and others provided a way of stepping outside of my immediate environment."

This "rebelling" and "stepping outside" is an interesting part of Powdermaker's growing up. It's also the way many other women social scientists describe their childhoods. Some have said that this kind of childhood makes social scientists. Social scientists—anthropologists, sociologists, historians—have to be able to look at the lives of others objectively, from a distance. And it may be that it all begins with a child who can "step outside" her or his own life and see what's going on. "It is doubtful," one sociologist has written, "whether one can become a good social

reporter unless he has been able to look, in a reporting mood, at the social world in which he was reared." That's how Powdermaker would describe her childhood. "Long before I ever heard of anthropology, I was being conditioned for the role of stepping in and out of society."

Powdermaker felt more comfortable with people outside her family, especially people her parents did not like. For instance, her German Jewish parents felt superior to Jewish immigrants from eastern Europe. As a child, she was taught to dislike them. But Powdermaker refused to dislike them. "Later, I went out of my way to meet recent Jewish working-class immigrants from eastern Europe, whom my family scorned. I liked them. They seemed to have a feeling of what I now call cultural roots, which I envied. They sang Russian songs, spoke Yiddish, and ate Jewish foods."

After high school, Powdermaker attended Goucher College. She majored in history. And there, too, she felt like an outsider. She was a day student, living at home, and so she was not a part of the campus life. But more important was her discovery that many people *considered* her an outsider. She was puzzled when she was not invited to join a sorority. She wasn't sure she wanted to join one, but she wanted, at least, to be invited. Soon the reason was clear, and Powdermaker learned something else about American society: Sororities did not want Jews as members. Powdermaker recalled later that this was "my first awareness of social restrictions on Jews, or at least, the first I remember."

The more Powdermaker learned about American society, the better she wanted to understand her place in it. She thought of studying sociology, but little was available to her at Goucher. She might have chosen anthropology, but there were no courses at Goucher, or any other undergraduate colleges for that matter. So she chose history. Her favorite periods in history were the Middle Ages and the Renaissance. And she took courses in literature, poetry, and philosophy. But for Powdermaker there was more to be learned about life off the college campus. "I 'discovered' the Baltimore slums and the trade-union movement. My belief in the latter was naïve, simple and ardent: poverty could be eradicated and the world would be better, if all workers joined unions." There was something else about the unions that also attracted Powdermaker—her family disapproved of them.

Powdermaker learned firsthand what it was like to be a poor worker in the United States. She spent a vacation working in a men's shirt factory. "I was scared by the power machine, as well as by the forelady. My body rebelled against sitting at the machine all day." She helped organize the local Women's Trade Union League and was sent as its representative to the Baltimore Federation of Labor. After graduating from Goucher, she worked full-time as a labor organizer. Later she looked back on her years of organizing workers as valuable experience for an anthropologist-to-be. She got a knowledge of the hardships of working-class life not to be found in textbooks. For Powdermaker this was part of the pattern to her life. "Before beginning to study anthropology, I had to experience stepping in and out of my own society—in the family, in college, and in the labor movement."

Powdermaker left the labor movement to travel in England. She decided to take a course in social anthropology at the London School of Economics. She enjoyed the class and especially the teacher, Bronislaw Malinowski, known for his work in New Guinea. She liked the way he thought out loud during his lectures so that his students could see his mind at work. "In the small seminars he made *us* think. If any one of the students had only half an idea, he encouraged and almost forced him, with kindly persistence, to follow through with it." Malinowski was the first to begin applying ideas from psychology to the study of culture. He often repeated to his students the Greek saying "Know thyself." Powdermaker became intrigued with anthropology and continued to work with Malinowski. Eventually she completed her work and received a Ph.D. degree.

What was Powdermaker's attraction to anthropology? It was what attracted many people, especially women, to the field: Anthropology requires many talents. And anthropologists must see life from different points of view. Anthropology also presents interesting problems. One writer describes the field this way: Anthropology is "a bond between subject matters . . . in part history, part literature; in part natural science, part social science; it strives to study men from within and without . . . the most scientific of the humanities, the most humanistic of the sciences." For Powdermaker it was not quite that simple. Yes, anthropologists strove to be objective, scientific. And, yes, because they were studying other humans, they must be understanding in a human way. But was this possible? Could one person be both objective and understanding? Could one even be scientific when studying human behavior? Powdermaker came back to these questions again and again throughout her life.

Powdermaker's interests were broader than most anthropologists of

her day. Her first fieldwork was done living among Stone Age people in Lesu, an isolated island in the southwest Pacific (1929–1930). Later she lived in the small rural town of Indianola, Mississippi (1933–1934), where she studied the interactions between blacks and whites. She then did a study of Hollywood, California (1946–1947). For another study she lived in an African mining township in Northern Rhodesia [now Zambia] (1953–1954). Each one of her field experiences was quite different from the others. And from each one she learned more not only about other people but also about her strengths and weaknesses as an observer.

Very early in her experiences Powdermaker became aware of something unique about anthropology. To study and understand other people, the anthropologist lives among them for a time. She or he might live in a separate place, or might live in a house with a family, taking part in its daily activities. Sometimes there are not only parents and their children in a family, but many generations living together. There might be grandparents, aunts and uncles, even people who are not kin, all living together under one roof.

Often, the family is quite accepting of its guest. And when this happens the anthropologist becomes part of the family, too. Anthropologists write about the sadness that parting with "their"

Thatching a roof on the island of Lesu. *From* Life in Lesu *by Hortense Powdermaker. (New York: W. W. Norton, 1971.)*

families and "their" villages brings. And they talk, too, of the joy of returning, not to visit the subjects of their studies, but returning "home," to their families. The visitor, then, has feelings about each member of the family—some are liked and some are not so well liked. And then each of the family members relates to the visitor in different ways. So anthropologists, Powdermaker realized, have a special problem. How much emotional connection with their subjects can anthropologists allow themselves? Can one become part of a family and still study it? When should one take part in family matters? And when should one step back and not get involved?

Powdermaker wrote in her autobiography, *Stranger and Friend*, about this problem. If you think about it, even the title of her book raises the question. "Field work," she writes, "is a deeply human as well as a scientific experience. . . ." This is the heart of the matter, she feels. Anthropologists not only observe and then record what they see, but they feel as well. "To understand a strange society, the anthropologist has traditionally immersed himself in it, learning, as far as possible, to think, see, feel, and sometimes act as a member of its culture. . . ." So how do you get around the problem of living in and, at the same time, trying to understand another culture? It's necessary, Powdermaker said, that we know something about the anthropologist. What role did she play in the family she studied? Was she like a mother, an aunt, a big sister, or a little girl? We need to know something about the observer's personality. We need to know what the family she or he grew up in was like. We need to know the observer's feelings about people who are different, very different, from herself or himself. Then we fully understand the anthropologist's impressions of other people. That's why Powdermaker felt it was important that anthropologists write their autobiographies.

These thoughts didn't just come to Powdermaker all of a sudden. They came to her during years of studying in school and then doing fieldwork. It began with her first field experience, at Lesu. You won't find Lesu on a map. Very few places that interest anthropologists are easy to find on a map. But it's on a little island near New Guinea,

almost on the equator. Powdermaker was the first anthropologist to study there. In fact very few outsiders had ever come to the island. It was important for her study that the culture be isolated. Sometimes anthropologists are interested in how a culture is affected by outsiders. But Powdermaker wanted to study a culture that was not touched by civilization.

The people of Lesu had a Stone Age culture when she arrived in 1929. Writing was unknown. No one had been to school. Their tools were simple— stone axes, seashell scrapers, wooden digging sticks and spears. She lived in a thatched house like the villagers. There were two rooms and a veranda, which is where tropical people spend much of their lives. Two anthropologists, an Englishman from a nearby island and an Australian, had come to help her get settled. They taught her some Pidgin—a language made up of English and native words—and gave her some useful advice on living there. The people from nearby villages welcomed her with gifts of food: yams, taro roots, and bananas.

This would be home for ten months. After a couple of weeks the visiting anthropologists left, and Powdermaker now felt terribly alone. Nothing in her life, certainly nothing in her schooling, had prepared her for that moment.

"Suddenly I saw myself at the edge of the world, and *alone*. I was scared and close to panic. When I arrived I had thought the place was lovely. Everything seemed in harmonious accord: the black natives, the vividness of the sea and of the wild flowers, the brightly plumed birds, the tall areca palm and coconut trees, the delicate bamboo, the low thatched-roofed huts, the beauty of the nights with the moon shining on the palm trees. But now the same scene seemed ominous. I was not scared of the people, but I had a feeling of panic. Why was I here, I asked myself repeatedly."

Powdermaker became more and more anxious about being there. The feelings of panic got worse. And she began thinking about leaving. Yes, that was it. She had decided to come, and she could decide to leave. Another boat would come by the island in six weeks, and she could leave then. Just knowing she could leave made her feel a bit better.

But during the next few days villagers came to visit her. There was Ongus, the man who had built her house, and his wife, Pulong, and their daughter, Batu. They brought baked taro, and Powdermaker asked them to sit down. They talked and Ongus taught her some native words. Other people came, and they sat and talked. One of her visitors was the village chief. "His wife announced that she was my sister, and it followed naturally that her mother became my mother. Their house was opposite mine, and from the beginning a warm friendship sprang up." Soon Powdermaker's fears faded away. "I was no longer alone, I had friends. I went to bed and fell asleep almost immediately. No more thoughts of madness or leaving entered my mind. Several years later I learned that a definition of panic is a state of unrelatedness."

The villagers welcomed her, made her feel comfortable in this strange setting. They felt responsible for her and cared for her. "The natives also took the position of instructors," she wrote later. "It was they who were teaching me the language, the magical spells, the myths and folk-tales, etc., and they took their job seriously." She was pleased to discover that they had a sense of humor, and in that she learned a lesson, too. "One day, after several months in Lesu, I made a rather amusing mistake while conversing in the native language. The verbal slip was repeated all around the village as a good joke, and I thought it was funny too. But not so an old man who had been my principal instructor in the language. Much annoyed, he came to see me. He asked if I didn't realize that everyone knew he was my teacher, and that when I made a mistake it reflected on him? I was properly humble and said meekly that I would try to do better next time."

This was Powdermaker's first field experience. Anthropology was such a new field that even the professors were just learning how to teach the subject. In those days students were not taught techniques for field study. They weren't even given a chance to go along with an experienced anthropologist to see how the work of collecting information was done. Instead, new anthropologists going into the field had to learn how for themselves. Powdermaker tried to prepare herself by talking to other anthropologists who had done fieldwork. And then, in Lesu, she began to learn on her own. Later she described her techniques in her study, *Life in Lesu* (1933). Anthropology students read her book and learned from her some methods they could use.

Here is Powdermaker's description of the way she worked: "I worked with the most intelligent natives, men and women, as informants. We had long sessions at my house . . . privately with one or two individuals at a time. Then, too, I attended every ceremony that took place during my stay and had long discussions about the rite after it occurred. I never went uninvited, but I was invited to everything. . . . I

would sit quietly to one side, munching a banana or taro, and taking notes. My notebook and pencil accompanied me everywhere, and the natives took it quite for granted that I should write everything down." The people of Lesu had no writing, so they were always curious about her note taking. "I explained that my memory was not good enough to remember everything they told me or that I saw, and so I wrote it down. This they understood, and some of them said that if they had writing, they would remember much better too."

Powdermaker observed every activity in the village and got to know as many of the 232 villagers as she could. She also learned to do the women's work.

I would go to the gardens with the women, sit with them as they prepared the food, or join them as they gossiped and took their ease after a day's work. In the casual everyday life I was much more with the women than with the men. I felt quite free at all times to wander through the village, visiting my friends, and they in turn would come and see me. At night I often listened to them telling folk-tales. Since most of the life was carried on outdoors I could stand on my doorstep and both see and hear the life of the hamlet about me. Here was a noisy quarrel going on, there some children playing, and in the distance, returning from the bush, some men with a wild pig they had just captured.

Part of fieldwork is learning new languages. There are thousands of populated islands in the Pacific Ocean and almost as many languages. Even if people on different islands originally spoke the same language, the islands are so far apart that over many generations the languages have changed. Since Powdermaker was the first person to work in Lesu for any length of time, there was no one else from whom she could have learned before she arrived. No one had even recorded the language in any way. So, like many anthropologists in those days, she learned the language from the people while she was there. That, she explained, "was the most difficult part of the work for me. I recorded texts [in writing] and then, with the aid of an interpreter, analyzed them. I collected a vocabulary as I went along. I listened to native conversation and gradually began to speak a little myself. . . ."

Upon returning from Lesu, Powdermaker received a fellowship at Yale University. She was also awarded a grant for the study of a rural community in the South. She chose Indianola, Mississippi, for her study of relationships between blacks and whites. It seemed almost impossible to do at the time,

but she lived with both white families and black families. She interviewed people of both races for over a year. Powdermaker attended black churches and white churches and other community gatherings. She visited schools to talk with teachers and principals and went out into the countryside to talk with sharecroppers. She ate meals with black families and managed to work comfortably and be accepted into both communities. She would include people of all social levels in her study. Her special interest was relations between the races. Here, too, Powdermaker sought a balance between her involvement with blacks and whites and the detachment necessary to do her work.

One of the things she tried to find out was how and when children first became aware of race. She had no experience working with children, so she talked with mothers. She asked them what kinds of questions their children asked, at about what age they began asking, and what answers the mothers gave. "I learned that many children asked the question of 'why': Why don't colored and white children play together? Why is his mother called 'Sarah' by a white person and 'Mrs.' by Negroes? The usual response to the 'why' was: 'I don't know, that's just the way it is.'" Often she would hear mothers follow up this answer with

Hortense Powdermaker around 1966. *Bachrach, New York.*

stern warnings about how to behave around white people.

Powdermaker's conclusions from her study in Mississippi were published in her book *After Freedom*. This was one of the first studies to describe patterns of black life in the South. It was also one of the first to speak frankly about interracial relationships and the codes of behavior in each racial community. Using the anthropologist's methods, Powdermaker was able to let her informants speak directly to her readers. Later, out of concern for what she had experienced, she wrote a book for young people called *Probing Our Prejudices*. Here she explained some of the causes of prejudice and suggested how people could change their attitudes about others.

After completing her fieldwork in Mississippi Powdermaker returned to teaching. She became a professor at Queens College and the New School for Social Research in New York City. She also lectured at the University of California in Los Angeles, at Columbia University, and at the University of Minnesota.

Over the years Powdermaker thought often about her talks with black and white people in Mississippi. One idea in particular stood out in her mind. She had noted that the main form of entertainment available in the rural South was movies. What's more, the movies were very important in the lives of the people she had talked to. More than just entertainment, the movies to many people were pictures of real life— they believed the stories in the movies were true. If that was so, she wondered, then how did movies affect people's lives? She began watching films in a new way, becoming an anthropologist in the theater. She made notes on the cultural patterns shown in the films.

Powdermaker realized that she could not understand movies by just watching them in the theater. To really understand movies, she would have to make an anthropological study of the people and places where the films were made. And so, in 1946, she was off to do fieldwork among the natives—this time in Hollywood, California. It turned out to be a complicated study. There were no models of similar studies for her to look at. So, once again, she would be breaking new ground. Later she would realize that there were a lot of problems with the work. But her book reporting on the study, *Hollywood: The Dream Factory*, says a lot just in its title. Powdermaker discovered that the filmmakers of Hollywood were changing American patterns of culture. Americans were not just going to the movies— the movies changed them. They began imitating the movies. Rather than

American life shaping films, Powdermaker found that films were shaping American life. Americans were actually acting out the fantasies of Hollywood writers, actors, and directors.

For her next study Powdermaker was on her way to Northern Rhodesia (now Zambia) and a copper-mining town. It was unlike anyplace she had ever been before. Some of her fieldwork would be done twenty-five hundred feet underground, to which depth she descended in a "cage," a kind of elevator. It was important to her to actually see where the men she was studying worked. "It enabled me to understand better an African when he described his first reactions to being underground. 'It looked like a rat's hole, and when you get down you are like a rat. . . . You cannot see the blue sky but only the rocks.'" In some ways it was like the Mississippi experience. Powdermaker would talk with Europeans as well as black African miners and tribal elders. She did something new here, though. Because she didn't have time to learn the language as she had

in Lesu, she trained Africans to do fieldwork. By and large, the African fieldworkers were better than the college students she was used to training at Queens College. The natives were more mature and had more life experiences than most American college students. Powdermaker felt comfortable here. "By the end of the first month or so, I felt more or less accepted by the Africans. . . . They had set me off from other white people. . . . Some of the interviews had the appearance of a social visit, ending with a cup of tea."

Powdermaker accomplished many "firsts." She added immensely to the understanding of human behavior. And she bravely took on the problem of race relations in the United States. To her, it was simply a journey. "In recounting my field experiences, I look inward as well as outward, with the benefit of hindsight. An anthropological voyage may tack and turn in several directions, and the effective field worker learns about himself as well as about the people he studies."

Mary Kawena Pukui

1895–1986   Hawaiian linguist and folklorist

Mary Kawena Pukui is celebrated among her people as one of the leading authorities on Hawaiian culture and language. Her life's work, from the time she was a girl, was collecting and translating Hawaiian folklore. She was a teacher to children and to scholars. She was an acclaimed author and composer, and an expert on Hawaiian history, music, and dance. She saved stories, expressions, chants, hula dances, songs, and poems that, were it not for her alone, would have been lost forever to her people today. In her last book, *'Olelo No'eau: Hawaiian Proverbs & Poetical Sayings*, are nearly three thousand sayings Kawena collected over her lifetime. She was regarded as a "living treasure," and though she never went to college, her research and her books and articles, along with her insights on Hawaiian culture, have preserved hundreds of years of the Hawaiian past.

Mary Abigail Kawena Wiggin was born on April 20, 1895, on Hawaii, the Big Island. She was called Kawena (pronounced Kavena) by her family and friends. Her full name, like many Hawaiian names, was long, a whole story in itself—Kawena-'ula-o-ka-lani-a-Hi'iaka-i-ka-poli-o-Pele-ka-wahine-'ai-honua Na-lei-lehua-o-Pele. The story tells of her family ties to the fiery volcano goddess, Pele. The family traced its history back to the earliest days, when the islands and the people were created. Pukui's great-grandmother was a descendant and priestess of Pele, and so was allowed to use Pele's name in the names of her children. Pukui translated her name as "The rosy glow in the sky made by Hi'iaka in the bosom of Pele, the earth-consuming woman. The crimson lehua wreaths of Pele." Her name, Pukui tells us, was revealed to one of her grandmother's sisters in a dream. The second part of the name, the flower wreaths, was given to Pukui by her grandmother. It was in memory of a sister, born before Pukui, but the time of her birth "sleeping," as the Hawaiians say, "through the summers and winters" in her grave on the east side of their house.

Pukui's life was the meeting of two cultures. She was what the Hawaiians call *hapa haole*, half foreign or half white. Her mother, Pa'ahana Kanaka-'ole, was native Hawaiian. Her father, Henry Nathaniel Wiggin, came to Hawaii from Salem, Massachusetts, in 1892 to be the overseer for a sugar plantation. Pa'ahana was known for her skill as a healer, and as a young girl was trained as a dancer and chanter of songs in the court of Queen Emma. During the years Pa'ahana was growing up, Hawaii was changing. The language and the ways of the people were being exchanged for the English language and European ways. But because she lived in Ka'u, a distant, isolated part of the Big Island, Pa'ahana kept to the old

ways longer than the people who were influenced by the missionaries and other foreigners. Among her people there was a saying: "We are like the *'a'ali'i* shrub, which holds fast with its roots to the rocky soil of the homeland, whatever winds may blow." So it was that Pukui grew up in two cultures, rooted in the ancient ways of her ancestors and the ways of the New World as well.

For the first part of her life Pukui was raised by her grandmother, her mother's mother, Po'ai. There was an old Hawaiian custom of *hanai*, in which children were given over by their parents to be raised by a close friend or family member in an informal adoption. This custom served to strengthen family bonds and political alliances. Often the firstborn child was given to his or her grandparents: Firstborn girls would be raised by their maternal grandparents, and firstborn boys by their paternal grandparents. It was a special honor, for that grandchild was chosen at birth to be the keeper of the family's history, lore, and rituals. In this way the family history was kept alive down through countless generations. This was especially important since the Hawaiians had no written language. Writing and reading would come with the missionaries from America in the early 1800s. Still, even after they had learned to read, many Hawaiian parents kept to the custom. On the day of her birth Pukui was given to her grandmother to become the *punahele*, the favored child who would learn and then pass on to the next generation the family's traditions.

After she was weaned, when she was about a year old, Pukui went to live with her grandmother. She was not far from her parents and saw them almost every day. Grandmother and granddaughter were never apart. "Wherever she went," Pukui later wrote, "the child went too—to the beaches, to the upland, to the Mormon church at Nalua, to the wharf at Honu'apo—everywhere! When Po'ai softened the earth around her potato mounds, the child was there asking questions about the caterpillars, cocoons, rat's nest or whatever she found. Every question was patiently answered."

As a *punahele* Pukui learned all of her family's stories, the family names and gods, their lives and their personalities. From the beginning she learned to listen. "A child must listen without interrupting. If there were questions, ask after the story was told—but never interrupt. One must not make noises, talk or walk around at story telling time lest it be distracting to the teller and interested listeners."

From grandmother to granddaughter passed the family's heritage. Pukui learned by observing Po'ai, then imitating her every movement and sound and asking questions. Always the lessons were spoken, and the chant was the spoken text. Pukui chanted with Po'ai at sunrise and sunset, praising the goddess Pele. By repeating chants, she memorized the names of the fifty *aumakua*, the family's guardian gods. She could chant long genealogies, the names of each of her ancestors, going back to before recorded time. She even had a chant for learning her multiplication tables.

Pukui learned to speak and think in Hawaiian from Po'ai and in English from her father. That was the way in her family. Her father—he always called her Tui, the name of a New Zealand mimicking bird—though fluent in Hawaiian, spoke to her only in English. With everyone else she spoke Hawaiian, and so, from her earliest years, she was thoroughly bicultural and bilingual.

In some ways Pukui was very modern, but she never forgot what her grandmother taught her. Even as an adult she followed the custom of always traveling clockwise—the direction of the sun's apparent movement—around an island. Whenever she and Po'ai left their house to go anywhere, they would chant to the *aumakua*, to protect their home while they were away. Pukui helped her grandmother gather healing plants and herbs, learning the names for all of them and the chants that accompanied the gathering. She learned the names of all the insects, flowers, and trees, and learned to dance the hula and play the ukelele. Together she and Po'ai spent their days in the garden growing sweet potatoes, watermelons, and herbs, and gourds, which Po'ai would make into bowls and cups and lidded pots for storing herbs.

As an adult Pukui remembered especially the hours in the kitchen with Po'ai. Much of the year they prepared meals in the outdoor kitchen, Pukui watching carefully as her grandmother made the traditional foods. She recalled playing on the mats covering the floor of the indoor kitchen. Cooking utensils were hung neatly on the walls, and hanging from the rafters high above her head were golden-brown gourds. A gourd would be cut so that it formed a bowl and a lid. It was then wrapped in a net, which was gathered at the top and tied to a rope. The rope was slung over the rafter so that it could be used to raise and lower the bowl to easily get at the contents. Pukui's father had given a fine set of dishes to Po'ai, but to Pukui the food tasted better eaten out of wooden and gourd bowls. She would never forget those days with her grandmother when she learned to cook. She had no toys, but since she never had them, she

didn't miss them. Every day was filled with the discovery of so many new things.

When Pukui was six her grandmother died, and Pukui returned to her parents. She was forever grateful to her father for the decision he had made the day she was born. Her early life had been shaped so beautifully by her grandmother Po'ai, and the loving relationship would continue to shape the rest of her life. Even at the age of six Pukui had a vast store of knowledge about Hawaiian traditions and customs.

She traveled with her family around the islands, and then was sent to school like other children. But school was nothing like learning with grandmother Po'ai. The worst of it was that schools were trying to erase all the things her grandmother had cherished and taught Pukui to cherish.

This was a time of change in Hawaii. Many things Hawaiian—language, customs, religion—were being given up for new ideas. The speaking of the Hawaiian language was forbidden in school and in some public places. That might be fine for children like Pukui, but most Hawaiian children, especially those from the country, knew only their native language. That's why Pukui broke the school rule and spoke Hawaiian to another student. She realized that her classmate could not understand the teacher, and so translated for her. The teacher overheard, and Pukui was punished for speaking the language she loved. Deeply hurt, she left the school and never returned.

Leaving school, for Pukui, did not mean the end of learning. She had already learned more than most children her age who were in school, but more important, she had a love of learning that would go on through the rest of her long life. Her father read to her the American writers Henry Wadsworth Longfellow, Nathaniel Hawthorne, and Ralph Waldo Emerson. Pa'ahana continued her mother's work, teaching Pukui more about Hawaiian lore. At fifteen, out of school and caring for an uncle who was seriously ill, Pukui began writing down the stories and chants she had learned from her mother and grandmother. Pukui's bilingual upbringing enabled her to make translations from the Hawaiian into English and, not realizing it yet, she was at the beginning of a lifelong career.

That career began when a neighbor, Laura Green, realized just how skillful a translator Pukui was. Green encouraged her to write down the stories she had learned from her mother and grandmother. She did that and then, on her own, began collecting and translating Hawaiian proverbs and sayings. "Every time I thought of something, I would jot it down. Otherwise, how would my children and grandchildren ever learn of their heritage?" Those jottings were the beginnings of a vast collection of Hawaiian lore and a work she would finish fifty years later, to be published as *'Olelo No'eau: Hawaiian Proverbs & Poetical Sayings.*

While collecting Hawaiian folklore Pukui found time to finish high school and graduate from the Seventh-Day Adventist Hawaiian Mission Academy. She was then twenty-eight years old and had been married to Kaloli'i Pukui for ten years. In the years to come Pukui would have *hanai* daughters of her own. Her parents adopted two Hawaiian-Japanese infants and gave them to her and Kaloli'i to raise.

Laura Green continued to encourage Pukui and to make her work known. She wrote letters to a cousin, Dr. Martha Beckwith, a professor of folklore at Vassar College, telling her about Pukui. "She is really wonderful with so much knowledge of Hawaiian in such a young person. Of course these stories are simple, but I am glad they can be kept, especially for the quaint sayings or proverbs that are attached thereto." It was Pukui's first introduction to the academic world, and it led to her first book with Professor Beckwith, *Hawaiian Stories and Wise Sayings.*

It was at this time that Pukui joined

the staff of the Bishop Museum in Honolulu. It was a dream fulfilled. She liked to tell a story about herself and the Bishop Museum. One day when she was about eighteen, she visited a cousin who lived across the street from the imposing stone building. They were sitting on the lanai, looking at the museum, when her cousin said to Pukui, "Someday you will work in that building." But Pukui protested that she was unqualified for the scholarly work done there. "Don't contradict me," her cousin said sternly, and as it turned out, he was right.

Her first work was translating Hawaiian newspapers and manuscripts for the museum, but eventually she did research of her own. When her workday at the museum was ended, she continued into the evening, teaching Hawaiian language classes, which included students like Dr. Kenneth P. Emory of the University of Hawaii (later Pukui and Dr. Emory would work together on a book). Another of her students with whom she would one day work on a book, Dr. Samuel H. Elbert, remembered those classes: "I had heard about her and wanted to meet her." Elbert already spoke Spanish, French, Marquesan, and Samoan fluently. "I told her I wanted to study Hawaiian. She was so good. She gave me lessons at her house and her mother was

there. . . ." Then, as if she weren't busy enough, Pukui, with her mother and her two daughters helping, also taught elementary-school classes in Hawaiian culture.

Pukui's skills as a translator became more widely known with each passing year. Dr. E. S. C. Handy of the Bishop Museum asked her to help him with his book on Hawaiian medicinal plants. He was asking for help with the translations and he got, in addition, Pukui's knowledge of plants that she had learned, as thoroughly as everything else she learned, from her family elders. Handy; his wife, Elizabeth; another friend, Eleanor Lilihana-a-I Williamson; and Pukui continued to work together, this time to interview and collect stories from Hawaiian elders. Wherever Pukui spoke to groups, she urged everyone, not just professional folklorists, to recall and write down bits and pieces of old Hawaiian life they remembered. Pukui, the Handys, and Eleanor Williamson hoped to save history and stories of the Hawaiian people, which would be lost with the passing of the older generation.

By recording the sayings of the elders, Pukui was preserving something very special about the Hawaiian language, called the *kaona*. The *kaona* is the hidden meaning of the language. The word *lehua*, for instance, means a kind of flower, but it can also mean a brave warrior or beloved person. In the same way the phrase *manu hulu*, which means feathered bird, can also be used to describe a prosperous person. As more and more foreigners came to Hawaii, the native people took greater delight in using the *kaona* as a kind of secret language that baffled outsiders.

Like other early anthropologists and folklorists, Pukui was not just collecting, but developing new techniques for interviewing people who had never told their stories to an outsider before. As in many cultures, the Hawaiians were uncomfortable telling their personal stories to strangers. In old Hawaii, asking someone personal questions about their ancestors and family was considered rude. Pukui collected a saying about this, that it was like "bleaching the bones of the ancestors in the sun," exposing family secrets, especially to a *haole*. It was Pukui's mother, Pa'ahana, who came up with an ingenious solution to the problem. "Go to my island—Hawaii," she told Handy, "and I will adopt you as my son." By adopting Handy, she could present him as a member of her family.

Pukui had a natural, low-key approach to her interviews, good advice today for oral historians. "We introduced ourselves and questioned—but not bluntly. If they were willing to talk,

fine, if not we didn't insist. We asked them such questions as how they lived and what they liked to do."

One of the books that came from this fieldwork, *The Hawaiian Planter*, contained some surprises for the reader of 1940. At that time most people thought of Hawaiians as fishermen. But Pukui was among the first to tell the story of Hawaiian farmers. True, the Hawaiians were great fishermen, but there were also tillers of the soil, especially the uplanders, as she called them. In *The Polynesian Family System in Ka'u, Hawaii*, the place where Pukui was born, she describes the setting, the kinship system, and the life cycles. Later she went on to compile *The Pocket Hawaiian Dictionary*, listing over ten thousand words that had not been included in three previous major dictionaries. This book she did with University of Hawaii linguist Samuel Elbert, who had once been in her language class, and Esther Mookini. Elbert was amazed at the way Pukui worked. She hadn't the time to trace thousands of words to their source, and instead simply recalled their meaning and origins from her memory.

Pukui's work continued almost up to her death, including books and scores of articles. *The Echo of Our Sound—Chants and Poems of the Hawaiians* she considered "one of my happiest proj-

Mary Pukui demonstrating string figures with children at the Punahau School. *Photograph by George Bacon.*

ects." Another of her projects, *Place Names of Hawaii*, includes four thousand names in Hawaiian, with English translations. *The Pocket Hawaiian Dictionary*, which she did with Elbert and Mookini, has been a best-seller—more than 84,000 copies sold since it came out. In all she was the author of over fifty publications.

As with her teaching, Pukui tried to help her people in more direct ways. For fourteen years, until she was too ill to continue her work, she worked with emotionally disturbed children at

the Queen Liliuokalani Children's Center. Because of her deep understanding of Hawaiian culture and values, she was able to help counselors and teachers working with young Hawaiians and the youngsters themselves understand how traditional beliefs and practices affected the lives of contemporary children. She collected case studies of her experiences with children and wrote about them in *Nana I Ke Kumu (Look to the Source)*. Being able to help came as something of a surprise to Pukui. "I never expected to be a 'social worker'—

Mary Pukui *(left)* listens to traditional musicians Pele Pukui Suganuma *(center)* and Ka'upena Wong *(right). Hawaii State Archives. Photograph by George Bacon.

I thought I would help out for one or two months. But I'm still doing it after all these years and will continue to as long as I can and they need me."

To help modern children Pukui looked to the old ways. Long before modern psychiatry and counseling, Hawaiians had found a way to help family members help one another with hurt feelings. As a small child Pukui recalled taking part in *ho'oponopono*, an early kind of family therapy. Its purpose was to keep families in harmony. The oldest family member called together everyone to talk about conflicts among them. By bringing problems out into the open and catching them early, small issues were prevented from exploding into anger and hostility that threatened the closeness of the family. Family members would express their hurts. Apologies would be offered and the conflicting members would become friends again. For Pukui *ho'oponopono* was a regular part of family life. "When I was a small child, I watched my grandmother set up a *ho'oponopono*—gathering of the family—whenever there were difficulties. Everyone talked out their differences. When my grandmother died, my mother carried on this tradition. We discussed our problems openly. Then we prayed. We forgave and were forgiven."

Using the past to understand problems of the present, Pukui's life linked the old and the new Hawaii. "She had a genius for explaining Hawaiian culture to others," Elbert remembers. "She had a tremendous memory. She would go talk to native Hawaiians and remember everything."

The life of Pukui adds up to something more than her research, writing, teaching, and counseling. Her life is best summed up by an old friend, Eleanor Lilihana-a-I Williamson, in her introduction to *'Olelo No'eau*. "Kawena has lived her life in accordance with a classic piece of traditional advice:

"E kanu mea 'ai o nana keiki i ka ha'i

"Plant edible food plants lest your children look with longing at someone else's.

"Kawena planted and nourished the seeds of Hawaiian wisdom in what became her own yard, that of the house of her beloved . . . Bishop Museum. She has left the fruits so that they may be picked by us, her Hawaiian children, and by all those who truly love Hawai'i."

Heinrich Schliemann

1822–1890   German archaeologist; discoverer of ancient sites in Asia Minor

In the eighth century B.C., there lived in Greece a poet named Homer. He is to some a great storyteller, setting down in his poems the myths of the ancient Greeks. And to some he is a historian, recalling in his poetry actual events. Little is known of Homer. He was said to be blind. And he lived in Athens, or perhaps Rhodes, possibly Argos, or could it have been Salamis? or maybe Smyrna? But one thing about Homer is agreed upon. His two long epic poems, the *Iliad* and the *Odyssey,* were the beginning of the Western literary tradition, and are thought by many to be among the most beautiful writings ever.

There's a problem with Homer as historian: The events described in his poems, centering around the Trojan War, happened some five hundred years before his time. It's an exciting story, which is why storytellers before Homer and ever since have told and retold it countless times. The story begins with Paris, the son of Priam, king of Troy, visiting Menelaus, king of Sparta. Paris falls in love with Menelaus's queen, Helen. He abducts her and takes her back with him to the great walled city of Troy. Menelaus and his brother, Agamemnon, assemble a fleet of ships to attack Troy and rescue the fair Helen. They are joined by the great warriors Odysseus and Achilles.

What happens next is one of the great stories of all time. The war raged on and on for ten years. Great battles were won and lost, and many Greek and Trojan warriors were killed. The Greeks had the bigger army, but Troy was well fortified. One day, the Trojans looked out across the plains from high atop their walls and saw that the Greek armies were gone. Then they saw that in front of the city gates was a huge wooden horse. Curious, they opened the great gates and pulled the horse into the city. That night Greek warriors concealed inside the horse crept out under cover of darkness, set fire to the city, and opened the gates to let in the Greek army. Troy was sacked and King Menelaus's honor avenged.

Was that the way it really happened? Was there even a place called Troy? And were there great warrior-kings named Menelaus and Agamemnon? Most agreed with the British historian Jacob Bryant, who declared, "The siege of Troy is a myth," and that was that. The *Iliad* and the *Odyssey* were beautiful poetry to be sure, but not fact.

Still, a few believed Homer's story to be true. In fact, they said, they knew where Troy was, at a place called Bounarbashi, a small village in present-day Turkey. One of those believers was a German businessman, who became an archaeologist and devoted his life to finding the ancient city.

The search began in the imagination and dreams of a young boy. Heinrich Schliemann was born in 1822 in the remote village of NeuBukow, in what is now Germany. As Heinrich grew up he, like the other children of the village, heard old tales told and retold, and believed them. Children then, as now, enjoyed tales of mystery, the more terrifying the better, and we can imagine a young Schliemann, wide-eyed, scared, holding his breath, the hair on the back of his neck bristling, listening to the village storyteller. One of the stories told of a ghostly maiden who, at midnight, rose out of the village pond, her arms stretched out before her, and in her hands, a gleaming silver bowl.

Many of the stories were of buried treasures. The villagers would tell that a great chest of gold and jewels lay buried beneath the walls of a nearby castle. Not far from where the Schliemanns lived, there was a strange earth mound where, according to legend, the child of a powerful German knight was buried, among great treasure, in a cradle of gold.

These stories enchanted young listeners, and so Schliemann grew up believing in fantastic happenings, mysterious figures moving in the night, and, in magic places, buried treasure. But something else was happening in his mind as he listened to the stories. Why, he wondered, didn't they just drain the pond and find out once and for all if the maiden and her silver bowl were really there? And all that treasure—just dig up the castle walls and find it or not. Then people would know, he reasoned, if there was any truth to the stories. But that didn't seem to occur to people in those days, and, besides, there was supposed to be a curse that would fall upon anyone who might even think of doing it. No, best to leave the legends alone, they all felt, except for Schliemann. He had begun playing with the idea that the way to find out if stories were indeed true was to test them.

Schliemann heard many stories at home. His father, the Reverend Ernst Schliemann, was the village pastor, poor like the peasants who came to his church. But he was also a self-educated scholar who loved to read about ancient history. Some of Schliemann's earliest memories were of his father telling him stories of times long, long ago, of Pompeii and Troy—memories he recalled later in his autobiography.

He also related to me with admiration the great deeds of the Homeric heroes and the dramatic events of the Trojan War, always finding in me a warm defender of the Trojan cause. With great grief I heard from him that Troy had been so completely destroyed, that it had disappeared without leaving any traces of its existence. My joy may be imagined, therefore, when being nearly eight years old, I received from him a Christmas gift of Dr. Georg Ludwig Jerrer's *Universal History*, with an engraving representing Troy in flames with its huge wall and the Scaean gate . . . and I cried out, "Father, you were mistaken: Jerrer must have seen Troy, otherwise he could not have represented it here."

"My son," he replied, "that is merely a fanciful picture." But to my question whether ancient Troy had such huge walls as those depicted in the book, he answered in the affirmative.

"Father," retorted I, "if such walls once existed, they cannot possibly have been completely destroyed: vast ruins of them must still remain, but they are hidden away beneath the dust of ages." He maintained the contrary, whilst I remained firm in my opinion, and at last we both agreed that I should one day excavate Troy.

So Schliemann would test the ancient legends someday, just as he wanted the local villagers to test the stories they told of ghosts and supernatural goings-on. And to prepare himself, he would continue to dream of Troy and to read Homer's stories, like his father, over and over again until he knew them by heart.

But there was no hope of his becoming a scholar, of having the education and, most important, the time and the money to go off to distant lands and dig for buried cities. His father could not afford to send him to the university. Schliemann's mother had died when he was still quite young, and there were now seven children in the family to be cared for. He was sent to live and continue his learning with his uncle and, though he worked hard, he found time to study. When he was only ten years old he sent his father an essay he had written in Latin. He attended secondary school, but the family fell deeper and deeper into poverty, and there was now no money to spare for tuition and books. Just before Schliemann was to take his first class in Greek and fulfill his dream of reading Homer in the original language, he had to leave school.

Schliemann went to work, first in a grocery store, then a fish market, then as a cabin boy, then as a messenger. At one time in his life he was so poor that he pretended to be ill so that he would be taken into the hospital and fed. But one day, when he was working in the grocer's shop, something happened that changed his life. A drunken miller came into the shop, an educated man who could grind wheat into flour and also recite Homer by heart. Schliemann remembered all his life what happened.

"That evening, he recited to us about a hundred lines of the poet, observing the rhythmic cadence of the verses. Although I did not understand a syllable, the melodious sound of the words made a deep impression upon me, and I wept bitter tears over my unhappy fate. Three times over did I get him to repeat to me those divine verses, rewarding his trouble with three glasses of whiskey, which I bought with the few pence that made up my whole wealth. From that moment I never ceased to pray to God that by His grace I might yet have the happiness to learn Greek."

It seemed an impossible dream. He worked five years in the grocery shop without earning enough money to return to school. He decided, in despair, to take a job on a ship sailing for South America. But instead of reaching South America, a shipwreck left Schliemann in Holland, where his new life began. It was here, while employed as an errand boy, that he began teaching himself foreign languages. He learned a new language by memorizing whole books and reciting them aloud. So, to learn English, Schliemann explained, "I committed to memory the whole of Goldsmith's *Vicar of Wakefield* and Sir Walter Scott's *Ivanhoe*." In six months he was fluent in the new language. In this way he also mastered French, Dutch, Spanish, Italian, and Portuguese—taking only six months to learn each language.

The Dutch firm for which Schliemann worked did considerable business

Early photograph of Heinrich Schliemann.

with Russia. Yet, Schliemann realized, not one person in the firm could speak Russian. So he learned Russian and bookkeeping as well, all of which started him on a path that would lead, a few years later, to his becoming a wealthy businessman. While on business in Russia he taught himself Swedish and Polish, modern Greek in six weeks, and ancient Greek in another three months. Now he had what he'd always wanted:

to be able to read Homer in the ancient Greek. Later he perfected the Latin he had begun learning as a child and, while on a short trip to Egypt, learned Arabic.

In 1863, now forty-one years old, Schliemann gave up his businesses and resolved to travel to places he had always dreamed of going, to study archaeology in Paris and take up the spade. But where to begin digging? Where were the ruins of the walls and the great city of Troy he had seen in that book long ago? That was his new challenge.

Remember that in Schliemann's day Homer's tales were considered myth. But those who did believe in the truth of Homer suggested a couple of possible sites for Troy. We know that one possibility already suggested was Bounarbashi in Turkey. Others believed a better choice would be a nearby village called Hissarlik.

Schliemann went to Turkey to see for himself, to see the two villages, and with him he carried Homer's *Iliad* as his guidebook. "At last," he wrote, "I am to realize the dream of my life, to visit at my leisure, the scene of those events which have always had such an intense interest for me, and the country of the heroes whose adventures had delighted and comforted my childhood."

Schliemann did not go to Turkey alone. With him was his new Greek wife, Sophia Engastromenos, who shared his love of ancient history and, yes, could recite whole passages of Homer from memory. She would be, Schliemann decided, not just a wife in the sense of those times, but a full partner in his researches and digs. They would make many important discoveries together. "Assuredly," he once wrote her, "your great pleasure will consist in writing a book in Greek on our excavations and publishing it under your own name, thus making the name Sophia Schliemann immortal."

Confronted now with the choice of Bounarbashi or Hissarlik, Schliemann turned to his "guidebook," the *Iliad*. His choice of site demonstrates not only Schliemann's skills as a historian, but the accuracy of his beloved Homer. Yes, Bounarbashi would be a good choice for a fortified town. But Homer wrote that the Greeks could travel from Troy to the sea several times in a day. Bounarbashi was eight miles from the shores of the Aegean, Schliemann reckoned, too far, in those days, to travel several times in a day. Hissarlik, however, was only three miles from the sea.

Something about the land around Bounarbashi didn't seem right to Schliemann either. According to Homer, there were outside the walls of Troy "two fair springs. One floweth with

Sophia Schliemann wearing ornaments of Helen of Troy. *Mary Evans Picture Library, London.*

warm water, and smoke goeth up there from around, while the other, even in summer, floweth forth like cold hail or snow or ice that water formeth." Schliemann searched and found many springs around Bounarbashi, but all of them were the same cool temperature. He was unable to find any springs at Hissarlik, but then, springs do dry up. So, he returned to Homer and read that "beside the springs are broad wash-

An engraving of Schliemann's excavations at Troy. *Mary Evans Picture Library, London.*

ing troughs of stone, where wives and fair daughters of the men of Troy were wont to wash bright raiment." Schliemann found the troughs, and now he had all the evidence he needed. He and Sophia would begin digging at Hissarlik.

Schliemann's decision that Hissarlik was the more likely site of Troy was an example of the kind of guesswork that historians and archaeologists do. It is this kind of guesswork that has led to many discoveries, not only in archaeology, but in science as well. Over and over in the history of exploration and discovery occur wonderful mo-

ments when a hunch or just a vague feeling turns out to be the right answer.

In April 1870 Schliemann began digging at the northwest corner of the mound. Soon a hundred laborers were digging a deep trench that would cut down, down through the centuries to the earliest settlements at the bottom. At first they discovered some artifacts from more recent times. Then they found a wall dating to Roman times. And then . . . Well, let Schliemann describe what happened next: "At a depth of 15 feet, I came upon huge walls six and a half feet thick and of

Heinrich Schliemann *(upper right)*, standing atop the Lion Gate in Mycenae, the legendary capital of the Greek king Agamemnon. Sophia Schliemann is seated at right in white hat. *From* Memoirs of Heinrich Schliemann, *edited by Leo Deuel. (New York: Harper, 1976.)*

most wonderful construction. Seven and a half feet down, I found that these walls rested upon other walls 8 1/2 feet thick. These must be the walls of the palace of Priam or the temple of Minerva."

Schliemann, it turned out later, had not discovered either of these things, but he was in the right place. In the Schliemanns' day there were not the scientific dating methods that archaeologists use today. So Schliemann could make only rough guesses about where in time he was as they dug down through the years.

But the Schliemanns did know what they were looking for. Once again the clues had come from Homer, who described vases and goblets of gold, weapons of copper, and silver dishes. And one morning, after digging for three years, it happened. Schliemann was walking through the excavations when a glint of sunlight off a piece of copper caught his eye, and near that, the gleam of gold.

What followed is one of the great chapters in early archaeology. Sophia Schliemann immediately dismissed the workers. From then on the Schliemanns would work alone. Sophia Schliemann had become so skilled and deft at working around and freeing artifacts from the soil that Schliemann entrusted this important work only to her. For the next twenty-five days she worked on her knees and, with only her bare hands and a pocketknife, removed piece after piece of gold from the crumbly soil. She cleaned each piece carefully and placed it in a basket. Among the pieces, the one most prized by the Schliemanns was the finely worked gold mask of a round-faced man with a mustache and full beard, his eyes closed peacefully in death. Schliemann had found, he believed, the death mask of his hero, Agamemnon.

Using more sophisticated techniques, later archaeologists found some of Schliemann's conclusions to be incorrect. The level he thought was Troy was deeper and older than Troy—he had actually passed through Troy on the way down. And archaeologists now know that the gold was not from Priam's treasure nor the mask that of the face of Agamemnon. But still the spirit, the dedication, and the love with which the Schliemanns worked remains an inspiration to young archaeologists to this day.

Michael Ventris

1922–1956   English architect who deciphered Linear B, the script of the Minoans

When Michael George Francis Ventris was fourteen, he visited an exhibition in London marking the fiftieth anniversary of the British School of Archaeology in Athens, Greece. He walked among the glass cases filled with relics from ancient Greece. He gazed at pottery, golden jewelry, stone carvings, and other beautiful objects from the civilizations he had read about in his history books. Like most English schoolboys of his day, Ventris was learning Greek (and Latin as well). So he knew something of the language, life, and times of the people who left these things behind. He was also thinking about something else exciting that would happen that day. Sir Arthur Evans, the grand old man of Greek archaeology, was at

the exhibition. Ventris would have a chance to hear him speak.

Evans was eighty-four years old, and he had spent his life in the dust of the past. Ventris listened intently to the small, gray-headed, mustached scholar at the lectern. Evans wore a white shirt, tie, and tweed suit, just as he did every day in the field (proper gentlemen in those days didn't wear work clothes). Ventris listened to the scholar recount his discovery of a long-forgotten civilization on Crete, a small island in the Mediterranean off the coast of Greece. Evans enchanted his audience with the story of how his search for an ancient people had begun in an Athens antique shop over thirty years earlier. It was there that he first saw the carved stone seals that the dealer said came from Crete. And it was there in that shop that Evans decided he would go to Crete, to a place called Knossos, and dig.

The story of Evans's work at Knossos is told in detail elsewhere in this book, but one chapter of that story remained without an ending. Ventris listened with growing interest as Evans talked of his one disappointment. The ruins of King Minos's palace turned out to be so extensive that Evans had decided to make it his life's work. He labored almost continuously from 1900 to 1932, excavating, describing, and restoring the palace. Evans came to know almost everything that could be learned about the Minoans—except one important thing. After digging only a few days, he had unearthed nearly two thousand clay tablets covered with mysterious characters. Evans called the script Linear B. (Evans also found inscriptions in what he called Linear A. He had guessed that Linear A was an even earlier form of Linear B, but that's another story.) And now, a third of a century later, he admitted sadly that neither he nor anyone else had any clue to the meaning of the characters.

Evans was not hopeful. But Ventris must have taken Evans's disappointment as a challenge. This was the first he had heard of the intriguing clay tab-

lets with inscribed pictures and symbols. Later he told friends that he had decided at that moment to study the Minoan tablets and be the first to decipher them. Just sixteen years later, Ventris's dream of giving voice to an ancient, long-silent language would come true.

Ventris was born on July 12, 1922, at Wheathampstead, Hertfordshire, England. His father, Edward Francis Vereker Ventris, was a lieutenant colonel in the British army and had served in India. Ventris's mother was Anna Dorothea Janaszówna, whose father had been born in Poland and had settled in England. She introduced her son to art and literature and saw to it that he spent his holidays traveling and visiting the British Museum. Ventris's earliest schooling was in Gstaad, Switzerland, where he was taught in, and was expected to read and speak, both French and German. While there, he learned the local Swiss-German dialect as well. When he was eight he returned to England to attend secondary school, majoring in the classics.

Ventris's close friend John Chadwick remembers that he always loved languages. When he was six Ventris taught himself Polish. And when he was seven he bought and read a German book about the Egyptian hieroglyphs. Later he learned Swedish after visiting the country for only a few weeks. "He had not only a remarkable visual memory," Chadwick recalls, "but, what is rarely combined with it, the ability to learn a language by ear."

Ventris never forgot that day when he first heard Evans talk about Linear B. When he was only eighteen, he sent an article to the scholarly periodical *American Journal of Archaeology.* He titled the article "Introducing the Minoan Language," and he was careful to conceal his age from the editor. The article was published. And although Ventris was later embarrassed by his conclusions—they were, it turned out, wrong—scholars still consider the article soundly written. It's worth looking at this early attempt because we, like Ventris, can learn a lot from mistakes.

Ventris knew of several ways to begin decoding a language. One way is to find another language that might be related to the unknown language and see if the known language holds any clues to the unknown. So he looked around, and considered the possibility of Etruscan. Ventris wasn't just guessing—he knew his history. The origins of the Etruscans are still a mystery to historians, but one theory has it that they came to Italy from the Aegean. If that were true, Ventris reasoned, then maybe the Etruscan language might somehow fit with Linear B. It didn't, and Ventris reported

Michael Ventris. *From* The Decipherment of Linear B *by John Chadwick. (Cambridge: Cambridge University Press, reprinted 1990.)*

his negative results. But he didn't give up his Etruscan theory for some time.

Ventris decided that he would like to be an architect, so rather than go on to a university, he entered the Architectural Association School in London. While in school he married Lois Elizabeth Knox-Niven, who was also an architecture student and later practiced architecture. Ventris's studies were interrupted by World War II, when he joined the Royal Air Force and trained to be a navigator. He navigated bombers throughout the war. He once told Chadwick that he had chosen navigation because "it's so much more interesting than mere flying." After the war and a year with the occupation forces in Germany, Ventris returned to his architectural training. When he graduated, he worked with the Ministry of Education, designing new schools. Ventris was recognized as a talented architect, but he never lost interest in the Minoan script. In 1952 he resigned from the group of architects with whom he had been working. He had decided to devote his time to "building a house, and working on the Mycenaean inscriptions. I have a backlog of archaeological work to complete before I can consider resuming architectural practice."

Ventris knew he faced an awesome task. Unlike Champollion, who'd had the Rosetta Stone with its Greek and Egyptian inscriptions, Ventris had no clues to the pronunciation of Linear B. He did know something about the history of Knossos, thanks to Evans. Knossos had been destroyed and rebuilt several times. And then about 1400 B.C. it was finally reduced to ruins. To this day, scholars do not understand what brought this early civilization to an end so quickly. Some have suggested an earthquake or, perhaps, a tidal wave

that destroyed the palace and all the dwellings. What is known is that the destruction of the palace was swift and that there was a great fire. That fire destroyed the palace, but it also preserved important documents. The heat that charred the great timbers of Knossos also baked hard the clay tablets covered with writing, the writing Evans later called Linear B.

With all the impossibilities he faced, Ventris continued to work at the pictures and characters on the clay tablets. "For my part," he wrote, "I was convinced that Linear B must contain 'Minoan' [a language older than Greek] and this did not make the chances of decipherment very bright: even the most painstaking statistics and the most penetrating analysis will not present you with a translation if the coded language is one you do not know anyway."

An unreadable script is very much like a secret code. Languages have been deciphered using the same methods a cryptographer uses to break a code. That's how Grotefend was able to decipher cuneiform (see his story elsewhere in this book). Ventris, too, was an amateur cryptographer and he understood the possibilities of using decoding methods. But he faced a serious problem. And to understand his problem we need to look at some of the possibilities to be considered by a decipherer.

Language is two things: There's the spoken language, the words we make with our voices. And there's the written language, the script, the symbols or characters that represent spoken sounds. Sometimes, though the script is a mystery, the language is known or partly known. That's what happened with Grotefend's decipherment of cuneiform. The script was unknown to anyone. But the underlying language became clear once Grotefend broke the code of the script. Once this was realized, not only could sounds be given to the characters, but the meaning could be learned as well.

There's another possible situation. With some ancient languages, the script is known but the language is unknown. This is how it is with Etruscan. Scholars can give sounds to Etruscan letters and words because the Etruscans used letters that look like ancient Greek. But even though we can pronounce the words and actually read Etruscan texts aloud, no one knows what the words mean. Even today, with the huge number of Etruscan texts available to scholars, the language remains a mystery.

There's also a third possibility. And this is the one that Ventris faced in attempting to decipher Linear B. The Minoan script *and* the language were unknown. It seems that this would make translation an impossible task. In fact it *was* considered impossible, unless a bilingual text could be found somewhere. That's what had led to the decipherment of the Egyptian hieroglyphs. The characters—the hieroglyphs—were unknown. And the language had not been spoken in so many thousands of years that nothing was known of it. Champollion was able to decipher the hieroglyphs only because of an amazing, accidental discovery. A large flat stone was found, called the Rosetta Stone, which contained the same text written three times—in hieroglyphs and another unknown Egyptian script, and repeated in Greek. It was possible then to match royal names in the Greek text with the same names in the hieroglyphs (see the story of Champollion). Once Champollion understood a few of the hieroglyphs, it was relatively simple to decode the rest. But no bilingual document containing both Minoan and a known language had appeared. There would have to be another way.

Ventris had a new method that Champollion did not know about. In the century between the decipherment of the hieroglyphs and the work on Linear B, some new techniques in cryptography had been developed. Cryptographers had learned that any code could be broken if many examples of the coded text were available. It's complicated, but here's how that works: The decipherer must determine the system being used in the language. There are three basic writing systems and, fortunately, it's not too difficult to tell them apart.

First attempts at writing thousands of years ago used pictograms, little pictures of things. The next step was the use of ideograms, symbols to represent ideas. The best example of this ideographic writing is Chinese. The earliest Chinese writing was pictographic. Eventually the language evolved to become ideographic, when the characters became symbols rather than pictures of things. Each sign or character in Chinese represents one word. Characters are also combined to make words. The ideograms, however, do not give any direct clues to pronunciation as letters and words do for us. The pronunciation of each character must be learned individually. There are many characters in Chinese. To become a good reader in China, one needs to know five or six *thousand* characters. A Chinese dictionary may contain fifty thousand different characters.

Another writing system, called a syllabic system, uses signs to represent sounds. Each sign stands for a sound. Except for words of one syllable, then, it takes many different signs to make up a word. A syllabic language uses

FIGURE 2

fewer signs than an ideographic language. But there must still be a different sign for each syllable. Japanese, which is a syllabic language, uses forty-eight signs, helped out by two little marks. The ancient language of Cyprus, an island near Greece, used fifty-four signs. The Cypriot syllabary is shown in Figure 2.

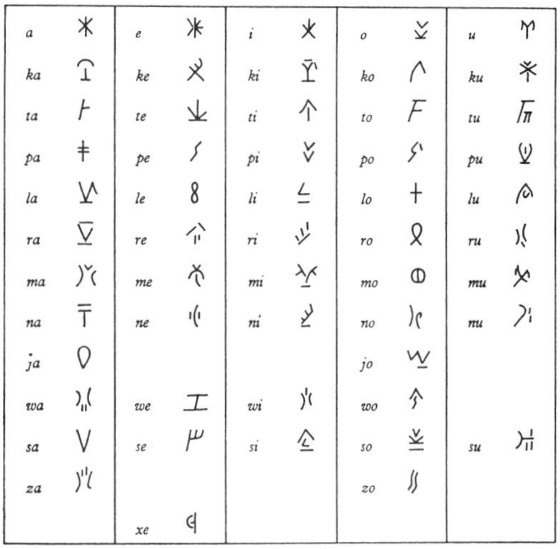

Notice that in a syllabic system the sign does not stand for one sound like an *a* or a *t* sound. Each sign stands for a syllable—*ka, wo, ku, si,* and so on.

And, finally, there's an alphabetic system. That's the basis of our writing. It goes back to the Egyptians and the Phoenicians, but our present alphabet comes from the Romans by way of Greece. In our alphabet we use twenty-six letters. Some are vowels—*a*, *e*, *i*, *o*, *u*, and sometimes *y*—and the rest are consonants. And that's an important characteristic of alphabetic writing—it uses very few signs compared to the other two systems.

The characteristics of different systems of writing provided Ventris's most important clue. The first thing he had to decide before he could go on was which one of these systems was used in Linear B. He went through all the tablet inscriptions he could and made a list of all the different signs. When he was through, he found that Linear B used eighty-nine different symbols (there's still some argument about this, but eighty-nine is close enough). The way he came to his conclusion seems pretty simple, but many of the researchers hadn't figured it out.

Is Linear B ideographic, syllabic, or alphabetic writing? Let's follow Ventris as he thinks it out. Ideographic languages need thousands of signs (a sign is needed for each word). Linear B has only eighty-nine signs, which are repeated over and over in different combinations, so it can't be ideographic. But there are too many signs for Linear B to be alphabetic. The most complicated extant alphabetic language is Russian, with thirty-two signs. Therefore, Linear B must be a syllabic language. Ventris concluded that each sign or character in Linear B represents neither a word nor a letter, but a syllable. If you guessed that Linear B was an alphabetic system, you're not alone: That was Ventris's first guess before he later tested it out.

So, to decipher Linear B, Ventris needed as many examples of the script as he could find. Fortunately, more and more inscriptions were coming to light. Ventris had access to the tablets Evans had found. And then he learned that an archaeologist at the University of Cincinnati had made a new discovery. Carl W. Blegen had excavated a palace at Pylos, on the Greek mainland. Among his finds were six hundred clay tablets with some kind of script inscribed on them. Ventris was able to examine a few of the inscriptions and recognized them as Linear B. This was an important discovery. Tablets written in Minoan had now been found in Greece as well as on Crete. Was it possible, Ventris began to think, that these tablets contained ancient Greek written in Minoan characters? This would mean giving up his first notion, that Linear B was Etruscan or some other language.

In the meantime, other scholars were working on the script. They were not able to decipher the language either, but with each small discovery came a better sense of Linear B. Ventris corresponded with several people around the world who were studying the Minoan script. One of them was American linguist Dr. Alice E. Kober. She was trying to find out something about the language by looking at the script, and she did find some interesting things. She discovered, for instance, that the language distinguishes between genders. Words might have several forms, one for men and one for women, another for animals, and still another for objects. She discovered also that the gender was changed by adding marks to the characters. Ventris was aware of her work—Kober was one of the many scholars he corresponded with—and her discoveries would play an important role in the eventual decipherment of the script.

Ventris, however, took a different approach from Kober's, using the new cryptographic technique. His first step was to make statistical tables showing the frequency of each sign—how often it appeared in the text. Then he counted the number of times each sign appeared at the beginning, the end, and other places on the sign groups. He found that three signs were most common at the beginnings of words. Other signs were found to be frequent final signs. Figure 3 shows what one of Ventris's syllabic grids looked like. You can see how he organized his information.

LINEAR SCRIPT B SYLLABIC GRID WORK NOTE 15
(2ND STATE)
DIAGNOSIS OF CONSONANT AND VOWEL EQUATIONS ATHENS, 28 SEPT 51
IN THE INFLEXIONAL MATERIAL FROM PYLOS:

		vowel 1	vowel 2	vowel 3	vowel 4	vowel 5
pure vowels?		30.3				37.2
a semi-vowel ?					34.0	29.4
consonant 1		14.8	32.5	21.2	28.1	18.8
2		19.6	17.5			13.7
3			9.2		3.3	10.0
4		17.0	28.6			0.4
5		17.7	10.3		4.1	10.2
6		7.4	20.5		14.8	14.4
7		4.1	44.0			
8		6.1	6.1		13.5	15.2
9			33.1		32.3	2.4
10		22.2		38.2	3.5	2.2
11		31.2	33.8	34.4	8.3	0.7
12		17.0			37.7	24.0
13			9.4	14.2		
14		5.0				
15		12.6				

MICHAEL VENTRIS

FIGURE 3

Ventris was also thinking about the sounds of Linear B. If he could actually pronounce a few syllables and then say whole words, the sounds would give important clues to the origins of the language. Ventris had studied the sylla-

Linear B	Cypriot	Value in Cypriot
⊦	⊦	*ta*
+	+	*lo*
⊤	⊤	*to*
⊬	⊬	*se*
‡	‡	*pa*
↑	⊤	*na*
⋏	↑	*ti*

FIGURE 4

bary of ancient Cyprus. He knew that it was related to Greek. And in one of those great leaps of the mind, he began to consider the possibility that the syllabary of Cyprus—which he knew how to sound out—might help give sounds to the long-silent Linear B. It turned out to be a good beginning. Figure 4 shows what Ventris found when he compared some Cypriot and Linear B signs.

Those tablets unearthed at Pylos in 1939 did not become immediately available to scholars. But over the years they were all photographed, and all were finally published in 1951. Now Ventris had additional information for his analysis, and he had something even more exciting. One of the Pylos tablets had a sketch of a little three-legged stand for a cooking pot at the end of a line. We would call it a tripod and the Greeks, *tripodes*. Suppose, Ventris thought, one of the words happens to be Minoan for "tripod." He was beginning to suspect that Linear B was actually a very early form of Greek. And something about the Pylos tablets suggested that they might actually be Greek—the ancient Greek he knew— written in Linear B.

The first confirmation of this theory came in a letter from Blegen, the excavator of Pylos and the tablets. He had applied Ventris's syllabary to the tablet that had caught Ventris's eye. He wrote to Ventris: "It evidently deals with pots, some on three legs, some with four handles, some with three, and others without handles. The first word by your system seems to be *ti-ri-po-de*. . . ." That was it! The syllabary had worked . . . or was it just coincidence?

Working excitedly with the inscriptions from other tablets, Ventris tried out his syllabary. Each time, he came up with a Greek word. The words not only looked like a very old form of Greek, but to his experienced ear, they sounded like Greek. Imagine his excitement as he sounded out the words he was now writing out with the help of syllabary—*a-to-po-qo* was very close to *artokopoi*, "bakers"; *pa-ka-na* sounded like *phasgana*, meaning "swords."

No.	Value	No.	Value	No.	Value
01	da	30	ni	59	ta
02	ro	31	sa	60	ra
03	pa	32	qo	61	o
04	te	33	ra₃	62	pte
05	to	34		63	
06	na	35		64	
07	di	36	jo	65	ju
08	a	37	ti	66	ta₂
09	se	38	e	67	ki
10	u	39	pi	68	ro₂
11	po	40	wi	69	tu
12	so	41	si	70	ko
13	me	42	wo	71	dwe
14	do	43	ai	72	pe
15	mo	44	ke	73	mi
16	pa₂	45	de	74	ze
17	za	46	je	75	we
18		47		76	ra₂
19		48	nwa	77	ka
20	zo	49		78	qe
21	qi	50	pu	79	zu
22		51	du	80	ma
23	mu	52	no	81	ku
24	ne	53	ri	82	
25	a₂	54	wa	83	
26	ru	55	nu	84	
27	re	56	pà₃	85	
28	i	57	ja	86	
29	pu₂	58	su	87	

Chart of eighty-seven Linear B signs with numeral equivalents and phonetic values. *From* The Decipherment of Linear B *by John Chadwick. (Cambridge: Cambridge University Press, reprinted 1990.)*

Among the words were names, the names of people and places he knew— *te-se-u*, Theseus; *ko-no-so*, Knossos; *a-mi-ni-so*, Amnisos, a harbor town near Knossos; and *tu-li-so*, Tulissos, a town in Crete.

Ventris would have to be sure that this wasn't coincidence or his reading into the signs more than was really there. He came upon an eight-syllable word. If his system worked with a word like this, there was no chance of a coincidence. Ventris wrote out the syllables, *e-te-wo-ke-re-we-i-jo*. It sounded to him like Eteocles, a Greek name he knew as well. Then it was true: The Linear B writing of Pylos was a form of Greek.

Ventris found that he was no longer decoding—he was translating and reading Linear B. Maybe his greatest joy was finding connections between his translations and his beloved Homer. Homer's accuracy was questioned on many counts. Most historians believed that the writings of Homer, though beautiful poetry, could not be historical. He could not possibly, they argued, have known about a time so many centuries before his own. One of the examples cited by these critics is the mention of a four-handled cup that King Nestor carried with him from Pylos to the Trojan War. Homer wrote of a "beautifully wrought cup which the old man brought with him from home. It was set with golden nails, the eared handles upon it were four. . . ." Blegen's decoding had been about tripods and vessels. It turned out to be an inventory of articles in the kitchen of Nestor's palace at Pylos. One of the articles mentioned in that passage was a *qe-to-ro-we*, a four-handled pot. Homer, by the way, learned much of what he knew about history through storytelling, the passing down of a people's history by voice from generation to generation.

Ventris fulfilled his boyhood promise when he was only thirty years old. The decipherment of Linear B took him about three years. There was more to be done, and surely he would have gone on to perfect the system he had discovered. Perhaps he would have broken the codes of other unknown languages. But he was killed in an automobile accident just four years later. Ventris is remembered especially by his friend John Chadwick, who continued the work on Linear B. "Ventris," Chadwick recalls, "was able to discern among the bewildering variety of the mysterious signs, patterns and regularities which betrayed the underlying structure. It is this quality, the power of seeing order in apparent confusion, that has marked the work of all great men."

Robert Eric Mortimer Wheeler

1890–1976 English archaeologist who excavated Roman remains in Britain and Harappa in the Indus Valley

What happened at [Maiden Castle] is plain to read. First, the regiment of artillery, which normally accompanied a legion on campaign, was ordered into action, and put down a barrage of iron-shod ballista (catapult) arrows over the eastern part of the site. Following this barrage, the infantry advanced up the slope, cutting its way from rampart to rampart, tower to tower. In the inner-most bay of the entrance, close outside the actual gates, a number of huts had recently been built; these were now set alight, and under the rising clouds of smoke the gates were stormed and the position carried. But resistance had been obstinate and the fury of the attackers was roused. For a space, confusion and massacre dominated the scene. Men and women, young and old, were savagely cut down before the legionaries were called to heel and the work

of systematic destruction was begun . . . the demolition of the gates and the over-throw of the high stone walls which flanked the two portals.

An eyewitness account of a terrible battle? Not exactly. The year is A.D. 43, and Roman legions are marching across Britain, attacking wherever they encounter resistance. This account was written by archaeologist Robert Eric Mortimer Wheeler in *History Was Buried*—nineteen centuries later! Wheeler wasn't there watching the attack, of course, so how could he describe the scene in such vivid detail? He read the land, the ruined castle, the scattered iron arrowheads (but not the kind used with hand bows), the bodies thrown, rather than placed ceremoniously, into hastily dug, shallow graves. He noted the ages and sexes of the thirty-eight skeletons whose skulls still showed the crushing blows of Roman swords. He read the arrangement of postholes marking huts, and the ashes around them. He read all of this like a book, but he added a measure of personal experience and understanding of human nature as well. "One skull, which had received no less than nine savage cuts," Wheeler observed, "suggests the fury of massacre rather than the tumult of battle—a man does not stay to kill his enemy eight or nine times in the melée.

"That night, when the fires of the legion shone out (we may imagine) in orderly lines across the valley, the survivors crept forth from their broken stronghold and, in the darkness, buried their dead as nearly as might be outside their tumbled gates, in that place where the ashes of their burned huts lay warm and thick upon the ground."

Robert Eric Mortimer Wheeler grew up on the land. From as early as he could remember, he roamed the countryside near Edinburgh, Scotland, with his father. "I trotted along at the level of my father's knees, which smelt delectably of Harris tweed. We sat by the roadside; high above us the telegraph-wires twanged their lonely music, and yet higher above the brown hills a lark

was singing, lonelier still." Wheeler's mother, Emily Baynes, was a niece of Shakespearean scholar Thomas Spencer Baynes of Saint Andrews University. His father, Robert Mortimer Wheeler, lectured on English literature at the university and later became a newspaper editor in Bradford, Yorkshire, where the family moved when Wheeler was four.

Father and son were very close. "His mind was a map of the by-ways of literature," Wheeler remembered, "a scholarly map full of exciting discovery. On wet afternoons I would curl up and he would extract dusty books from the backs of his double-stacked shelves, reading and expounding a multitude of things, some of which I did not understand and others which I understood better than he knew. From my earliest years he treated me as an adult mind, and I mentally hopped and skipped alongside his talk as I hopped and skipped beside his long striding legs on our frequent walks together."

Wheeler entered the Bradford Grammar School at nine. He recalls learning little of importance there and not much enjoying it. But his interest in archaeology had already begun. "Looking back," he wrote, "I can see how in these impressionable years the insidious poisons of archaeology were already entering into my system. On one day it might be the discovery of a strange medieval kiln in a clay-pit at Baildon; or, further afield on another, the filling of our pockets with Roman potsherds where a stream cuts the flank of the Roman fort at Ilkley. Or again, the sight of the strange crosses in the Ilkley churchyard or of the still stranger cup-and-ring marks on the hillside above the town, or the picking up of an occasional flint knife or 'scraper' on Rumbold's Moor."

Young Wheeler grew up not only in the outdoors, but with a houseful of pets. When he talked about his animal friends there was a wonderful sense of mischievousness and humor that came out even in his serious, scholarly writing as an adult.

There were innumerable creatures that we assembled around us (my two sisters and I): two mongrel collie-dogs, mother and son, which we had for years, a semi-Persian cat, a venerable and seemingly immortal wood-owl of unspeakable wisdom that lived outside in an enormous pen of a cage, a dozen fantail pigeons (silly, puffed-up creatures), hedgehogs and tortoises that roamed perilously about the wilderness of the garden, guinea-pigs, green tree-frogs, newts netted in the moorland pond, and, not least, grass-snakes which had a tremendous nuisance-value in my constant guerrilla warfare with my countless maiden aunts. A snake in an aunt's bath was worth any petty punishment that might ensue.

When Wheeler was fourteen the family moved to London, where his father became head of the newspaper's bureau there. He was given special permission to take the entrance examination for University College, which was usually not permitted for any student under sixteen. Wheeler attended the university with honors and at the same time attended art school. Long before he thought of archaeology, he dreamed of being a painter. He spent his holidays alone or with young artist friends in the art room of the school. "Every spare moment of my busy boyhood was used up in the production of an endless succession of water-colours, oil-colours, pastels," he wrote. "To me every thought, however abstract, assumed (and assumes) a shape and colour. Friday was privately yellow to me long years before I read, with sharp and jealous surprise, James McNeill Whistler's impatient remark 'Of course Friday's yellow.'"

Wheeler graduated with his B.A. degree in 1910. For the next two years he studied for his M.A. degree. He had been working as the private secretary to the dean of the college and also found time to continue with art school. "Still my passion was to be an artist. My happiest haunt was a room at the Victoria and Albert Museum into which at that time was crowded an incredible number of precious water-colours that invited unending discovery; and next came the long-repeated pilgrimage up the silent stairs to the Diploma Gallery, which Michelangelo and Leonardo shared privately with me and none other." Wheeler later remembered these years as especially important in his life. He became engaged to Tessa Verney, whom he married in 1914. She would become an accomplished archaeologist in her own right and her husband's most important assistant in much of his fieldwork. Among her accomplishments was taking charge of the important excavation of the Roman amphitheater at Caerleon.

Wheeler wasn't yet really interested in archaeology when he first heard about and decided to apply for a grant to study archaeology. His real reason was to avoid becoming, as he put it, "a permanent cog in the machine." Among the scholars who interviewed him was Sir Arthur Evans, the discoverer of the Minoan civilization at Knossos in Crete. Wheeler proposed to his admissions committee that he would study pottery from the Roman period in Britain. His choice impressed the scholars. Recent discoveries of pottery at Roman sites in Britain had become an important subject in British archaeology, yet no one was studying the new finds. Now Wheeler would have an op-

portunity to do important and original work. It was the beginning of a new time in his life. "I was accepted, and left the room with a sudden sense of responsibility and anxiety. . . . My future was indeed fixed; I was to be an archaeologist; but all else was quicksand."

It turned out to be a busy and rewarding time. That same year, Wheeler was recommended for a position as "junior investigator" on the staff of the Royal Commission on Historical Monuments in England. It would be an honor to be accepted, but Wheeler's education had been in the classics, not in architecture, which the position required. To qualify for the appointment, Wheeler attended University College's architecture school at night, studying elements of building construction and architectural drawing. These were skills, he discovered later, that he'd use all the rest of his life. "The training was one which I should recommend to all archaeologists, whatever their chosen path." World events would bring some unexpected turns in the young archaeologist's life. "Three months later I was one of the three probationers chosen for permanent appointment. . . . Tessa and I celebrated the occasion by getting married. It was now 1914 and, before we knew where we were, the war was upon us."

In August 1914, war broke out all over Europe, and it soon became a world war, World War I. Wheeler received an officer's commission in the Royal Field Artillery. He remained in London for a few months as an instructor in the University of London Officer's Training Corps, and it was there that his son Michael was born. Wheeler was impatient with his assignments in Scotland and England, wanting to get to the front. In 1917 he got his wish and saw action with his artillery unit in France and Italy. He participated in the occupation of Germany and then returned to London and civilian life in 1919.

Even during the war years Wheeler managed to get in some digging. It happened in 1917 while his field-howitzer unit was stationed at Colchester. There was a secret plan to place the unit on a barge and tow it across the North Sea to the Belgian coast where it would be landed behind German lines. "Happily for myself," Wheeler remembered with relief, "the Germans got wind of the projected landing and it was abandoned. Meanwhile, during the summer evenings I was quietly conducting an offensive upon the Balkerne Gate of Colchester." The Balkerne Gate was one of the most important ruins dating back to ancient Britain. This was the entry to the Roman city of Colchester when one was traveling along the road from London.

After the war, Wheeler returned to his work with the historical monuments commission. Like many young men of his generation, his life and work had been interrupted for almost five years. But it was worse than that, much worse. World War I was the terrible tragedy of Wheeler's time; an entire generation of young men had been lost. And he recalled a desperate sense of isolation and loss. "We had been blotted out. . . . It is a typical instance that, of five university students who worked together in the Wroxeter excavations of 1913, one only survived the war. It so happened that the survivor was myself." Wheeler was one of only a handful of young archaeologists who returned to the university after the war, receiving his doctorate in 1920.

Wheeler faced another problem when he returned to fieldwork after five years. He was deeply disturbed by the state of archaeology in the early twentieth century. It was clear to him that the techniques used by archaeologists—the techniques he had learned—for the recovery and analysis of buried relics were inadequate. Most of the archaeological work Wheeler saw around Britain was, in his words, "a free-for-all" in which artifacts were being dug up "like potatoes." Archaeological methods were not then taught in the universities. Students were not required to take part in digs. Indeed, most archaeology students completed their academic work, to their doctorates, without even having seen an excavation. It was common for untrained diggers who were no more than treasure hunters to tear into important sites and destroy crucial evidence. Wheeler was painfully aware of the potential for damage, damage that could never be undone. "There is no right way of digging," he once said, "but there are many wrong ones."

Wheeler himself, even at this advanced stage in his career, had no formal training in excavation techniques. But good techniques were not unknown, and he vowed to learn them and make others aware of them as well. For these higher standards he sought, Wheeler would look to an earlier example, the work of Augustus Pitt-Rivers.

General Pitt-Rivers had conducted research and experiments leading to new developments in army rifles. He researched the history of firearms and then developed ways of keeping records of his research so that they could be easily retrieved. When he retired from the British army, the general became an avid collector of all kinds of artifacts—weapons, shields, masks, ivory and bronzes from Africa, even canoes.

Eventually he put together one of the largest and most important collections in the world, which he donated to Oxford University. He inherited an immense estate, Cranborne Chase, in the south of England. Everywhere on Cranborne Chase he found evidence of ancient burial sites and earthworks. Pitt-Rivers decided to devote his retirement years to exploring the sites on his land. He died when Wheeler was only ten years old.

Perhaps the best clue to Wheeler's character was his refusal to continue excavating without learning all he could about methods. And to learn, he would return to Pitt-Rivers's several volumes on his investigations at Cranborne Chase. "I peered anxiously into the future. Manifestly, my path thither lay backwards, to the forgotten standards of Cranborne Chase, before advancing to new methods and skills."

Pitt-Rivers was well ahead of his time. He used Cranborne Chase as a laboratory to test out his scientific notions of excavation. He applied to archaeology the principles he had learned in his army work. Every detail of his digging was recorded in a way that would make it easy to find for research. "I have endeavored to record the results of these excavations in such a way that the whole of the evidence may be available for those who are concerned to go into it." He also realized what most archaeologists and amateurs of his day had overlooked: All archaeological excavation is destruction. It is permanent destruction. If a mistake is made, it cannot be made good again and done over. Most excavators of his day were collectors who scooped up relics for museums, for sale, or for their own private collections. But Pitt-Rivers understood that the artifact is not as important as its place in the site. The position of an artifact—its depth in the soil, its location on the site, established by careful measurements—gives, to the trained eye, clues to time and place.

Pitt-Rivers's sense of discipline, Wheeler realized, was what modern archaeology needed if it were ever to become more than just guesswork. Pitt-Rivers made sure every excavator who worked for him was thoroughly trained. He made "before" and "after" models of the sites so that visitors could see what the sites had looked like originally. His basic principles of digging are the archaeological standards of today. "No excavation ought to ever be permitted except under the immediate eye of a responsible and trustworthy superintendent." It's always better, he warned, to err on the side of being too cautious. At a time when excavators were interested primarily in the most spectacular, artistic finds, Pitt-Rivers demanded

they pay more attention to odds and ends that had been thrown away as rubbish. "It is by the study of such trivial details that archaeology is mainly dependent for determining the date of earthworks."

Hundreds of hours of work had gone into each of the Pitt-Rivers reports that Wheeler read. Here was the model Wheeler and, he hoped, every archaeologist after him would follow. Sites were documented with detailed plans, charts showing stratigraphy, the arrangement of strata, and precise measurements of all the artifacts found. Nothing was overlooked or considered too small and insignificant. Everything, from tiny animal bones to potsherds to stone walls, was measured and described.

Wheeler took Pitt-Rivers's suggestions to heart. He applied the same principles to his work on Roman sites in Britain and ancient places in India. His colleagues respected his work. He was noted for his meticulous methods and the thoroughness with which he trained young archaeologists who came to him.

Educating a new generation of archaeologists was one of Wheeler's greatest concerns. After the war, the demand for archaeologists was increasing. There was a growing need for trained excavators, not just in Britain, where impor-

Mortimer Wheeler relaxing with a group of students at the Maiden Castle excavation site. *University College of London, Institute of Archaeology.*

tant new discoveries were coming to light almost every day, but all over the world, especially in the Near East. And the number of students interested in archaeology was growing. Wheeler drew up a proposal and, in 1927, together with his wife, Tessa, urged the University of London to create the British Institute of Archaeology. The institute became a reality in 1937, the first school of its kind anywhere in the country. Wheeler was appointed honorary director.

Wheeler would follow Pitt-Rivers's example in another way. Later he wrote a book for archaeology students, *Ar-chaeology from the Earth*. It was one of the first modern practical textbooks on field archaeology. It covered planning and carrying out excavations; organizing the supervisors and staff; preserving, recording, and photographing relics; and writing archaeological reports. "The archaeologist," Wheeler told his reader, "is not digging up things, he is digging up people." Excavation required skill with a hand trowel, but even more important, it took accurate observation and imagination. Over and over he emphasized the need for accuracy in recording architectural features. Mapping and photography were used to record the exact positions of skeletons and pottery in burials, down to the tiniest artifact. Wheeler's students learned to keep their trenches tidy and always in order so that nothing was overlooked or lost. Wheeler was one of the first archaeologists to make extensive use of photography. Whenever a burial was found, for example, everything contained in it was carefully exposed and then photographed in position before removal.

Excavations, Wheeler told his students, were not just for finding artifacts. Artifacts were important, but more important was the information they revealed about human beings. The objective of all excavations, he believed, was to find facts about life long ago. These facts help us to understand the complex and always-changing relationship between people and their environment. All this care was what enabled him to describe in such detail and with such feeling the Roman attack on Maiden Castle that opens this chapter. Most recent excavations, and those going on today, build on the basic principles that Wheeler, Pitt-Rivers, Leonard Woolley, and a few others set out.

Another war, World War II this time, would intrude on Wheeler's life, and this one, too, would change the direction of his work. He served with General Sir Bernard Montgomery's forces in North Africa. In 1943 Wheeler was promoted from colonel to brigadier general and was assigned to direct the air coverage for the invasion of Italy. Up until then, Wheeler's interest had been the archaeology of ancient Britain. He and his wife had been directing diggings to investigate the earliest settlements and towns. Their discoveries at Maiden Castle went back beyond the Roman occupation to a time before 2000 B.C., to what the Wheelers called the "first occupation" by settlers of the Neolithic era. But now war had taken Wheeler to another part of the world. In 1944 he was assigned to the post of director-general of archaeology in India. Indian officials questioned the appointment: "I had dabbled in Roman Britain: but what had Roman Britain to do with India? The question was a not unreasonable one, and I can now only retaliate by saying, 'See below.'"

After the war Wheeler conducted excavations in India. There were still many unanswered questions about ancient India, and archaeology was the way to get at the answers. Something was known of the Indus Valley civilizations around 3000 B.C. This was the time of the early kingdoms in Mesopotamia, and there had been contact between these two parts of the ancient world. But then there was nothing to be found until the sixth century B.C.—

a silence of almost three thousand years. What's important about this period of which nothing was known is that it was the time when Indian civilization was developing.

Wheeler had many questions he hoped to answer. What was the connection, if any, between the early Indus cities and later Indian civilization? Who were the original people who settled there? Where did they come from, and when? And what about so much Indian literature and art that seemed to come out of this period of silence—what were its origins? And what about South Indian history? In this part of India there was no record of contact with Mesopotamia. There was, in fact, almost nothing until the seventh century A.D. Wheeler proposed to use archaeology to begin filling in the long blank spaces. And he proposed to train the younger generation of Indian archaeologists who would continue the work after him.

It was a huge task—India is an immense subcontinent—and here's how Wheeler began: "In my room at the top of the Railway Board building, now and then snatching books and papers from the paws of an intrusive monkey, I sat down and drew up a list of the many Roman coins which, since 1775, have been recorded from the soil of South India. I then sent for two of my officers, went through the list with

them, and dispatched them on a four thousand miles' tour with instructions to select one or more of the named sites where significant association with an Indian culture seemed a fair gamble and where excavation might be feasible."

Wheeler's search led to the little dusty town of Harappa in what is now Pakistan. Its name tied it historically to one of the two greatest cities in the Indus Valley civilization. The other great city was Mohenjo-Daro, which Wheeler would also explore.

It was here, in the Government Museum, that Wheeler found the first clue in his search. "In a workshop cupboard my hand closed upon the neck and long handle of a pottery vessel strangely alien to that tropical environment. As I looked upon it I remember recalling that provocative question . . . 'What has Roman Britain got to do with India?' Here was the complete answer. Here was indeed much more than the complete answer. In my hand I held the first key to the prehistoric archaeology of South India, of a half a million square miles of Asia. . . . A wine-jar from the Mediterranean had not arrived alone; its presence indicated infinite possibilities."

More clues followed in quick succession. Wheeler's first hunch was right. "An inner room of the public library contained three or four museum-cases.

An excavated street in Mohenjo-Daro. *From* Early India and Pakistan to Ashoka *by Sir Mortimer Wheeler. (New York: Frederick A. Praeger, 1959.)*

I strode hopefully forward, and, removing the dust with an excessively sweaty arm, peered into them. For the second time within the month, my eyes started in their sockets. Crowded together were fragments of a dozen more Roman amphorae, part of a Roman lamp, a Roman intaglio, a mass of Indian material. . . . After much searching, the keys were discovered and I found myself handling the fragments of cups and dishes of the time of Augustus and Tiberius from the famous potteries of Roman Arezzo. My search was nearly over. . . ."

Sixty-one Indian archaeology students joined with Wheeler and the work began. He trained them in excavation methods and the preparation of field records. He taught them surveying, field photography, and drafting. Lecturers came to talk to the students about topics in history, anthropology, and archaeology. They excavated walled cities of wide main streets and houses solidly built of burned brick. Below the streets was a system of brick drains that carried sewage from each house. The people who had lived here, Wheeler and his students discovered, could write and work metals—copper, bronze, and

A photograph of Mortimer Wheeler in later life. *University College of London, Institute of Archaeology.*

gold. They were artisans and merchants carrying on international trade. They were apparently Aryans, invaders from the northwest. Here, then, was the civilization that filled in the blank space in India's long history. And we are reminded once again of Wheeler's comment to his students: "The archaeologist is not digging up things, he is digging up people."

Charles Leonard Woolley

1880–1960   English archaeologist whose most important discovery, among many, was Ur of the Chaldees

Leonard Woolley (he never used his first name) smiled every time he told the story of how he became an archaeologist. As a boy, it seems, he was destined for a life as a minister. He was born in London on April 17, 1880, the son of the Reverend George Herbert Woolley and his wife, Sarah Cathcart. Young Woolley attended schools especially for the sons of ministers, and then Oxford University, where he studied the classics and theology.

It was while at Oxford that Woolley's future profession was actually chosen *for* him. He recalls in *Spadework in Archaeology* how one day, in 1904, he was summoned to the office of the dean of New College, William Archibald Spooner. (Spooner, by the way, became famous not as a clergyman or scholar,

but for a funny habit. He had occasional lapses of speech when he would transpose the sounds of words. So when he meant to say "sons of toil," it might come out "tons of soil"; or "blushing crow" instead of what he meant to say, "crushing blow." We all do this now and then, and when we do it's now called a spoonerism.) Dr. Spooner asked Woolley if it was true that he had decided not to be a minister like his father and, if so, what he intended to do. Woolley answered, "Well, I want to be a schoolmaster." The dean fixed his eyes on the young man and said in his commanding way: "Oh yes, a schoolmaster, really. Well, Mr. Woolley, *I* have decided that you shall be an archaeologist."

Woolley remembered later that he

was not quite sure what an archaeologist did, and that he was not entirely happy with the finality of the decision. "For me, and I think for the Warden too, archaeology meant a life spent inside a museum, whereas I preferred the open air and was more interested in my fellow men than in dead-and-gone things; I could never have guessed that after a short—and invaluable—apprenticeship in the Ashmolean Museum at Oxford, all my work was to be out of doors and, for the most part, out of England; and I had yet to learn that the real end of archaeology is, through the dead-and-gone things, to get at the history and the minds of dead-and-gone men."

So Spooner had his way, and upon graduation Woolley was made the assistant keeper of the Ashmolean Museum. This was an honor. The Ashmolean is one of the oldest museums in the world, having been opened in 1682. Here Woolley could spend his days among archaeological finds. It was here, too, that he had his first opportunity to do fieldwork, when he was put in charge of excavating Roman sites in Northumberland. His first attempts were successful—beginner's luck, he always said—for he discovered some wonderful things, among them the Corbridge lion, a fountain, a Roman granary, and terra-cotta reliefs. A year later he was invited to direct a dig in Nubia, which uncovered the first cemetery of the ancient Meroitic civilization ever found. He was, at twenty-seven, already a seasoned archaeologist. To his knowledge of Greek, Latin, Italian, French, and German, Woolley now added various spoken dialects of Arabic, which were essential for the directing of diggings in the Near East.

Woolley's life was to be filled with not only great adventures but also meetings with remarkable men. At thirty-two he was given his first independent command of a dig, a British Museum expedition to Turkey, to the ruins of Carchemish, the capital of the ancient Hittite empire. There he worked with archaeologist T. E. Lawrence, who later would become known throughout the world as the soldier-adventurer Lawrence of Arabia. "I had known Lawrence since my time in the Ashmolean Museum when as a shy schoolboy, with a friend even more tongue-tied than himself, he used to bring me bits of medieval pottery found by workmen digging house foundations in Oxford, and I was very glad to have him now as my sole assistant." They became close friends and lived together in a rough stone house built near the site.

Woolley enjoyed Lawrence's sense of humor. "The lintel over the entrance door was made of a single block of soft

Leonard Woolley. © *The Hulton-Deutsch Collection Limited, London.*

limestone, and Lawrence amused himself by carving on it the winged sun-disk which was the emblem of the Hittite god-head. Only a month or so ago a distinguished archaeologist sent me a photograph of the doorway anxiously inquiring what had happened to this fine and unpublished monument of Hittite sculpture! Lawrence would have enjoyed the joke immensely."

Woolley and Lawrence's team uncovered wondrous objects from a civiliza-

tion whose splendor had remained buried for thousands of years—great temples, sculptures, relief carvings, and a statue of the Hittite god Atarluhas sitting on his lion throne. The greatness of the city overwhelmed Woolley. "Very magnificent must Carchemish have been," he wrote in his introduction to archaeology, *Digging Up the Past*, "when its sculptures were gay with colour, when the sunlight glistened on its enamel walls, and its sombre brick was overlaid with panels of cedar and plates of bronze; . . . but even now, when it lies deserted and in heaps, it has perhaps in the melancholy of its ruin found a subtler charm to offset the glory of its prime." Woolley returned from the excavations at Carchemish to work as an associate at the British Museum. Being associated with one of the great museums of the world, dating back to 1759, was yet another honor. Still, Woolley would spend as much time as possible excavating. Yes, there was much to be gained by reading and working with the museum's collections, but it was no substitute for digging. "It is the field archaeologist who," Woolley said, "directly or indirectly, has opened up for the general reader new chapters in the history of civilized man; and by recovering from the earth such documented relics of the past as strike the imagination through the eye, he makes real and modern what otherwise might seem a far-off tale." The young archaeologist could not even have imagined at the time that some day, at the British Museum, there would be the Babylonian Room, a gallery devoted entirely to the treasures found by Woolley at Sumer.

The adventures continued—some unwanted. While serving as an intelligence officer with the British army during World War I, he was captured and imprisoned by the Turks for two years. After the war he continued his fieldwork in Turkey, Iraq, and Syria. He returned to Carchemish. Then he went to Egypt to work at the site of the capital built by the great pharaoh Akhenaton (see the story of Howard Carter and Lord Carnarvon). And then, in 1922, Woolley began the great work of his life.

For nearly forty years, Woolley's attention would be focused on a mound surrounded by an unremarkable stretch of sand in present-day Iraq. The Arabs called this place Tal al Muqayar, "the Mound of Pitch." It lies about halfway between the city of Baghdad and the Persian Gulf. Woolley describes what he saw when he first climbed to the top of the tell, a mound made up of the rubble of ancient settlements: "Standing on the summit of this mound one can distinguish along the eastern skyline the dark tasseled fringe of the palm-gardens on the river's bank, but to the north and west and south as far as the eye can see stretches a waste of unprofitable sand. . . . It seems incredible that such a wilderness should ever have been habitable for man, and yet the weathered hillocks at one's feet cover the temples and houses of a very great city."

You've perhaps wondered why the past must usually be reached by digging down into the earth. In his book *Ur of the Chaldees*, Woolley raises the question so that he can help us to understand it:

How do houses and cities sink below the earth's surface? They do not; the earth rises above them. . . . As the frail mud huts fell into decay and over the ruins of them new huts were built, only to collapse and be built over in their turn, the ground-level rose, just as it does in any modern mud-built village of the Near East, and what had been a low island became a hill. Many generations passed: the acropolis of Ur rose higher and higher into the air as the refuse of its houses was piled in the streets or flung out over its walls.

In his digging at Ur, Woolley often found that he would reach a floor level within the foundation walls. Then he'd keep digging until a few feet below he found another floor, and a few feet below that yet another. Each successive house had used the foundation of the previous one and kept building up over centuries and generations at the same place. "When a house was pulled down and rebuilt the site would be partly filled in, and the new ground floor set at or above street level. In the Near East the rate of rise is faster. In Syria and Iraq every village stands on a mound of its own making, and the ruins of an ancient city may rise a hundred feet above the plain, the whole of that hundred feet being composed of superimposed remains of houses, each represented by the foot or so of standing wall which the collapse of the upper part buried and protected from destruction." He continues in *Ur of the Chaldees*, "Rubbish mounds 40 feet high must represent a long period of time, a period certainly to be reckoned in centuries. . . ."

Even before he began digging here, Woolley knew the name of the buried city, Ur of the Chaldees. It was a city from the Bible, the original home of Abraham. It was at Ur where, as the story is told in the Old Testament, the flood occurred following a rain of "forty days and forty nights," and where Noah—his Sumerian name was Utnapishtim—built the ark. There had been earlier excavations here and at the nearby settlements of Eridu and Al-'Ubaid, and they offered the promise

of important finds. Now Woolley would lead a joint expedition of archaeologists from the University of Pennsylvania and the British Museum, a task that would take him twelve winters.

Woolley did not discover the site of Ur. J. E. Taylor, a British consul, found the tell in 1854 and even predicted it would be a valuable site. But after Taylor's discovery there was little further work on the site. It was Woolley, however, who is credited, more than any other archaeologist, with revealing not only to scholars but also to the interested reader what it was like to live in Sumer.

Ur was a large, bustling city; a commercial, cultural, and religious center, like big cities today. And as Woolley excavated more and more of the old city, he was able to form a clearer picture of what life must have been like there. He estimated that within the four square miles of Ur there lived half a million people. "The streets were unpaved, with surfaces of trodden mud which in wet weather would make deep slush, and they were so narrow that no wheeled traffic along them was possible. Wheeled vehicles had of course long been familiar (incidentally, a model chariot was found in the quarter) but it must have been debarred from the city, where everything must have been carried by human porterage or on donkey-back, for which reason the masonry at street corners is nearly always carefully rounded so that passersby should not graze themselves on sharp brickwork. . . ."

As Woolley's team unearthed one house after another, he began noticing the interesting similarities among all of them. No two were exactly alike—the differences in the sizes and shapes of the building plots required small changes—but there was an ideal type. There were, Woolley guessed, three reasons for this: climate, the traditional Arab desire for privacy at home, and custom. Woolley was especially interested in the role of custom in architecture. Sumerian architects had to observe the rules of the "House Omen Texts," which prescribed the shape and size of parts of the house. In his description of a typical house in Ur, Woolley quotes from passages in the texts that apply:

The front door was small and unpretentious ("if the door of a house be very large, that house will be destroyed") and opened inwards ("if the door of a house opens outwards the woman of that house will be a torment to her husband") and you passed into a little brick-paved lobby having in one corner a drain over which would be set a jar of water so that you might wash your feet before going farther; the second door, leading to the house

proper, was in a side wall so that there might be no clear view in from the street . . . and there was a step down in the doorway ("if the threshold of the court be higher than that of the house the mistress shall be above the lord") taking you into the central court.

Much of what Woolley "knew" about a house thousands of years old he learned from houses he saw in Iraq. He knew that in many traditional societies customs persist for a very long time, for thousands of years, remaining alive even today. Because he was observant and willing to make a guess, Woolley was able to recreate for us things that might not otherwise be known. For example, nothing of the furniture remained in any of the houses he excavated, but he used several sources to reconstruct a house interior.

It would have been for the most part of a very simple nature. Folding chairs and tables are represented on seals and we know of chests of wood or wickerwork for storing clothes; many coloured rugs would be laid on the floors, and plenty of cushions; for light at night there would be oil lamps, little saucers with a wick floating on the oil. . . . Such a house as I have described, with its paved court and neatly-whitewashed walls ("If the plaster of a house is painted white, it brings luck," but "If in the interior of a

The temple of Ur, restored. *From a drawing by F. G. Newton. By permission of the Society of Antiquaries of London.*

house the walls show the plaster falling off, destruction of that house"), its own system of drainage, its ample accommodation of a dozen rooms or more, implies a standard of life of a really high order. And these are the houses not of particularly wealthy people but, as the tablets found in them prove, of the middle class, shop-keepers, petty merchants, scribes and so on whose fortunes and idiosyncrasies we can sometimes trace quite vividly.

Woolley paid careful attention to even the smallest details. Nothing, he had learned, was too small or seemingly too insignificant for his attention. "One

has to look out for all such little things," he wrote, "for the thin powdery white streak which represents the matting that once lined the pit, for the holes in the soil where once were the upright wooden ribs of a wicker coffin, for the rim of a tall clay vase standing in the grave and not crushed flat by the earth's weight; on encountering any such thing the well-trained Arab pick-man will stop his work and report to the foreman the likelihood of a grave; then the pick will give place to the knife for careful work, and the excavator will get out his notebooks and his measures."

Once, while digging at Al-'Ubaid near Ur, Woolley found an immense temple and beautiful mosaics of lions and deer. And he found thousands of bits of things, among them a tiny gold bead. Others might have simply put it aside, but Woolley, in accordance with his own strict rules, examined it carefully. The little bead turned out to be one of the most significant finds of the entire excavation. On it was a name, a clue to who had built the temple, A-anni-padda. Later Woolley found a limestone tablet with an inscription in cuneiform revealing the identity of the name on the golden bead: "A-anni-padda, King of Ur, son of Mes-anni-padda, King of Ur."

Much of the information Woolley found was written. In one of the houses, owned by a scribe, Igmil-Sin, he found two thousand tablets. Igmil-Sin, Woolley read from the tablets, was the headmaster of a boys' school. He held classes out in his courtyard and in a guest room that is not of the usual shape. Looking through the tablets, Woolley found many that were the shape and size of those used by students for exercises and dictation. And on these tablets could be read religious texts, histories, mathematical material, and multiplication tables.

The tablets presented a special problem for Woolley and, for us, some inter-esting insights into his inventiveness. Most of the tablets found at Ur were unbaked. The usual process was simply to leave the finished tablets out in the sun to dry. After thousands of years in the ground, the unbaked tablets had soaked up water and had softened to the consistency of cheese. Any attempt to remove them obliterated the inscriptions. So Woolley came up with an idea in the desert.

At Ur any lumps of clay looking like tablets are lifted from the ground still encased in their covering of earth, and are packed in metal boxes filled with clean sand; after they have been left for a few days to give the clay a chance to dry, the boxes are put into a rough-and-ready kiln heated by vaporized crude oil and are baked until the tins are red-hot and the clay is turned into terra cotta. Then the tablets are taken out; their colour may have been altered, which matters little, but they are hard and strong; broken bits can be stuck together, the faces can be cleaned by brushing without any risk to the legibility of the characters; no inscription, however fragmentary, can be overlooked, and its preservation is assured.

One of the ideas Woolley came up with to assure good work and honesty from his workers was the payment of baksheesh. There were two serious problems confronting a conscientious archaeologist like Woolley. The first was getting careful work from unskilled, uneducated workers. The second was making sure the workers didn't steal valuable finds and sell them for a great deal more than they earned. This was a problem especially when many of the finds contained gold and silver and precious stones and the workers were very poor. Woolley's plan was simple. At the end of each day's work, the foremen lined up in front of him with their work parties' finds for that day. Woolley listed each find and placed a value on it based on what he knew the worker could get for it in the market. He then paid the worker this amount in addition to his wages. It wasn't all that costly, and it eliminated the motive for stealing. "On an average season," Woolley noted, "the 'baksheesh' bill may amount to 15 percent of the wages." And the system encouraged careful excavation. Baksheesh was paid only for objects that were not broken through carelessness.

If you've never been on an archaeological dig and seen the care it takes to remove and then reconstruct an object, it's hard to imagine what that must be like. Woolley pioneered several new methods and perfected as many old ones in his years of excavating. At Ur he discovered an identical pair of beautiful pieces he called "The Ram Caught in the Thicket." Later, Woolley described the work that went into recover-

ing this treasure. Both pieces were crushed and broken, the wooden parts decayed to dust. "Nothing except the earth around them kept the fragments of lapis and shell inlay in position, and if that position were once lost, there would have been no guide at all for the restoration of the figure." His team carefully covered the parts and the soil around them with molten wax and muslin so that when the wax hardened the whole thing could be lifted from the earth as a piece. Then the work of restoration began.

With gentle heating the body could be pushed out into its original shape. . . . The legs were straightened, and with slender tools inserted down the tubes of them, the dinted gold was pressed out again. . . . The head presented greater difficulties, because the thin gold leaf was broken into eighteen small fragments and these were badly crushed and bent; each had to be unfolded, worked out to its original curve and strengthened from the back. . . . It was a jigsaw puzzle in three dimensions, but in time the head took shape and character. Few people, looking at such an object in the glass case of a museum, realize what it cost to get it there.

The restored ram stunned Woolley and everyone who saw it. No one had thought that there were people over 4,500 years ago capable of such craft.

Woolley's team made many dramatic discoveries during its seasons of excavation. Perhaps the most dramatic was its uncovering evidence of the flood, the biblical flood for which Noah built the ark, the rain that lasted "forty days and forty nights," when, according to the Book of Genesis, "the waters prevailed upon the earth an hundred and fifty days." That story, Woolley knew, dated back long before the Bible to Sumer, where, in one of the king lists, it was written: "The flood came: and after the flood, kingship was sent down from on high." In other words, civilization had been destroyed or, at least, badly disrupted, and the people had to start again after the disaster, including starting a new dynasty. Woolley knew that the Hebrew story in Genesis probably evolved from a much earlier story told by the Sumerians. Still, there was no proof of an actual flood. There was no proof, that is, until Woolley began sinking a deep shaft down through the strata at Ur. He tells in his book what happened.

The shaft went deeper, and suddenly the character of the soil changed. Instead of the stratified pottery and rubbish, we were in perfectly clean clay, uniform throughout, the texture of which showed that it had been laid there by water. The workmen declared that we had come to the bottom of everything, to the river silt of which the original delta was formed, and at first, looking at the sides of the shaft, I was disposed to agree with them, but then I saw we were too high up. . . . I sent the men back to work to deepen the hole. The clean clay continued without change . . . until it had attained a thickness of a little over 8 feet. Then, as suddenly as it had begun, it stopped and we were once more in layers of rubbish full of stone implements, flint cores from which the implements had been flaked off, and pottery.

I got into the pit once more, examined the sides, and by the time I had written up my notes was quite convinced of what it all meant; but I wanted to see whether others would come to the same conclusion. So I brought up two of my staff and, after pointing out the facts, asked for their explanation. They did not know what to say. My wife came along and looked and was asked the same question, and she turned away remarking casually, "Well, of course, it's the Flood."

The facts will never be known. Woolley's hypothesis is a guess, but a very informed one, based on his wealth of experience and knowledge. "The discovery that there was a real deluge to which the Sumerian and the Hebrew stories of the Flood alike go back does not of course prove any single detail in either of those stories. This deluge was not universal, but a local disaster confined to the lower valley of the Tigris

and Euphrates, affecting an area perhaps 400 miles long and 100 miles
across; but for the occupants of the valley that was the whole world!"

Woolley had proven one interesting
fact from the story as told in Genesis.
The Bible says, "Fifteen cubits upward
did the waters prevail." A cubit is an
approximate measurement based on the
length of the forearm from the elbow
to the end of the middle finger, generally agreed to be about 18 inches. A
little math tells us that 15 cubits is 270
inches, or about 23 feet. Woolley calcu-
lated it this way: "Eleven feet of silt
would probably mean a flood not less
than twenty-five feet deep." It would

seem that Woolley and Genesis agree.

Woolley brought many talents to his
archaeological work, especially the ability to recreate, from piles of rubble and
stone, poignant images of day-to-day
life thousands of years ago. He was recognized by his fellows as a thorough,
talented scientist. One of them, Seton
Lloyd, paid him the finest compliment:
"In Sir Leonard Woolley's camp at Ur
the technique of extracting valuable objects from the ground, preserving and
interpreting them, and finally the art-
istry connected with their publication,
reached a very high degree of accom-
plishment."

Yigael Yadin

1917–1984   Israeli archaeologist who excavated the ancient city of Hazor and the fortress at Masada

Yigael Yadin seemed destined from birth to be an archaeologist. He was born in Jerusalem, Israel, one of the longest-inhabited, most ancient and holy places in the world. His father was a professor of archaeology at the Hebrew University, and together father and son would work on one of the most significant archaeological discoveries of all time.

Yadin's homeland was the land of the Bible. He grew up among places that are thousands of years old. As a boy he walked along ancient winding streets on paving stones worn smooth by the feet of countless generations. Jerusalem had risen on the ruins of the ancient city of David, built by the Israelite king three thousand years ago. It was here, Yadin read in his Bible, that Solomon, son of David, built a great temple. "And it came to pass in the four hundred and eightieth year after the children of Israel were come out of the land of Egypt . . . that he began to build a house of the Lord."

Solomon's temple must have fascinated Yadin, as it has so many archaeologists who have dreamed of finding it. Its construction is described in detail in Chronicles. All who saw it were struck with awe. It was built of white stone blocks and gilded with gold, which reflected the light of the sun and dazzled the eyes. "He overlaid also the house, the beams, the posts, and the walls thereof, and the doors thereof, with gold; and graved cherubims on the walls." Nothing remains of Solomon's temple today. It was destroyed by the Romans.

History is a way of life in Israel. Even

today the people live in a biblical world. The names on the map—Bethlehem, Mount of Olives, Golan, Nazareth, Gilead, Gilboa, Lebanon, Gaza, Sinai— are still living places. Schoolchildren go on outings to the remains of Jericho, the Church of the Nativity and the birthplace of Christ, the ruins of the cities of Solomon and David, or a synagogue whose walls have heard the prayers of generations upon generations. They might visit the synagogue at Maon and stand at the edges of its mosaic floor, laid in the sixth century A.D. Thousands of tiny square pieces of pottery—yellow, brown, white, red, and blue—were carefully arranged to make a picture of a menorah flanked by two fierce-looking lions. The children would be sure to notice that the seven-branched candlestick in the mosaic is not much different from the ones many of them have in their homes.

In Israel the Bible is more than an ancient book. It is the basis of modern Israeli law. Much of that law goes back to biblical times, and back another thousand years before the Bible, to Sumer and Babylon and the ancient law codes of the great kings Lipit-Ishtar and Hammurabi. Law and justice were important to the Sumerians, and we can read much of their law from thousands of clay tablets, the first legal documents, written in cuneiform. Those principles

of law and justice were passed through generations of Jews and Christians to the present day.

Even the Hebrew language, the spoken sounds and the beautiful writing, echo a time thousands of years ago. But there is a sad side to this history as well. Much of the anger and violence in the Middle East today can be traced to hatreds with histories as old as the land.

So the past is always present in Israel. One cannot put a shovel into the ground there without unearthing some reminder of the past. The synagogue with its beautiful mosaic floor was uncovered by a bulldozer scraping the ground to build a road. Another synagogue and mosaic pavement were discovered by farmers digging an irrigation ditch. In Jerusalem workers digging a trench for the foundation of a new house break through into an open space. The open space turns out to be a tomb dating back to the second century B.C. No wonder that in Israel archaeology is a national pastime. Schoolchildren, soldiers, farmers, pharmacists, waiters, lawyers, clerks, accountants, secretaries, factory workers—anyone you can think of—will, in their spare time or on vacation, be out digging in the hot sun. Among them are many who, as children, dreamed of being historians and archaeologists, of making exciting discoveries about their ancient ancestors. Yadin was one of them.

Yadin was born in Jerusalem on March 21, 1917. His father, Eleazar Sukenik, was the first professor of archaeology at the Hebrew University. His mother, Chassia Feinsod, founded the first kindergarten in Palestine in the years before her children were born. Yadin attended high school in Jerusalem, and it was as a student that his life began heading in two different directions.

Israel had been struggling for its independence as a Jewish state and a home for Jews all over the world who had suffered oppression and the horrors of the Holocaust. The birth of Israel, like the birth of most nations, was not a peaceful transition. Independence would have to be won by force. Jews formed an underground army, the Haganah, which Yadin joined when still in high school. He began as a runner and then took on more and more responsibility. All the time he continued his education. He graduated from the Hebrew University and then went on to get his M.A. degree in archaeology. By now he was also chief of operations for the Haganah.

For a time Yadin's military career would take precedence over archaeology. The state of Israel was proclaimed in May 1948, and the Haganah became the Israel Defense Forces. In a few months the new nation and its army would be tested by an attack by Arab forces. Yadin's brilliant leadership helped bring about a quick victory. In 1949 he was appointed chief of the general staff of the Israeli army. At thirty-two, he had also become Israel's youngest general. Three years later he retired to return to his graduate work in archaeology. In this busy life he also found time to pursue his interests in underwater fishing and collecting Middle Eastern stamps with an archaeological theme.

Yadin's first important contribution in archaeology came working alongside his father. In 1947 seven ancient scrolls had been found by a shepherd boy in a cave on the shore of the Dead Sea. This set off a search for more of what became known as the Dead Sea Scrolls. Several more were found in nearby caves. Some of the scrolls were written on parchment and some on papyrus, mostly in ink made of powdered charcoal. One was engraved on copper sheets. It was Yadin's father who first recognized the age and significance of the scrolls. They contained all but one of the books of the Bible as it existed at the time of Christ, and they had been written one thousand years earlier than the oldest known copy of the Old Testament. Yadin helped his father with the

A photograph of Yigael Yadin taken in 1968. *Jewish Theological Seminary of America.*

translations. Later, along with another Hebrew University archaeologist, he helped decipher the seventh scroll. The parchment had become so brittle that it took the most careful work just to open and unroll the scroll so that it could be read. This scroll, it turned out, contained stories from Genesis.

The Dead Sea Scrolls enabled scholars to understand for the first time the origins of Christianity. The scrolls were written by members of a Jewish sect called the Essenes, whose beliefs, Yadin explained, were "nothing less than a missing link between . . . standard Judaism and Christianity." One of the most exciting scrolls and the longest—twenty-six-and-a-half feet—reveals more than was known before about early Jewish and Christian life. Included in this scroll are descriptions of the festivals, offerings and holy gifts, the Temple and its courts, the laws of uncleanness and purity, and the laws of the king. Sadly, Professor Sukenik died before seeing several of the scrolls, which had been sold and were in the United States. It was his son who eventually arranged their purchase by, and their return to, Israel.

In 1955 Yadin received his doctorate degree in archaeology from the Hebrew University. And it was in that same year that he began one of his most important expeditions, to find the city of Hazor. Yadin was interested in Hazor for many reasons. First of all, little was known about the Canaanite and Israelite peoples who lived there. Hazor's enormous size and its features suggested that it was unique among Palestinian cities. For Yadin, Hazor offered the possibility of answering many questions. "Some of the most controversial and acute problems in biblical history concern Hazor," he wrote, "and only the spade could help solve them."

Hazor was an important city in biblical times. It was a powerful political and military force, perhaps the most powerful of its day. This Yadin knew from biblical references as well as from documents found in other cities. According to the Bible, a group of kingdoms united their armies and prepared to attack Israel. "And they came out, with all their troops, a great host, in number like the sand that is upon the seashore, with very many horses and chariots. And all these kings joined their forces and came and encamped together at the waters of Merom, to fight with Israel" (Joshua II: 4–5). We learn from the Bible also what happened in that battle. "And Joshua turned back at that time, and took Hazor, and smote its king with a sword; for Hazor formerly was head of all those kingdoms. And they put to the sword all who were in it, utterly destroying them . . . and he burned Hazor with fire" (Joshua II: 10–13).

So from just a few references in the Bible, Yadin had learned much about the kingdom of Hazor. If he excavated there, would he find evidence of Joshua's burning of the city? Would he find charred wooden beams and ashes everywhere? Yadin hoped that excavations at Hazor would help scholars confirm the events in the Book of Joshua and shed new light on his life.

References to Hazor were found in the documents of other cities as well, some as far away as Egypt. For instance, Babylonian texts revealed to Yadin that the great king Hammurabi had sent special ambassadors to Hazor:

Two messengers from Babylon
who have long since resided at Hazor,
With one man from Hazor

as their escort, are crossing to Babylon.

But why? The reason was most likely trade. In a document found in another city, Mari, Yadin read this accounting:

30 minas tin, for Ibni-Adad king of Hazor
20 minas tin for Ibni-Adad for the second time;
20 minas tin for Ibni-Adad for the third time.

From this document Yadin learned not only the name of the ruler of Hazor but something of its importance in the tin trade. Tin is an essential metal for making bronze, which was used for fashioning weapons and tools.

Yadin had his first clues from the written documents. "We were therefore in a position to reconstruct the history of Hazor from historical documents and then confront our theories with the results of the excavations—an exciting situation in archaeological practice."

Hazor was a populous city, perhaps the most populous of its time—some 30,000 people lived there. And it was immense. At the end of his excavations Yadin realized just how immense. "Despite the fact that our expedition was among the largest of its kind in this part of the world, after five years of hard work we managed to excavate only a small fraction of the area. It would require another 500 years of digging to uncover Hazor's secrets completely."

Yadin's military experience proved quite useful in his new life as an archaeologist. The logistics of an archaeological dig are like those of a military campaign. There are large numbers of workers to house, feed, and move around. Tools and equipment must be gotten into isolated areas, sometimes far from any roads. The workers must be trained, organized into teams, and supervised. The camp of an excavation team, with its rows of tents, looks and runs much like a military camp. Water must be gotten to the site. Large amounts of soil and rock must be moved. Sanitation must be tended to. At Hazor, Yadin introduced a new archaeological tool, the helicopter. Military helicopters were called in to survey the site, locate campsites, and, during the dig, take aerial photographs of the excavations. Since the introduction of the helicopter as an archaeology tool, many sites that couldn't have been found on the ground have been discovered around the world. In Israel, archaeology takes on a military look for other reasons. Yadin's workers were often under threat of attack. Army rangers, volunteers taking their vacation leaves to work as amateur archaeologists, kept their weapons at their sides to protect the team.

Yadin had studied his subject thoroughly, so when he began excavating, it was as though he knew what he would find before he began digging. There's a story told about this sixth sense of his. He knew that long after Joshua's destruction of Hazor, Solomon had rebuilt the city. Solomon had also rebuilt the ruined cities of Megiddo and Gezer at about the same time. Yadin was well acquainted with Solomon's plans for cities and with a gate found at Megiddo. He took careful measurements of the gate and used them as a guide for his excavations at Hazor. "We traced the plan of the Megiddo gate on the ground, marking it with pegs to denote corners and walls, and then instructed our labourers to dig according to the marking, promising: 'here you will find a wall,' or 'there you will find a chamber.'" His predictions proved correct, to the amazement of the workers.

Yadin was not only a scholar but a considerate expedition leader as well. He was always keenly aware that the people working with him were as interested as he in what would be uncovered and what would be discovered about life in ancient Israel. He and his archaeologists gave lectures on the history and archaeology of the site. Later, at Masada, they conducted thorough archaeological tours of the rock fortress on the Sabbath. But most impressive was the way he treated his workers as professionals. "One of the means we used to increase the interest of our workers in the dig," Yadin explained in *Hazor*, "was to assemble them occasionally and explain what we had found and how we had come to our conclusions. This gave them a feeling of involvement and made them a part of the team."

Yadin's sense of what might be hidden under the earth is especially intriguing when we stop to think about what his teams found when they first arrived. "Before the excavations began," he wrote in his book *Hazor*, "nothing could be seen on the surface except traces left by ploughshares and stalks of harvested wheat." Nonetheless, this seemed to Yadin to be the best place to begin, and he would stick with his hunch.

The first days of the excavation were rather disappointing . . . so much so that some members of our staff began to doubt the expediency of exploring any further. But there is a firm rule in excavations: do not give up until you are quite certain that you are really in virgin soil. And indeed, soon afterwards we were rewarded with the major discovery of the season and, I may now add, of all the five seasons of excavations. Just about one metre below the surface, we struck remains of buildings with cobble-stone floors, well preserved walls and great quantities of pottery. Here, indeed, we had the first sign that the area had not been an enclosure or camp but a fully built-up city.

Eventually Yadin's teams unearthed the remains of twenty-one cities and settlements, the earliest dating to five thousand years ago.

Perhaps because he had been a soldier, or maybe just because there are so many military episodes in the Bible, Yadin's archaeological interests were military as well. Originally he had chosen to write his doctoral dissertation on military strategy during biblical times. And then he changed his mind. One of the Dead Sea Scrolls discovered by his father turned out to contain a detailed description of Jewish military tactics. Certainly a great many people would be curious about an army that could defeat the combined armies of several powerful kingdoms or legions of the Roman Empire. But for Yadin this subject was a very personal choice. For his doctorate he translated what he called *The Scroll of the War of the Sons of Light against the Sons of Darkness*. From the descriptions in this scroll, he was able to reconstruct Roman as well as Jewish weapons, uniforms, shields, and infantry and cavalry maneuvers.

Yadin found in the ancient scroll some interesting comparisons with his own military experience. For instance, he read in the scrolls how men were assigned to military duties by age. The age of conscription was 25, sometimes 20. The youngest men (20–30) were used only for services and support. "The age of the actual fighters," Yadin read in the scroll, "is from 30 to 50. The middle group [30–45] is employed in assault tasks requiring both physical and spiritual strength, while the next oldest [40–50] is employed in static fighting. . . . The senior group [50–60] is used for performing special additional duties which do not demand physical stamina and ease of movement." This, he realized, was almost exactly how the Israel Defense Army was organized.

For Israel's youngest general there was something very special about his expedition to Masada. Here on a mesa, a natural rock fortress high above the desert floor, the Jews had made their last stand against Rome. In the first century A.D. the Romans occupied Jerusalem. Occasional rebellions by the people of the city were easily put down by the Roman army. But then, in A.D. 66, the people rose up in rebellion to regain their city and their freedom. Rome sent legion after legion of soldiers and, finally, after four years of fierce fighting, Jerusalem was taken again. The rebellion was over except at one outpost—the fortress of Masada.

From Masada, the Jews made attacks on Roman garrisons. And the Romans, determined to crush the resistance, marched on Masada. After a three-year siege the Romans breached the walls around the fortress. But as the first soldiers burst in, they were not met with a volley of arrows or the shouts and rush of attackers. As the Jewish historian Josephus reported, "they were astonished in the highest degree on not hearing any noise but the crackling of flames," and, upon reaching the palace, they found that "including women and children, no less than nine hundred and sixty persons were slain on this occasion." Rather than become slaves to the Romans, the Jewish defenders had chosen suicide over surrender. Josephus left us a vivid description of the reaction of the Roman soldiers that morning: "And so met the Romans with the multitude of the slain, but could take no pleasure in the fact, though it were done to their enemies. Nor could they do other than wonder at the courage of their resolution, and at the immovable contempt of death which so great a number of them had shown. . . ."

Why is Masada so important today? For Yadin and the young Israeli volunteers especially, it is a sacred place. As Yadin explained, it was special "because it had been the dream of every Israeli archaeologist to fathom the secrets of Masada; and because an ar-

chaeological dig here was unlike an excavation at any other site of antiquity. Its scientific importance was known to be great. But more than that, Masada represents for all of us in Israel and for many elsewhere, archaeologists and laymen, a symbol of courage, a monument to our great national figures, heroes who chose death over a life of physical and moral serfdom."

Volunteers came to dig at Masada from twenty-eight countries all over the world—a nurse from Denmark, a young artist and a doctor from London, a French cab driver and his wife, a British naval officer, a student from South Africa. Among them were homemakers, pilots, a violin maker, bankers, potters and sculptors, librarians, priests, shepherds, actors, architects, and on and on—even an elephant tamer. The youngest was sixteen; the oldest in their seventies. Together they worked to unearth thousands of artifacts. They found relics of everyday life, including clothing, lamps, coins, sandals, food jars, pottery, utensils, wall paintings, mosaics, baskets, gold rings, belt buckles, and many other things. They found the oldest synagogue discovered to date in Israel. They found scrolls containing chapters from the Book of Psalms, the Book of Deuteronomy, and the Book of Ezekiel. The psalm texts were a thousand years older than any biblical manuscript yet discovered.

One of the huge cisterns, excavated from solid rock, that supplied water to Masada. Sunshine streams from the hole in the ceiling through which rainwater filled the cistern. *Photograph copyright © David Harris, Jerusalem.*

And what was the most important find of all, to Yadin and his volunteers? "If I were pressed to single out one discovery more spectacular than any other, I would point to a find which . . . certainly, when we came upon it, electrified everyone in Masada who was engaged in the dig, professional archaeologist and lay volunteer alike." The find was eleven ostraca, small jagged pieces of broken pottery with writing on them.

Upon each was inscribed a single name, each different from its fellow, though all appeared to have been written by the same hand. . . .

As we examined these ostraca, we were struck by the extraordinary thought: "Could it be that we had discovered evidence associated with the death of the very last group of Masada's defenders?" Josephus writes:

They then chose ten men by lot out of them, to slay all the rest; everyone of whom laid himself down by his wife and children on the ground and threw his arms about them and they offered their necks to the stroke of those who by lot executed that melancholy office; and when these ten had, without fear, slain them all, they made the same rule for casting lots for themselves, that he whose lot it was to first kill the other nine, and after all, should kill himself.

Had we indeed found the very ostraca which had been used in the casting of the lots?

Yadin made important contributions to biblical studies and Jewish as well as early Christian historical knowledge. Why did he do it? The role of archaeology in Israel today, Yadin believed, is "to uncover the relics of Biblical Israel and thus make the Book of Books more understandable to all people whose lives have been shaped by its teachings."

Further Reading

Titles marked by an asterisk are most suitable for young readers.

GENERAL

*Allen, Agnes. *The Story of Archaeology.* New York: Philosophical Library, 1958.

*Braidwood, Robert J. *Archaeologists and What They Do.* New York: Franklin Watts, 1960.

*Ceram, C. W. *Gods, Graves, and Scholars: The Story of Archaeology.* New York: Alfred A. Knopf, 1968.

*———. *Hands on the Past.* New York: Alfred A. Knopf, 1966.

*———. *The March of Archaeology.* New York: Alfred A. Knopf, 1958.

*Cottrell, Leonard. *The Land of Shinar.* London: Souvenir Press, 1965.

*———. *The Lion Gate: A Journey in Search of Myceneans.* London: Evans Brothers, 1966.

Golde, Peggy, ed. *Women in the Field: Anthropological Experiences.* Chicago: Aldine, 1970.

*Hackwell, John W. *Signs, Letters, Words: Archaeology Discovers Writing.* New York: Charles Scribner's Sons, 1987.

*———. *Digging to the Past.* New York: Charles Scribner's Sons, 1986.

*Lasky, Kathryn. *Traces of Life: The Origins of Humankind.* New York: Morrow, 1989.

*Lewin, Roger. *In the Age of Mankind: A Smithsonian Book of Human Evolution.* New York: Morrow, 1989.

*McEvedy, Colin. *The Penguin Atlas of Ancient History.* London: Penguin, 1967.

*Mellersh, H. E. L. *Archaeology: The Science and Romance.* Exeter, England: Wheaton, 1966.

*Moore, Ruth. *Man, Time, and Fossils: The Story of Evolution.* New York: Alfred A. Knopf, 1967.

*Poole, Lynn, and Gray Poole. *Men Who Dig Up History.* New York: Dodd, Mead, 1968.

*Robbins, Lawrence H. *Stones, Bones and Ancient Cities.* New York: St. Martin's Press, 1990.

*Silverberg, Robert. *Lost Cities and Vanished Civilizations.* Philadelphia: Chilton, 1962.

BENEDICT

Benedict, Ruth. *Patterns of Culture.* Boston: Houghton Mifflin, 1934.

Caffrey, Margaret M. *Ruth Benedict: Stranger in This Land.* Austin: University of Texas Press, 1989.

*Mead, Margaret. *An Anthropologist at Work: Writings of Ruth Benedict.* Boston: Houghton Mifflin, 1959.

————. *Ruth Benedict.* New York: Columbia University Press, 1974.

BOAS

Benedict, Ruth. "Franz Boas as Ethnologist." *American Anthropologist* (July–September 1943): 27.

Caffrey, Margaret M. *Ruth Benedict: Stranger in This Land.* Austin: University of Texas Press, 1989.

Emeneau, Murray B. "Franz Boas as Linguist." *American Anthropologist* (July–September 1943): 35.

Herskovits, Melville J. *Franz Boas: The Science of Man in the Making.* New York: Charles Scribner's Sons, 1953.

Kroeber, A. L. "Franz Boas: The Man." *American Anthropologist* (July–September 1943): 5.

Mason, J. Alden. "Franz Boas as an Archaeologist." *American Anthropologist* (July–September 1943): 58.

*Mead, Margaret. *An Anthropologist at Work: Writings of Ruth Benedict.* Boston: Houghton Mifflin, 1959.

Reichard, Gladys A. "Franz Boas and Folklore." *American Anthropologist* (July–September 1943): 52.

BREASTED

*Breasted, Charles. *Pioneer to the Past.* New York: Charles Scribner's Sons, 1943.

CARTER and CARNARVON

Carter, Howard. *The Tomb of Tutankhamen.* New York: E. P. Dutton, 1954.

*————, and A. C. Mace. *The Tomb of Tutankhamen.* 3 vols. New York: Cooper Square Publishers, 1963.

*Desroches-Noblecourt, Christiane. *Tutankhamen: Life and Death of a Pharaoh.* New York: New York Graphic Society, 1963.

*Edwards, I. E. S. *Tutankhamun: His Tomb and Its Treasure.* New York: Alfred A. Knopf, 1976.

*Glubok, Shirley. *Discovering Tut-ankh-Amen's Tomb.* New York: Macmillan, 1968.

*Mertz, Barbara. *Red Land, Black Land: The World of the Ancient Egyptians.* New York: Coward-McCann, 1966.

EVANS

*Horwitz, Sylvia L. *The Find of a Lifetime: Sir Arthur Evans and the Discovery of Knossos.* New York: Viking, 1981.

FLETCHER

Gay, E. Jane. *With the Nez Perces: Alice Fletcher in the Field, 1889–92.* Lincoln: University of Nebraska Press, 1981.

Mark, Joan. *A Stranger in Her Native Land.* Lincoln: University of Nebraska Press, 1988.

————. "Alice Cunningham Fletcher." In *Four Anthropologists: An American Science in its Early Years.* New York: Science History Publications, 1980.

GOODALL

*Goodall, Jane van Lawick-. *In the Shadow of Man.* Boston: Houghton Mifflin, 1971.

*————. "Life and Death at Gombe." *National Geographic* (March 1979): 592–621.

*————. *My Friends the Wild Chimpanzees.* Washington D.C.: National Geographic Society, 1967.

*————. "New Discoveries Among African

Chimpanzees." *National Geographic* (December 1965): 802–831.

GROTEFEND

*Chiera, Edward. *They Wrote on Clay*. Chicago: University of Chicago Press, 1966.

Wellard, James. *Babylon*. New York: Saturday Review Press, 1972.

HURSTON

Hemenway, Robert E. *Zora Neale Hurston: A Literary Biography*. Chicago: University of Illinois Press, 1977.

Howard, Lillie P. *Zora Neale Hurston*. Boston: G. K. Hall, 1980.

*Hurston, Zora Neale. *Dust Tracks on a Road: An Autobiography*. Urbana: University of Illinois Press, 1942, 1970.

*Lyons, Mary E. *Sorrow's Kitchen: The Life and Folklore of Zora Neale Hurston*. New York: Charles Scribner's Sons, 1990.

*Nathiri, N. Y. *ZORA! A Woman and Her Community*. Orlando, Florida: Sentinel Communications Co., 1991.

KROEBER

Kroeber, Theodora. *Alfred Kroeber: A Personal Configuration*. Berkeley: University of California Press, 1970.

*_____. *Ishi in Two Worlds*. Berkeley: University of California Press, 1961.

Steward, Julian H. *Alfred Kroeber*. New York: Columbia University Press, 1973.

LAYARD

Kubie, Nora. *Road to Nineveh*. London: Cassell, 1964.

Layard, Austen Henry. *Nineveh and Its Remains*. New York: Putnam, 1849.

Waterfield, Gordon. *Layard of Nineveh*. London: John Murray, 1963.

Wellard, James. "Layard in Babylonia." In *Babylon*. New York: Saturday Review Press, 1972.

L. S. B. LEAKEY

Cole, Sonia. *Leakey's Luck*. New York: Harcourt Brace Jovanovich, 1975.

Leakey, L. S. B. *Adam's Ancestors*. London: Methuen, 1934.

_____. *By the Evidence: Memoirs, 1932–1951*. New York: Harcourt Brace Jovanovich, 1974.

*Moore, Ruth. "The Leakeys, East Africa and Man." In *Man, Time, and Fossils: The Story of Evolution*. New York: Alfred A. Knopf, 1967.

*Payne, Melvin M. "Family in Search of Prehistoric Man." *National Geographic* (February 1965): 194–251.

MARY LEAKEY

*Leakey, Mary. *Disclosing the Past*. New York: Doubleday, 1984.

*_____. "Footprints Frozen in Time." *National Geographic* (April 1979): 446–456.

RICHARD LEAKEY

*Leakey, Richard. *One Life: An Autobiography*. Salem, New Hampshire: Salem House, 1983.

LOWIE

Lowie, Robert H. *Robert H. Lowie Ethnologist: A Personal Record*. Berkeley: University of California Press, 1959.

Murphy, Robert F. *Robert H. Lowie*. New York: Columbia University Press, 1972.

MALLOWAN

Mallowan, Max. *Mallowan's Memoirs*. New York: Dodd, Mead, 1977.

*_____. *Nimrud and Its Remains*. 3 vols. New York: Dodd, Mead, 1966.

MEAD

Howard, Jane. *Margaret Mead: A Life*. New York: Simon and Schuster, 1984.

*Mead, Margaret. *Blackberry Winter*. New York: William Morrow, 1972.

Metraux, Rhoda, ed. *Margaret Mead: Some Personal Views.* New York: Walker, 1979.

PARSONS

Hare, Peter H. *A Woman's Quest for Science.* Buffalo: Prometheus Books, 1985.

Spier, Leslie, and A. L. Kroeber. "Elsie Clews Parsons." *American Anthropologist* (1943): 244–255.

POWDERMAKER

Powdermaker, Hortense. *Life in Lesu.* New York: W. W. Norton, 1971.

_____. *Stranger and Friend: The Way of an Anthropologist.* London: Secker and Warburg, 1966.

PUKUI

*Pukui, Mary Kawena. *'Olelo No'eau: Hawaiian Proverbs & Poetical Sayings.* Honolulu: Bishop Museum Press, 1983.

SCHLIEMANN

Ludwig, Emil. *Schliemann: The Story of a Gold Seeker.* Boston: Little, Brown, 1931.

*Poole, Lynn, and Gray Poole. *One Passion, Two Loves: The Story of Heinrich and Sophia Schliemann, Discoverers of Troy.* New York: Crowell, 1966.

VENTRIS

*Chadwick, John. *The Decipherment of Linear B.* Cambridge, England: Cambridge University Press, 1967.

*Cottrell, Arthur. *The Minoan World.* London: Michael Joseph, 1979.

WHEELER

*Wheeler, Mortimer. *Archaeology from the Earth.* Oxford: Clarendon Press, 1955.

*_____. *History Was Buried.* New York: Hart Publishing, 1967.

*_____. *Still Digging.* London: Michael Joseph, 1955.

WOOLLEY

*Cottrell, Leonard. *The Quest for Sumer.* New York: G. P. Putnam's Sons, 1965.

Woolley, Leonard. *Excavations at Ur.* London: Ernest Benn, 1954.

*_____. *History Unearthed.* London: Ernest Benn, 1963.

*_____. *Ur of the Chaldees.* Harmondsworth: Penguin Books, 1929.

*_____. *Ur: The First Phases.* London: Penguin, 1946.

YADIN

*Pearlman, Moshe. *The Zealots of Masada.* New York: Charles Scribner's Sons, 1967.

*Yadin, Yigael. *Hazor.* New York: Random House, 1975.

*_____. *Masada.* New York: Random House, 1966.

_____. *The Scroll of the War of the Sons of Light Against the Sons of Darkness.* Oxford: Oxford University Press, 1962.

Index